Escaping Rej

Game Of Wolves: Book 2

Lindsey Devin & Skye Wilson

© 2023
Disclaimer

This is a work of fiction. Names, places, characters, and events are all fictitious for the reader's pleasure. Any similarities to real people, places, events, living, or dead are all coincidental.

This book contains sexually explicit content that is intended for ADULTS ONLY (+18).

Contents

Chapter 1 - Kira...5

Chapter 2 - Wyatt...22

Chapter 3 - Kira...42

Chapter 4 - Wyatt...64

Chapter 5 - Kira...87

Chapter 6 - Wyatt...103

Chapter 7 - Kira...127

Chapter 8 - Wyatt...156

Chapter 9 - Kira...173

Chapter 10 - Wyatt...202

Chapter 11 - Kira..241

Chapter 12 - Wyatt...261

Chapter 13 - Kira..277

Chapter 14 - Wyatt...292

Chapter 15 - Kira..315

Chapter 16 - Wyatt...336

Chapter 17 - Kira..366

Chapter 18 - Wyatt...393

Chapter 19 - Kira..415

Chapter 20 - Wyatt...445

Chapter 21 - Kira..458

Chapter 22 - Wyatt...485

Chapter 23 - Kira..508

Chapter 24 - Wyatt 519
Chapter 25 - Kira..536

Chapter 1 - Kira

The scream continued to tear from my throat as the witch transported me. She released me in the new area, then vanished.

Stumbling forward, I hit the ground, panic still arcing through me like sparks through a broken wire. Wyatt was gone. Probably halfway across the island, wounded and exhausted, with Leif attacking him. That last image of the other alpha leaping toward Wyatt, his jaw gaping, etched itself in my memory. I had to get out of this stupid obstacle course as quickly as possible and find a way to save Wyatt.

I stood, then bent to brush the dirt from my pants. Had I not done that simple action, everything would have been over in an instant. No sooner had I leaned forward than a massive blade swung from left to right. A hidden mechanism had sent the huge ax head across the pathway I stood on. The blade glided past the back of my head, so close my hair fluttered as the air whooshed past me. A loud, meaty *thwack* came from the other side of the path, where the blade buried itself inches deep into the trunk of a palm tree.

Reflexively dropping to the ground, air burst out of me, but I managed to look up and see how close the trap had come to ending me. The crescent-shaped blade was still quivering. A wooden handle bigger than my wrist stretched back into the undergrowth, where an apparatus hummed and whirred as it tried to reload the trap. But the blade had wedged itself so deeply, it couldn't reset itself.

There could be more of those damn things. I stayed low, crawling almost a hundred yards until I was sure I was away from any spring-loaded traps. Alone and out of danger for the moment, I had a few seconds to let what I'd seen sink in.

Leif had turned feral. He'd attacked us, attacked Wyatt. For all I knew, Wyatt was dead. My hands trembled at the very thought, and a black, gaping pit opened in my stomach. I shook my head viciously, trying to throw the idea out of my mind. Yes, Wyatt had been hurt, and yes, Leif appeared to be feral and out of his mind, but Wyatt was a trained Tranquility operative. His skills were beyond reproach. As much as I hated to admit it, he was probably on par with me. If anyone could survive a fight while injured, it was Wyatt. In a one-on-one fight between the two alphas, I would bet on Wyatt. Plus, feral or not, Leif was *not* a trained fighter. Wyatt would be fine. He had to be.

Wyatt was fine. Wyatt was fine. Wyatt was fine. I held onto the thought like a pinwheel spinning around my head, the only fuel that could keep me going as I proceeded down the obstacle course.

In the distance, I heard a scream, then the howl of a wolf. Not Wyatt, someone else. It sounded like they were scared—scared or hurt. A fist clenched in my chest as I thought about the others. I couldn't let another person die, but there was nothing I could do while stuck out here with my head on a swivel to watch out for traps.

Still, I rushed forward, crossing a foul, bubbling green stream by racing along a narrow tree trunk that had fallen across it. The path was easy to follow, and it led me to something ominous: large rock outcroppings, too tall to scale and too wide to run around, lined the trail on either side. A three-foot-wide hole at the base of the rocks looked like the only way through. It angled into the pitch-black underground, with no way for me to see what awaited inside.

"Son of a bitch." Gods knew what was hiding down there, but I had no other choice. If I wanted to do *anything* to help Wyatt, I'd need to get out of here fast.

Dropping to my knees, I gazed as far into the earthen tube as I could. The canopy above diffused the sunlight, which didn't help me at all. The faint light only provided shadows. Huffing in irritation, I dived headfirst into the hole. My elbows quickly grew raw as I used them to pull myself along. The space was big enough for the male alpha wolves to get through, but it felt like the walls and ceiling were closing in on me. It was awkward as hell for me to get through in my human form. Obviously, we were meant to travel through this passage in our wolf forms, but Abel and I, with the shift-suppressing potion still coursing through our veins, would have a hard time. Hell, I was *already* having a hard time. After a few more yards, the tunnel arched upward, making movement more difficult as I struggled against gravity.

My toes ached from being jammed into the tips of my boots. I ignored the pain and pushed deep into the dirt to propel myself forward. I'd probably lose at least one toenail if I kept moving this way, but what the hell. Plus, the goddamned tunnel felt like it might collapse at any second. To make matters worse, I'd already come across two offshoot tunnels and had no way of knowing if I should keep going straight or take one of those.

Darkness draped me like death, and even my shifter night vision did very little to show me the way. If I took those other tunnels, I'd be totally lost. No, I had to keep going straight. The thought of crawling around under the earth for hours, lost in the darkness, induced twinges of panic.

Leaving the offshoot tunnels behind, I inched my way another hundred or so feet. A rattling hiss and a strange bird-like mewling had my every muscle tensing. The reptilian smell hit me then, making me freeze mid-crawl.

Basilisk. Fuck.

I swallowed hard and tried to glance backward, but the tunnel didn't have enough leeway for me to see behind me. When the rasping sounds of scales on dirt reached me, I gathered all my strength and willpower and pushed forward faster.

A full-grown basilisk could kill with not only its venom but its gaze. I'd seen one days ago in the swamp challenge—a juvenile, thankfully; otherwise, several of us would have died when it slithered out of the mud. From the sounds coming from behind me, this one was huge. Like any shifter, I could heal quickly and from almost anything, but a basilisk's venom might be enough to kill me.

With a new surge of energy, I crawled and scraped forward as quickly as my limbs allowed. Ahead of me, the pitch blackness gave way to a faint gray light illuminating the tunnel ahead. I had to be close to the exit. I dug my toes into the dirt yet again and pressed myself forward. Behind me, the rasping sounds grew louder, more insistent, as though the creature had heard or smelled me. My breath hissed in and out of my nose in spastic gasps as the sounds behind me grew closer. I could almost feel the damn thing's breath on my feet.

"Is somebody in there?" a voice rang out from the end of the hole. Faint, but not far away.

"Help!" I screamed. my fear shoving away any pride I might have had. "Help me!"

"Kira?"

"Abel?" I recognized his voice.

"What's wrong? Are you stuck?"

I clawed forward even faster, knowing salvation waited around the next bend in the tunnel. I just had to get there before the monster creeping along behind me reached my frantically kicking legs.

"Basilisk!" I shouted, barely able to breathe. "Keep your eyes closed, Abel! Don't look!"

"Holy fuck, Kira, hurry!"

Ahead of me, the tunnel grew brighter, slicing through the suffocating darkness and giving me a view of the end. Abel had his arm thrust into the tunnel, fingers wiggling, beckoning me. Tingles shot through the nerves in my arm as I reached forward and clasped his hand mere seconds before a deep, stinging agony bit into my calf.

I screamed and kicked at the thing, pain and panic making it hard to think straight. The creature's teeth dug in deeper, its fangs scraping against my bones, sending a grating feeling through my entire skeleton. The pain enveloped me, forcing the air from my lungs, not even letting me scream. The world spun around me faster and faster, and my stomach roiled. I had no idea if it was from fear or the venom.

The basilisk yanked me backward, but Abel held strong. With the death grip he had on me, I could focus on breaking free rather than fighting for the exit. I pushed my free foot into the jaws of the beast, shoved my boot into its mouth, and pried its mandibles open. One of its long, delicate fangs snapped off beneath the heavy rubber sole of my boot. The pain must have surprised it because the creature's mouth burst wide open and an alien screech—a mix of a rooster's crow and a hiss—erupted in the narrow tunnel, threatening to burst my eardrums.

The release allowed Abel to pull hard and drag me free of the tunnel. I sucked in huge lungsful of air and pulled myself up against his body. The second I was on my feet, I dragged him away from the hole before the goddamned thing in there could emerge and finish what it had started. We ran together until we couldn't see the tunnel exit.

The basilisk's venom had already wormed its way into my body. My vision blurred, fading in and out, and a ringing like a high-pitched insect screaming echoed in my ears. I did my best to ignore it.

Gasping, I bent over, hands on knees. "I'm glad you're okay."

"Uh, yeah," Abel said, panting. "If I hadn't been, I think you'd be about halfway down a giant snake's throat."

"It's not a real snake," I said, shaking my head. "They're magical creations from millennia ago. They're like a combination of a cobra, chicken, and alligator. No legs, though, so that's why people think it's only a giant snake."

Abel gaped at me. "Um, okay, Professor Monster-lady. Anyway, are you all right? Did it bite you?"

I pulled my pants leg up, showing him the vivid red puncture wounds on my calf. "Hurts like a bitch."

"Come on, I'll help you." Abel gingerly placed one of my arms over his shoulders. He put his arm around my back and supported me as we headed down the path.

"Have you... ugh... seen Wyatt?" I asked between gasps of pain.

"No. Was he with you? Did he get stuck in that tunnel?"

I winced as a hot ice sensation lanced up my leg. "No, we got separated. Last I saw, he and a feral shifter were fighting." I didn't add that the feral was Leif. One thing at a time.

We had to be close to the end of the course. The tree line indicated we were near the mansion. Abel helped me through the last few obstacles, my leg growing heavier and more leaden with every step. The venom slowed me and made my brain all fuzzy. Fire ran through my veins. Were I not a shifter, I'd probably already be dead.

Even as I struggled with the agony and the obstacles, I tried to catch Wyatt's scent, desperate for even the faintest whiff—but nothing. Images of Leif ripping Wyatt's throat out flashed through my mind, but I pushed them away. He had to be okay. I refused to believe anything else.

"Look!" Abel cried out, his voice thick with relief. "The mansion! We're almost there."

I could see the courtyard ahead of us, less than fifty meters away through the trees. Not even the pain clawing at me could make me forget what happened the last time I crossed the boundary into the courtyard without someone I cared for. The showrunners would never let me back into the jungle to go after Wyatt. They hadn't for Zoe, so why would this be different? If I stayed, I could backtrack and try to find him.

Abel noticed my hesitancy and tugged me gently. "Are you okay? Need me to carry you?"

"Let me!" a voice called from behind.

Abel jerked in surprise, and I turned toward the voice. Every movement was slow and sluggish due to the venom slowly creeping through my veins. Gavin was jogging up the path, a cavalier smile on his face.

"Where'd... you come from?" I wheezed.

He threw a thumb over his shoulder. "Made it through the last of the obstacles. Did you guys see that damn basilisk?"

"We did more than see it," Abel said, gesturing to my leg.

Gavin's eyes went wide when he saw the punctures. "Oh my gods, Kira. We have to get you to the healers. Even your metabolism isn't enough to flush that kind of toxin out."

"That's what I'm telling her," Abel said. "The courtyard is right there. I think she's too tired to go farther."

The pain and lethargy of the venom was too great for me to argue. It took all I had to stand. My exhaustion wasn't entirely about me being in pain, though. Most of it came from thinking about Wyatt.

Too weak to fight off his offer of help, I let Gavin scoop me into his arms and held onto him as he hurried the last few yards along with Abel. We crossed the boundary into the courtyard, and a small part of my mind cried out.

Wyatt was stuck out there. I would be of no help to him.

We'd come in last. Chelsey sat off to the side with Mika, J.D., and Tate. They all looked pretty dirty and beaten up, but to my chagrin, none looked like they'd needed to be carried like an invalid.

"And here is our other prize mate," Von said as Gavin gently set me on the flagstones. "You had us worrying for a bit." He wagged a finger at me in disapproval. "You may need to invest in a map the next time you go out. You're *very* directionally challenged from the looks of things."

I wanted to spout some smartass comment, but all I could do was moan as the healers worked over me.

"Drink this, sweetie," an older witch said, handing me a small vial.

I quickly downed the bright green concoction. It tasted like vinegar, garlic, and what I imagined wet dog would taste like. I gagged but managed to keep it down.

"You weren't the only one of our merry band to get lost," Von said. "Mika ended up hopelessly lost at one point."

Across the courtyard, Mika rubbed a hand through his hair, looking more irritated than embarrassed.

I tried to speak, to ask about Wyatt, but all my energy had vanished. The potion and spells were working, but not fast enough. Von went on.

"I'm sure our fans are going to be a little disappointed. A remarkable number of cameras were damaged during this challenge—far more than is typical. So, unfortunately, the footage will be a little sparse. We saw almost none of Mika until J.D. found him and helped him back. Nor did we get much from Kira or Wyatt." Von glanced back into the jungle and frowned exaggeratedly. "It seems Mr. Rivers may not be joining us any longer."

"Do you know where he went missing?" I asked. My voice sounded stronger now that I was healing. "Send someone in after him."

Von turned to me and cocked an eyebrow. "Hmm. Really, Kira? Is that what you want? It appears to me that Miss Durst may not be as finished with Wyatt Rivers as she might have us believe."

Shit. I had to remember the plan. If Von thought the hatred between Wyatt and I was fading, he'd drop the bombshell that we knew each other before coming on the show.

"Just because I don't like someone doesn't mean I want them dead," I said, getting to my feet unsteadily. "I wasn't a huge fan of Nathaniel or Omar, but I didn't enjoy seeing them die." I pointed back toward the jungle. "I despise Wyatt. I'd rather tongue-kiss a harpy than end up with him as my mate. But he deserves a chance to live."

Maybe the vampire bought my act, maybe not. His noncommittal shrug gave nothing away. "We tried to send a witch in to teleport him back to the main path once you were taken care of. That staff witch has yet to return." He shook his head sadly. "Sometimes, our poor staff members fall victim to the dangers of

Bloodstone Island." He leaned conspiratorially toward one of the cameras. "That's why they sign waivers before each season. Can't be too careful, can we?"

Ignoring my glare, Von and the floating camera migrated to the other housemates. He took a seat next to J.D. and put a friendly arm around the alpha.

"J.D., can I catch a few words with you? It looked to us via the camera feed that you went through the obstacle course in a rather lackluster manner. Can you give us some reason as to why that was? I'm sure the viewers would love a little look into your mind and how you tick. In fact, it looked like you weren't even going to complete the course alive until you heard Mika screaming for help."

I crossed my arms and glanced at the jungle again, but allowed my attention to go back to the interview. Mika had almost died? How many of us had been close to death today?

J.D. gave a perfunctory shrug. "He got torn up pretty bad and needed help. What was I supposed to do? Leave him to die?"

Von laughed and slapped a hand on his thigh. "Yes, my boy! That's the game. One less alpha means one less person between you and Chelsey or Kira.

But," he nudged J.D. jovially, "I can understand your hesitancy to leave one of your own behind. I think it's one of the reasons our fans are rooting for you. I truly believe you would be a great mate for Chelsey or Kira. Either one. Though..." Von smiled wide and looked across the courtyard at me. "You will be having a very sexy date with Kira in the mating chamber tomorrow. Perhaps you can *really* show her what you're capable of tomorrow night, hmm?"

He tried to nudge J.D. playfully again, but the alpha wasn't having it. J.D. still looked miserable. No doubt he was still pining for Leif.

At the thought of Leif, my gaze snapped back to the forest. Von continued trying to get soundbites from J.D., but everything they said became background noise—distant and unimportant. Wyatt was out there, fighting for his life.

Unless he's already dead, a wicked voice in my head murmured.

No. I gritted my teeth and focused all my attention on the jungle, mentally willing Wyatt to appear. He couldn't be dead. I refused to believe it. Leif had been shockingly ferocious, powerful, and quick, urged on by the feral rage and hunger boiling inside him. Still, Wyatt had trained as an operative. I'd seen him deal with things far more dangerous than a feral shifter. He hadn't faced them as injured as he'd been earlier, but that shouldn't matter. Even hurt, a TO could handle a wolf like Leif... unless something else had happened. A second feral? A demon? Any number of things could have joined the fight and swung things against Wyatt's favor.

Nausea welled up in my stomach. It wasn't from the venom—that was already fading from my system, thanks to my healing and the witches. No, this came from worry and fear. The jungle, dark and malevolent, towered over me as if it was gleeful of my anxiety. I put my hand to my mouth, hoping the others didn't see the look on my face, see how badly I wanted Wyatt to come jogging up the path.

"Please, Wyatt," I whispered into my hand so quietly that I could barely hear myself. "Please come back."

Chapter 2 - Wyatt

Birds. That was the first sound I noticed—the chirping and cawing of birds. Was that what the afterlife was? Darkness and birds chirping for eternity? Maybe I was in hell.

Before I opened my eyes, I took stock of my body. I'd never died before, so I had no frame of reference. But everything on my person felt whole and uninjured.

As I slowly opened my eyes, green assaulted me. I saw green everywhere, and treetops. I was staring at the jungle canopy. Lying there, I blinked and listened to the cacophony of birds, frogs, and gods knew what other animals, singing the songs of their given species.

Click, click, burr, click, click, burr. A mechanical whirring and clicking sound came from somewhere nearby. That made no sense. From what I could see, I was in the middle of the jungle.

My mind began to clear, and I recalled the last things that had happened—Kira being pulled away by a witch, my arm throbbing and hanging almost uselessly at my side, and Leif jumping toward me, teeth bared, ready to tear my throat out. Had I lost so much blood, I'd passed out? If so, why wasn't I dead?

I sniffed the air. Leif. And nearby, from the strength of his scent. The realization forced me to move. I sat up quickly, rolled to the side, and jumped to a crouch, ready to fight. If Leif was still here, how had I survived? He'd been bloodthirsty and out of his mind. I should have been a red smear on the forest floor, especially if I'd lost consciousness.

A sniffing sound came from my right. Snapping my eyes over, I saw Leif. What I found sitting near me looked nothing like the savage and deranged wolf that had attacked me and Kira. A man in human form sat on the forest floor, clutching his bowed head, rocking back and forth. He was crying and muttering to himself, but his voice was so low, I couldn't make out the words.

Everything in my mind screamed at me to run, to get away before he came to his senses, but something about his demeanor drew me in. My curiosity might get me killed, but I *had* to know what the hell was going on.

"Leif?" I ventured, my voice raspy. I'd kill for a glass of water. "Are you okay?"

"I can't, I can't, I can't, I can't..." The words repeated over and over, punctuated every few seconds by another sniffle.

"What..."

The words died in my throat as I finally took in the scene around me. After waking, I'd been too focused on the fact that I'd survived and that Leif sat next to me. Now? What lay around me sent a chill up my spine. Three other feral wolves were strewn about the clearing we sat in. Two had their throats ripped out, and the third looked like its stomach had been split open, its insides tumbling out in a steaming pile. I grimaced and looked away.

On the opposite side of the clearing, a massive mountain loomed above us, casting a shadow over our location. It was the dormant volcano, one of the most iconic images of Bloodstone Island. Up a slight incline, I noticed an opening, perhaps a cave? That weird mechanical noise was coming from the entrance. What the hell was this? Could this be the place Kira had talked about? The location where Zoe and the rogue shifter were camped out at?

"Fuck you!" Leif's scream pierced the afternoon air.

Spinning back to him, I realized he wasn't talking to me. He glared at a tree in front of him, his eyes glazed over. His teeth were bared, and a thin string of drool hung from one lip. Something had gone terribly wrong with him.

Self-preservation won out over my curiosity. I took two unsteady steps backward, putting distance between us. On my third step, a stick snapped underfoot, and Leif jerked his eyes toward me.

"Where are you going?" He slowly rose to his feet, the madness in his eyes slowly returning.

I held up my hands in a warding-off gesture. "Hang on, buddy. Leif? It's me. It's Wyatt. Stay cool, my man."

"You can't leave." The last word turned into a howl as he shifted.

"Ah, fuck."

I whirled and ran, sprinting into the forest. My escape ended at less than a dozen yards when Leif's jaws clamped down on my boot. With a wicked jerk of his head, he pulled my legs out from under me, sending me crashing to the ground. My face slammed into the forest floor and stars exploded across my vision, threatening to send me back into the dark abyss of unconsciousness. Rather than immediately eviscerating me, Leif pulled and yanked at my foot, dragging me back the way we came. Blood oozed from my nose and my head rang.

After a few seconds, I got my bearings again and realized what Leif had planned as he dragged me up the hill toward the opening in the volcano. Something about those strange sounds made me uneasy. Some deep and instinctual part of me did *not* want to see what waited inside.

I brought my foot down on Leif's face, the heel of my boot slamming into Leif's muzzle. Yelping in pain, he released my foot. Taking advantage of his confusion, I pulled myself away and shifted, backing away as I bared my teeth at him.

A deep growl reverberated from Leif's chest as he lunged at me. I'd seen it coming and was prepared. I dodged to the side, bit the side of Leif's neck as he flew past, and spun the full weight of my body to the side. Leif's momentum and my movement caused him to tumble toward a tree to my left.

He crashed into the trunk, head slamming into the wood with a meaty *thwack*. His body crashed to the ground in a heap. I didn't think I'd killed him, hoped I hadn't, but I couldn't take the chance to stand around and find out. This was my chance to escape. I ran for it, my paws hissing over the leaves and moss beneath my feet.

Why had he been trying to drag me to that place? It made no sense. Nothing about the way Leif had acted made sense. How had he gone feral so quickly? Going feral was a long and agonizing process. What the actual *hell* was happening on this island?

My thoughts were scattered as something lunged at me from the undergrowth and slammed into my side. I lost my footing and skidded across the ground. What I saw standing above me irritated me more than it scared me.

The chupacabra's glowing red eyes glared at me. The creatures looked like scrawny hairless dogs but with bigger teeth, strange reptilian spines along their backs, and that godawful tongue. The thing hung from its mouth, twisting and writhing like it had its own mind. It could latch on and suck the blood out of other creatures, hence the nickname "goat sucker." They were more of a pest than a danger.

Righting myself, I stood and growled deep in my throat, then took a heavy step toward the beast. It yowled at me, hesitantly stepping back. It had realized it had overstepped its abilities by attacking a shifter. Even the average human would have had a decent chance of fighting it off, but it against me? No way, and it knew it. I lunged at it, snapping my jaws for emphasis, and the thing tucked tail and vanished back into the jungle.

I shifted back to my human form and continued heading away from the volcano back toward the obstacle course. From the sun's position in the sky, I'd been knocked out for a while. Was the challenge even still going on? I couldn't remember if Von had given us a time limit. However long I'd been out, it hadn't been long enough to fully heal. My body still felt like I'd been hit by a bus.

"Where goes the shifter man?" a female voice whispered from an outcropping of rock to my left.

I jerked in surprise and almost fell over as I tripped on a tree root. "Who's there? Who are you?"

"We three. The three that be. That's who are we." This voice was different from the first.

From beneath the outcropping, a face slowly emerged. My stomach dropped as the thing revealed itself. A fae, but one twisted by black magic. Its skin shimmered a sickly, almost transparent white, and the eyes were completely black with no white showing. Strange red veins crisscrossed her skin. She lifted a hand with talon-like black nails. Two more faces appeared as her friends oozed out from their hiding places like snakes. All three had once been female before being corrupted.

I took another step back, my mind racing. The lead fae crawled along the rock almost like an insect, sending a chill up my spine. She was naked and smeared with dirt and debris, leaves stuck in her jet-black hair. I knew she could have cleaned herself up in seconds with a spell, but apparently she didn't care.

Those lifeless black eyes bore into mine. "Give us the liquid of life—blood, semen, or sweat. Wonders, we can show you if you would be our little pet."

"Indeed, sister," the second fae said. "Feast on his power. Take the delicious shifter man. Long life you want? Long life we give."

The third fae slithered across the stones to join her sisters. She grinned up at me and clacked her black teeth together. "Suckle it, we would. Pleasure, we would give. Spell, we can cast. Then bite it off, we will. Blood will end it at last. Like us, you can be."

I took another step back. "I'm, uh, gonna have to take a rain check on that, okay? It all sounds, um, delightful, but I've got to go. I'm not a big fan of the whole biting-the-dick-off thing."

The three fae women chattered in some mad language like chittering locusts, then the lead fae stood to her full height. She extended her hands to her sides, claw-like nails raking at the air.

"No magic? Useless, you are. Food, you will be. Play with your body, we will."

The three women lunged forward like they were made of water, writhing and slithering, the red veins crossing their flesh glowing with inner magical power. I screamed, shifted, and ran. Around me, trees exploded as the fae sent spells after me. The manic screeches of the women were the only thing I could hear. I sprinted, hoping to lose them.

Ahead of me, the ground sloped drastically into a ravine. Pushing myself, I increased my speed, then leaped. Wind rippled through my fur as I propelled through the air. The landing would be rough, but it had to be better than whatever those freaky fae had planned for me.

Half a second before I landed, I tucked my head and hit the forest floor, rolling madly. Thankfully, the ground was thick with rotting palm fronds and ferns. Instead of feeling like I'd been beaten with a sledgehammer, it felt more like a couple of guys had kicked me a few times.

Coming to a stop, I flipped over and looked up. The fae hadn't followed, but I couldn't bank on them staying put. I shifted back into my human form and began to run. The ravine led back to the path, and within minutes, I came to an obstacle—a large wall covered in barbed wire. I breathed a sigh of relief that I'd at least made it back to where I needed to be.

The wall proved easy to climb, but it wasn't my body that worked overtime, it was my mind. Kira. Was she okay? Had she finished the course without getting hurt? My thoughts took a surprising turn when I began to worry about the others, too. J.D.? Mika? Were any of them dead? The idea made me queasy. I'd initially come on the show to protect Kira, but now I saw things from her point of view—or started to, anyway. A lot of the guys here didn't deserve to die on this island. In my mind, Mika, J.D., and Abel all deserved a happy ending, a chance at life away from this hellhole.

That kind thought didn't quite extend to Tate and Gavin, though.

Thirty minutes later, soaked with sweat and with a few more bumps and bruises, I jogged out of the jungle into the mansion's courtyard. Cameras flocked toward me as I almost keeled over in exhaustion. Off to the side, Von started clapping, and my gaze tracked over to see Kira, Abel, and Gavin.

Kira's eyes went wide at the sight of me. Oh, thank the gods, she was alive and safe. Relief flooded my entire being at the sight of her. It took everything I had to keep my composure. We still had an act to follow.

"My, my, my, Mr. Rivers, you gave us quite a scare," Von said. "We were certain you'd been turned into hamburger meat by some terrible beastie. Welcome back. You do have a flair for the dramatic, don't you?"

"Water," I gasped, waving to one of the support staff. "Water." I'd never been so thirsty in my life.

Kira took a few steps closer, concern blazing in her eyes. I wiped the sweat from my brow, crooking my fingers as I did to make a gesture like the peace sign but with the index and middle fingers bent and the thumb between them. It was a common hand signal for operatives. Basically, it meant, *All good, debrief later.*

Kira nodded almost imperceptibly. One of the witches brought over a crystal pitcher and glasses. I bypassed the glasses, yanking the entire pitcher off the silver tray to guzzle the water.

"How very masculine," Von remarked as he watched me gulping down the water between gasps of breath. The icy liquid poured down my mouth and the front of my shirt. It felt amazing as it cooled me off, but it tasted even better.

Finally done, I handed the empty pitcher back to the witch. Von stepped over, that ever-present camera hovering behind him. He threw an arm around my shoulders. "You know, it's difficult to impress a vampire. We live such long lives, and we've seen so much, yet here you are, shocking the pants off me. I was certain you'd been eliminated. Tell us, Wyatt, how did you get out of that jungle alive? The fans back home must be positively drooling to find out how things went for you. And, of course..." Von gestured back toward Chelsey, who had emerged from the mansion. She was a little pale, but it seemed she'd fully healed from the wolfsbane tea she'd drunk earlier. "Our lovely Chelsey must be beside herself now that she knows you are okay."

"A rough day, for sure," I said.

Seeing that was all he was going to get out of me, Von cocked an eyebrow. "You don't say. Very verbose, aren't you, Mr. Rivers? Anyway, don't let me hold you two kids up from being reunited. We all know you are Chelsey's top choice. Come, my lady, and say hello to this strapping alpha."

Chelsey looked uncomfortable as all the hovering cameras turned their lenses on her. Flicking my eyes, I saw Kira watching her as she stepped forward. Chelsey opened her arms and took me in a hug. As I hesitantly embraced her, I couldn't help but wish it was Kira's body nestled against my chest instead. I still felt nothing for this woman. Chelsey had a kind heart, beauty, and from everything I'd seen thus far, a sharp mind. But there was zero chemistry between us.

I wanted Kira. *Needed* Kira.

"I'm so glad you made it back," Chelsey said as she broke our embrace.

"Glad to be back," I said, giving her the best fake smile I could muster.

"Okay, Wyatt, enough tiptoeing around the subject," Von said. "How on earth did you get so far off-track out there?"

He wasn't going to give up until I gave him something. Deciding to be as vague as possible, I gestured toward the forest. "Hard not to get really turned around in there. Trying to survive those traps and obstacles, you know? I ended up off-trail and lost my way. Simple as that." Deciding to throw in a bit of truth, I added, "Three dark fae almost got me, and I fell down a ravine. That led me back to the course."

Von's eyes brightened. "The Three Sisters? Very interesting, aren't they?"

"Uh, yeah. Lots of rhyming. Not a fan."

Von chuckled and punched me lightly in the shoulder like we were buddies. I smiled, but my anxiety was eating at me. I wanted to find out what the hell was going on here. What had happened to Leif? Kira stood right there, less than fifteen feet away, yet I couldn't talk to her. It was maddening. The ever-present cameras had become even more of a nuisance than before.

Von turned back to his lead camera and smiled his shimmering grin at the world. "Well, I have to say, I'm surprised and a little disappointed that we didn't have any additional eliminations for this challenge. I'm sure you folks at home are saddened as well. We all love drama, am I right?" He held up a finger. "But do not worry. There are still some juicy moments coming up. A special arena match *and* two lucky couples get to enjoy the use of the mating chamber. We've decided to have the chamber dates on two separate nights. Better to draw out the sexiness, yes? I'm sure you all agree. Until next time. Remember, everyone loves an underdog."

Once he signed off, the lights on my bracelet changed, and the hovering cameras all zipped back toward the mansion.

"Well, kids, it's been fun, but I'm famished," Von said, then licked his lips. "A delectable young stud has been dropped off in my room for me to

partake in. I'm sure you'll understand if I make haste."
He winked at Chelsey. "Don't worry, I won't drain him
dry. I want a little fun afterward."

The host hurried off toward the mansion.
Chelsey shuddered. "That's creepy, right?"

I imagined male and female volunteers offering
Von their necks for food and their bodies for pleasure.
Bile rose in my throat at the thought. If it was just sex,
who cared? Do what feels good with whoever you
want. The whole sucking-blood-from-your-neck part
was where I drew the line.

Kira stood off to the side, talking to Gavin. I
needed to talk to her, but even without the cameras,
we had to be careful. How the hell would I get her
alone?

"You look like you could use this." I turned to
find Abel offering me two bananas.

I glanced at the fruit, hunger clawing at my
stomach. "Thanks," I said, taking the bananas and
tearing one open to devour the flesh inside.

"I'm going to go get changed," Chelsey said.
"Are you all right?"

The concern in her eyes and voice made my
heart hurt. All this woman wanted was someone to

love her, and she'd set her eyes on a man who didn't desire her. I nodded and smiled at her, doing my best to be cordial. "Yeah, I'm fine. You go ahead."

As Chelsey walked toward the house, Abel nudged my arm. "How bad was it? Out there, I mean?" He nodded toward the jungle.

"Lots of bad shit out there. Those dark fae were the worst, though," I said as I chewed the banana. "Crazy as hell. I couldn't tell if they wanted to eat me, use me as an ingredient for a spell, or have sex with me. Super creepy and gross."

Abel chuckled. "Well, at least you were able to shift. I've never had to go through something like that without relying on my inner wolf to come out and help. I don't know how Kira does it. Gods, it's really impressive. I'm glad I stumbled on her when I did. Otherwise, I don't think she'd have made it."

Warning bells screeched in my head, and I turned to him, the second banana forgotten. "What happened?"

"Basilisk in a tunnel she had to crawl through. If you took a certain route through the course, that was the only way to advance. I pulled her out, but it got its teeth into her. Gavin and I basically had to carry her back. It looked painful." He furrowed his brow. "I think it messed with her head. She acted like she didn't want to cross the finish line. Almost like she didn't want to leave the jungle."

My inner wolf was raging. Kira had been bitten and shot full of venom. From the sound of it, she'd nearly died. It pissed me off that I hadn't been there to help her.

Pushing the rage and sense of impotence down, I schooled my face into a mask of disgust and scoffed. "No surprise there. Kira's always in some sort of trouble." I raised my voice so everyone could hear me. "She's basically a walking disaster, barely scraping by. She'll end up getting someone killed if she isn't careful. That's not something I have to worry about with Chelsey."

"Oh my god, Wyatt," Kira snapped from across the courtyard. "Get over yourself."

"Was I talking to you?" I asked. I was laying it on thick, but it was all part of our cover. "I think Abel and I were talking privately, weren't we? Maybe go back to what you were doing and leave us alone. How about that for an idea?"

We'd done this so often over the years that falling back into the pattern of bickering was no different than putting on an old, comfortable coat. At work, at her house—anywhere—we'd always squabble. The only difference this time was that the fighting wasn't real. We were putting on a show that would hopefully help keep us both alive.

Kira took a few steps closer and jammed her fists into her hips. "Yeah, you weren't talking to me, but you should maybe keep my name out of your mouth if you don't want me to speak up. Surely you can't be so dumb to think I wouldn't say something. Or maybe you are." She shrugged. "You tell me."

I rolled my eyes and laughed. "Gods, you're so full of drama. You probably get off on all these people watching you on TV. It wouldn't surprise me."

"I don't. Honestly, if anyone enjoys it, it's probably you, Wyatt. You keep bouncing from girl to girl. Poor Chelsey could do so much better." She glanced pointedly down at my crotch. "She could find some*one* better and some*thing* bigger, if you know what I mean."

Abel, eyes wide with surprise, backed away from me, obviously not wanting to get pulled into

Kira's tirade. Behind her, Gavin had a shit-eating grin on his lips. Mika, however, stared at us in disbelief. He knew the deal, yet our show must have been so believable that it surprised even him.

"You know what, Kira?" I said. "Stop trying to keep the attention on yourself. Maybe head back up to your room and get some *beauty* sleep." I looked her up and down and sneered in disgust. "You fucking need it."

Her face went red, and she looked for all the world like she wanted to tear my throat out, but her eyes revealed the truth. She was fighting back a laugh. To cover the smile that threatened to spread across her face, she bared her teeth as though she were enraged.

"You are an asshole, Wyatt Rivers."

Chapter 3 - Kira

I bit into the side of my cheek to keep from laughing, hard enough to make my eyes water. A nice touch, if I said so myself. Having wet eyes really helped sell the whole thing. Wyatt was laying it on thick, maybe even too much.

"You know what, I don't have time for this," I said. "I'm going up to get checked out by the healers again. I feel sick to my stomach. Maybe that's the basilisk venom, or maybe it's looking at you, Wyatt. Whatever it is, I need to get it figured out. Why don't you go read a book or something?" The look I gave him was heavily suggestive, and I hoped he understood what I was trying to get across. A small library sat down the hall from the healing room in the mansion.

To my relief, Wyatt ran a hand down his chest, his thumb tucked in, hidden behind his palm. Another hand signal from the TO: *understood*. With a sigh of relief, I spun around and stomped away from him.

"Damn. Better you than me, bro," Tate said as he chuckled.

"Why are you guys like that?" Abel asked, sounding beyond confused.

Now that I'd said I was going, I needed to at least make an appearance in the healer's room. If nothing else, it would give Wyatt time to break away from the others. If he left too soon after I did, it would look suspicious.

Whenever I went into the healing room, it always struck me how antiseptic and monochrome it was compared to the rest of the mansion. Bland and austere compared to opulent luxury. When I walked in, only one member of the healing staff was available—the rest must have been outside. The fae woman was young compared to the others and smiled as I closed the door behind me.

"Can I help you?" she asked as I stepped in.

"Um, yeah, a basilisk bit me. So, I just want to make sure there were no complications."

Her eyes went wide. "Goodness. I heard about that. So scary. I am *not* a snake person, so that sounds like the most terrifying thing ever." She grimaced. "Were you really underground when it came after you?"

A shiver ran up my spine at the memory. "Yeah. Anyway, my leg still hurts. Not bad, but I can feel where it bit me every time I take a step. Is there anything you can give me until it fades?"

She bent and dug around beneath the counter. "I have just the thing. That kind of venom is nasty. Even the best spells and potions can't flush it all away. Some of it will have to work its way out." She glanced up and winced. "I hate to say it, but the next time you pee, it won't be super-pleasant. Most of it will be expelled through the bladder."

"Wonderful," I said dryly.

She shrugged and pulled out a small vial of pills. "Here you go."

I took the bottle and glanced at the label. My jaw dropped. "Ibuprofen? Seriously?"

The fae nurse grinned and rolled her eyes. "Sometimes human remedies end up being the best. Rarely, mind you, but *sometimes*. These pills have a weird interaction with magical venoms, especially once they've been diluted by other magical means. It puts a buffer between the body's nerves and the peptides in the venom. Honestly, I don't get it. All I know is that it works. Take one now and another about ten minutes before you go to bed. After that, you should be good to go."

The little brown pill looked so insignificant in my palm. Tossing the tablet into my mouth, I swallowed it dry as I tucked the little bottle into my pants. "Well, thanks. Hopefully, this is the last time you'll see me here."

"Fingers crossed. Good luck," she called as I exited.

Once the door closed, I glanced down the hall, listening intently and sniffing the air. Only one person was nearby, and I knew that scent better than anyone's. I ducked into the small library and found Wyatt perusing the books on the shelves. He turned and held up a book.

"Did you know these are all fake?"

"What?"

He opened one, showing me blank pages. "Fake. These aren't real books. Hell, the leather binding isn't even *real* leather. It's all for show. I fucking *hate* this place."

The door clicked shut behind me, and I locked it to ensure we'd have a bit of privacy.

"What the hell took you so long to get back?" I hissed and punched his chest.

"Ow, shit." He rubbed the spot where I'd hit him. "That freaking hurt."

"Spill it. What happened after the witch took me?"

"Damn, no foreplay? We're gonna dive right in, huh?"

Our banter always drove me crazy, but it endeared him to me even more. A month ago, I wouldn't have believed that I'd enjoy being around Wyatt, joking around with him. It was strange but pleasant in a weird way. Though I really *did* want to know what was going on.

"Were you hurt?" I asked, glancing up and down his body.

His smile faded as he slipped into a more professional attitude. "Not badly. Scrapes and cuts, but nothing as bad as a damn basilisk bite, if that's what you mean."

A shaky sigh escaped my lips. I'd been so worried about him, and now that I knew he was fine, a massive weight lifted from me. I wanted to reach out and touch him, to feel his body and make absolutely sure he wasn't hurt, but we had no time for where that would inevitably lead—where it always led when we were alone together. As nice as a few minutes of carnal excitement sounded, we had to stay on task. My eyes found his and my face flamed.

"Are we *absolutely* sure there are no cameras or microphones in here?" I asked.

"I checked the whole place while I waited for you. We're good." His confidence meant a lot.

I sighed in relief. "You had me worried to death. You know that, right?"

The grin Wyatt gave me was sad. "Welcome to my world."

I couldn't help but laugh. "Fair enough." My smile faded when I remembered how I'd left him in the jungle and what had been about to happen. "Leif? Did you... well, you know?" I couldn't say the rest. It would hurt too much.

Wyatt's eyebrows rose and he sighed. "That part is weird."

He told me about his blackout, waking up in a different part of the jungle, and Leif's odd behavior. The part about the volcano and the weird tunnel leading into it was even stranger.

"Could that be where Zoe's hiding?" Wyatt asked. "Some hidden underground bunker inside the volcano? Whatever's in there, Leif tried his damnedest to get me inside. Something about it was *off*. Creepy and wrong. I can't really explain it. Just a gut feeling."

At the mention of Zoe, I told Wyatt about finding her and the one-eyed wolf named Crew. It took a few minutes, but I gave him the gist of my plan for staging eliminations to get the other alphas off the show and out of danger. He looked more and more surprised as I continued talking.

"Kira, this is huge. The fact that people are living and surviving on Bloodstone Island is crazy. It shouldn't be possible."

"I know. I was just as surprised, but it's true. They think they can help us, though. We have to give it a shot."

"We can't go into this without more information. There needs to be some kind of foolproof plan in place before we start trying to get guys like Abel and J.D. off the show. If we don't do this right, they'll end up dead regardless."

That was something that had been playing at the edges of my mind for a while. "Do you think they'd kill us on purpose? To keep it a secret?"

Wyatt's mouth twisted as he thought. "This show makes hundreds of millions of dollars every year. Almost all of that is predicated on the fact that Bloodstone is the most dangerous place on the planet. If it came to light that wasn't true? Well, people have been killed for a lot less."

He wasn't lying. I'd seen enough in my time as an operative to know that was true. "Well, we'll have more help than we initially thought."

"What does that mean?"

"Chelsey. She's *pissed* the people in charge kidnapped her brother. He's back home now, but she wants to tear this fucking show apart from the inside, too."

Wyatt's eyes widened in surprise. "Wow. I get it, but I'm still a little surprised. She's tailor-made for this show. Her turning on them says a lot."

"I don't have a full plan yet, but if it's the last thing I do, this will be the last year this show is on. I want it gone. I don't want to think about how many people have died for this shit for no damn reason."

Wyatt's eyes narrowed. "I don't like the way you phrased that."

"Huh?"

"You said, 'If it's the last thing I do.' I don't like that. Taking the show down would be great, but I don't want it to be the end of you. If it comes down to it, you need to stay safe. Someone else can be the revolutionary. Not you."

"I know what I'm doing," I said. Did I, though?

"The people in charge are powerful, Kira. Tons of money, tons of influence, and a *lot* to lose. Think about it. They're already killing alphas in this fucking game. If it looks like their cash cow might be in danger, the gloves will really come off. That's all I'm saying."

He made it sound like nameless and faceless monsters were in the background, pulling the strings, which was probably true. But it irritated the crap out of me when he treated me like this. After everything we'd been through, he still acted like I couldn't handle myself.

Before I could press him on that matter, he redeemed himself. "As difficult as it may be, if anyone on earth can tear this show apart, it's you. It doesn't stop me from worrying about you. I want this over as much as you do, but there's only so much one person can do."

He was right about that. One woman against a host of millionaires and billionaires, and whatever awful people they had to send against us? The odds weren't great. One person couldn't fight an army. If we were going to bring this thing toppling down, we'd need the rest of society to help. How the hell did you do that when *everyone* loved the show?

"Anyway..." I said. "I need to get back out there. Make sure to keep up the act. I think we did a good job out there."

Wyatt raised an eyebrow. "Did you really have to say my dick was small, though? Low blow."

"You called me ugly."

"Actually, I said you needed beauty sleep. It was only inferred, not outright stated."

"Semantics. Now shut up, we need to go. You first."

Wyatt chuckled and cracked open the door, glancing around the hall. "All clear."

"Hang on." I put a hand on his arm. "If we're going to keep snipping at each other, we need to have some code words. So we know what's really going on."

"Such as?" he asked, quietly latching the door again.

I thought for a second. "Well, if I say, 'You're pissing me off,' it means... I don't know, how about, 'Thank you?' Does that work?"

"And when I call you an 'annoying little brat,' it means 'I love you,'" Wyatt said with a mischievous smile.

The words slammed into me, explosive and heavy with meaning. Had he really just said that? Butterflies burst in my stomach. He'd stated it so nonchalantly, I couldn't tell if he was serious.

Before I could say anything, he opened the door and stepped out into the hallway. I hurried after him, not giving a damn if anyone saw us together. I needed to know if he meant what he'd said. After the library door closed behind me, I grabbed Wyatt's arm, forcing him to turn and face me again.

"What did you say?"

Wyatt stared into my eyes. "You heard me."

"But... but..."

"Hey, leave her alone!"

I flinched in surprise as Gavin stalked toward us, glaring at Wyatt.

"Oh, good. The *second* most annoying person in this house," Wyatt said.

Gavin hurried over to me and put a hand on my shoulder. "Was he being a dick?"

"It's fine, Gavin, seriously," I said, though I wasn't sure if it was. Wyatt's words still bounced through my mind like a pinball.

Wyatt made a disgusted face and waved a hand in dismissal. "I need to get out of here. Have fun with this annoying little brat."

He looked me in the eyes when he said it, and the slow, burning coals that had been smoldering inside me burst into flame. I watched him walk away with a strange sense of loss and excitement. I didn't want him to go, but he had to. Otherwise, Gavin would pick up on the reality of our relationship.

Gavin brushed a finger along the bottom of my chin. "You look worn out. Have you eaten since you got back?"

As though jerked from a dream, I blinked and shook my head. "Um, no. Not really. I had some water. That's all."

"Do you need to see the healers? You look sort of out of it. Is the venom still messing with you?"

"Already been," I said, coming back to my senses as Wyatt vanished around the corner. "Food would be good, though."

Gavin smiled and took my hand, leading me toward the kitchen. Once there, he waved down one of the staff chefs. Within ten minutes, we were sitting at the kitchen island. I bit into a club sandwich.

"Feeling better?" he asked.

Physically? Yes. Emotionally? No. I couldn't stop thinking about what Wyatt had said. *I love you.* Three words I'd never heard from anyone other than Mom, Dad, or Kolton. In all the years Jayson and I had been paired, he'd never uttered those words to me. They made my head spin, making it difficult to concentrate on Gavin. My wolf was in a strange state of bliss that I'd never felt from her before.

The TV above the island clicked on automatically, drawing me out of my inner thoughts.

Von's face filled the screen. My hunger almost vanished at the sight of him.

"Good afternoon, everyone. This broadcast is for our contestants only. I'm sure all of you are very tired after this exciting day. As such, you'll have the afternoon and evening off to recover and recuperate. Filming will start at breakfast tomorrow." His smile grew even wider and his eyes glittered mischievously. "And don't forget, tomorrow night, Wyatt and Chelsey will have the mating chamber all to themselves. Kira and J.D. will follow the next evening. Until then, enjoy your afternoons."

The TV clicked off, leaving us in silence. Grateful to be rid of Von again, I resumed eating. The only thing that pulled me out of my food reverie was Gavin's voice.

"Kira, can I ask you a question?"

Oh, shit. I swallowed. "Sure. What's up?"

He tapped a finger on the marble countertop, then his shoulders slumped. A very sullen look crept across his face. "Why did you pick J.D. for the mating chamber?"

There it was. Exactly the thing I knew he'd ask. He was obviously a little pissed about it. I wiped my hands on a napkin, but before I could say anything, Gavin went on.

"It's just that I thought our date went really well. We *connected*, or at least it seemed that way to me. Ever since I got here, I've been trying to show you that I'm here for you, to take care of you and show you that we're meant to be together."

Now he wasn't the only one who was a little pissed off. "Gavin, I'm not sure if you've noticed yet, but the chamber is completely my choice. I can do what I want with my own body. Or are you saying you somehow *deserve* to go in there with me? Is that what this is? You think that because you feel a certain way about me, you get to control what I do?"

His face gave away his reaction—he realized he'd overstepped. The pissy expression vanished and he raised his hands in surrender. "Wait, no. That isn't what I meant, it's just—"

"Stop," I said. I didn't want to stop now that I'd started. "If I want to take someone in there and fuck their brains out, that's my prerogative. It's my body, my pleasure, my life. That's not even the biggest part. I actually do *like* you, Gavin. Way more than I thought I would when you first got here."

His eyes brightened and a faint smile flickered across his lips. "You do?"

"Shut up and let me finish. Yes, I do like you, though I have to say, it makes me uneasy that you want to overthrow your pack and have mine absorb the remainder."

Gavin's brow furrowed. He couldn't have looked more confused. "Wait, aren't you on board with that? Surely you hate my pack even more than I do."

I shoved my plate away. My appetite had suddenly disappeared. "It doesn't matter what I think about your pack. What rubs me the wrong way is that you show zero emotional connection or affection for the group of people you were raised with."

Gavin leaned forward, lacing his fingers together like he was praying in Heline's temple. "But they're terrible, Kira. You saw how my dad and Jayson treated you. They're all like that. I can't stand what they are. They need a change in leadership. *Something.*"

"Listen, I'm not an idiot. I'm a realist. All packs have problems, some more so than others. I get that. Even my pack can be frustrating to deal with at times, but the pack is family. Shifters, especially wolf shifters, are meant to protect and love their packs no matter what. It's been that way since before recorded history, and the idea of you using me to turn all that on its head makes me feel... dirty, I guess."

He shook his head vehemently. "I don't want to *use* you. I'm sorry if that's how it came across when I explained it. I *genuinely* want you for my mate. To be with me forever, whether anything happens with my pack or not. I don't want you to think I hate all packs. It's super honorable that you're so fiercely loyal to your pack. I get it. I'm not trying to disparage your pack when I say this, but..." He leaned in close, locking his eyes on mine. "Can't you see how everyone's blind devotion to packs can be dangerous? Giving everything you have to protect them up while they do awful shit?"

His words reminded me of Wyatt's history. His pack had turned their backs on him, refused to acknowledge that his fated mate had been terrible and would have ruined his life. They hadn't even fought for him. I frowned as I thought about my own situation. The pack elders had pushed my father to kick me out and force me to become a lone wolf because I'd been rejected at the altar. Wyatt had been so disgusted by it all that he'd voluntarily left his pack, leaving all the wealth and prestige behind. Gavin despised how his father and Jayson had handled things.

Was I the one who had it wrong? Did Wyatt and Gavin have the right of it while I simply followed along like an obedient little pack girl? The thought unsettled me.

"Can we not discuss pack politics right now?" I said, desperate to change the subject. "I can worry about that stuff later, after I've survived this damn show. Speaking of, I need to check on Chelsey. I haven't had the chance to see how she's doing since she drank that stupid tea."

"Sorry," he mumbled.

As I stood to leave, his expression turned pensive. He wanted to continue the conversation, but my brain was fried. I needed to get away, and I really did want to check on Chelsey. Hopefully, her scare with the wolfsbane hadn't put her off helping me. I walked away before anything else could be said, leaving Gavin to stew.

Chelsey was on the back patio overlooking the courtyard closest to the helipad. She wore sunglasses and stared out at the sea. As I approached, she lifted a mug to her lips and sipped, then grimaced and set it back down.

"That looks pleasant," I said.

She glanced my way, then looked down at the mug's contents and wrinkled her nose. "The witches gave me this tea—jewelweed, basil, ginger root, and something called yarrow. It's freaking gross, but it does help. The healers said I needed to drink four cups of the stuff today to flush out the rest of the toxins that their spells and potions didn't take care of." She pushed the mug away from the side of the table. "What's up? Looks like you want to talk."

Taking the seat opposite her, I gazed out at the rocky shore and ocean beyond. The view was like something from a movie—beautiful and majestic. I could hardly believe we were on the most dangerous piece of land in the entire world.

While I scanned the horizon, I tried to figure out what to say to Chelsey. Telling her about Zoe, Crew, Haven, and the plan to get everyone out with fake eliminations was out. For one, I didn't want to get her hopes up. Not until Zoe sent word again. Until Wyatt and I had a concrete plan in place, it would be best to keep things vague.

Pulling my eyes away from the sea, I looked at her. "Didn't come to talk. Not really. I saw you out here and wanted to make sure you were doing okay."

She gave the mug a sidelong look. "Other than having to drink that vile shit, I'm okay."

"So your, uh, head's still in the game?" I asked pointedly.

She caught my meaning and glanced around for any cameras before leaning in close. "Still on the same page, yeah. These assholes almost killed me earlier. I'm done. Do we have a plan? Like maybe a press release or something?"

A press release? As if that was possible. Even if it was, no one would care. Everything that had happened so far was all part of the show. The fans back home would probably eat it up if we tried to raise a stink over stuff that had happened every season for over thirty years.

Chelsey was a bit naïve when it came to overthrowing powerful organizations. Not that I could call myself an expert, either.

"I don't think talking to the press will do much for our cause," I said. "Right now, everyone's alive. No one was lost during the last challenge. That's something to celebrate. Until I figure out what we're going to do, we have to keep playing the game. Like the... mating chamber tomorrow, and the next day."

Despite my best wishes, talking about the mating chamber sent an image flashing through my mind. Wyatt, slick with sweat, grunting and thrusting into Chelsey, her head thrown back as she screamed in ecstasy. I blinked it away quickly, but the image had already seared itself into my brain. What made it worse was that Chelsey probably had the same thoughts running through her head, but instead of disturbing her, they probably excited her.

My inner wolf snarled and growled. If I didn't have such heavy control of her, I thought she might try to force me to shift and rip Chelsey's throat out. I did my best to soothe the beast within me.

Chelsey took another large swallow of her tea, shaking her head in disgust. "Okay. Let me know if anything changes. I'm ready whenever you are. Say the word."

I smiled at her as I stood to leave.

She leaned forward and put a hand on mine. "Kira, I know this isn't the best place to be, or the safest, but I'm glad we met. I was so worried you'd hate me once I came onto the show, but you've been nothing but kind. It's really made this whole thing easier to get through."

Guilt washed over me. "Hey, no problem."

Chelsey released my hand and leaned back. "Thank you. Especially for everything you've done to help me and Wyatt be together." She chuckled. "I think he's still a little hesitant about it, but maybe between you and me, we can turn him around."

Shame like cold mud coated my skin. I nodded, not knowing what else to do. "I'll let you rest."

"Okay." Chelsey took up her mug again and went back to gazing at the ocean. Feeling like the world's biggest asshole, I hurried away.

Chapter 4 - Wyatt

My body was wiped out from everything I'd gone through during the challenge and the weirdness that followed. I collapsed in my bunk almost as soon as Von told us we had the rest of the day off, then slept for fourteen straight hours. Nightmares had me in their grip the entire time.

I dreamed that Leif had been successful in dragging me up the volcano. In the dream, the mountain hadn't been dormant; it had hissed and spit sparks and lava. Massive clouds of ash plumed out of it, lightning arcing through the black clouds in great spiderwebs of light, like the storm had come from hell itself.

The dark, foreboding tunnel echoed with the sounds of the erupting volcano. Drumbeats reverberated off the wall. The closer we got to whatever destination Leif dragged me toward, the louder the mechanical whirring and clicking sounds grew. Eventually, those sounds drowned out all the others.

My fingernails tore as I desperately clawed at the stone floor to get away. Leif continued dragging me somewhere I did not want to go. The madness in his wolf's eyes iced my insides over. He pulled me to my doom, and there was nothing I could do to stop it. A great wooden door swung open at the end of the tunnel.

I woke with a start, nearly tumbling from bed. Sweat coated my body, and my breath shivered out of my lungs in great, shuddering gasps. The fitted sheets were twisted and torn from the corners of the mattress. I must have clawed at them in my sleep. Unsteadily, I rose and dressed. While my body felt rested, my mind was still exhausted.

The clock on the wall showed me how long I'd been asleep, and my eyes nearly bugged out of my head. It was almost time for lunch. I'd missed dinner and breakfast while that nightmare had its hold on me. My stomach gave a warning rumble, and I hurried out to get some food before I passed out from hunger.

The mansion was droning with activity by the time I arrived downstairs. The other alphas had already migrated to the kitchen and dining room. J.D. sat in the corner, picking at a salad, staring miserably into the bowl. Tate, Abel, Mika, and Gavin sat at the breakfast nook, chatting and eating. They were acting pretty friendly. Strangely so. From the corner of my eye, I caught the hovering cameras. I glanced at my wristband and saw the green light. We were recording. That meant everyone had to put their game faces on.

J.D. glanced up as I walked in and nodded a greeting to me. I returned it and headed toward the buffet they'd set up for us.

"Mr. Rivers? Panini?" a chef behind the table asked as I stepped up.

"Huh?"

He motioned toward a sandwich press and a pile of ingredients and loaves of bread. "Panini sandwich?" he offered. "Would you like one?"

"Um, yeah, sure."

"Excellent. Prosciutto, mozzarella, and capicola? Some spinach and caramelized onions?"

I waved his question away. "Yeah, yeah. Sounds good. Thanks."

While he made the sandwich, I loaded my plate with pasta salad, a slice of quiche, and a massive slice of cheesecake. I'd been hungry when I woke up, but once I saw the food, the sensation grew ever more intense. The chef placed the steaming grilled sandwich on my plate, and I headed over to join the conversation, leaving J.D. to his thoughts.

"Hey, guys. How's it going?" I said as I sat. "I'm glad you all made it through yesterday."

I meant it. I didn't want anyone else to die. But Tate must have assumed I was being a smartass because he snorted. "With what a douchebag you've been lately, I bet you're lying about that. Probably pissed you aren't the only alpha left, right?" He laughed. "Shit, you probably want both the girls to yourself. Is that what you're going for? Hoping the show will let you have a little harem of your own or something?"

"Even if that was what he wanted," Abel said dryly, "that's not how it works. One male and one female together." He glanced over his shoulder. "Don't give them any ideas. They might do that next year for ratings." He turned to me. "Change of subject. Tell us how the hell you got so turned around yesterday. The course was pretty cut and dry. Didn't seem like something you'd struggle with."

I swallowed the bite of pasta salad I'd been chewing and shrugged. "I let myself get distracted worrying about Chelsey."

Mika, knowing my game, rolled his eyes and continued eating. The others weren't as pleased with my answer.

"Oh, what bullshit," Gavin sneered.

Tate cocked an eyebrow and grinned at me. "I guess it's good you're so caught up on Chelsey since you'll get to be in the mating chamber with her tonight." He glanced around at the others, and his grin grew wider. "Though, old boy here probably doesn't know how to get a girl off, anyway. I bet that's why Kira's so over him and it got his panties in a bunch. Is that why you don't like Kira anymore, Wyatt? Couldn't find the clitoris?"

I bobbed my eyebrows and tilted my head. "Well, I found your mom's fine. So no, I haven't had any trouble."

Mika had to turn sideways when the water he'd just sipped spurted out of his mouth with a laugh. Tate glared daggers at me. In all honesty, I'd forgotten all about the mating chamber. Images of the last time

I was in there with Kira filled my mind. I pushed them away before I could get too worked up.

"I think Chelsey will have a good time. I can't wait to see what kind of talents she has in the sack." I felt gross talking about her like that, but I did my best to project a douchebag façade. "Kira was good, but I think Chelsey will be better."

Gavin and Tate both looked pissed now. Tate called out to J.D., "Hey, bro, you better enjoy your night with Kira. Once she's with me for good, she'll forget all about every other alpha she's been with." Tate leaned forward, resting on his elbows, and stared into my eyes as I ate. "When we're fucking? It'll be my name she screams."

"Fuck off," Gavin growled. "Who the hell says she ends up with you?"

The two men bickered back and forth. I stole a glance at J.D. He'd never acted interested in Kira, but that didn't stop my jealousy from rearing its ugly head. The mere thought of another man being intimate with Kira sent my wolf into a spitting, growling rage. Kira had probably chosen J.D. to appear impartial—and because he seemed the least likely to pull something on her. J.D. was an honorable and good shifter, and he wouldn't do anything without consent. But I couldn't help wondering what any man might do with someone as gorgeous as Kira in that chamber.

Almost as though my thoughts had summoned her, Kira walked in. It took all my willpower not to stare at her. I kept my eyes down and worked on my sandwich.

"Hey, guys," Kira said. "How is everyone? J.D.?"

J.D. smiled at her. "I'm good. Thanks."

Kira took a seat at the table with the rest of us. "Did everybody have a good morning?"

She purposely ignored me and began chatting with the others. Her scent wafted toward me, and that alone made my cock hard. My fork slid into the cheesecake, and it took all I had not to imagine our bodies slipping together the same way.

"We were actually talking about you before you came in," Tate said.

Kira rested her chin on her hand and grinned at him. "Really? Do tell." She winked. "Was it something naughty?"

My eyes were halfway through rolling when I caught myself. The sexy, flirty act must have been exhausting, but she played it up well.

"Yeah, a little. You know, Kira, there's still time for you to change your mind about who to take into the mating chamber."

She arched an eyebrow. "Oh? Think you'd do better, do you?"

"I've never had a partner who wasn't satisfied." Tate's cockiness made my skin crawl. "I'd do things to you that you never imagined. You'll be calling out to the gods before we're even halfway done."

"Would you shut the hell up?" Abel snapped.

Thank fuck he'd said it first because I'd been about half a second from shoving my fork into Tate's throat.

Kira remained the perfect and composed actress. She giggled seductively. "Oh, I'm sure you know what you're doing, Tate. I'm looking forward to spending some time with J.D., though. He's really an amazing guy."

From her tone and inflection, I could tell the compliment was genuine. J.D. looked up from his food and smiled. He still looked down, but her praise was cheering him up.

"I think you're great, too, Kira." He sighed and glanced around. "All I really want is for you to be happy. I want *everyone* here to be happy. We all deserve a happy ending, right?"

"Aw, so sweet. No wonder the fans love you, J.D.," Von Thornton said as he strode into the room.

J.D.'s eyes clouded over and he went back to staring at his food.

Von put a hand on J.D.'s shoulder. "Such a loveable alpha. Our social media accounts show you're the favorite among the contestants."

J.D. looked uncomfortable under the vampire's gaze. He probably wanted to swat the other man's hand off his shoulder.

"Poor Jordan Darkham has lost so much, including his close friend Leif on this show, that our viewers are rooting for him to end up with a fated mate of his own."

"I forgot his name was actually Jordan," Mika muttered. He tossed his fork down and glanced sideways at Von. "I've lost my appetite."

Mika was one hundred percent over the show and Von's goofy showman antics. He hadn't wanted to be here to begin with, and everything that had happened so far had only made things worse for him.

If Von heard Mika's comment, he ignored it. With one last pat on J.D.'s back, Von turned to address all of us again. "As you all know, there will be an arena match tomorrow afternoon. However, this time, it won't be one on one. The producers have decided to switch things up a bit and have teams. Very exciting, I know. As the challenges get more dangerous, more alphas will be eliminated, and at a much quicker pace." Von winked at us. "Things are getting absolutely exhilarating now."

If by "exhilarating," he meant dangerous, sadistic, and gut-wrenching, then he was right. Kira was listening to Von with rapt attention, but her eyes were stormy with rage. She had the same opinion about all this as me, and it became harder by the minute to keep acting like we were good little boys and girls having a good time on the show.

"I've already informed Chelsey about this change. She needed a bit more looking after by the healers after yesterday, so don't worry. She's already heard the news." Von smiled and then glanced at me, then at Kira. "We don't want to leave our viewers wanting and wondering what could have been, so rather than waiting until tomorrow night for the second mating chamber date, we've done a quick remodel of one of the vacant bedroom suites and turned it into another mating chamber. Tonight, the two happy couples will be able to enjoy a night of wanton debauchery before tomorrow afternoon's arena match."

Von raised his arms, apparently waiting for us to applaud or something. When we didn't react, he didn't miss a beat. "This way, our fans will have a better idea of which alphas are, shall we say, masters of the bedroom domain. This will definitely spice things up. When our beloved alphas fall in battle during the challenges, it will tug at the heartstrings even more and might lead to some outbursts— catfighting, or even fistfights. We haven't had to break up any brawls yet this season, so here's hoping."

"Sounds great," Kira said in a strained voice.

Von clapped once. "I knew our leading ladies would be on board. I'll leave you all to your lunch." He turned to one of the cameras. "Until tonight, ladies and gentlemen. See you then. Grab your popcorn and get ready."

Von rushed out of the room in deep discussion with one of the assistant directors.

"So, what do you think the arena match will be?" Abel asked once Von walked out of earshot.

Gavin scoffed. "Oh, I'm sure it'll start with us all getting a full body massage, maybe even with a happy ending. Then? A leisurely stroll through a field of daisies, followed by catching butterflies, along with lollipops made of sparkles and sunshine." He rolled his eyes. "More likely, it'll be a swimming contest with a shark or something—with some raw and bloody meat strapped to our legs, of course."

Tate leaned over in his chair to put an arm around Kira's shoulders. "Well, whatever it is, I'll be there to keep Kira safe." He gave her a reassuring grin. "Don't worry, babe. You're safe when I'm around."

I gritted my teeth and kept my eyes down, but every fiber of my being wanted to smash my fist into Tate's nose. Once I had myself under control, I decided to play on the friends-to-enemies act Kira and I were putting on.

Pointing at her with my fork, I said, "Good luck with that, brother. This one will probably end up getting you killed for the trouble. She's a pain in the ass and *has* to be independent all the time, even when someone tries to help her."

"Oh, Wyatt, don't act all holier than thou. Like you were some damned white knight trying to save the damsel in distress," Kira said scornfully. "That couldn't be further from the truth. You want everyone here and back home to think you're some big hero."

"That's not true. You just don't want to admit that the way you always try to do things is dangerous. Damn annoying little brat."

A red flush crept into her cheeks, and she pursed her lips at the use of my little code phrase. She cleared her throat and glared at me. "Well... you, uh, you—"

"You know what?" I said, cutting her off as I stood. "I'm done eating. You guys have fun. I need to rest up for the mating chamber tonight. Have fun with the annoying little brat."

I handed my empty plate to one of the staff and walked out.

"You're driving me fucking crazy, you know that?" Kira called out.

Once I was out of sight of the cameras, I allowed myself a little grin. She had to be telling the truth. It made me happy to know that I drove her as crazy as she drove me.

That evening, I dressed in the alpha den, preparing for my night with Chelsey. I was uneasy about the whole thing. Would she try to pull something? She'd made it clear that she liked me and didn't try to hide her attraction for me. I really did not want to have to peel her off my body, but I would if it came to it.

"Excited for the big night?" Mika said as he strolled into the den, giving me a sarcastic grin.

All the other guys had gone to the game room to watch on the big TV. Thankfully, the chamber didn't have cameras *inside* it. At least the showrunners hadn't resorted to broadcasting homemade porn. There would be some build-up, though—the men and women getting escorted down, plus probably some talk from Von about what everyone thought might be going down inside.

"Not really," I said.

Mika flopped down on his bunk and pulled out a book. "Figured."

"Staying in tonight?" I don't know why I even asked. He always stayed in.

"Yup. I have no desire to watch this thing unfold. Have fun. Well, as much as you can without the woman you really want."

I opened my mouth to respond, but a knock at the door made me turn. One of the half-demon security guys stood there.

"Mr. Rivers? It's time," the man said in a deep rumble.

"Okay."

"Knock 'em dead, big guy," Mika called to me as I left.

A camera followed me and the security guard as he led me to the official mating chamber. Apparently, Kira and J.D. would be in the makeshift chamber. The thought alone made my eye twitch. I shook the thought away before my imagination could run away with me.

He escorted me inside, where Von and his dumbass smile waited for me. A second camera hovered behind his head.

"Welcome, Wyatt. An exciting night awaits. Chelsey will be here soon, but I wanted to greet you and show you the refreshments." He swept a hand to a small table by the door. "Champagne, red wine, a selection of dark chocolates, strawberries, and homemade whipped cream." Von stepped over and leaned toward my ear, pointing to the nightstands beside the massive bed. "I think you already know this, but we've stocked some grade-A items in there for when things get hot and heavy. Standard things like lubricant, but also more adventurous items: handcuffs, nipple clamps, a riding crop. Hmmm, delicious, isn't it? Well, I'll leave you to welcome Chelsey. Enjoy yourselves. I *do* mean that."

Von left, and the cameras departed with him, leaving me alone to peruse the room as I waited for Chelsey. I poked around in the drawers. My eyes went wide with surprise, shocked to find a drawer packed full of vibrators of various sizes and lengths, lube, handcuffs, and a barrage of other items.

"Holy shit," I hissed and slammed the drawer shut, wincing in disgust.

A moment later, the door opened again. Straightening, I turned to see Chelsey stepping in, looking both excited and nervous.

"Hey, Wyatt."

"Hey."

From the way she looked at me, I could tell she truly thought something would happen between us. I couldn't toy with her emotions. I would not be having sex with her. Even if someone put a gun to my head, I couldn't even look at another woman in that way, much less do what the whole world thought we would be doing in here.

"Chelsey?" I said, taking a few steps toward her.

"Yes?" Her eyes were wide with hope, and I felt like a dick for what I was about to do.

"Listen, can we sit and talk for a second?" I motioned toward the two seats in the corner rather than the bed.

"Oh. Umm, okay." She walked over and sat, obviously confused.

I took the seat opposite and leaned forward on my elbows, keeping eye contact with her. "I've got something I need to tell you because you deserve the truth."

"Uh oh," she said. "This isn't going to be good, is it?"

"I'm so sorry, Chelsey. I didn't want to lead you on or hurt you in any way, but I don't care for you in the way you deserve. I'm head over heels in love with Kira. I always have been." It was the first time I'd said that internally or out loud. It felt good. "Anyway, I don't see my feelings ever changing. I know she and I have been acting strange toward each other lately, but this show is like fifty percent survival and fifty percent acting. The best way for me to protect Kira is by acting. The same goes for her." I paused. "I'm not entirely sure she feels the same as I do, but I don't know if she's just acting to keep me safe. I wanted you to know the truth."

I took a breath and waited to see what her reaction would be. Chelsey stared at me, worrying her lower lip between her teeth. Her shoulders sagged and a sad smile spread across her lips.

"I should have known." She slapped a hand to her forehead. "I'm an idiot. It was so obvious if I'd wanted to see it." Chelsey sounded discouraged and sad, but not heartbroken or devastated. I'd take that as a win.

"Are you okay?" I asked.

"This sucks," she blurted. "All of it. Being on this show, being stuck here. It's all so fucking awful. I've only been here a few days. I can't imagine what you and Kira went through. I can't blame you guys for doing what was needed to stay alive."

A shaky, relieved breath shuddered out of me. "So, you're good?"

"I suppose." She glanced forlornly at the bed. "I still don't know why Kira tried to get you and I together. That part doesn't make any sense. Could she have been screwing with me?"

"No." I held up my hands. "She wasn't. That's what I meant when I said I wasn't sure if she felt the same for me as I do for her. She wanted me to get off the island alive, and she thought being paired with you would be the best way. She, uh..." Should I tell Kira's biggest secret? I had to, especially if this woman was going to help us get off this island alive. "Kira isn't planning on taking a mate. All she wants is the favor from Heline."

Chelsey's eyes widened with surprise. "Seriously? I don't think anyone has ever chosen that before."

"I know, but it's a secret. You can't tell anyone, it'll—"

"I get it, Wyatt. I won't say anything." She laughed sarcastically. "You think I want to throw Kira under the bus when these assholes kidnapped my little brother? Put him out in the jungle to die? No. Fuck those guys. I hope Kira does win and tells Heline to set this whole island on fire." The venom in her voice filled me with relief. Our secret would be safe with her. The anger in her voice wasn't easily faked.

"Sorry, I didn't want to imply you weren't trustworthy."

She waved my comment away. "It's fine. I just really wanted a fated mate, you know?" Tears filled her eyes. "If I could have what I dreamed of, things would have been different with the mate who rejected me. I loved him so much. I know a lot of people end up paired with people they don't care for or strangers or whatever, but he was different. I miss him, Wyatt. I really do. Other than my family and pack, my mate was the most important person in my life. Until he wasn't."

She sniffled, and I hurried to a nightstand to grab some tissues. "Here you go."

"Thanks," she said thickly, taking the tissues.

I felt terrible for her. Unlike Kira, Chelsey had not only been devastated by being rejected, but she'd had her heart ripped out because she'd actually *loved* her fated mate. I could have told Chelsey things would work out and she'd find love with someone other than the guy who'd rejected her, but anything I considered saying sounded cheesy and hollow. This was not the time for fake platitudes. I decided to get her mind off her heartbreak by focusing on her anger at the showrunners.

"I know Kira talked to you a little about what she wants to do. Breaking the show?"

Chelsey nodded, her tears already drying up. The muscles in her jaw flexed and rippled as she gritted her teeth. "Yeah. I told her that once she had a plan, I was all in."

"Good." I nodded. "We'll need help, but I don't want you risking your life for it. I want the show done, too, but not if you or Kira get hurt. I'd never forgive myself if you were hurt, and I think I'd die inside if something happened to Kira."

"My brother, Hunter, is back home. They sent him back the same night I rescued him, but who's to say they won't abduct him again? I'll do whatever it takes to fuck these people over. No one deserves to be hurt like that. I'm down for whatever you guys need to do."

I smiled. Gods, a mountain had been lifted off me. Another ally. The more, the merrier. First Mika, now Chelsey, *maybe* J.D. soon. Plus, Zoe and that Crew guy out in the jungle. The more people we had on our team, the more faith I had that we might actually succeed.

"So," Chelsey said, glancing over at the table. "Those strawberries look really good. Do you mind?"

I laughed. "Go to town. Just... don't look in the nightstand drawers. Unless you're curious what a footlong dildo looks like."

Her mouth formed a perfect *O* of shock. "Duly noted. I think I'll stick to the treats and alcohol."

Over the next forty minutes, we indulged in the chocolate, fruit, and whipped cream. I had one glass of red wine to calm my nerves, but Chelsey finished an entire bottle of champagne and passed out on the bed, snoring lightly. I settled down on the velvet couch beside the gas fireplace to sleep. There were only a few moments when I wondered how things were going in the other mating chamber, but I forced my mind to go blank. Gradually, I slipped into darkness.

Chapter 5 - Kira

I'd opted for the least revealing dress in my closet. Zoe had brought a ton of stuff, but nearly everything looked like something I'd wear to work a few hours at a strip club. The camera followed me as I strolled down the hallway behind the fallen angel bodyguard.

Rather than leading me to the mating chamber on the third floor, he guided me down the stairs to the second floor of the west wing. I'd been to the mating chamber the night Wyatt had almost died. That room had been much smaller than my suite, but almost more luxurious. Chairs and sofas all around, the massive bed, lighting, and mirrors—none of it had left any doubt as to the room's use.

We rounded the corner and came to a door just as Von approached from a separate hallway, tailed by his own camera.

"Oh, right on time," Von said and stepped forward to give me a peck on the cheek. I suppressed a shudder when his icy lips touched my face. "J.D. arrived a few minutes ago and is waiting for you inside. I have to say, you look gorgeous." He turned to the camera. "Doesn't she, folks?"

"Thank you, Von."

"Tell me, did you come up with this look all by yourself?"

I wasn't sure if he was goading me or just wasn't smart enough to realize what he'd said. The smile on my face sat brittle on my lips. "Well, actually, I did. You see, my best friend was my stylist, but someone dragged her out of the mansion and took her to the jungle, never to be seen again. I wonder why I would have to get myself ready?"

Instead of being taken aback, Von laughed. "Oh, Miss Durst, you are a feisty one. Save some of that fire for inside the mating chamber. I'm sure J.D. will love a little excitement. He has seemed a bit forlorn lately. Perhaps," he winked, "a nice roll in the hay will bring him around, hmm?"

The fact that he talked about J.D. and me like we were sex dolls made me want to gag. When Von addressed the cameras again, some of the tension in my muscles eased. I'd been seconds away from punching him in his perfectly white teeth.

"As everyone knows, the mating chamber is one of the most exciting and erotic parts of *The Reject Project.* Two shifters throw caution to the wind—along with their clothes, of course—to enjoy a night of unrelenting passion. It's romance, it's lust, it's everything we love to see. And who knows, the person our lead mates take into the chamber may very well end up being the mate that the goddess Heline pairs them with at the end." Von put a hand to his chest and nodded slowly. "So much beauty. So much love. I *adore* these nights as much as our fans do."

My god, would he ever shut up? I'd had enough of pandering to the cameras. I snapped. "Von, I'm really tired. I'd like to go to bed, okay?"

Von laughed like I'd just told the funniest joke in the world, but instead of answering me, he turned back to the camera. "Ladies and gentlemen, it appears that Kira is itching to get under those sheets with J.D. My goodness, is he in for a wild ride." He looked at me again. "Go to it, young lady. I only ask that you don't break the poor boy. Leave some for Chelsey. She might have a chance with him later, and we want all his parts in working order. Enjoy."

He strolled away, leaving me by the door. Seething, I watched him walk away, then shrugged it off and yanked the door open. The room was nice. If anything, it was even more luxurious than the regular mating chamber. Satin curtains hung from the ceiling, draping around the bed. The bed itself took up a huge portion of the room; it was just as big as the other mating chamber's. Where the hell did they even get this stuff?

J.D. was sitting next to the fireplace but stood when he saw me. "Oh, hey."

"Hey."

The poor guy looked dejected. It broke my heart to see the toll the show had taken on him so far. He'd been such a lively presence from the beginning, but ever since Leif had been lost, he'd become more and more withdrawn. I really wanted to tell him the truth, but that could hurt him even more. Being feral was almost as bad as death. Maybe even worse. The body still lived, but the mind was shattered and forever lost in a pit of madness. Did J.D. really need to know Leif's fate?

"You look beautiful tonight," J.D. said as he rounded the bed to approach.

I glanced down and slid my hands down the dress to straighten any wrinkles. "Oh, this old thing? I threw it on at the last minute. I usually wear this when I mow the lawn back home."

J.D. laughed, and it was good to hear. It sounded real. It didn't last long, though. After a minute of awkward silence, he gestured to an oak table. "You want anything? They left a bunch of stuff. Wine or... whatever?"

I shook my head and took a step closer to him. I wasn't interested in the snacks or booze. "How are you doing, J.D.? Really?"

An obviously fake smile greeted me. "Oh, I'm great. Fantastic. I get to spend the night getting to know you a little better." He glanced nervously at the bed. "Um, it's a little weird, though. Like, actually being in here. Where the whole world is expecting you to... uh... you know. It's sort of uncomfortable. At least, it is for me."

He couldn't have looked more anxious if he tried.

"Believe me, I find it just as uncomfortable." I laughed to relieve some tension. "J.D., you know I didn't choose you for the mating chamber so we could have sex, right?"

He blinked. "What? Really?"

"Surprised?" I sat down on the bed. "You shouldn't be. All I wanted was some time alone with you to see how you're doing. I wanted a night of conversation. Plus..." I chuckled. "I thought you'd like a night away from that alpha den. I'm sure it gets stinky in there. And loud."

J.D. visibly relaxed and grinned as he sat next to me. "You have no idea. Tate is terrible when he snores. He literally sounds like a lawn mower when he's asleep. I like Abel, but he talks in his sleep— nonsense stuff, but loud enough to be annoying. The worst snorer was Ryan, but he wasn't here very long."

Ryan. Gods, I barely thought about him anymore. The first of the alphas to die. His body, or whatever was left of it, might still be out there somewhere. The first blood spilled, but not the last.

J.D. must have seen something in my face because he put a hand on my forearm. "I want you to know, I don't think any of the eliminations have been your fault. I didn't mean it like that."

I patted the top of his hand. "I know you didn't. It's awful to think about."

"You know, you're different when the cameras are on, but you've always been really nice to me. I hope you end up with someone you really love at the end. You deserve a fated mate who will make you happy. I still can't believe someone rejected you."

More guilt gnawed at my heart. None of these men had known they were signing up to get used by not only the showrunners but also the lead mate. When I signed up, I was fine with tossing them all aside to get what I wanted. Between that and how I used to treat Wyatt, who *wouldn't* reject me? Being here had changed me in ways I never would have believed. I now felt responsible for all the remaining men.

A war waged in my mind. How did I protect and save these men, but also protect and save my family and pack from war? It wasn't only the wolf packs at risk, either. The last time a war broke out within our species, it spilled over. Humans, witches, fae, other shifter races—all the sentient creatures of the world got swept up in it. I had so much responsibility, so much to worry about. I *had* to get my wish from Heline, but I also had to make sure that whoever was left with me could be safely taken to Haven like the others. If there were others. I still had no clue if our plan for staged eliminations would work.

J.D. frowned. "Are you okay?"

I snapped my gaze to him, shaking off the thoughts that had been pulling me under. "Oh, sorry. Yeah. I was, uh, just thinking about my rejection."

"Shit. Sorry. Didn't mean to open old wounds."

"No problem. Water under the bridge, right? I'm not the only one who never should have been rejected. You got the short end of the stick, too. You're a great guy, J.D. You deserve to have your special someone."

To my horror, J.D.'s face crumpled, and his eyes went misty. He tried to nod, then shrugged instead. "Yeah. I just, uh, I didn't figure out who that special person was until it was too late. I can't even think about being with someone else. Not when that person is gone, and I never even had the chance to say goodbye."

Anyone could see he meant Leif. At least, anyone who knew the two men and wasn't blind. J.D.

had obviously begun to develop feelings for the other alpha that Leif hadn't even noticed. They may have been on the verge of something, and now J.D. thought Leif was gone forever. His heartache was too much for me to bear. I couldn't let him continue to believe Leif's corpse was rotting on the island.

I rested a hand on J.D.'s shoulder. "I need to tell you something. About Leif."

J.D. blinked rapidly, sending a single tear cascading down his cheek to rest on his chin. "What? Oh, gods, were you there when it happened? Did you see him die?"

"Huh?" I shook my head. "No, no, no, he's not dead, J.D. Wyatt and I saw him out there during the last challenge. He's feral, but he is most definitely alive."

J.D. stared at me for several seconds. His eyes grew wider by the second as my words sunk in. "He's alive?" A disbelieving smile replaced the sorrow on his face.

"Yes, but he is feral. You can't get your hopes up. You know what that means."

A shifter going feral was pretty rare. Anyone coming back from that type of madness would be even rarer. There were ancient stories about it, and every few decades, a news story would come out about someone miraculously recovering from it. But for the most part, those poor souls were in for a lifetime of psychosis and rage.

"No, I get that." He wiped furiously at his eyes. "If he's alive, then there's a chance. However small. Holy cow, man, this is awesome news."

A switch had flipped in J.D., and it was like he was coming back to life—a parched and lifeless plant getting water and springing back up.

"I thought you should know, but you can't tell anyone," I said. "I have no clue what's going on. Leif went feral in, like, a day. That shouldn't be possible. Something weird is going on, and I have no clue if the show's producers know about it. I'll do my best to help him, but until then, I need to make sure you aren't going to put yourself in danger to look for him."

J.D.'s head bobbed. "I get it. You're a Tranquility operative, a badass. I'll follow your lead. Don't worry. But if this is true, then there might be a chance to save him somehow."

If our plan to stage eliminations was going to work, the people we wanted to save would have to know everything. That was the only way things would go smoothly. J.D. was one of those I desperately wanted to save. Why not tell him now? When would there be a better time to bring him into the plan?

"What would you say if I told you that you could survive Bloodstone Island without having to deal with the show?"

"Are you serious?"

"I am. I'm still working on the plan, so I can't tell you everything, but it's possible. I need you to trust me and be patient. Can you do that?"

"Yeah, for sure." I hadn't expected him to look so excited. "Don't say anymore. I'm not a good actor, so it's best if you don't tell me too much. Like, for real, I'm awful at lying."

He was already acting more like his normal self, which might pose a problem. "Okay, but you should probably still try to pretend to be sad. I don't want anyone getting suspicious about your sudden change in mood."

"Got it. I'll do my best." He blushed. "Um, we could say that, uh, well…" He shrugged one shoulder. "We could say I feel better because we actually *did* the deed here. That could be a good reason for me to be acting different."

I almost laughed, but he was right. It *would* sell the act Wyatt and I were putting on. If everyone thought I'd slept with J.D., it would make it that much more believable that Wyatt and I hated each other.

"That's a really good idea," I said. "If Von or anyone asks, we had the time of our lives in here. No need to go into gory details, though. Let their imaginations do the work." I laughed.

J.D. laughed, too, and it was that old infectious laughter. "Well, now that that's settled, do you want something to eat?"

I rolled my eyes. "Sure, why not?"

We ate caviar, chocolates, and strawberries covered in whipped cream. J.D. managed to become tipsy on red wine before his metabolism could flush it out. Eventually, he passed out on a chaise lounge with a wine glass in his hand. I gently took the glass, then tucked a blanket over him before falling asleep on the bed.

The next morning, I woke early. J.D. was still asleep on the sofa, snoring softly. Maybe I could get back to my room before the cameras came to interfere.

After slipping on my shoes, I opened the door a crack and peeked out into the hall. Still deserted. Slipping out, I closed the door and hurried down the hallway. The sun wasn't even up yet. I couldn't help but grin to myself, thinking of how pissed Von would be when he realized he couldn't corner me the moment I stepped out of the chamber. It almost made me want to stay behind to see the look on his face.

My thoughts quickly slid from Von to Wyatt. I wondered how his night with Chelsey had gone. It was ridiculous to be jealous of Chelsey, especially when Wyatt had made it clear he had no interest in her. Yet, I couldn't keep the intrusive thoughts away. What if Chelsey had tried to seduce him? They'd probably had alcohol in their room, too. Who knows what might have happened if things got a little intimate? A mental image of Wyatt's face buried between Chelsey's legs flashed across my mind, and a bloodcurdling rage ignited in my wolf.

As I hurried through the halls, the thoughts and images kept playing around in my head. Unbidden and unwelcome. Unstoppable. By the time I returned to my room, I was seething with anger, my wolf only fueling it. I closed the door and almost screamed in surprise when I saw what waited for me in the room.

A small white parrot waddled across the desk by the window. Seeing me, it tilted its head to the side and made an *ohr-ohr* sound. A small and tightly wound tube of paper was tied to its leg with twine.

What the hell?

I inched closer to the bird. The creature didn't freak out or fly away—a good sign.

"Hey, little buddy. Did someone send you?" I felt dumb talking to it, but what else was I supposed to do? It was a parrot, so maybe it could talk. "Can you speak?"

It tilted its eyes toward me. "Can you speak?" it echoed in a croaking bird voice.

I sighed, irritation boiling up inside me. "Oh, for fuck's sake."

"Fuck sake," the parrot responded.

It nudged my fingers with its head as I untied the note. As soon as the paper was in my hand, it leaped off the desk and swooped out my window. I stared after it, watching it flap and glide beyond the mansion grounds and back into the jungle.

As I unrolled the note, my stomach began doing little excited flips. I had a hunch who'd sent it, and when I began to read, a smile formed on my lips. I was right. Zoe.

Me again. That mansion is really hard to get into with magic. Like, freaking crazy-hard. Crew had an idea. The little guy that brought you the note is named Mr. Feather Pants. I named him myself. An eagle shifter here at Haven trained the parrot to carry letters and notes. It looks like the wards around the mansion only keep out dangerous or magical creatures, whoever the witches and fae decide can't cross the wards. But normal creatures can still get through—rats, birds, bugs, stuff like that. This should work well for passing you information, as long as the dumb bird doesn't get lost or eaten by something on the way.

I'll send another letter soon. While you wait, just stay nice and safe, preferably in those big, muscly arms of Wyatt's. You guys are really cute together. Ah! I love this. I can't wait to hear all the

naughty details when I see you again. Oh, and like
last time, watch your fingers.

The letter burst into flames once I read the last word. I let it go, and exactly like the previous time, all that remained was a tiny wisp of ash. A sense of relief filled me. Having a better form of communication would help. We'd still have to be careful. I didn't want to think of what would happen if some staff member intercepted the parrot. Until Zoe sent another letter, I had to play the game—stay alive, and keep all the others alive.

No big deal. Super easy.

Chapter 6 - Wyatt

Sunlight streamed through the window beside the fireplace. The shimmering rays on my eyelids woke me up. Squinting at the sudden light, I rubbed a hand over my face. The stubble made a rasping sound beneath my palm, and I rolled over to look at the bed. Chelsey lay strewn across the middle, arms out wide, mouth slightly agape, still deeply asleep.

The thin cashmere throw blanket I'd slept under had slipped off me sometime during the night and lay pooled on the floor. The fireplace was still warm, and I was a little too hot from sleeping fully clothed. I stood and looked out the window. The sun had barely crested the horizon. If I hurried, I might get out of here before Von showed up.

After putting my shoes on, I double-checked that Chelsey was still asleep before creeping toward the door. The knob spun soundlessly under my hand, and I left the room as quietly as possible. I eased the door closed with the slightest *click*, turned, and—

"Good morning, handsome. Did you have a wonderful night of debauchery?"

I jerked in surprise and whirled around to find Von Thornton and two hovering cameras behind me. "Holy shit."

"Not so far," Von said with a thoughtful tilt of his head. "A wiccan priestess tried holy water on me in 1833, but holy shit? Can't say I've ever seen that before. Enough about me, though. How were the festivities last night?" He gestured toward the cameras. "Our fans are drooling over it. There are even some bets on which positions you two used to get things started."

"Can we do this later, Von? I'm still trying to wake up."

Von made an exaggerated frown and shook his head. "I'm afraid not. We need to get this interview out of the way now. What if you're horribly mutilated or killed in the arena match this afternoon? I can't interview a corpse, can I? No offense, obviously."

"Obviously," I grunted.

"Anyway," Von went on, "we're getting deep into the season, and we really need to heighten the tension. What better way than to talk about the debauchery of last night? When the viewers know how much fun you and Chelsey had together—or Kira and

J.D.—they'll be even more emotionally involved during the next challenge."

"Yeah, yeah, I get it," I said, rubbing my forehead. As I did, I saw my wristband wasn't glowing green. "Are the cameras not on yet?"

"Not yet. Are you ready to begin?"

I let out a relieved breath and pushed past him. "Not a chance in hell."

I stifled a groan as Von hurried after me and stepped in next to me, easily keeping up with my pace. "Wyatt, you know this is a requirement. We must know how things went last night. Surely you understand that?" Von threw his arm out in front of me, forcing me to stop. When I glared at him, a vicious smile tugged at his lips. He raised an eyebrow. "Unless... something happened that caused you not to enjoy your night? A little performance anxiety, perhaps?"

"Von—"

"You know, it's not the first time things like this have happened on the show. Five seasons ago, a young alpha named Brock couldn't, for the life of him, get his little soldier to attention. Had to send a witch in with a potion to *speed things up*, if you know what I mean. Shifters are known for their drive and virility, but things happen."

"I'm done here," I said, slapping his arm away.

"Or maybe you were thinking of another gorgeous young lady?" Von called.

My steps faltered, and I almost tripped over my own feet. "What?" I asked, looking back at him over my shoulder.

Von's smile grew more predatory as his gaze slid down my body. I suddenly realized how I looked—wrinkled and disheveled. You'd have to be stupid not to know I'd slept in my clothing.

Von narrowed his eyes. "It looks like you slept a little too well, Mr. Rivers. Not at all like someone who spent four or five hours writhing in passion. How could someone spend an entire night in a bedroom with someone as beautiful as Chelsey and not look exhausted, I wonder?"

My heart hammered. Von was suspicious. We *had* to keep up the act. If Von thought Kira and I were faking, then he'd be compelled to release the information he had. I had to do whatever I could to keep the facade going.

Turning on the charm, I smiled and gave a condescending shake of my head. "Von, I think you remember from my interview with Callista back in Fangmore City that I'm a gentleman. And a gentleman never tells. I didn't tell that woman what happened between Kira and me in the chamber, and I'm not going to tell you what happened with Chelsey and me." I walked closer to him. "As for my *little soldier,* as you put it? He's very tired. Chelsey and I had a fantastic night. We did finish up early, though, hence my well-rested appearance." I gestured to my clothes. "And if you're wondering why I look like a slob, it's because all this got tossed aside when the party started. Simple as that. And the answer is still no. I'm not going to tell all the voyeurs in your audience what happened. You'll have to get over that, okay? That's final."

"Hmmm." The suspicion in his eyes faded, replaced with disappointment. "Well, I suppose I can't force you. A shame, but I understand. If there's one thing we at *The Reject Project* understand, it's the desire for privacy."

The fuck you do.

"I only hope the others are a bit more forthcoming," Von went on. "At least I'm sure to get some juicy details from J.D. That young man is like an open book. I'll probably have to slow him down on the play-by-play."

"Yeah, sure," I grunted, and to make sure I laid it on thick, I added, "With how fucking annoying Kira is, I doubt his *little soldier* stood at attention. Better him than me."

Von tittered a laugh, then rushed back down the hall, probably to catch Chelsey as she woke or to check in on J.D. and Kira. The vampire vanished around the corner, but I continued to stare even after he left. What if Von was right? J.D. *was* an open book. He might tell him he had no interest in Kira. Would that increase Von's suspicions that Kira and I were playing a game?

There was no way to know, and standing in the hallway wasn't going to solve anything. Instead, I headed downstairs for breakfast. If I was lucky, the other alphas would still be sleeping so I could eat in peace.

Unfortunately, it wasn't my day to be lucky. The kitchen and dining room were bustling with activity. Much to my surprise, J.D. was sitting at a table with Abel and Tate.

"Bro, it was such a fantastic night. You'll never believe how great it was. Kira, like, has something about her. I can't explain it."

Tate glared at him. "Can you shut up?"

I forced myself not to mimic Tate's glare. Cameras buzzed around the men as they ate and talked. I did my best to hide my irritation. My wolf was demanding blood, wanted to throw down with J.D. right there, but I forced him down and tried to appear calm and collected on the surface.

"I know, bro, but I can't help it," J.D. said to Tate. "But I feel better than I have in days. It's all thanks to Kira. It really was a magical night. She totally blew my mind."

I couldn't tell if he was lying. Gritting my teeth, I headed to the buffet and filled a bowl with cereal even though my hunger was rapidly vanishing. I controlled my temper and took a seat at a separate table, trying to feign disinterest in the topic.

Tate, however, had trouble controlling his own anger. He leaned across the table and leveled a finger at J.D. "I like you, and that's the only reason I'm giving you this warning: stop talking about Kira like that. She is *my* fated mate. I'm going to see to it. Yeah, we get it, you had the time of your fucking life in the mating chamber. Enough." Red-faced and furious, Tate turned and spotted me. "Change of fucking subject. How was your night, Wyatt?"

"Fine," I grunted. "Not anyone's business but mine and Chelsey's, though. All I can say is I'm feeling much better after a night alone with her."

It wasn't a lie. Now that I'd laid everything out to Chelsey, a massive weight had lifted off me. It wasn't a sexual release, but a mental one.

Before Tate could say another word, Kira strolled into the dining room. It took everything I had not to stare at her. As usual, she looked gorgeous. She had no trouble cloaking herself in her TV persona and shining that thousand-watt smile at everyone.

"Good morning, guys. How's breakfast?"

"Great," Tate grumbled, then shot J.D. a spiteful look. "Sounds like you two had a good night."

Kira walked around the table, put her hands on J.D.'s shoulders, and kissed him on the cheek. "It was a pretty amazing night, wasn't it?"

I almost bent my spoon from gripping it too hard. Desperate thoughts and reassurances pulsed through my head, but the way Kira and J.D. smiled at each other made me stifle a growl before it could come out of my throat. She was playing for the cameras. That's all it was, and I knew that. Kira had been acting since she got on the island. Still, I didn't like it. It was silly and stupid, but dammit, I couldn't help myself. Would she feel the same if I were bragging about my night with Chelsey?

Unable to help myself, I tossed my spoon into my bowl. "I had an amazing night, too. Chelsey and I were a much better match in bed than the last time I was in the chamber. No offense, of course," I added offhandedly to Kira.

Kira shot me an icy glare. "Wonderful to hear. I'm glad Chelsey took that map I drew."

"Huh?" I frowned, confusion clouding my mind.

"Oh, the one for her to find your cock. It's so small, I told her she'd need a map to figure out where it was."

Tate snorted and nearly dropped his glass as a jet of milk shot from his nose.

"Damn, man." Abel gave a sad shake of his head. "You're being a real ass, Wyatt. Leave it alone."

Kira put a hand on Abel's shoulder. When she looked at me again, I could see I'd actually pissed her off. "Thank you, Abel, but I can handle myself. God, I'm so glad you showed your true colors so early, Wyatt. You and I really aren't a good match. Not just emotionally, but in bed as well. You never could give me what I needed." She sent J.D. a suggestive smile. "Another alpha, however, gave me exactly what I wanted last night. *Multiple* times." She smiled wickedly at me. "And again this morning in the shower. You and I are nothing but water under the bridge now, Wyatt."

I'd spent years training to control my emotions. As an operative, I'd found myself in various situations during missions where I had to keep my calm and cool. But all that training fell away now. Before I could stop it, an image flashed across my mind. Kira bent over, water from the shower cascading down her back, J.D. behind her, his cock buried in her pussy. Kira moaning as he drove deep into her.

"Enough!" I barked. "I'm done talking about this."

Kira arched an eyebrow. "Well, you were pretty eager to talk about how your night was. I thought we were having story time."

"I was also trying to eat. I don't need to hear what you two did together. I'd prefer to *not* regurgitate my food."

"At least you know how to eat cereal, Wyatt. You weren't very good at eating something else, if my memory serves."

"Holy fucking shit," Abel muttered, looking like he'd rather be anywhere else.

Somehow, Kira and I had slid off the rails of acting and stumbled into an actual fight. About shit that hadn't even happened. For some reason, I couldn't stop. What the fuck was wrong with me?

"I didn't hear Chelsey complaining last night. She asked for seconds *and* thirds."

Kira narrowed her eyes, her nostrils flaring. "How wonderful for you."

She spun on a heel and stomped out of the room. I'd fucked up. I'd let my jealousy get the better of me and said things I shouldn't have. Why in the name of the gods had I pushed it that far? It was supposed to be an act, not a fight. Fuck.

Pushing away from the table, I stood and went to follow her, but J.D. leaped up to block my way.

"Let her go, bro," he said, shoving his palm into my chest and making me rock back on my heels. I'd never seen him look so pissed. For the first time since the show had started, J.D. looked like he wanted to fight someone.

He was looking out for Kira, wanting to give her a little peace after the fight. The problem was, my inner wolf saw it as a challenge. Not only that, a challenge from the man who had been playing in a movie in my head moments before—a movie of him fucking Kira. I clenched my fist and gritted my teeth, shaking with anger as I did all I could to stop myself from knocking him out.

After a few deep breaths, I stepped back and raised my hands in surrender. "Sorry. I'm outta here."

As I left, Tate's laughter followed me. Probably a joke about me, but I kept walking, ignoring my surging anger. One foot in front of the other. Keep moving.

I walked through the mansion, letting my temper dissipate. When I finally stopped walking, I was mildly surprised to find that I'd ended up right at Kira's door.

"Crap." I groaned.

Better to get the apology over with sooner rather than later. At least this way, she couldn't stew on it any longer than necessary. I'd throw myself on my sword, fall to my knees, and beg—whatever it took. I was still beating myself up over it. Maybe she'd be able to see that in my eyes.

Sighing, I knocked three times.

"What?" Her voice, petulant and pissed, came through the door.

"It's me. Can I come in?"

For a few seconds, I was worried she'd simply ignore me, but then the locks turned and the door opened. Kira's hand shot out and grabbed my shirt, wrenching me into the room. The move was so sudden, I nearly fell flat on my face.

"You jackass! You didn't have to get so deep in the act." Kira crossed her arms over her breasts. "Do you have any idea how much you pissed off my wolf? It took all my control not to go and claw Chelsey's eyes out."

"Seriously? I'm out there picturing you and J.D. fucking in the shower. How do you think I felt? Did you really need to lay it on that thick? You did everything but draw a damn diagram."

"I'm sorry, I thought we were trying to make it believable. You were the one who brought it up. I just followed your lead."

"It's how you touched him, Kira." I had to clench my fists to contain my temper. "If I had to watch your hands on J.D. for another second, I was gonna lose it."

Kira took a step forward, uncrossing her arms. "Am I hearing that right? Is Wyatt Rivers telling me who I can and can't touch? Do I belong to you in some way? I didn't realize you saw me as a piece of property."

Gods, she could be irritating. "I never said that or even implied it. All I said was that I didn't like seeing it."

Kira pressed close to me, the heat of her body radiating onto mine, her nose only inches from my face. "Why?"

My inner wolf lost it. He surged forward, nearly forcing a shift—not from rage and anger, but from desire, lust, and need. I couldn't stop myself if I wanted to, and I sure as shit didn't want to.

"Because you're mine." I curled my hand around the back of her neck, pulling her close so I could crush my lips to hers.

Kira yelped in surprise, but her mouth opened, her tongue meeting mine in a frenzied dance. Her hands roved up my back until her fingers ran through my hair, and she pressed my face even closer to hers.

My hands moved of their own accord and unbuttoned her pants. The animal inside me took over, and all I could of was having her, making her mine. The urge to take her was stronger than it had ever been. Almost painfully unbearable.

I backed her farther into the suite toward the bed, our lips never parting. Kira's breathing became heavier and more excited as the backs of her knees hit the side of the bed. Finally, I pulled my lips from hers and gasped for air as I yanked her pants and panties down around her knees. I spun her around and bent her face-first over the bed, then dropped to my knees and shoved my tongue into her pussy, digging my fingers into the glorious flesh of her ass.

"Fuuuck," Kira moaned into the blanker, her voice muffled.

I slid my tongue across her clit, circling it, then pressing deep into her, fucking her with my mouth. Kira reached back and grabbed my head, urging me on. She pressed her hips back against my face, grinding against my mouth. Her pussy almost suffocated me, but I couldn't imagine a better way to die.

Pulling my face away to catch my breath, I slid two fingers into her and reached around her to rub her clit. Kira gyrated her hips in rhythm with the thrust of my fingers.

"Gods," Kira moaned. "You're gonna make me come."

"That's the idea," I whispered, moving my fingers faster.

Her panting and moans became desperate. I felt her muscles tense—she was close. I leaned in, licking her ass while my hands worked. She cried out, her body spasming as the climax took her. When her trembling subsided, she twisted around and looked into my eyes. The hunger there frightened and excited me at the same time.

"My turn," she purred, her voice barely a whisper.

In seconds, we were both naked, and I was on my back on the bed. Kira nestled between my legs, her hand wrapped around the base of my throbbing cock. She locked her eyes on mine, flicking her tongue over the thick head.

"Want me to take care of you?" she asked.

I nodded, unable to form words. Grinning, Kira lowered her head and took me into her mouth. I groaned at the heat of her mouth as she took every inch of me. She bobbed up and down, stroking me with her hand as she sucked. With every passing second, my need for her grew. I watched her devour me and fantasized about biting her, fully claiming her as mine. I had to push that thought away. It was too far to go. Even now, with my body ablaze with pleasure and need.

I couldn't take any more. In one fluid movement, I pulled out of Kira's mouth and flipped her onto her back, gazing deep into her eyes as I slid into her. Eyes locked on mine, Kira moaned in delight as I filled her. My wolf gnashed its teeth, urging me on.

I ground my hips against her, driving my cock deeper into her pussy. Kira clawed at my chest, lifting her hips to meet mine. There was no way I could hold back any longer. My thrusts quickened as I plunged into her until we became one. Kira's magnificent breasts bounced as I fucked her.

"Harder. Fuck me harder," she said with a wicked smile.

The groan that left me was almost a laugh as I obliged her. Flesh slapped against flesh as our bodies came together with each thrust. We pulled each other close, embracing as we descended into an abyss of pleasure.

Kira dug her fingers into my back, wrapped her legs around my ass, and pulled me ever deeper into her. Our sweat mingled, and again, I fantasized about claiming her. My lips brushed her shoulder, and I salivated with the desire to take her. Instead, I pulled my head to the side and kissed her again.

Kira moaned into my mouth, trembling under me as another orgasm neared. Her pleasure was too much for me. My cock twitched and spasmed, electric bolts of ecstasy shooting through my balls and up my back until it coursed through my entire body. I shuddered as I came, my thrusts never ceasing.

Pulling her lips from mine, Kira gasped and let out a guttural sound. The veins on her neck stood out as the orgasm took hold of her. Spent, I still moved within her, desperate to give her everything she desired. I wanted to make sure she had every second of pleasure. After an eternity, we both collapsed, exhausted and satisfied.

As I lay there with her in my arms, all my earlier anger and frustration evaporated. Peace unlike any I'd ever experienced washed over me. Kira ran a hand along my chest. Apologies were in order.

"Hey, I'm sorry about earlier," I said. "I shouldn't have been so hard on you out there. I lost it, and I shouldn't have."

She traced a finger along my abs, circling my belly button. "It's fine. I was a bitch, too. I think we both went overboard on the whole act."

"So, how did your night *actually* go?" I asked.

"Fine. J.D. and I talked a lot. I told him Leif's alive and feral. I couldn't handle how pitiful he looked. He needed to know."

"Well, that explains why he was in such a chipper mood this morning."

"Yeah," Kira said. "We decided to act like we had sex to explain his sudden shift in mood since he's such a terrible actor." She looked up into my eyes. "I also told him I'm planning on getting people out of here alive."

"How did that go?"

"He said he'd do whatever it took." She tapped her finger on my abs. "Uh, how were things with Chelsey?"

She still looked worried and uncomfortable. Couldn't she see how I felt about her? Or did she think she wasn't good enough to be loved? Ever since her first shift, she'd had these walls up. I'd always assumed it was to protect people from the threat she thought lurked deep inside her. That was part of it, sure, but perhaps she also thought she was such a terrible person that no one would ever care for her.

"I told her I was in love with you. That you and I are faking the whole fighting thing, and that while I like her as a person, there will never be anything more than friendship between us."

Kira's eyes widened. "Wow, uh, okay. How did she... um, is she good with that? Like, does she hate us both now?"

"No. She's disappointed, but she understood. She's pissed at the show more than anything. She's ready to claw Von's eyes out for kidnapping her brother." I rubbed a hand down Kira's bare back. "I feel bad for her. She's really not over her last fated mate. She'd been head-over-heels in love with the guy. Part of me thinks she latched onto me out of desperation to heal her broken heart or something. Either way, she'll help us ruin this show once and for all, no matter what it takes."

Kira sagged in relief. "Thank goodness. I like Chelsey, but the way she kept looking at you all the time was getting under my skin. If someone didn't tell her the truth, I think my acting might have gone out the window." She huffed. "I can't understand why my wolf gets all pissy about stuff when it has to do with you."

Interesting. My wolf reacted the same way to her. It was part of why I'd gone so overboard at breakfast. Even the *idea* of someone else being with Kira sent it into a raging tailspin. I opened my mouth to say something, but a pounding at the door interrupted me.

Kira sat up quickly, slapping a hand over my mouth. "Hello?" she called, loud enough to be heard through the door.

"It's Von, my dear! I have cameras rolling. I somehow missed you leaving the mating chamber. I need to get a word."

"Shit," Kira muttered.

"Is something wrong?" Von asked, his voice muffled. I could still hear the glee in his tone. "Are you... indisposed?"

Fuck. He knew I was in here with her. The son of a bitch knew, or at least suspected. I took her hand off my mouth and hissed, "Get up. We have to get dressed. Hurry."

I bounded off the bed in search of my clothes. Kira hustled off the other side, finding her panties in the corner. I'd barely gotten my underwear on when the door crashed open and a hulking fallen angel stumbled inside.

Kira yelped in surprise and threw an arm across her exposed breasts—thank the gods she'd gotten her panties on in time. Von stepped through the door, followed by cameras. My wristband flashed from white to bright green. The fucker was filming this.

Von clapped gleefully. "Oh, goody. Just as I expected."

"Get the fuck out of here!" Kira screamed, her face flaming with anger and embarrassment. She did her best to pull a T-shirt over her head without showing the whole world her tits. "Now, Von. Get out."

Ignoring her shouts, Von turned to one of the cameras. "Ladies and gentlemen, now you see why we went with a special live broadcast. Exciting, isn't it?"

Live? Holy fuck. That meant everyone on the planet saw this, including the other alphas. Oh, gods.

"This morning, we have a *big* reveal," Von said. "It seems that we have a first on *The Reject Project*. Never in our history have a lead mate and one of the contestants known each other prior to filming."

"Don't, Von," I snapped.

"Now, now, Mr. Rivers. Don't try to steal my thunder. People of the world, I bring you an exclusive, juicy secret that Wyatt and Kira have been hiding from everyone."

Kira buried her face in her hands. She knew what awaited us. It was like watching a train crash. You couldn't do anything, didn't want to see it, but you couldn't pull your eyes away.

"Kira Durst and Wyatt Rivers knew each other before the show started. They partook in carnal delights with each other prior to the premiere. They have tried to play the system. This entire season has been rigged from the start. Rigged by these two duplicitous lovers behind me," Von declared, then swept his hand back toward us.

The cameras zeroed in on us, like gun barrels ready to fire.

Chapter 7 - Kira

Rage wiped out all my surprise. The fucking bloodsucker had busted down my door and caught us with our pants down, literally. Had I ever been this angry? This worried? Wyatt would take most of the backlash for this, be the main target for ire. As the lead mate, I'd probably get the benefit of the doubt, though that was debatable. Either way, I needed to protect Wyatt as best I could.

Summoning all my inner strength, I forced myself not to gut Von right there and took a step forward.

"This was *not* rigged," I said desperately. "Yes, okay, we did know each other before coming on the show, but nothing was ever rigged in Wyatt's favor. I had no idea he was coming on the show. You've got this all wrong. It was... um... a coincidence. That's all."

Von wagged a finger at me. "Now, now, Kira. I'm sure you can see how that sounds. Besides," he gestured at us and our half-clothed state, "it appears you two just finished having a *very* good time."

Heat rushed to my cheeks. I was wearing nothing but a T-shirt and panties. Wyatt stood on the other side of the bed, clad only in boxers, his chest still sporting the faint marks from where I'd clawed him while he'd fucked me.

Yeah. This looked bad.

Von turned back the cameras again, laying his surprise on thick for the audience. "Can you believe it? These two in here, doing only the gods know what to each other mere hours after their sordid nights with two other contestants." He sighed and shook his head. "What would poor Chelsey and J.D. think of this?"

Wyatt looked as pissed as I did, but he knew it was pointless to argue. Von would spin this however he wanted to make us look as bad as possible. Wyatt sat on the edge of the bed, teeth clenched, and stared at the ground while Von kept flapping his jaw.

"Our viewers at home have never seen something as underhanded as this. In all the decades of *The Reject Project,* there has never been a couple as shameful and malicious as this."

I couldn't handle it anymore—he needed to shut his mouth. I took a few steps in his direction, ready to break his jaw, but the fallen angel stepped in front of me. The massive bodyguard towered a foot and a half over me.

"Don't think about it, miss." His voice was like mud-covered rocks cracking together.

The guy had arms like tree trunks, but I could take him. But God only knew how many others might be out in the hall, waiting to jump in if necessary. It made me feel impotent. All I could do was sit there and listen to Von tear us apart while hundreds of millions of people watched.

"Kira and Wyatt have twisted what is supposed to be a beautiful game. Shifters come on this show to find love and hope and happiness. Yet, here these two are, screwing their brains out behind everyone's backs, throwing all the other contestants under the bus to ensure they end up with fame, riches, and honorary membership to the First Pack. All without facing any real danger or searching for genuine love."

"No real danger?" Wyatt snapped. "Are you shitting me?" He stood and leveled a finger at Von. "You can make up whatever shit you want about me and Kira, but the people back home will never have the full story. Not if it comes from your bloodstained lips. All you do is lie."

Von put a hand to his chest and opened his mouth in overdramatic shock. "How dare you, sir? You think you can besmirch my good name? All I do is broadcast the truth." Von pointed at Wyatt, then at me. "What I know is that there will be repercussions. I have no idea what they will be, but something will need to be done. You two have thrown off the balance of the game since the moment you got here."

"This is bullshit," I muttered, crossing my arms.

Von ran a hand down his suit, smoothing out non-existent wrinkles. "You may think that now, but we'll see what you say in a few hours." He turned to the cameras, that showman smile of his back in place. "In a move never before seen on *The Reject Project*, I will be summoning the showrunners here to Bloodstone Island so we can discuss how to proceed. I suggest everyone tune in a few hours from now for a once-in-a-lifetime episode. You don't want to miss this."

Von swept his hand at the cameras and they fled from the room. The vampire slid a phone from his suit pocket and quickly swiped and tapped it a few times. His smile widened and he pumped his fist.

"That was *fantastic*," he said, looking up at us.

"What was?" I spat. Our worldwide humiliation? "You've got a lot of fucking nerve to—"

"The ratings," Von interrupted, waving his phone at us. "We're already getting initial numbers in. They went through the roof during that little fiasco. This is very exciting. Audience engagement on social media is like nothing we've ever seen before. My gods, look at all these comments in the last few seconds alone." He looked like a kid in a toy store with a blank check.

"Everyone *hates* you two right now," he continued gleefully. "Most people think Wyatt is a scumbag and that Kira is a... well, let's see what terms they're using." He scanned his phone. "Looks like 'whore' and 'slut' are two popular euphemisms, along with 'backstabber' and 'bitch.'" He shoved his phone into his pocket. "This could not be going better."

"So treating us like shit is good for the show? Why am I not surprised?" Wyatt said.

Von rolled his eyes. "Wyatt, Wyatt, Wyatt. This is show business. When you have a hook, you have to use it, really dig it in deep. Once it's there, the audience can never look away. Plus, that was all live.

The reaction?" He snapped his fingers. "Instantaneous. It goes to show that we have what is possibly the most successful season yet. You two should be happy."

"Happy?" Wyatt growled and took an angry step toward Von. The bodyguard moved to intercept, giving Wyatt a warning shake of the head.

"Yes, happy. Everyone involved should be happy with our success. Though..." Von put a thoughtful finger to his chin. "I'm not sure how long either of you will remain on the show. The showrunners will be very upset about this getting out."

"They must have known," I said. How could Von possibly think they hadn't? Everyone from my pack watching would have known immediately.

Von sighed dramatically and looked at me like I was an idiot. "Of course they *knew*, sweet woman. You think this is the first time we've had contestants who knew each other? In thirty-one seasons? You cannot be that dense. No, they'll be upset that the news leaked out to the public."

It was like someone had shoved an electric cable into my brain. "You're the one who told!" I screamed. I had to be going crazy.

Von rolled his eyes. "Well, yes. You two pissed me off, so... I don't like to be played with, you see." He narrowed his eyes. "I'm not a toy for silly wolf games. As soon as Mr. Rivers here told me your little secret, I wanted to use it for the show, but you two decided to act like you were at each other's throats. You forced my hand, really. Had you two played the game the right way, we could have had fun with it. But now? Things have escalated.

"A word of advice. Never screw with a vampire. When you've lived as long as I have, you learn to hold a grudge. Also, prepare yourselves to be called into the meeting with the showrunners. They'll want you there when they discuss how to handle these issues."

Wyatt and I shared an incredulous look. Wyatt pointed at Von again. "But *you* told. *You*. Like Kira said, you'll be in trouble, too."

Von waved him away and smirked. "I'm the star, darling. Stars don't get in trouble."

"Aren't we the stars as well?" I asked.

Von stifled a laugh. "Of this season? Yes. Of the entire show? Afraid not."

"Gods, you really don't give a fuck about us. I bet you actually enjoy watching us die out there," Wyatt said.

Von's face grew somber and he pressed a hand to his heart. "Wyatt, that hurts. I've lived for centuries, and the years and lives flit by more rapidly each time the calendar page turns. It's nothing personal. Mortal deaths are like changes in the weather for me. You must see that. It's part of nature. Do I cry when a leaf falls from a tree in autumn? No. Do I weep when the snow melts in spring? Of course not. But make no mistake, I genuinely like the two of you."

"Seriously?" I tilted my head. "You could have fooled us."

"Oh, of course. You two have made this season very exciting, and if there's one thing the undead love, it's excitement. After living for centuries, we're rarely surprised anymore. The living always think they're special or one of a kind, when in reality, you're all simply retreads of someone who lived a few decades or centuries ago. My life will get much less exhilarating when you two are knocked off the show, believe me. Which I'm sure will be any day now," he added offhandedly.

Wyatt yanked his shirt off the floor. "I'm glad we could entertain you."

Pulling out his phone again, Von grinned. "Thanks are not necessary. You two should go ahead and get dressed. I just received confirmation that the showrunners are heading to the helicopters and will be arriving within the hour. These are *very* rich and *very* powerful people. I doubt you'll want to meet them in your current state of undress."

"Why would we meet them?" I asked. "Aren't you guys just gonna put your heads together and figure out some sadistic way to get Wyatt and me killed?"

Barely paying attention as he tapped away at his phone, Von nodded absently. "Yes, yes, you'll more than likely be eliminated soon. Still, they'll want you there. Best to keep your mouths shut unless they ask questions." He glanced at the hulking fallen angel. "Come, Samael, the helicopter will be here soon. I want to have refreshments ready for our guests."

Von vanished out the door. The fallen angel followed him, walking backward to keep an eye on us until he was at the door. With a final glance, he turned and left the room.

"We're fucked," I groaned, running my hands through my hair.

Everything was falling apart. J.D. and Chelsey knew our secret, but the others—Abel, Tate, Gavin—would be blindsided. Gavin knew, but he didn't understand the depth of my and Wyatt's relationship. Tate would be *pissed*, and gods only knew how he'd react. Abel? If I had to guess, he'd be hurt or dejected by the betrayal.

Then there were the fans. Even if we survived whatever punishment the showrunners threw at us, I was sure Von would add more chances for the audience to vote, and you could bet your ass they'd be voting against us at every turn.

Wyatt must have seen on my face that I was spiraling. He strode over to me and put his hands on my arms. "Calm down, we'll figure this out."

"How? We worked so hard to make sure it wouldn't be so bad when he revealed it. He caught us fucking on camera. It can't get much worse."

Wyatt smiled humorlessly. "Well, he at least didn't catch us in the act. I think that could have been worse."

I moaned in frustration. "You know what I mean. All this has been for nothing. If we get kicked off the show, then I won't be able to help the others survive. I won't be able to ask Heline to stop the war. My pack will be defenseless. All this would have been a waste of time. How the fuck will I help Zoe get off the island? This is a nightmare I—"

"Enough," Wyatt cut me off. "We can fix this. Let me think about it."

There was no way out of this that I could see. Instead of trying to fix it, we needed to figure out a way to survive. Wyatt frowned in deep thought. All I could think of was how he'd look dead, torn apart by some beast because the show had put him in even worse danger than usual. This had all gone bad too quickly.

"Okay, we can play it like this," Wyatt said. "We knew each other before, yeah, but I was stalking you. I coerced you into sex one night, then followed you on the show. I'm like a psycho and twisting things to my benefit. You can go on camera, crying and talking about how unsafe you felt. Maybe even say I forced myself on you today."

He might as well have kicked me in the chest. He didn't give a damn about himself. That story would only put him in more danger. If we went that route and he somehow *did* survive and get home, his reputation would be ruined. Even his unofficial pack would kick him out if they thought he was a stalker and a rapist.

No. Absolutely not. I wouldn't allow him to throw his good name in the gutter to make me into some blameless princess.

"Wyatt, shut up," I snapped.

He blinked, surprised. "What?"

"You're a dumbass." I leaned forward and kissed him. After pulling away, I could see he was in shock. "We aren't doing that. In fact, we don't even need to worry about a plan until after this meeting. Quit trying to think up ways to make yourself out to be a monster. We may never even get the chance to say anything. The people coming hold all the power. They may just kick us off the island immediately."

"Maybe not," Wyatt said. "My uncle Rob might be one of them."

"What do you mean?"

"He's the one who pulled the strings to get me on the show. A bunch of people in my family work for the studio that owns the show, but he's one of the main execs who runs things. There's a chance he could be one of the people who comes. I'm not sure who he answers to, but it might be an ace in our deck." He shrugged. "Possibly."

If Wyatt did have a relative that deep in the inner workings of the show, then it might help us. If nothing else, we'd at least have one person arguing for us.

"Let's get ready," I said. "The last thing I want is to be late for this thing."

We showered together, and it was as unsexy as could be. We were both too consumed with what was to come. A lot hung in the balance. I had a worrying thought that they might kill us on the spot. Technically, the deaths on the island were "collateral damage." We'd all signed legally binding paperwork that basically gave the show the rights to our lives while the show was going on. Even our dead bodies weren't sent home if we were found; they were left to rot on the island. Who was to say they wouldn't get us out of the way and give the authorities some story that we'd suffered a tragic end in the jungle?

Thoughts like that kept bouncing through my head while I dressed. As I finished tying my shoes, there was a knock at my splintered, destroyed door. A staff witch entered without waiting for me to invite her in.

"I'm to lead you to your meeting. Mr. Thornton says it's time."

"Are you good?" I asked Wyatt, his hair still damp from the shower.

"As ready as I'll ever be," he said.

We joined the witch at the door. She gestured at the ruined entryway. "I'll have someone come to fix this while you're out. A few spells and some elbow grease, and it should be good as new."

"While we're out?" I said. "Does that mean we'll get to come back?"

The older woman chuckled as we walked. "Oh, I have no idea. I just thought it would be nice if things were back to normal if you did return." She clucked her tongue disapprovingly. "You know, I was rooting for you and J.D., sweetie. You've done that poor boy dirty."

Great. Even the staff thought Wyatt and I were pieces of shit. That didn't bode well for the upcoming meeting.

"There you are!"

The three of us stopped and turned to see Tate barreling down the hall toward us.

"Shit," Wyatt muttered.

"You two motherfuckers!" Tate spat. "I can't believe the shit I just heard, what I saw on the damn television. You've been playing us since the goddamn beginning, fucking us over left and right. Doing everything you can to make sure the two of you can win!"

"Tate," I said. "It's not what you think. We—"

"Oh, fuck off, you dumb cunt."

"Whoa!" Wyatt shoved Tate back. "Watch your fucking mouth."

Tate regained his footing and laughed bitterly. "Oh yeah, big man. Let me guess, she's pulling the strings, huh? You're just along for the ride on the pussy, right?" He sneered at me. "I've spent all this damn time trying to win you over, trying to get you to like me. In the end, you looked at me like I was nothing but a little bitch. I was only shit to scrape off your shoe and leave for dead on this goddamn island. Fuck, man, I almost lost my arm for this shit."

J.D. and Abel rounded the corner, drawn by the shouting. Things were getting worse by the minute, but blessedly, there were no cameras around. Abel looked upset. J.D. was obviously worried, but he caught my eye and gave me a reassuring nod.

"Tate, calm down," Abel said listlessly.

"I am calm!" He jabbed his finger my way. "I hope they kick your asses out—both of you. I hope they shove you out into the jungle to fend for yourself. I'll laugh my ass off while you get ripped to fucking shreds."

"Holy shit, man," J.D. said. "Too far."

"Keep talking, Tate. See what happens," Wyatt said, glaring daggers at the other alpha.

I was too shocked to speak. Of all the remaining alphas, Tate was the one I'd liked the least, but he'd basically been jovial. He'd complimented me and done all he could to stand out and win me over. He'd never acted like Omar or Nathaniel, but this betrayal had either triggered something that had never been there before or revealed his true personality. I hoped it was the latter. I didn't want to think our deception had turned a moderately good guy into whatever lunatic was screaming at us now.

"Miss Durst, gentleman," the witch said, looking frazzled. "We really don't have time for this. You three," she pointed at Tate, Abel, and J.D., "need to go on. We have time-sensitive things to attend to."

Abel grabbed Tate's shirt and tugged him back. For a moment, it looked like Tate was about to fight him off, but he allowed Abel to pull him away. He waved a hand at us like he was swatting away flies. "Fuck them. I need to go find Chelsey. At least she's for real." He shrugged away Abel's hand and stomped off.

J.D. waited until Abel followed before mouthing, *I'm sorry.* He shook his head sadly and followed the other two.

"My," the witch said, her hand on her chest. "That was rather more intense than I thought it was going to be. Come on now. We need to hurry."

We didn't get far. When we reached the landing on the third floor, Gavin stepped out of an alcove to greet us.

"Hey." When he looked at me, I could see sadness and confusion in his eyes. He'd still held out hope that I'd fall for him. Another person hurt by my lies and deception.

"Mr. Fell," the witch said testily, "we are on our way to a meeting. These two have some explaining to do."

"Well, I'm going, too," Gavin proclaimed.

"What?" Wyatt, the witch, and I all said in unison.

"I'm part of this. Kira and I knew each other before the show started as well. In fact, my older brother was the one who rejected her. The only reason he's here," he pointed at Wyatt, "is because he's a possessive asshole and thinks Kira will fall for him instead of me. What he doesn't understand is that Kira and I are fated to be together. I know it. If I come along, I can explain. Once the showrunners hear what I have to say, they'll understand everything."

Gavin sounded delusional. I had no idea why he thought professing his undying love for me or telling the showrunners his theory that the blood test between Jayson and I had gotten mixed up would solve anything.

The witch seemed to think the same thing. "Goodness, you shifters are full of damn drama. It's one thing after another," she hissed as she put a firm hand on Gavin's chest. "You stay here. Mr. Thornton and the others are only expecting these two. Go on. You can bat your eyelashes at Kira later."

Gavin was already shaking his head before she finished speaking. "But—"

"No buts. Get out of here before I cast a spell to sew your mouth shut. You're going to make us late, which will get me in trouble. Go!"

The other alpha glared at her for a moment, but the prospect of having his mouth literally sewn shut made him relent. We moved past him. Gavin glared at Wyatt, but gave me a reassuring nod. He reached out as though he wanted to take my hand, but I pretended not to see the gesture.

We headed up a final set of stairs to the outdoor patio on the roof. The witch opened the door and gestured for us to go first. "Good luck. You'll need it," she said before closing the door behind us.

On the patio, a table had been set up and multiple people sat around it. They all carried themselves with power and authority. Almost as one, the group turned to look at us as we walked forward.

Hoping that Wyatt recognized his uncle among the crowd, I looked at his face. Wyatt's tight jaw and confused face told me all I needed to know—his uncle was not in attendance.

As we drew nearer, I realized that I recognized two of the six people at the table. One was the wealthy media mogul Garth Sheen—Mika's father. The other was the strange and enigmatic man who'd been at the auditions. The psychic who, if I had to bet money, was the one who'd pulled the strings to help get me on the show in the first place.

"One's a psychic," I whispered to Wyatt, hiding my lips by pretending to scratch my nose. "Guard your mind."

"Got it."

The others all appeared to be generic rich business people—all but one. A woman sat at the middle of the table, striking in her beauty. She held herself in an aloof manner, almost as though the people around her were of no consequence. Her white dress stood out like snow among the men's charcoal and black suits.

I tried to scent her, but came away with no clue if she was human, shifter, fae, or something else entirely. She made me uneasy, even more so than the others.

Von stood nearby and circled the table to meet us. He wore sunglasses and a ridiculous wide-brimmed hat to block out the sun. "Kira, Wyatt, welcome. I present to you the board of directors for *The Reject Project*. If you would, please tell them your story. Say your piece. If they like what they hear, they may use it to spin things on the show and do some damage control."

"Where's Robert Rivers?" Wyatt asked. "He should be here. He's on the board."

Garth Sheen scoffed. "Rob? He's been expelled from the board. No longer with us."

"What?" Wyatt looked shocked and confused. "Why? Shouldn't there have been some word? A report on the news or—"

"Enough," Garth barked at him. "We ask the questions, not you, son. Your uncle can't pull the strings anymore. Understand?" He jammed his fingertip onto the table. "Speak. You have thirty seconds each to tell us why we shouldn't toss your asses out in the jungle to die right now."

He really was an alpha asshole. No wonder Mika didn't want to go home. If he'd been my father, I'd have taken my chances on this island, too.

"Explain your connection," Garth prodded.

So, Wyatt's uncle had kept almost everything hidden from the rest of the board. That must have been part of why they were mad—they'd been blindsided by Wyatt's and my relationship as well. Could that be why good old Uncle Rob had been kicked off? I bet it was. Fantastic.

Wyatt gritted his teeth, and that muscle in his jaw ticked like it always did when he was annoyed. Sighing, he told them that we'd known each other for years, that he and my brother were best friends, and we were co-workers in the TO.

"Why aren't you interrogating Von, too?" I asked, unable to hold my tongue.

Von raised his eyebrows and put his hand to his chest demurely. "Me?"

"Yes, you, dammit," I snarled, scanning the other board members' faces. "He's the one who told the whole fucking world. Why isn't he out here getting crucified with us?"

Garth glanced across the table at Von, a dark expression clouding his face. "She's right, Von. What the absolute fuck were you thinking? You could have kept this all under wraps and made our lives a lot less difficult."

Von shrugged, and I was upset to see that he didn't look the least bit chastened at being singled out. "Ratings, darling. That's the name of the game. I was shooting for the stars to try and land on the moon." Von gave Wyatt and me a sidelong glance. "Let's be honest, these two haven't been the best team players. I thought it was a good play to make." He rolled his eyes. "I had no idea so many people would lose their collective minds about this. My apologies, of course."

Garth and the others grumbled a bit, then the bearded man addressed Von. "You're damn lucky that you're so popular. Otherwise, you'd have a lot to answer for."

Von raised a finger and winked. "But I am popular. You just admitted it."

To my disgust, the board members shared a subdued chuckle and turned their attention back to us. You had to be fucking kidding me. That was all Von got for doing this?

"Speak up, you two," Garth went on. "This connection you two have, where did it start?"

Defeated, I gritted my teeth and shrugged. "Um, his pack also lives in my pack's territories."

"What the fuck does that mean?" a man sitting to the left of the woman in white asked.

Wyatt gave a resigned sigh, and I explained. "Um, I'm part of the Eleventh Pack. Wyatt is in an unofficial pack."

Various looks of disdain and disgust flickered across everyone's faces. Most of these people were from high-level packs and had deeply ingrained prejudices against lone wolves and unofficial packs.

Garth's face was a mask of derision. "Your uncle never said anything about his nephew being a lone wolf."

"I'm not a lone wolf," Wyatt argued. "I have an unofficial pack. When I left Second Pack, my parents and family were ashamed and covered it up. I sort of, I don't know, disappeared from sight."

A dark-skinned man sitting beside Garth leaned back in his chair and folded his hands in his lap. "So, not only did you have Rob pull strings to get you on the show, you also lied about being in a pack?

The Reject Project has never had a contestant from an unofficial pack before. This is worse than I thought."

Wyatt clenched his jaw, his body tense. I'd seen that expression before—he was about to argue. "Wait a minute," he said. "I don't see how—"

"Hold your tongue," Von said, wagging a finger at him. "Let the board call on you if they want to hear anything from you."

"Yes, sir," Wyatt hissed through his clenched jaw.

Ignoring us, the group began to argue about what to do.

"We shut it down. Right now. Today," the dark-skinned man said.

Another man with a bushy beard rolled his eyes. "Do you have any clue how much money we've sunk into this thing already? My gods, we've already sold the marketing rights to the finale. Do you have any clue how much money that was? How much we'll have to pay back to the sponsors?"

"Clark is right," a man on the opposite side of the table said. "We can't write off tens of millions of dollars. It'll hamstring the company for years, if not longer. Hell, if we cancel, the sponsors may be hesitant to come back. Then where would that leave us? It could cause us to fold completely."

The dark-skinned man pointed toward us. "What does it matter if the show goes on if those two have already ruined that game? And that *thing*," he said, sneering at Wyatt, "has ruined the prestige. If some mutt from outside the pack hierarchy can have a chance to win, then why even bother?"

Wyatt growled so low and soft that only I could hear it. I wanted to rip that fucker's head off. What a total bigot. Had that been the way I'd looked at everyone who didn't belong to a pack? I tried to recall how I'd responded to lone wolves and others like Wyatt. Had I really been such a bitch? It sickened me to think about it now.

Garth waved a hand around flippantly. "I think we do shut it down. Send these two out into the jungle to fend for themselves and try for a quick turnaround on the new season. I'm not worried about the sponsors. Give me a day, and they'll be begging to sign up for the new season. Maybe we can even play this as a new angle—we could take the remaining cast and add some more alphas. We can spin this however we want once the lovebirds are rotting corpses in the jungle."

The way he heartlessly condemned us to death shocked even me. Mika's childhood and upbringing must have been awful. It disgusted me. Garth was screwing with his son's life, which meant far less to him than the profits and money brought in by the show. The remaining men and Chelsey had already gone through so much, and now he wanted them to start all over? To undertake even more dangerous challenges? That sounded like literal hell. He must really want his son dead if he was suggesting that.

"No, Garth," the psychic said. "The reviews will tank us. If we try to reset with the current cast and throw a bunch of shit at the wall to see what sticks, we'll get blowback. If it sounds lazy to me, just imagine what the fans will think."

"Well, what the hell do you suggest?" Garth spat.

"I *suggest* we use an angle that will pull the viewers in. My best idea? We test these two," the psychic said as he pointed at us. "We have Von really buckle down on them. Show the audience whether they truly are committed to each other. We could show them as star-crossed lovers. People eat that shit up. The lone wolf there had been pining away for her for years, then she gets rejected but still won't be with him, so he weasels his way onto the show. Boom. Ratings bonanza."

The dark-skinned man looked incredulous at the suggestion. "Well, she'll obviously pick Wyatt at the end. Where's the drama?"

"Easy," the psychic said. "We keep Chelsey on. The remaining guys will pursue her. That's the 'traditional' portion of the show," he said, making air quotes. "Then we have these two fighting for their lives and their future together. It'll be like having two shows in one."

Everyone around the table took his words into consideration. Several of them looked like they thought the idea had merit. There was no way I could let this continue. They were literally playing games with our lives, so we should have some say in how things went. I couldn't just stand here while they dictated what would happen to us. I opened my mouth to speak.

"*Hush, child*," a voice whispered. It took me a second to realize it came from inside my head.

"*Who is this?*" I asked in my head.

The woman in white at the table tilted her head, the corner of her lips lifting into a knowing smile. "*You know.*"

How the hell had she barged into my head like that? I'd put up all the mental walls I could to keep the creepy psychic out of my mind, but this woman had slid in like the doors were wide open.

"*We both know the real reason you came on this show,*" the woman said. "*And it was not to get a mate, but a wish. A favor?*"

An icy-cold finger pressed deep into my belly. Who was this woman? A tickle at the back of my mind gave me a warning. I had to step carefully. As powerful as the men were at the table, this woman might be the true power behind the scenes.

"*Tell me, Kira. Are you as sure of yourself and your plan now that Wyatt's life is on the line? Now that his survival is solely in your hands?*"

Chapter 8 - Wyatt

The men kept bickering and haggling back and forth. The whole time, I stood there, rage and panic coursing through my veins. I didn't know a single person at this table other than Mika's father, and I'd only met him in passing when I was a kid. Worry snaked through my mind. Was my uncle okay? Bitter regret and shame roiled in my belly. I'd ruined his life by asking him to get me on the show. He'd done a favor for his only nephew, nothing huge. Yes, that favor had broken rules. It was laughable, really, when the *rules* on *The Reject Project* weren't worth the paper they were written on.

Along with the panic, rage, and shame was fear. These people were talking about Kira and me like we were nothing but pawns on a chessboard. Playthings to be used and then tossed away. Everyone in the world thought the show was so exciting and luxurious when in reality, it resembled a car crash more than a game. A well-produced and marketed car crash, but a car crash all the same. No one who truly knew how this show worked would ever want to be on it. These people had the whole world fooled.

"What I'm saying," Garth said, eyes flashing with anger, "is that if we leave them both on the show, there is still a slim chance that they'll make it to the end." He slammed his fist on the table. "I am not authorizing honorary membership into the First Pack to a fucking lone wolf. Not happening."

One man, who didn't have the scent of a shifter, leaned back in his chair and smiled placatingly at Garth. He had to be the psychic Kira mentioned. He smiled, but the look in his eyes held deadly seriousness. "Garth, you can't go changing the rules because of your prejudices. The rules clearly state that the winners receive cash prizes, a penthouse apartment in Fangmore, *and* honorary membership in the First Pack and all the benefits that come from that membership. If you yank that away, you'll alienate a lot of wolf-shifter viewers. It's one of the main draws of the show."

Garth looked ready to explode, but held his tongue. The men then devolved into another round of arguing about sponsorship rights and other legalese that made no sense to me. It was surreal. These talks should have been happening in a glittering office building, not on a rooftop patio in the middle of a dangerous jungle. The people spouting off at each other seemed to have no clue about the magnitude of what was going on. All they cared about was lining their pockets and getting the most bang for their buck. That, and keeping their precious little show going. It made me wonder how all this had come about in the first place. What had made these men and all those before them want to be connected to this fucking spectacle?

"Black Fang Brewery has been known to invest in troubled IPs before," a bearded shifter said. "If this goes sideways, we can probably offer them some kind of exclusivity deal for a season or two in exchange for a hefty investment."

Garth waved that comment away. "Absolutely not. I know the owner. Emilio is a cocksucker. If he invested that much, he'd want a seat on the board. No way. Over my dead body."

The muscles in my jaw ached. I forced myself to relax and unclench my teeth as their conversation played out. Only one thing mattered: Kira. No matter what the board decided, I had to ensure that she got off this island safe and sound. She'd fight it kicking and screaming if I didn't go, too, but I was willing to take that risk.

Her pack had always been fairly traditional, and there was no way of knowing how they would react to her if she returned home without winning anything, but that would be better than being dead. I could try to send word to my unofficial pack to have them take her in. My friends would do that for me. I opened my mouth to demand Kira be sent home, but my words were cut off by another loud voice.

"For fuck's sake," the psychic said, leaning forward. "Enough! We have to get this figured out now. What do we do with those two?" He pointed at me and Kira. "All this other stuff can be handled back on the mainland. I didn't come all the way out to this godsforsaken place to talk about commercials and legal fees. Which route do we want to take with them?"

There were a few seconds of contemplative silence before the bearded shifter shrugged his shoulders. "I like your idea. We use them as a secondary storyline. Play it up hard before they get eliminated."

"Who said we're getting eliminated?" I said.

"Hush," Von muttered.

Garth cast a withering glare at Kira and me. "Don't worry. We'll be making things very difficult for you. I give it two days tops before you're both dead." He waved a dismissive hand at the psychic. "Fuck it, fine. Do what you want. Don't come crying to me if there's a disaster, though."

The others quickly acquiesced, but I could see none of them thought Kira and I would last long. Most probably even relished that idea. Glancing over, I tried to see what Kira thought of the whole situation. She looked confused, like she wasn't even paying attention to the conversation. Her brow was furrowed, and she stared at the woman in white—the only person who hadn't said a word.

I nudged Kira's arm and whispered, "Hey? What's wrong?"

Kira flinched when I spoke, almost as if some trance had been broken. She shook her head quickly. "Nothing. I'm fine."

She seemed anything but fine. She watched the woman in white warily, almost fearfully. I was curious to know what the hell was going on, but Von would only chastise me again if I spoke up.

The psychic turned his attention to the vampire host. "Okay, Von. They stay on the show. Push them hard and really see how deep this *connection* they have goes. It should make for some rather dramatic television for a while."

"Very well," Von said with a placating nod. "I think we'll put out a poll for the fans to vote on whether team *Kwyatt* can stay or not. It's good for the audience to have a say in how things go." He waved a hand through the air. "Regardless of the final tally, we'll make sure the vote goes to them staying, obviously. I mean, we're really in charge, not the fans." He chuckled.

"Whatever," Garth growled. "Just turn the heat up on the cast members. Not only these two, but the others as well. If you can keep viewership at an all-time high, we can use it in negotiations with the sponsors and investors for next season."

This guy was a piece of work. His own son was on the show, and he was telling Von to make things more difficult. He'd more or less sentenced his son to death with nothing more than a wave of the hand. Of course, this was the same asshole who'd been fucking his own son's fated mate on the sly and then decided to be pissed off when Mika rejected her. My own father hadn't been the best, but he hadn't been such a douchebag.

The upper packs had always been power-hungry and immoral. Seeing how the alpha of the strongest pack acted in a situation like this was enough to make me want to tear down the whole system. Not just the show, but the entire pack hierarchy. The whole thing left a bitter taste in my mouth. Not only had *The Reject Project* shown me exactly how shady it really was, but the men and women running it were even worse.

"I'll have the media team send the poll out right now," Von said, pulling out his phone and rapidly typing. "In the meantime, we'll get some good footage of the other alphas interacting with these two. It'll get some good playback on the mainland and should help influence people to vote. Fan interaction does wonders to grow viewership."

Unable to hold my tongue anymore, I finally blew up. "Why the fuck are we even here? Was there a reason Kira and I had to sit here and listen to you talk about us like we're objects instead of people?"

The bearded man sat forward quickly and leveled a finger at me. "Watch your mouth, son. You're lucky we didn't decide to toss your ass off the roof."

The woman in white let out a soft laugh. It was the first sound I'd heard her make during the meeting. I locked eyes with her, and a shiver ran down my spine as she smiled at me. She said nothing, just laughed softly again, then fell silent as her stare seemed to penetrate deep into my soul.

"Come on now, friends," Von said, herding me and Kira away like we were kindergarteners.

It wasn't until we were back inside and heading down the stairs that I could breathe easily again. The men up there didn't intimidate me, but they'd still basically held my life in their hands. And that strange woman had made the whole thing seem almost dreamlike.

The witch who'd guided us up to the roof was waiting at the bottom of the first flight of stairs.

"Enola, can you please escort Kira to her room? I want to take Wyatt to the alpha den to have some time with him and the other alphas on camera. We want some male-on-male tension before the females are brought back into the mix." Von pushed a button on his phone, and within seconds, two cameras rushed in from around the corner. The light on my wristband suddenly glowed green.

The witch nodded. "Absolutely, Mr. Thornton."

"Kira, I'll fetch you in a bit," Von said. "Come, Wyatt."

"Am I a dog now?" I asked bitterly.

Von laughed and patted me on the shoulder. "No, my boy, though you are in the canine family. Come on, drama awaits."

Kira reached out and grabbed my hand, giving it a squeeze before I followed Von down the hallway. Thankfully, the vampire was too concerned with sending emails and texts to pay me much attention as we walked. A small blessing.

On the ground floor, he finally tucked his phone away. "Good news. All the alphas are in the den. It's going to be fantastic."

"Yeah. Can't wait."

A camera floated directly behind my left shoulder. It was all I could do not to grab it and slam it against the wall.

"Here we are," Von said, twisting the doorknob.

He opened it and gestured for me to step inside. The camera followed, but there was already one in the room. The others had been relaxing, but upon my entrance, the mood changed palpably. Abel glanced at me warily, J.D. and Mika gave me worried looks, but Gavin and Tate looked like they wanted to tear my face off. Gavin just glared at me, but Tate couldn't hold back.

The large alpha jumped off his bed and walked toward me. "Wow, he's still alive. I guess the showrunners didn't want to kill your ass off yet."

Behind me, I heard Von clapping faintly. "Oh, good. Right off the bat."

Tate pressed his chest against mine, pushing me back. "You know, I wish I could say I've calmed down, but that'd be a fucking lie. How about you and I figure out who's the top dog right now, huh?"

I raised an eyebrow. "I suggest you back the fuck up unless you want to spend the next ten minutes picking your teeth up off the ground. I've dealt with enough in the last hour. I don't want you chirping in my ear."

Tate laughed, but there was no humor in it. "Oh-ho, big man. Still thinks he's the best. Liars usually do, don't they? Let's go, then."

Tate clenched his fists and was in the process of raising his hands when Mika leaped between us. He shoved a hand into my chest, pushing me back, and did the same to Tate. "Enough. You two both need to cool off."

"Right," J.D. said. "Can't we just talk or something? I'd like to *actually* hear the truth."

"Oh, shut up," Gavin snapped. "We already know the truth. Wyatt is some damn lovesick puppy. Kira turned his ass down back home, then came here to find a *real* mate, and he followed her here like the little bitch he is. It's pretty simple. And because of him, Kira's in danger. This whole charade has been her trying to make the best of a bad situation."

"Please, bro," Tate said, rolling his eyes. "You've got your nose shoved so far up her ass, you can't see what's going on. She played us. All of us, and *this* prick," Tate pointed at me, stabbing his finger in my direction, "helped her."

"Stop," Mika barked at Gavin. It was the most worked up I'd seen him since getting on the show. "Everyone chill, okay? Gods."

"Is what Gavin says true?" Abel asked. "Did you follow Kira here? Is that what all this is about?"

The cameras whizzed around the room, getting different shots and angles. Von was probably drooling over how this would be one of the juiciest and most dramatic situations ever. All live-streamed, I was sure. No time for editing when you could broadcast the bickering and fighting to the masses immediately. I could almost feel the vampire vibrating with excitement behind me.

Something Von had said up on the patio came back to me before I answered Abel. He'd talked about how the fan vote would influence things. Kira and I staying was already set in stone, rigged by these assholes. But there might be other votes that could help or hurt us depending on how things went. I could still play the game, even if it meant bending the truth to my will. Even if it was only a one-percent chance of helping keep Kira safe, I had to do it.

Plus, it wasn't a true lie. Kira had no any idea I'd be on the show until I stepped out of that limo at the premiere.

I held my hands up in surrender. "All right, fine. You guys want the truth?"

"Uh, yeah," Abel said.

"Okay. I've been in love with Kira for years. She had no clue and basically hated my guts most of the time we knew each other. I had to live knowing she was fated to another. It made me miserable, but then, he rejected her. I thought it would finally be my chance to swoop in and steal her away. Except instead of coming to me like I'd hoped, she tried out for this show."

"I fucking knew it," Gavin muttered bitterly.

"Anyway," I continued, "I couldn't handle the idea of her being here without someone to protect her. No offense, but I didn't trust any of you to keep her safe. I hadn't even met you guys. For all I knew, you'd be idiots or douchebags. I would do anything to keep Kira from danger. I'd die if I had to. Nothing would be too far. *Nothing*. I didn't come here to win her, I came here to make sure she gets back home alive. Even if that means I die."

The others were silent for a moment. I'd been far more open and vulnerable than I'd intended. Had that been a mistake?

"Aw," J.D. said. "Okay, bro, you've done it. Full one-eighty for me. I'm a Kwyatt fan again, a hundred percent. You two belong together. That's really sweet, man. I know you guys have been pissy with each other lately, but you're meant to be with Kira. One hundred percent."

"Wait, wait, wait," Abel said. "Hang on. I get having a falling out, but you two were fucking other people." He turned and looked at J.D. incredulously. "Like, dude, she just had sex with you. Then a few hours later, she's fucking Wyatt. Now you're *rooting* for her to be with him. None of this makes any sense." Abel's voice sounded like he was on the verge of having a nervous breakdown from confusion.

"I'm not buying it," Tate said. "His little *I-love-her-but-she-doesn't-love-me-back* sob story doesn't hold water with me. It sounds like a load of horseshit. You are a lone wolf. We found that out a few minutes ago. That's fucking disgusting, I might add."

Looking over my shoulder, I glared at Von. He smiled back and shrugged in a "who me?" sort of way.

"You and Kira did this to try and get into the First Pack," Tate continued ranting. "She's all the way down in the Eleventh Pack, and you're in an unofficial pack full of mutts. You twisted this whole thing to get the prize and screw the rest of us over. Admit it."

"Kira wouldn't do something like that," Gavin snapped, getting right in Tate's face.

Tate, finally turning his ire from me, grinned maliciously at Gavin. "Gods, bro. You haven't even seen her naked yet and you're already pussy-whipped. Damn." He wrinkled his face in disgust and took a step back from Gavin. "Whatever. You guys can have the lying bitch. From here on out, I'm after Chelsey. I don't know what to believe anymore, but it looks like she's *actually* here for a mate."

Heading for the door, Tate made sure to shoulder-check me as he went, making me stumble back. Hot, vicious anger welled up inside me, and my wolf gnashed his teeth, ready to fight. It took every ounce of self-control not to attack the other alpha. Shaking with rage, I clenched my fists and let him go.

"Cut!" Von shouted in giddy excitement. The hovering cameras swooped out of the room and into the hallway. "That was exactly what I'd hoped for! You guys were perfect."

"Glad we could be of service," Gavin snapped, his angry gaze still locked on my face.

"I need to get Chelsey's reaction," Von said. He pulled his phone out and swiped a few times. "It's looking very interesting, Wyatt. The viewers are really torn. The voting on whether to send you home or keep you is neck and neck."

"Like that matters," I retorted. "You guys already decided we were staying."

Von swatted my comment away like a pesky fly. "No matter. Anyway, I'm going to find Chelsey. Don't forget, gentlemen, the arena match is soon. We can't be late for that."

"Don't wanna be late for our own funeral, right?" Mika asked sarcastically.

Von was too busy scrolling his phone to take in those words. "Yes, Mr. Sheen, very good." The vampire finished whatever he was doing and tucked his phone into his pocket again, returning his attention to us, that game-show host smile reappearing. "I think we really have something here. This is already the highest-rated season ever, and it's only going to get better with the new twists we're adding. Especially now that we have all this *aggressive* alpha energy bouncing around. Ah, it's going to be so much fun. See you all at the arena match." Without another word, he vanished out the door.

So much fun? For Von, that meant backstabbing, blood, and danger. If I had to guess, the rest of the show would be a wet dream for him. Unless Kira and I could change things.

I had to hope we could, now that the crosshairs were firmly on our heads.

Chapter 9 - Kira

"Follow me," the witch said as Von and Wyatt went downstairs to the alpha den.

"I know where my room is," I said.

She sniffed. "Well, that may be, but you've shown a propensity for going places you shouldn't. As well as doing things and *people* you shouldn't."

"Excuse me?" I rounded on her, my nostrils flaring. How dare she?

She gave me a bored, tired look. "Sweetie, don't take it personally. I've worked on this show for fifteen years. You aren't the first female lead who liked to *get around,* if you know what I mean."

"That's not... I didn't... ugh, you don't know what the hell you're talking about," I sputtered, caught off-balance.

"I know. It's very difficult. All these virile and sexy shifters, the sexual tension. It's tough." She glanced around to make sure we were alone, then leaned in conspiratorially. "I'll tell you a secret. In my first season here—newly divorced, mind you—I had a bit of heartache to contend with. I was forty-three years old and wide-eyed from the spectacle of it all. Things moved quickly, and the mansion buzzed with sexual energy. Well, I may or may not have given the male lead a little," she nudged me with her elbow, "you know, oral satisfaction. It happened one afternoon after I'd healed him from an arena match. It was all very sudden and exciting, but it made a middle-aged woman feel like a kid again. It was delightful, honestly. Especially when he reciprocated—"

"Ew! Please, can we stop talking?"

She shrugged, and we continued down the hall to my room. The mental image of this almost sixty-year-old woman sucking off some shifter nearly two decades ago wouldn't stop playing in my brain. Would everyone back home look at me the way Tate had? Like some opportunistic hussy who wanted to screw and then *screw over* the alpha contestants? Would Wyatt and I be hated and despised when we went home? Dear gods, what would Kolton think? My parents? They must have seen the footage of Wyatt and me practically naked. Even if I managed to get out of this fucking show alive, how would my family react?

"Home sweet home," the witch said, gesturing to the now-repaired door.

"Thanks." I hurried inside, closing the door in her face.

I frantically searched the room for the TV remote. I was on the verge of a breakdown when I finally found it twisted in the bedsheets that were still rumpled from my and Wyatt's lovemaking this morning. Snatching it up, I turned the TV on to see what might be happening. Sure enough, Von had set the cameras to a special live feed for the whole world to see.

On the screen, Tate was chest to chest with Wyatt, chewing him out. The scene played on, and I worried that the fans might look at Wyatt the way Tate and Gavin were—like he was a problem that needed to be dealt with. It didn't matter that we weren't going anywhere. The fans could still make our lives difficult.

As things grew more heated, Wyatt finally made a heartfelt admission.

"Okay. I've been in love with Kira for years. She had no clue and basically hated my guts most of the time we knew each other. I had to live knowing she was fated to another. It made me miserable, but then, he rejected her. I thought it would finally be my chance to swoop in and steal her away. Except, instead of coming to me like I'd hoped, she tried out for this show."

I gaped at the screen. *I've been in love with Kira for years.* Something about that sentence sent a warm, pleasant shiver up my back. Had he really admitted that to the entire world? To Kolton and the rest of my family, his unofficial pack mates, and every other sentient creature on the planet? The statement could never be taken back. Once something like that was out there, you couldn't reel it back in.

The rest of the scene in the alpha den played out as expected. It looked like Mika and J.D. were firmly in our camp. Gavin and Tate looked like they would rather stab Wyatt in the back than look at him, and poor Abel seemed confused and turned around. The poor guy looked like he was having a hard time making heads or tails of the situation.

After Tate stormed out, the feed cut to a commercial for a luxury resort off the Sapphire Coast. While the ad break dragged on, I busied myself by making my bed. It was pointless and silly, but I had to do something other than watch a commercial for hemorrhoid treatment potions.

When the show resumed, Von was sitting opposite Chelsey. The other woman looked a little shell-shocked, but I had the sneaking suspicion it was because Von had stormed into her room for an interview, not from seeing Wyatt and me together earlier. Thankfully, Wyatt had been honest with her in the mating chamber the previous night. I'd have hated for her to see the footage while she was still pining for Wyatt.

"Well, Miss Rein," Von said. "A very interesting day today, don't you think?"

Chelsey's smile was awkward. "I suppose it has been, uh, eventful."

Von chuckled in that way that always made my skin crawl. "Indeed! Well, after seeing everything that transpired this morning, I have to ask: do you feel cheated in some way? Especially after the romantic evening you spent with Wyatt last night?"

Chelsey surprised and delighted me by shaking her head firmly. "Absolutely not."

"No?" Von looked shocked.

"No. I mean, isn't this how the show is supposed to go? You, I don't know, *play the field*, so to speak? Find who fits with you and would make a good mate? And try to survive. I think Wyatt and Kira were only doing what they needed to survive. Honestly, I find it all pretty romantic."

"That's true, but the fact that they knew each other prior must give you some pause, no? That throws a wrench into the entire game, does it not?"

Chelsey grinned. "Well, there's never been a second lead mate before either. I could say that me being here throws as much of a wrench into things as anything else."

"Oh, I love you, girl," I muttered to myself. It was nice to see she was also on our side. At least, she was acting like she was.

Von, looking uncharacteristically put off by her answers, went on. "How do you think this will all play out, then?"

Chelsey chewed on her lip for a moment. "I think—*hope*—Kira and Wyatt will keep watching each other's backs. That's one of the main things a mate is supposed to do—they protect. Everyone deserves someone like that. People deserve to have a person who loves them and watches over them. I hope I eventually find the same, even if it isn't Wyatt. I'm never going to fault two people for finding love." She narrowed her eyes at Von. "I mean, really, what kind of person would?"

"Very illuminating and romantic insight from Chelsey Rein, everyone. We'll be back soon with our arena match. Before our commercial break, though, we have to remind everyone there are only a few minutes left to vote on whether Wyatt and Kira get to stay on Bloodstone Island. Hurry and vote. Don't be left out of the decision." A moment later, the screen clicked to a commercial.

"The *decision*," I mocked.

This whole place was so fake, it might as well have been made from plastic. Sure, they let fans vote for things, but the big stuff? That was all decided by those bigwigs I'd met earlier. Now, I had to sit around until we were taken to whatever new hellish game Von and the others had cooked up.

I couldn't sit still and worry about it. Jittery, I got to my feet and paced the room. Part of me wished that I'd never decided to come on this dumb show to begin with. If I hadn't, then Wyatt wouldn't have followed me and put himself in danger. The idea washed out of my mind almost as soon as it entered. How could I wish that, after everything that had happened because of it? Yes, Wyatt would have been safe, but if I hadn't come here, I never would have seen Wyatt as more than my brother's best friend. He was no longer my bossy and annoying coworker. He was... what was he to me, exactly?

Chewing at my thumbnail, I continued zig-zagging across the room, deep in thought. It wasn't something I typically did, especially when Wyatt was involved. I'd built up all these walls over the years that it was hard to see over them or bust through. But soon it became pretty clear that I didn't want to even *think* about a time when I might not have Wyatt. When I tried to imagine my life without him, terror and sadness welled up inside me. I didn't want to lose him. I... I loved him.

The words echoed through my head and forced me to freeze in place as the implications of that one thought exploded in my mind. I loved Wyatt Rivers. The more I said it, the more the walls receded. My love for him wasn't new. I'd loved him for a long time, but I'd been too stubborn to realize it, too angry and afraid of what I'd done during my first shift. That had left me terrified of allowing myself to feel any emotion for the boy who saved me—the one person who had pulled me out of that cave, calmed me, and kept my secret all these years.

In all my shame, I'd been blind to the fact that the one person who *did* know what I'd done had never looked at me like the monster I thought I was. Wyatt had never condemned my actions or looked down on me. All he'd ever done was try to stay near me and keep me safe. All I'd done for years was be an ass to the one person who I should have been able to confide in. Through it all, my feelings for him had grown, but they'd been shoved down deep inside, along with my inner wolf.

The revelation shattered me to my very core. Desperate to get my mind off it for a few minutes, I went to the closet and dressed for the arena match. As I dressed, I kept thinking of Wyatt and the way he'd cradled my bloody form when he carried me out of those woods. All the times he'd risked his life to protect me on the job. How it always felt like he was staring all the way into my soul when he looked into my eyes. And finally, the way his body made mine feel when we were together. The pleasure and connection was indescribable.

When the knock came at the door, I was so deep in my thoughts and emotions, I yelped in surprise. Hurrying to the door, I yanked it open to find the bloodsucker standing outside my door.

Von leaned over the threshold, glancing around. "Any naked post-coital alphas in here?"

"Very fucking funny. What do you want?"

"Well, it's about to be shown, but I thought you would want to hear it first. The fans have voted for you and Wyatt to stay. It was very close indeed, but even had we not already made *special considerations*, you two would have stayed on the island."

"Really?" As much as I didn't want to talk to the vampire, this information wasn't to be taken lightly. I'd truly believed that the fans would want us to be eliminated.

"Yes, really," Von said. "It was almost a fifty-fifty split, but you all came out on top. I've already been in contact with the board. This has made them feel more certain they made the right call on keeping you two. Aren't you excited?" He looked like he was preparing for me to jump up and hug him.

"I'm delighted," I said, my voice lifeless and monotone.

"Oh, stop," he said, swatting my arm playfully. "Look at the fans, they're going crazy."

He turned his phone to me, showing the current feed from the show channel. Clips of groups of fans all around the world flashed by. They'd gathered in city centers to watch the show on the massive electronic billboards. People were crowded together like sardines, holding up placards and homemade signs. It looked like half of them were ecstatic that Wyatt and I had *won* the vote, while others were booing and hissing. It was still surreal to think that millions and millions of people were watching what was happening to us. Not only watching, but actively rooting for and against us and our survival. Were these people really that bloodthirsty that they didn't give a damn whether we lived or died?

Not for the first time, I wondered if this show might be part of why the shifter packs were as messed up as they were. Or, maybe it was vice versa. Had the pack dynamics influenced the show itself? Could people like Gavin and Wyatt be right? Maybe the packs didn't need to be totally destroyed or shunned, but there was some kind of cancer in the traditional system that I was only now starting to witness.

It hurt my brain. My entire life, I'd been blindly devoted to my pack and the system that governed it, but now it all seemed trivial and silly. All the strict traditions and rules seemed pointless after being on this island.

"That's great, I guess," I finally said.

Von tucked his phone away. "Quite a close vote. We even allowed a write-in option for fans to vote on—an alpha brawl between you and Wyatt to see who survived and could stay."

"Are you fucking serious?"

Ignoring my shock and disgust, the vampire went on. "I stopped by to tell you we're meeting downstairs in five minutes for the arena match. I think the others have already begun trickling that way. See you soon. Hmm…" He leaned forward, grabbed my chin, and forcibly tilted my face back and forth. "Maybe a bit more makeup. I know you don't currently have a stylist, but that's no reason to look slovenly. Goodbye, dear." He let go of my face and strolled away, humming the song's theme show.

"Prick," I growled under my breath.

I waited a few minutes before leaving so I wouldn't catch up with Von and have to walk in with him. Once enough time had lapsed, I left and went to the main living room. I was the last to arrive.

The atmosphere in the room could only be called tense. Everyone sat in hushed silence. Gavin sat on one side of the room, his eyes shooting daggers at Wyatt where he was seated with J.D. and Mika. They didn't look angry like Tate and Gavin, but they still wore pensive and worried expressions. We all knew danger was coming and that some of us might not survive.

Tate sat on a loveseat with Chelsey, murmuring something to her. The poor woman looked like she'd rather be anywhere but there. Gavin tore his eyes from Wyatt and spotted me. His face softened and he leaped up to meet me.

"Kira, hey. I'm really glad you guys are staying on the show. You have no idea how worried I was that *someone*," he sneered at Wyatt over his shoulder, "had put your place here in jeopardy. You don't deserve any of the criticism." He put a hand to his chest. "I understand that none of this is your fault. I really do."

"Yes, yes, we're all very happy our cast gets to stay together," Von said as he stepped into the living room, flanked by a camera. "Thank you, Gavin. I'm sure the many fans who voted to keep Wyatt and Kira feel the same."

"I didn't say I was glad Wyatt was still here."

"Of course." Von's lips curled into a smile. "And there are many out there who feel that way too. In fact, nearly half the voters wanted both of them off the show. By keeping them here, we have appeased half the fan base, but in order to appease the other half, we need to turn up the heat."

"Oh, good," Mika said, his voice dripping with sarcasm. "We wouldn't want things to be too calm."

Von pointed at him. "Exactly, Mr. Sheen. More excitement, more danger, more drama. That is what we will bring to you and our fans today."

"Thanks a lot," Tate grumbled.

"I kind of expected it, honestly," Chelsey said. "It's always been this way on the show. Once the cast gets smaller, the challenges get tougher."

"That is true, Miss Rein. And as such, today's arena match will not take place in the arena. Instead, we will be making our way to the beach."

J.D. paled. "The beach?"

"Yes." Von's eyes glittered with excitement. "Today's arena match will be a team event rather than a one-on-one match. You will be participating in a boat race across the dangerous Bloodstone Bay."

Tate swallowed and his usual bravado disappeared. "In the water?"

Von nodded slowly and spoke as though he was addressing a slow-witted child. "That does tend to be where one would use a boat, yes."

The mood in the room dropped even further. The water around Bloodstone Island was legendary for how dangerous it was. The mermaid clans here were the most bloodthirsty and violent on the planet, and several other creatures had made their home in the bays and along the beaches. Unlike tourist beaches elsewhere, there were no spell boundaries to keep the things away. It was even more dangerous than the jungle. At least out on the island, you could run, jump, climb, and fight. In the water? There wasn't much you could do but die.

"It appears that you are all as excited as I am about this little task," Von said. "The first team to get to the other side of the bay will receive a bit of additional help during the next big challenge. The losing team will end up with a penalty for that challenge." He slid his eyes to Wyatt, and I thought I could see even more malice in the vampire's gaze than usual. "Speaking of penalties, Wyatt came in last during the obstacle course, and his penalty for that poor performance will come into play during this arena match. Unfortunately, with this being a team event, his penance will affect his entire team."

Wyatt slumped back on the couch and crossed his arms, glancing at me. He didn't look surprised. We'd both known he'd pay for coming in last.

"We do have an odd number of contestants, so the teams will be a little lopsided. Names were selected at random earlier. Abel, Chelsey, Tate, and J.D. will be going up against Wyatt, Mika, and Kira."

I rolled my eyes. I couldn't help myself. Random, my ass. We'd been grouped together on purpose. The only surprise was that Mika had been lumped in with me and Wyatt. Had his father pushed for that? After meeting the man and knowing the background between the two, I had a sneaking suspicion that he had. Wyatt and I would be in the most danger, and putting Mika on our team had to be a way of getting him eliminated as quickly as possible. Once we were all gone, Chelsey would be the main star. The two people who had *rigged* the game would be out, and the son of one of the showrunners would be out of the way as well.

Right when I thought the show couldn't be more fucked up, it showed me that it still had ways to be horrible.

Rather than spiraling into hopeless depression, determination surged through my being. I'd be damned if I let these assholes push us around like this. They thought it was a done deal that the three of us would be killed? Well, it was time to change the paradigm. I would do everything possible to make sure we won this challenge.

"For this match, you'll be equipped with specially enchanted fae weaponry. These weapons will help you fend off the merpeople, sea serpents, and various other beasties. Each member of Chelsey's team will receive a weapon. Due to Wyatt being penalized, only one weapon will be provided for Kira's team."

"Can't we do this with me being the one without a weapon?" Wyatt said. "Why is my whole team being punished?"

His face was twisted with fury. If I knew anything about Wyatt, it was the fact that he protected people, especially those he cared about. The thought of the others being penalized for something he did was probably eating away at his insides.

"Sorry, Wyatt. Rules are rules. Now, as I was saying, the weapons will be elementally based—wind, water, electricity, fire, and ice." Von snapped his fingers, and six witches marched into the room, each holding a different item. "Chelsey, your team will receive the wind, water, electricity, and fire weapons. That leaves your team, Kira, with the ice weapon."

The witches doled out the weapons. Each looked like gnarled tree branches about eighteen inches long, but the tips had been enchanted to look like what each weapon was made to do. The fire weapon had a glowing ember embedded in the tip, and small flames flicked from it. A bright blue gem with a tiny vortex spinning around it adorned the tip of the wind weapon. Strange weapons indeed, and very old-fashioned. The fae weaponry we used in the

Tranquility ops was more advanced. These things looked like weapons the fae had used centuries ago.

"Now that you have your supplies, if you all will follow me, we can make our way to the bay. If you all could, please try to look dashing and intense. I want a dramatic shot when we walk out the front doors of the mansion."

Von led us out to the massive marble-floored foyer and through the front doors, the cameras following. A slight breeze tickled my face as we exited, and my hair fluttered behind me. Off to the side of the stairs, a witch held her hands up. It was all I could do not to roll my eyes. Even the wind was manufactured. When this segment aired, Von would probably replay this shot in slow motion, set to dramatic music.

The ice weapon was heavy in my hand. The heavy gray ice chip that sat at the top spat and sputtered flecks of snow and ice as it swung at my side. What good would it do once we got into the heat of battle? Was it strong enough to freeze an entire merperson? Could it fully freeze the bay's surface so we could run across it and be done? I'd have to wait and see.

Once we'd crossed the patio and descended a set of steps that led down the hill away from the helipad, the bay came into sight. A huge crescent of land surrounded dark blue water. Three greenish lumps appeared on the surface, then vanished beneath. A sea serpent. Great. The creatures had already come out to play.

Two long rowboats were moored at the water's edge closest to the mansion. Staff members stood on each boat, holding oars. The beach wasn't sandy but covered in small, smooth pebbles that shifted as we walked.

"Here we are," Von said as we reached the boats. "The lovely Bloodstone Bay. Its depths hold much beauty, and even more danger. In these gorgeous azure waters, the Bloodstone Merpeople take refuge. Multiple other creatures reside here with our finned friends. Sea serpents, large carnivorous water scorpions, and possibly a few feral crocodile or alligator shifters."

"Oh, for fuck's sake," Tate grumbled.

"Your weapons will be very useful. Keep them ready as you row," Von said. "And, while I know wolves can be good swimmers, I would caution anyone from attempting to simply shift and swim. Fast as you might be, our friends in the water are much faster. The merpeople will probably have you dismembered before you even have time to drown. Our staff of witches will transport whatever remains of both teams back to the mansion once the challenge is over.

"The winning team may do well not to finish *too* far ahead of their rivals. You will need to fend off any enemies that may attack while you wait for the other team to finish or perish. Have a *wonderful* time, everyone," Von finished with a huge grin and wide-open arms.

The witches handed us our oars and we boarded our separate boats. Wyatt pulled Mika and me together once we were seated. "Kira, I think you should keep the weapon. Mika and I are the strongest. We'll paddle for our lives, push as hard as we can for the opposite shore, and Kira will watch our back with the weapon. Does that sound like a plan?"

"Sounds good to me," Mika said.

I gripped the ice weapon harder, the wood sliding across my palms. "That's fine, but I'll help row until we see danger."

"Everyone ready?" Von asked.

We all nodded or gave a thumbs-up of agreement, everyone silent as we prepared ourselves.

"Very well. Ten seconds."

J.D. waved at me from his boat. "Good luck, guys." He looked more worried than usual.

I smiled back at him and raised a hand to return his wave. "You too."

Von held his fingers up as he counted down. "Three... two... one. Go!"

Mika, Wyatt, and I dug our oars into the water, slashing at the ocean with the wooden tools. With more rowers, the other team leaped into the lead quickly, moving half a boat's length ahead. As I rowed, I gritted my teeth. We were about twenty feet from shore when the light blue water suddenly became a deep, dark sapphire as the shore dropped away to deep water.

Seconds later, a merperson appeared below us. The creature was pasty and pale white with long, spindly arms that ended in heavily webbed fingers and claws. Thick, gross-looking gills ran along their neck. Hypnotized by the sight, I stopped rowing and stared down into the depths as the merperson swam beside us. Its face was semi-human but lipless, and it had eyes like a fish. Its malevolent glare met my eyes and it gnashed its teeth.

"We have company," I finally said.

Wyatt glanced over his shoulder. "Mermaids?"

"Yup. And this one is pissed," I said, putting my oar aside and picking up the weapon.

"What the hell is that?!" Abel screamed from the other boat.

I spared a glance to see he was pointing up at the sky. Three shadowy creatures were descending from one of the mountain peaks. It took a few moments before I could identify them.

"Thunderbirds!" I screamed.

Mika and Wyatt didn't bother looking. They lowered their heads and rowed even faster. I'd never dealt with a thunderbird before. They typically lived in the deserts near the Western Wastes. The beasts grew massive and lived off bats, smaller birds, and other flying creatures. Juveniles like these *only* had a wingspan of twelve feet, but they were strong enough to carry any of us off to their nest. From there, things would not go well. I didn't intend to end up as bird shit two days from now.

The other team stopped rowing to aim their weapons at the skies. Blasts of elemental magic arced through the sky. Abel hit one bird with the wind weapon and sent the thing tumbling into the ocean. A second later, the water exploded in a huge geyser as a gigantic sea serpent broke the surface and swallowed the thunderbird.

"What the hell was that sound?" Wyatt called back, having not seen the display.

As an answer, I screamed, "Row faster!"

I didn't think the serpent was big enough to swallow our boat, but I didn't want to hang around and find out. The other birds retreated back to their mountaintop. Since the other team had stopped rowing to fight off the intruders, we were in the lead, nearly one-and-a-half boat lengths ahead.

Our advantage didn't last long. A thumping sound came from beneath our feet, the impact vibrating through the whole boat. Before I had time to realize what was happening, a fist-size hole shattered through the wood. A merperson's coral spear pushed through, jerked side to side, and then snapped off, leaving the tip in the rapidly spreading water at the bottom of the boat.

"Shit." The boat would sink in seconds if I didn't do something.

I aimed the fae weapon at the hole. The stick shivered in my hand as energy surged through it. A frigid beam of light erupted from the tip and froze the water in the breach, blocking more from flooding the boat.

Before I could check to see if the quick repair would hold, a shout from the front of the boat drew my attention. Mika was struggling. He'd dropped his oar and was trying to pry himself out of the embrace of the merman who had leaped from the water.

"Help," Mika grunted, pulling at the webbed hands. The creature had dug his claws in, and blood was blossoming where the talons had broken Mika's skin.

Wyatt dropped his oar and spun in his seat to help Mika. Because of that, he didn't see what was coming from the side. A mermaid lunged over the side, gripping a coral knife in her hand. I had no time to scream or warn him. She drove her weapon down, stabbing Wyatt in the thigh. He bellowed a scream and fell to the bottom of the boat, clutching at the wound. The female wrenched the knife out and raised it over her head to slam into Wyatt's chest. I blasted her with the weapon, freezing her head into a block of ice. She fell sideways, slamming her temple against the side of the boat. The mermaid's head exploded in a shower of blood and ice before her body slumped into the water.

On the other side of the boat, the merman attacking Mika had twisted the alpha's body around and pulled his head underwater. Mika's fingers gripped the edge of the boat, knuckles white with strain as he tried to pull his head from the water, but he wasn't able to counteract the creature's strength.

The fear of another contestant dying slammed into me. I could almost see Mika's lifeless body lying on the mansion floor after the challenge. Eyes dead and gaping, staring at me in accusation.

No. I was not going to let that happen. Dropping the weapon, I stood and grabbed Mika's shoulders, heaving back on his body, playing tug-of-war with the creature under the water. Mika thrashed and flailed; I could almost feel the panic and terror vibrating through his body. Behind me, Wyatt jerked around and cussed something. From the corner of my eye, I watched him pick up the ice weapon and freeze a massive, feral alligator shifter moments before its jaws clamped onto his throat. Another one was trying to climb aboard. Wyatt punched and kicked at it while I tried to save Mika.

I was losing the tug-of-war. Mika's body began to go limp, exhausted from the fight and lack of air. Then, like a light switch clicking on, I realized we weren't using all our weapons.

"Mika!" I screamed, hoping he could hear my words through the water. "Shift. Mika, shift!"

He must have heard me because his body shifted into his wolf form. Instead of shoulders and shirt, I held his fur and his front legs. Under the water, I saw his jaws snap and clamp on the face of the merman. A second later, the blue water became a red mist as Mika ripped its face completely off.

What remained of the merman sank down into the water. Mika fell backward, shifting back as he did. He hit the bottom, gasping and coughing. "Holy shit. Thanks."

Wyatt managed to fight the other alligator shifter out of the boat and grabbed his oar, wincing when he put weight on his injured leg. Mika and I grabbed our own oars and paddled. From some distance away, I could hear the other team screaming and fighting. Too worried about my safety, I didn't spare a glance in their direction. The sounds of magic, fighting, and shouting followed us as we slowly but surely left them behind.

We were less than a hundred feet from the shore when a serpentine head rose from the water directly in front of us. Yellow eyes glared at us. It was not as large as the sea serpent that had killed the thunderbird, but more than big enough to bite one of us in half or drag us into the depths of the water.

It watched us for several seconds, as though judging whether we were worth attacking. Another movement caught my eye—a shark fin. It surprised me to see something as boring as a shark swim by after fighting so many magical creatures. Though, if we fell in, the shark would eat us all the same.

The serpent, seeing an easier meal, dived straight down. Mouth gaping, razor-teeth exposed, it seized the shark and began to feast. Blood bloomed in the water around it.

"Hurry," Wyatt said. "While it's eating."

The three of us paddled around the monster and eventually made it to the opposite side. The sound of the boat coming to shore had an almost dreamlike quality to it. Had we really made it?

Mika and I helped Wyatt out of the boat and walked twenty feet up the beach to cross the finish line. Dazedly, I realized we'd won. A glance behind showed that the other team, battered and soaking wet, was only now paddling toward the beach. They looked even more exhausted than I felt and were still almost a hundred yards away.

"I gotta say," Mika said, collapsing on the ground next to Wyatt, "that was much worse than I thought it would be, and that's saying a lot."

My eyes were still on the other team, my anxiety for them growing by the second. Still, I managed to look at the other two men. "You know, we make a pretty good team," I said.

Chapter 10 - Wyatt

My leg throbbed where the merbitch had stabbed me. It wasn't healing right. I poked it gingerly, hissing as pain seared straight up my leg.

Kira turned away from watching the other team struggle. "What's wrong?"

"I think a piece of that coral knife broke off inside my leg."

Before I could talk myself out of it, I shoved my fingers deep into the wound. "Argh." My eyes watered.

"Damn," Mika said. "You want help?"

"No," I grunted through gritted teeth.

My index finger and thumb pushed deep, pinching, trying to find the damned little thing inside. Finally, blessedly, I felt the rough nub of the foreign object. I tugged, and it slid out half an inch. A string of curses left my mouth as my fingers lost their grip on it. After catching hold of it again, I ripped the thing out of my leg. The one-inch tip of the spear sat, bloody, in my palm. The dark beige of the dead corral must have broken off when it hit the thigh bone. I tossed it toward the ocean in disgust. Now that the offending object was out, my healing abilities kicked in.

Kira knelt to check the cut, but I was more concerned about her. She had to swat my hands away after I tried pushing her sleeves up, looking for wounds.

"Stop it! I'm fine, Wyatt."

"I need to make sure you aren't hurt."

"I said I'm fine. Only you and Mika were hurt." The usual irritation wasn't in her voice. For years, she'd always bristled when I tried to check on her. I'd gotten so used to it, I did a double take.

"Are you really okay? You didn't call me a bossy asshole or tell me to mind my own fucking business."

She checked the wound in my leg, tenderly probing the outer edges, her skin cool and refreshing on my inflamed skin. Kira glanced up at me from under her lashes before returning her gaze to my leg. "I've... well, I've decided to be a better person."

The words came out haltingly, almost as if she really wanted to say something else, but I knew her well enough to leave it be. No reason to look a gift horse in the mouth.

Leaving her to tend my wound, I checked on Mika. He wasn't concerned with our little exchange and had his neck craned around to scan the jungle. The look in his eyes wasn't one of fear or terror but consideration. He'd made his plans known to me before. He intended to sneak off the show and try to fend for himself in the jungles of Bloodstone. This was not a good opportunity, but he didn't appear to understand that.

I leaned over, putting my hand on the back of his neck to pull his head toward mine. Mika's brow furrowed, confused by the brotherly gesture as I brought our foreheads together.

"Wyatt, what—"

"Now is not the time," I whispered, keeping my voice as low as possible.

"Huh?"

"I saw you looking in the jungle. *Now is not the time.*" I glanced sideways, and he followed my eyes to the camera floating ten feet away. "They're watching. You can't run off."

Understanding my meaning, Mika patted a hand on my shoulder. His arm blocked our mouths from the view of the camera. Anyone watching the feed would think we were having a moment of camaraderie after surviving the terrors of the bay.

"I can't stay here much longer," he said.

"Kira and I are working on a plan. We're going to fake the eliminations and get the contestants off the show. If you hang in there a little longer, we'll get you someplace safe so you won't have to go it alone out there."

Mika blinked rapidly, almost like his brain had short-circuited and he was doing his best to reboot it. "Wait, what? How is that possible?"

"No time to explain now. We've got a lot of shit going on. Stay strong, and we'll talk later."

"You bet your ass we will," Mika said with what I took to be a relieved grin.

I slapped his shoulder and pulled away, laughing and putting on a show. "You're right about that," I said, raising my voice so the camera could hear. "I thought that sea serpent had us."

Taking his cue from me, Mika laughed along. "Yeah, I was pretty sure we were done."

The wound in my leg already felt better. With a little help from Kira, I stood and watched the other team struggle to finish the challenge. Their boat came ashore with the sound of scraping stones. They were soaking wet.

Chelsey shakily got out of the boat, her fae weapon snapped in two. Abel appeared to be the only one who'd been injured. He cradled his arm to his chest, avoiding the row of punctures from what I could only assume was a merperson bite.

Tate tossed his oar back into the bay in anger. "Fuck you!" he screamed at the water.

The other team hobbled up to cross the finish line. Chelsey's eyes were wide with surprise when she spotted us. "How the hell did we all get out of that alive?"

She had every right to be confused. That had been an especially lethal arena match. Knowing what I knew now, I would have thought at *least* one of us would have died. Apparently, Lady Luck had decided to take us under her wing today.

Almost as if my thoughts had jinxed us, a bright flash blocked out all sight and sound. For a single second, there was nothing, and then that familiar, awful tugging sensation came over me. A moment later, we were all back at the mansion courtyard.

Von walked down the steps from the mansion, slow-clapping as we regained our bearings. "What an exciting match. I think I can speak for our fans when I say I never believed you would all make it through unscathed. Very impressive. It seems that everyone is having a lot of fun and no one wants to be eliminated."

Sure, that was it. We were having fun—that's why we didn't want to die. Did this guy actually believe the words coming out of his mouth? It had to all be for show, or else he'd truly lost his mind over the last few centuries.

Von strolled over toward us, cameras fluttered all over the place, recording every possible angle. "Now that you've all returned, I can give you the good news. It's exciting."

"Oh no," Abel groaned from behind me.

I had the exact same thought. "Exciting" meant bloody and dangerous in Von-speak.

"That was only the warm-up," Von said. "A simple and basic challenge to get you ready for an even bigger and more thrilling task."

Tate pushed through the front of our group, looking like someone had just pissed in his cereal. "No way, man. We're exhausted. We need a break after that. We almost died out there."

Von, oblivious to Tate's anger, laughed and shook his head. "Oh, Tate, you give yourself very little credit. We all saw how well you did out there. To me, and probably everyone at home, it looked like a leisurely morning row on the water. A little cardio to get the body ready for the rest of the day.

"As much as everyone enjoyed watching that last little display of strength and wits, our fans crave danger and zeal, and danger and zeal we will give them. As for a rest, I think that can be arranged since we still have some preparations to make." He clapped his hands together. "You all will need to get changed and healed. Thirty minutes should be enough time."

Tate's shoulders sagged as he realized his argument wasn't getting us anywhere.

"Change for what?" J.D. asked.

"Pick out something rather formal. Think of a cocktail party or something similar." He held up a warning finger. "There will be a fun little twist, though. I can't wait to get started. Thirty minutes, everyone."

Something about the way Von said "a fun little twist" turned my insides to ice. He had something planned, and it couldn't be good.

I sat beside Kira, not wanting to leave her. If something awful was coming, I wanted to ensure I could protect her. My plan ended up being thwarted when a pair of witches came forward and led Chelsey and Kira away from the men to take them to their rooms.

"Gentlemen," Von said, "I'll see you soon."

Mika took the lead and headed toward the mansion. The rest of us followed. None of us looked excited about what was to come. Back in the alpha den, I found a tuxedo in a zipped-up garment bag. The outfit hung beside my bed, and glossy leather dress shoes sat beneath it.

"Are we going to a freaking wedding?" Tate asked as he unzipped his bag.

"More like a funeral," Abel muttered morosely.

J.D. sat on the edge of his bed to take off his soaked boots. "I'm glad I'm not dead in a casket right now. I never said anything, but I've always been freaking terrified of mermaids. I'll only go surfing on a beach where there are spells keeping them away. Even the friendly ones freak me out, but those things out there?" He nodded to the window. "I'm going to have nightmares for years."

"Does anyone else think that whole thing was just to tire us out for whatever Von has planned next?" Tate asked as he buttoned his tux. He tugged his lapel in frustration. "And why the fuck do we have to wear this shit? What the hell do we need to be dressed up for? It's freaking me out."

For once, I agreed with Tate. I doubted Von had planned a nice, leisurely date for us. Before I could voice my agreement, though, a knock at the door interrupted us. A witch and one of the fallen angels stood in the entryway.

"Everyone ready?" the witch asked.

"Apparently so," Mika said as he finished tying his dress shoes.

"Good," she said with a smile. "For the purposes of this next challenge, you will be brought down one by one." She extended a hand. "Gavin, you'll be coming first."

The other alpha took one of his rare breaks from glaring at me to frown at the woman. "Me? Why?"

"Purely random. No worries. Come on, dear."

Gavin's brow furrowed. He looked like he wanted nothing more than to refuse, but he shuffled off after her down the hall. The bodyguard stayed put.

"Think we're gonna run for it?" J.D. asked.

The fallen angel looked bored. "You can try."

I wasn't completely sure I could take the guy. The dude was like a walking wall of muscle. The others had zero chance unless they caught him by surprise, which wasn't likely. We couldn't really run, anyway. He'd been assigned here to prevent us from trying to catch a peek of where we were being taken.

Something didn't feel right, and I didn't like it.

Over the next ten minutes, the rest of us were escorted separately. Abel and I were the last two, and they called him before me, leaving me alone. Why was I last? Was this *truly* random? From my experience, not a damn thing on this show was random.

When Von Thornton himself came to retrieve me, it did nothing to assuage my fears. "Wyatt Rivers," the vampire said in that grating, used-car salesman voice. "Are you ready?" A camera hovered over Von's right shoulder.

"Better late than never. Gonna give me a hint?"

"Nice try, but no. You'll all receive your special information once you're together again."

"So, we will be together? Why'd you separate us in the first place?"

"You'll see," he said as we started walking.

The guard's footsteps thudded along behind us, reverberating through the halls. I followed Von to a set of stairs that led to a deeper level of the mansion. A basement, maybe? Whatever it was, I was sure I hadn't been there yet.

Our walk ended at a set of ornate wooden and glass double doors. The glass glimmered with artificial frost, keeping me from seeing what lay beyond. From out of his jacket, Von extracted a small vial with a little rubber stopper. He pulled the cap and handed it to me.

"Drink that, and you'll be free to head on in," Von said.

I remembered Chelsey nearly dying from drinking something laced with wolfsbane. "That's gonna be a hard pass for me. I've seen your taste in drinks, Von, and I'm not talking about blood."

"Very clever, Wyatt," Von said. "But rest assured, every contestant was given the same drink.

No dangerous shenanigans in this vial. It's simply a potion that will nullify your shifter sense of smell— nothing else. You'll retain standard human senses, though."

I narrowed my eyes. "So, I won't be able to scent anyone? What are we doing? Orgy in the dark?"

Von swatted my chest. "You cad." Then he smiled. "No, but I may jot that down as an idea for a future season. Go on, Wyatt. You'll love what we have planned."

There was no point in arguing. If I raised a huge stink, I'd only get held out of this challenge. Then what? Kira was probably in there, and I had to be with her. Whatever they had planned, I needed to keep her safe, and there was only one way to do that.

Before I could go through any more internal arguments, I downed the whole vial. The taste was bitter and almost alkaline, like drinking pool water mixed with baking soda. As I swallowed, my shifter senses vanished. Everything became a thousand percent less intense. I couldn't even smell the blood on Von's breath that I'd noticed only a moment before. If this was how humans scented things, it was incredibly boring. I didn't know how they made it through the day.

"Good boy," Von said. "Let's proceed."

Von unlatched the door and stepped inside. I followed, then froze in place. The dark gray walls were accented with gold and silver fixtures, and the ceiling was solid black with tiny lights randomly spread out to mimic the night sky. Massive chandeliers hung in each corner. The lighting was dim but not dark enough to obscure the rest of the room. All the others were mingling around a few cocktail tables as some of the staff walked through with trays for canapés and champagne flutes.

The whole thing jarred my mind. It took me back to the kind of high-class parties I'd been to when I was still part of the Second Pack. The wining and dining, golf, horse races, water polo, yachts—all the rich-people shit everyone in the upper packs *loved*.

None of it had ever been my speed. I'd gone along simply because it was what everyone expected me to do, or because my father or my fated mate Serenity had dragged me along. Being thrust back into something like this gave me mental whiplash.

Across the room, I spotted Kira chatting with Abel. She looked amazing. Her dress hugged her body perfectly. A pearl necklace circled her neck and hung down to her chest. She laughed at something Abel said, then caught me looking at her. Her smile lit up her eyes, but before I could join her, Von began his announcement.

"Good evening, everyone. Glad we could all make it."

It was all I could do not to remind him that we'd basically been forced down here, but I told myself that wasn't prudent.

"Hopefully, you'll all partake of the refreshments the staff is providing. Tonight is a wonderful opportunity for you to get to know each other better than you already do."

Von had completely lost it. He had to be out of his mind. He was treating this like nothing more than a dinner party. Maybe he'd gone senile, like older vampires do before they became feral. Maybe this time next year, he'd be one of the emaciated creatures running around in the jungle.

I was wrong, though, once he said his next words.

"If the cameras could make sure they catch all the contestants' faces? I want to capture their reaction. One of the contestants in this room is not who they appear to be. Each of you drank a potion that nullified your shifter-enhanced sense of smell. That means that none of you know the truth. One among your number is not a shifter. There is a changeling in your midst, mimicking one of the contestants."

We all froze. J.D.'s champagne flute slipped from his fingers, the sound of breaking glass echoing the air.

A lead ball dropped into my stomach. A changeling? They were one of the most terrifying creatures on earth. Those beings could alter their appearance and voice to mimic anyone perfectly. The way their bodies could morph also gave them incredible strength and endurance. But what made them truly horrifying was their propensity for eating still-living meat. Their strength was also on par with even the strongest shifters. Von had basically just told us we were locked in a room with a buzzsaw that wanted to eat us, and with our senses on lockdown, we couldn't see or anticipate the threat.

"Ha, I knew I could get a reaction from you," Von said cheerfully. "You have no clue how difficult it was for us to procure such a creature and negotiate its willingness to participate. I hope you all understand what an amazing situation you find yourselves in. Anyway, you all are obviously well-versed in changelings and their abilities. Not only can they mimic with perfection any individual's image, but also their voice and tone. They also have an eidetic memory. With only a few minutes of observation, they can impersonate all mannerisms, personal tics, and even incorrect pronunciations. The best part? This particular changeling has been watching most of the episodes of this season. They've had plenty of time to get each and every one of you down pat."

"So, what's the play here, Von?" I asked tersely, my eyes scanning everyone. Which one was the monster?

"I'm glad you asked, Wyatt. This evening will go on as it has for the next ten minutes. Once that time is up, the changeling will kill a specifically chosen cast member. That is, unless the imposter is discovered and killed first. So, it's quite simple. I will caution you to be careful whom you align yourselves with tonight. Changelings are the perfect actors, the greatest liars on the planet. You may not know who your friends are until it's too late." He glanced at his watch. "Oops, getting a little long-winded as usual. The time starts now." Von retreated through the double doors, and then came the heavy *thwack* of the thick deadbolt being slid into place, locking us in.

The staff in the ballroom set their trays down and rushed for a door toward the back of the room. In seconds, that door also locked from the outside. All that remained in the ballroom were the cameras and us.

Around the room, the other contestants eyed each other warily. Even though a changeling could impersonate anyone and anything, it didn't stop me from trying to see *something* off about the others. Was Abel holding his glass weird? Had Chelsey always tugged on her ear like that when she was nervous? Was J.D.'s look of horror genuine? My eyes bounced between them all like a ping-pong ball, searching for some kind of tell that would give the changeling away.

I'd been an operative for years, but since coming to this island, I'd realized there were a lot of creatures and threats I hadn't come up against yet.

This creature would be added to that ever-growing list. I knew about changelings from legends, books, and movies, but dealing with the real thing had to be much more difficult. Knowing a creature could imitate someone down to the finest detail was one thing. Seeing it in action was another. No one here looked different. None of them were acting *off* in any way.

"What the fuck are you looking at?" Tate asked Mika. "Why are you staring at me like that?"

Mika held his hands up in surrender. "Easy, my man. We're all looking at everyone at the moment."

Tate scowled. "Yeah, but you were eyeballing me pretty damn hard."

The two men bickered back and forth, but nothing serious. They were both acting as they normally would—Mika, calm and brooding; Tate, blustering and irritated. Trying to be as nonchalant as I could, I walked to a table where the staff had left their trays. I snatched a champagne glass, then popped an appetizer into my mouth. Scanning the room, I sipped on the bubbly liquid.

Gavin glared at me. I didn't even have to imagine what he thought—he probably hoped I *wasn't* the changeling. If I had to put money on it, he probably had his fingers crossed that it was someone else so that it could turn and rip me to shreds. Of course, that theory only held if Gavin himself wasn't the imposter.

Kira was doing the exact same thing I was— glancing at each individual, taking in their appearance and mannerisms before moving to the next. Textbook TO training. Assess the situation, identify the threat, and plan for all eventualities. I strolled over to join her.

"Any clues?" I whispered as I took my place by her side, though I stayed out of reach of her hands in case she wasn't Kira.

"This is stupid," she said. "How do you find an imposter when they look and do every damn thing the person they are mimicking does? I have no idea how to figure it out."

Before I could respond, music pumped from the speakers, and I flinched in surprise. A second later, a huge eighty-inch TV clicked on, showing Von's smiling face.

"To try and figure out who's who, I think the ladies should dance with the gentlemen. Getting good and close might make for better detective work." After that helpful "advice," the screen clicked off.

A moment later, Gavin stepped up to Kira. "Well, what do you say? Want to cut a rug?"

I put a hand on his chest and pushed him back. "Whoa, no way. Not happening."

Gavin slapped my hand away. "I didn't hear anyone make you Kira's master. She's free to say yes or no on her own."

Before I could retort, Kira touched my arm. "It's fine, Wyatt."

"I don't want any of these guys near you," I said. "Not until I know who is or isn't the changeling. For all we know, it's Gavin, and he's supposed to kill you."

Kira, locked in her TV persona, smiled. "Wyatt, a little dancing won't hurt anyone. Besides, there's still around eight minutes until the timer goes off. Everyone is safe until then."

As I opened my mouth to argue, Kira stopped me with a subtle wink and a nearly imperceptible nod. She knew what she was doing. Maybe she even wanted to get close to Gavin to figure out if he was the imposter. Grudgingly, I stepped aside, huffing out a breath as Gavin took Kira's hand, a victorious smile on his face.

A shiver of fear worked its way up my spine. Why would she go with him so willingly? Was she really just being nice to determine if he was the changeling? Gods, what if she was the monster? That thought revolted me in a deeply visceral way, and I did my best to push it aside.

I backed away, crossing my arms, and kept my eyes glued on the two as they danced. I alternated between eyeing Gavin and Kira and checking on the rest of the cast. Tate walked over and asked Chelsey to dance. The other woman agreed reluctantly. As the seconds ticked by, my anxiety grew.

One thing that changelings were unable to mimic was memories. The creature would never have a clue what a person had experienced unless it was something talked about on an episode of the show. If I could try to weed out possibilities, it would make things less stressful. I needed an ally.

Crossing the room, I stepped close to Mika. The man flinched back, a look of fear and surprise in his eyes. "Wyatt?" The way he said my name told me he wasn't entirely sure I was who I looked like.

Dropping my voice to a whisper, I said, "What happened earlier when we crossed the bay?"

A look of understanding dawned in his eyes. "You, uh, you stopped me from running away from the show."

"Oh, thank the gods," I said, heaving a sigh. "It's you."

Mika grinned. "That's pretty smart. I guess that means you're you."

I stood beside him, settling in and watching Kira dance with Gavin again. "Seems so. Have you noticed anyone acting weird?"

Mika shook his head. "Everyone looks totally normal. Honestly, I can't believe anyone isn't who they say they are. These things are freaking weird."

"I'm going to talk to the others. See if I can figure it out using memories."

"Well, good luck with that. Those cameras are everywhere. Most of your interactions were caught on film. Who knows what that thing has watched."

"Yeah, thanks." I moved off to mingle.

My first stop was Abel and J.D. The two men stood together, eyeing the other like each might be a hungry manticore ready for a meal. A quick conversation about some of the interactions we had in the limos and helicopters when we first arrived at the island had me fairly convinced it wasn't either of them. When I left them behind, both were more at ease.

Tate and Chelsey were harder to get to. I had to wait until they stopped dancing, and the whole time, the clock ticked away in my head. A few questions, and I could be sure they were who they looked like.

"Tate? I need to ask you something," I said, walking toward him.

He eyed me warily. "Fuck off, bro."

"I'm serious. It'll just take a few seconds."

Tate put a hand on my chest and not so subtly pushed me away. "Nah. For all I know, you're that fucking thing. Get out of here."

Could he be the changeling? The thought twisted my guts into knots. It would be a good reason not to want to answer any questions. Pissed off, I left him where he was. There was no reason to keep pushing. The look in his eye told me it was a lost cause. Instead, I turned my attention to Chelsey.

"Hey, Wyatt," she said as I took my place beside her. "Sorry about how he acted," she added, glancing at Tate as he walked away.

"That's fine," I said, shaking her comment off. "Quick question. When we were in the mating chamber, what were you drinking before you fell asleep?"

She frowned and blinked, obviously confused by the question. "I'm sorry?"

Sighing, I tried to ask again, this time with a bit more tact. "Sorry, I'm trying to figure out who's the changeling. Only you and I would know what you were drinking. That's why I wanted to know."

Chelsey smiled in relief, but then trepidation entered her eyes. "Well, what if you're the changeling? Maybe you're trying to get close to me so I trust you, and then you'll try to kill me later."

Fuck. I had no response to that. Whatever I said could go either way. If I told her something about that night to prove I was who I said, then I would just be giving her info to use if she was the monster. Another variable.

"I'm going to head over there," she said. As she stepped away, she gave me a wide berth.

Great, now I had two people who could be the damn changeling. My plan wasn't going like I wanted. Instead of eliminating targets, I was adding to them.

Gavin and Kira were still dancing. Fear welled inside me. It had to be Gavin. He was the only option left. I'd spoken to Kira, and while I hadn't asked her any questions, I was certain she wasn't the changeling.

This was the plan, then. Use Gavin to kill Kira. That must be what Von and the showrunners wanted.

Before I sprinted to the dance floor to tear the two of them apart, the song ended, and Gavin walked Kira to the one of the cocktail tables. Walking over to join them, I decided to make absolutely sure I was right. We only had two or three minutes left at best.

"Gavin?"

"Wyatt, I don't remember either of us asking you to interrupt. I'm trying to have a conversation with Kira."

Ignoring him, I pushed forward with my questions. "What color suit did you wear to Kira and Jayson's mating ceremony?"

"I *said*, I didn't ask you to come over here. If you're trying to get Kira alone again, it's not going to happen. I know she's who she's supposed to be. We're fated to be together. You think I wouldn't know the real Kira? Fuck off."

I balled my hands into fists, about to lay him out, but Kira gave me a warning shake of the head. She mouthed, *It's not him.* That brought me up short. Not him? Shit.

Spinning away from them, I checked the others again. Had I fucked up? Did the changeling know more than I'd thought? I didn't see how it could be possible, but if it wasn't Gavin, then who?

"That dude isn't acting right," Abel said, pointing at Tate. "Has anyone else noticed it yet?"

"Yeah, well, I don't like the way Mika's over by himself in the corner, watching us all," J.D. pointed out.

Anxiety filled the room as the time ticked closer to zero. Everyone grew warier by the second. We had to figure this out soon.

A hand shoved me from behind. I turned to find Gavin pointing at me. "You're acting suspicious as fuck. I've seen you walking around talking to everyone. That's weird."

Everyone besides Mika gave me a wide berth. Their paranoia had them taking Gavin's words to heart.

"Gavin?" Kira said, looking at him with renewed interest and confusion. "Leave him alone. It's fine. It isn't Wyatt."

"Bullshit," Gavin said, shoving me again. "It has to be him."

I backed away, holding my hands up. "I guess we'll find out soon."

"Right," Gavin grunted. "I'm keeping my eyes on you. Got it?"

"Got it."

The other alpha moved back to the cocktail table and downed a glass of champagne in one gulp. I pulled Kira aside.

"I thought you said it wasn't him," I whispered.

"I didn't think it was. He said some stuff while we were dancing that made me sure, but now? I don't know." She scanned the crowd as small arguments and accusations flew back and forth.

"What's your inner wolf saying? Mine's too freaked out from having our shifter senses blocked to help me make a read."

"Same," Kira muttered, still glancing around. "I don't have a good connection to her, anyway. This is making it worse. I'm starting to think the changeling is Gavin, though. Did you see the way he freaked out on you?"

A tremble of unease shot through me, and hot, nervous sweat trickled down my back. "Kira, where did I find you that day twelve years ago?" The question burst out of me before I even realized I was going to ask it.

"Wyatt, focus, we don't have time for this. We both know where you found me that day. What we need to worry about is which of these people is about to flip out and try to kill us."

Grabbing her arm, I spun her roughly to face me. "Tell me, right now, where I found you and what happened. The night of your first shift. Tell me right fucking now."

Kira's first shift was probably the single most important moment of her entire life. The trauma, pain, and horror were as deeply ingrained in her as her parents' faces. If she didn't respond to my question, then I'd have my answer.

Kira glared at me and shoved her finger into my chest. "I don't feel like walking down memory lane when Gavin is about to change into some monster and rip someone apart."

That was when I noticed it. My shifter sense of smell might have been nullified, but my inner wolf still stalked through my mind, awake and watching. It felt no connection to this woman. There was no pull, no desire, no need. My inner wolf knew the truth my eyes couldn't see. The hairs on my arm stood on end as I took a hesitant step away from her.

I needed to kill it. There were seconds left until the timer ended, but I couldn't do it. She looked, moved, spoke, and acted exactly like Kira. I couldn't force myself to hurt the thing, even though I knew in the depths of my soul that it wasn't her. Even the thought of crashing my fist into that beautiful face made me want to throw up. My body froze with indecision as my breath came in quick, panicked gasps. I couldn't tear my eyes from her.

Seeing my distress, Kira frowned and took a step toward me. "Wyatt? What's wrong? Are you okay?" She took a step toward me.

"Don't," I gasped, holding out a hand to ward her off.

Her face softened and her voice dropped to a whisper. "What's the matter? Did you see something you didn't like?" she cooed. A hungry and wicked spark flashed in her eyes.

A scream ripped through the room, and she and I turned to look. Abel had broken a champagne bottle and now brandished its jagged edge toward Tate.

"Back up, motherfucker. I *know* you're the changeling," Abel snarled through gritted teeth.

Terrified, Tate took a step back. "Hey, man, watch it with that thing. It's not me, I swear."

Abel lunged, swiping at Tate with the makeshift weapon. "That's exactly what a changeling would say."

A deep, resonant bell chimed, ending the ten-minute timeframe.

Kira turned back to me. "Isn't that cute? The little shifter thinks he knows what I'd say."

Her face twisted into a grin of determined rage, and she leaped toward me, slashing a hand at my face. When her palm struck me, I felt pain through my skull like I'd been hit by a car. I fell backward.

"Oh, shit," I grunted, pushing away from her.

Kira stalked toward me as the rest of the contestants ceased their own arguments and backed away. Even as I watched her walk closer to me, I couldn't force myself to believe that it wasn't actually Kira.

"Holy shit," Tate barked, pointing toward us. "It's Kira. She's the changeling."

"What's wrong, Wyatt?" she said, drawing nearer. "Didn't like my little love tap? Maybe you should spread your legs, and then I can show you what I can really do."

Scrambling to my feet, I held my hands out in front of me. "Stay back. Stop, Kira. Stop it."

Now only a few feet away, she jammed her hands onto her hips and put on a fake pouty frown. "Aww, don't you like me anymore? Come give me a kiss. Then we can make up. Maybe..." She raised an eyebrow. "I can have you for dinner. Oops, I meant, have you over for dinner."

A surprised shout exploded from my throat as the Kira-thing leaped toward me again. On pure instinct, I shifted, dropping to all fours and sidestepping her as her fingers grasped the air where

I'd been a moment before. The Kira-thing stopped mid-stride, spun, and kicked out with her foot, catching me in the side. It was like being kicked by a horse. I spun through the air, landing on a cocktail table. Glasses of champagne went flying through the air. Gods, this thing was strong.

The table shattered under me, and as I fell, I flipped and landed on my feet. Everything in my mind screamed at me that this was not Kira, it was the changeling. Knowing that, I still hesitated to attack. I couldn't do it. What if it was her, and the fuckers running the show had given her some kind of potion to screw with her head? For all I knew, she was some kind of distraction from the actual monster.

"Wyatt, watch out!" The warning came from J.D. as he took a few steps toward me as though to help.

I shook my head and gave a warning growl.

J.D. frowned but did as I'd asked. None of these alphas had my training. I wasn't about to get someone else killed.

The Kira-thing advanced again. I had to do something. Even if this really was Kira, whatever they'd done to her had made her go crazy. I had to incapacitate her somehow. Jumping forward, I slammed all four of my paws into her chest, shoving her back. She tumbled and fell, cracking her head on a table as she went down.

The dull thud as her skull hit the table made me sick inside. Part of me wanted to rush to her side and see if she was okay, the other part screamed at me to finish the fight. Before I could decide what to do, the Kira-thing sat up. She didn't look like she was in pain at all, even with the blood pouring from the gash in her head.

"Enough playing," she hissed at me.

Terror had me almost shifting back spontaneously. The horror that rose in my chest was beyond anything I'd ever felt. Kira's face melted away, revealing a warped and twisted maw of twitching tentacles, writhing and dangling to her chest. Her shoulders slumped then rose, turning into pointed and jagged protrusions, almost like horns. Her delicate fingers and hands swelled and elongated into mottled, green-skinned digits tipped with razor-sharp talons.

"What is that?!" Abel screamed.

"Are you good?" Mika asked, taking a lunge forward.

The thing lashed out, backhanding Mika in the chest and sending him tumbling to the ground. Mika cursed in irritation rather than pain.

The tentacles that made up the thing's mouth rose up like snakes, and a wet, guttural scream erupted from the depths of its mouth. Inside the lipless mouth, rows of shark-like teeth gleamed, ready to shred my flesh. Screams from the others echoed my fear, but I couldn't take my eyes off the thing as it rose to its feet.

Moving faster than it had any right to, it leaped at me, swiping the air with taloned hands. I lashed out with my jaws, catching one of its arms by the wrist. I twisted my head, biting down as hard as I could until the bone snapped between my jaws. With one savage twist of my head, I tore the hand clean off. The beast yowled, but it sounded more like anger than pain.

In another burst of speed that made my head spin, the changeling flipped me onto my back and straddled me. My hind legs were useless, so I pawed at its chest, trying to push it away. Lighting quick, it slammed the one good hand it had left into my shoulder and chest. The talons speared the flesh and skin. Even in my panicked agony, I noticed a hovering camera position itself directly above my head, a perfect spot to catch a close-up shot of me getting my throat ripped out.

Blood spurted from the wounds in my shoulder, sending a spray of it across my face. The coppery tang of my own blood sent a surge of adrenaline through me. I thrust my paws up, shoving the monster away from me, even as its face tentacles tried to clutch at my throat. Finally gaining purchase on the monster's ass with my back legs, I pushed at it with all my remaining strength.

The beast tumbled over my head and slammed into the ground. Adrenaline had me flipping onto all fours and lunging at the creature. I sank my teeth into the flesh behind its neck. The thing tasted like rotten fish, brackish water, and mud. Shaking my head violently back and forth, I did my best to break its spine. My strength wasn't where it needed to be, with my shoulder and chest still in agonizing pain.

A clawed hand swung toward my face, and I released the thing just in time to roll away. The talon missed my eyes by an inch. Righting myself again, I snarled at the creature as it lumbered to its feet. The others had backed away, pressing themselves against the walls, staring at the battle with wide-eyed horror.

The changeling's feet had no claws or talons; they were flat and almost frog-like. They slapped against the floor as it rushed toward me. My body trembled, but I didn't move. I waited for my chance. I needed this to be over soon. This thing was too powerful and fast, and I wasn't sure how long I'd survive.

The changeling opened its arms wide as it moved closer, one arm ruined, one glittering with my own blood. Holding myself steady until the last second, I sprang forward. I angled my jaws to hit beneath the writhing mass of tentacles and closed my jaws on its throat. Knowing it was caught, the beast's steps faltered. With the sound of cracking tendons, breaking cartilage, and tearing flesh, I bit down hard and yanked my head to the side. A massive wad of flesh tore free, and inky black blood spurted through the air.

Hitting the ground, I spat out the hunk of flesh and shifted to my human form in time to see the changeling twisting and thrashing on the floor. In seconds, the black puddle had grown massive, and after several minutes, the thing twitched one last time and then stilled.

As it did, though, it changed into the last thing it had been before the fight. For one moment, I saw Kira, her eyes glazed and sightless, her throat a shredded, bloody ruin. I gasped in horror at the sight.

Blessedly, the image vanished when, at last, the entire body sank into itself with a hiss of greenish steam. Then the body was gone, leaving nothing behind but a bubbling green and black puddle. It smelled like shit. I backed away, covering my nose, trying not to gag.

"Holy shit, man," Abel said. "That thing was crazy. Are you okay?"

I clutched my wounded chest. My fingers went slippery and wet with blood, but my body had already begun healing. "I'll be fine," I growled. Then I lifted my head and screamed at the door, "Von! Get your ass in here."

J.D. walked over and put my uninjured arm around his shoulders to help me stand. A moment later, the double doors to the ballroom opened and Von swept in with a cadre of other staffers—a healing witch, a security guy, and two men who looked like butlers. The two men went to work cleaning up the mess that had been the changeling. The healing witch helped J.D. get me to a couch set against the back side of the ballroom. She began casting healing spells on me while Von addressed the cameras.

"I hope everyone at home enjoyed that. It's not often anyone gets to see a changeling in action, especially not in their natural form. Wyatt Rivers must have really made that one mad. A pity it didn't survive." He frowned, and I thought he might be serious.

"Where's Kira?" I barked at him. I couldn't get the image of her corpse on the floor out of my mind.

Von turned to smile at me. "Ah, yes, the question of the hour. You know, Wyatt, we let the folks at home in on the secret. We thought it was juicier that way. They all knew that wasn't the real Kira."

The witch finished her spell, and the relief at having the wound gone was nothing compared to the anger raging inside me. I jumped off the couch and stalked toward Von.

"That was horseshit. You picked me to die, didn't you? You said that thing already had a target."

Von rolled his eyes. "Of course we did. But as with the boat teams earlier, it was all randomly chosen and—"

"Bullshit. Shut the fuck up and tell me where Kira is. Now."

Von gave me a huffy, affronted look. "No need to be so angry. You did manage to win. Sweet Miss Durst was knocked out. Her vial was filled with a sleeping potion rather than a shifter-sense nullifier. We took her to her room for a little nap."

Before I could do something I regretted, I shoved past him and stomped out of the ballroom. All I could think of was seeing Kira. The image of her transforming into that monster wouldn't stop flashing through my mind. Nothing would help until I was with her again. The *real* her.

Chapter 11 - Kira

"Kira? Oh, gods, Kira, are you okay?"

Muffled words swirled through my head. Someone was calling out to me. Where was I? Why did I feel hungover? When I opened my eyes, everything looked blurry and shadowy. Hands probed at me, checking me for something.

The last thing I could remember was the witch leading me to a pair of double doors. She'd given me something to drink and then... nothing. Whatever they'd given me must have knocked me out cold. Some sort of sleeping potion, probably.

After blinking a few more times, my eyes cleared enough to see a hulking form standing over me. The form slid up my sleeves and gently tilted my chin to the side. The room was dark, but enough light filtered through the curtains for me to make out the face.

"Wyatt?" my voice croaked. I felt like I'd swallowed fireplace ashes. "Water. Please," I rasped.

"Yeah, of course. Hang on."

The bed bounced slightly as Wyatt stood and ran to the minibar at the far end of the room. He returned a moment later, unscrewing the top off a bottle of water.

He handed me the glass. "How do you feel?"

"Like shit," I said, gulping the water. I drained the whole thing in five or six chugs and wiped my mouth. "Oh, sweet gods, that's good."

The water did wonders for my mind. The confusion and blurriness faded, and I could finally take in what I saw before me. When the image clicked into place, the bottle dropped from my hand. Wyatt was covered in blood, his suit shredded and punctured on the shoulder and chest.

I gasped and crawled across the bed to him. "What the fuck happened to you?"

He took my hand before I could probe at the torn clothing. "I'm fine. The dinner party didn't go quite as planned."

"Huh? What are you talking about?"

Wyatt sighed, and from the stormy look on his face, I could tell it had been bad. "They shoved us all into a ballroom down in the basement. Locked us in with a changeling."

I clapped my hand to my mouth. "No. Are you serious?"

He nodded sadly. "It... um..." His voice cut off in a choked sound, something that wasn't quite a sob.

Instead of finishing his sentence, he grabbed me and pulled me in close, wrapping me in a tight embrace. I flinched in surprise, then melted into his arms. He rubbed my back and held me tighter than I'd ever been held in my life.

"I just need a second, okay?" Wyatt whispered.

"Okay. Sure. Take all the time you need." I rubbed his back in return and pressed my cheek to his chest.

He must have been through something terrible. From the way Wyatt was reacting, I had a suspicion, but I waited for him to calm down before saying anything. After a few minutes, his body went rigid and stiff. He pulled away and held me at arm's length, a look of abject horror on his face.

"Where did I find you twelve years ago? After your first shift?"

He knew I didn't like talking about that day. It was the worst day of my life, and the last thing I ever wanted to talk about. But the terror in his eyes prompted me to answer.

"The cave," I said. "Covered in blood. You held me just like this while my world fell apart. Wyatt, what happened with the changeling?"

The horror melted from his face and the tension eased out of his muscles. "Oh, thank the gods." He wouldn't meet my eyes when he began to explain. "It looked like you. I killed it. It looked *exactly* like you. I knew it wasn't you, but..." He trailed off, shaking his head.

"Hey," I said, flattening my palms on his cheeks and forcing him to look at me. "That wasn't me. It's okay."

"It's not okay." The fervent way he said that and the shame in his eyes broke my heart.

I'd spent years knowing Wyatt Rivers as a calm and steady influence. As structured and steady as a marble statue. Emotional but controlled, empathetic and kind, businesslike and dependable. This wasn't like him at all. Killing that creature had really messed him up.

"I'm fine, Wyatt. You can calm down. It's all over. I promise we'll get through this stupid show.

We'll come out the other side okay." I said the words and hoped he believed them because I wasn't as confident as I sounded.

Wyatt sighed wearily and ran a hand roughly across his face, his demeanor changing fast. The sorrow and regret vanished, replaced with anger and worry.

"I can't believe they knocked you out," he growled. "Those fuckers. How do you feel? Any headaches or anything?"

Despite the situation, I smiled. "I'm all right. Maybe a slight headache, but nothing too bad. Honestly? You look worse than I feel."

He glanced down at his ruined suit and chuckled ruefully. "That thing got a pretty good hit in. The witches healed me."

"As good as you look in what's left of that suit, I think you need to get cleaned up. Come on." I climbed off the bed and took his hand to lead him to the bathroom.

Wyatt didn't argue. He was still tense and stressed, and I wanted to help him calm down. He needed to have a clear head to survive whatever the show had planned for us next.

"Here, give me that jacket and your shirt," I said.

Wyatt stripped off and handed me the items. The jacket was stiff with drying blood, and the dress shirt was shredded. I looked at them, shook my head, and tossed them in the trash can beside the sink. Crimson still streaked Wyatt's chest and stomach where it had dripped from his wounds. Even his waistband was soaked through.

"You're a mess," I said. "Let me turn on the shower."

"Shower?" He raised an eyebrow at me, and a hint of a grin crossed his lips.

While turning the water on, I looked over my shoulder. "Oh, unless you don't want one. I can turn this off."

"Nope, didn't say that."

"Okay, then. Finish getting undressed and toss the clothes in the trash."

He did as I asked, and once the water was hot enough, I stripped off my own clothes and pulled Wyatt inside the massive shower. His eyes roved hungrily over my body. We stood under the steaming water and just held each other. More and more tension drained from Wyatt while we stood there. Finally, I pulled away and grabbed the soap.

"You're gross. Let's get you clean."

He chuckled as I soaped my hands and scrubbed at his neck, shoulders, and chest. The blood drained off, swirling in a pink-tinged whirlpool at the drain. Whatever Wyatt had been through had been rough. I'd spent the entire time fast asleep. I couldn't have been there to help him, but this was one way to take his mind off everything. I *wanted* to make him feel better.

Wyatt sighed as my soap-slicked hands massaged his chest and shoulders, kneading the tension out of his body. After a few moments, his hardening cock brushed against my leg.

"Does this feel good?" I whispered, dragging my fingertips down his chest and across his abs.

"Yeah," he breathed.

Smiling to myself, I went lower, wrapping my fingers around his rock-hard erection. Wyatt gasped as I stroked him. Moving slowly and gently, my fingers slid along his full length to the tip and back down to the base.

I looked into his eyes. "Do you want more?"

He nodded fervently. I moved aside, letting the jets from the shower rinse the soap off him, and dropped to my knees. His cock twitched and throbbed in my hands, and when I took him in my mouth, the heat of it radiated across my lips and tongue, making me moan around him.

Wyatt leaned back against the tile wall, sucking in a breath as I moved my lips lower and lower until the full length of him was in my mouth. The head of his dick pressed at the back of my throat, a sensation so erotic and sexy that my pussy was soaked in an instant. Something about making him feel good sent my wolf into a frenzy. She pushed aside all rational thought and urged me on. I wanted to make Wyatt's eyes roll back with pleasure, his hands ball up in ecstasy, and his mouth scream with delight as I made him come.

Digging my fingers into his ass, I pulled him in and back out, fucking him with my mouth. Wyatt thrust his hips in time with my movements. Delirious with excitement, I sucked at the head of his cock, grabbing the shaft and stroking him as I massaged him with my tongue.

"Holy fuck, you're gonna make me come."

Pulling my mouth away, I grinned up at him. "Good."

Before he could say anything, I went back to work, again taking him deep into my throat. Before I could finish him off, Wyatt yanked his hips back, pulling his cock free from my lips with an audible *pop*. He yanked me to my feet and pushed me back against the opposite wall, directly under the water. With a hungry look, he pressed his lips to mine, shoving his tongue into my mouth. I greedily accepted it.

A finger slipped into my soaked pussy, making me moan into his mouth. Wyatt added a second finger. My knees went weak as he thrust the two digits into me, fucking me with his hand. I pulled away from the kiss, gasping for air, and cried out as his thumb rubbed my clit.

Wyatt lowered his head until there was the delicious pressure of his lips sucking at my nipple. Tingling electric sparks blasted off inside my head as his tongue slipped and swirled around the tightening nub of flesh. I almost cried out in disappointment when he pulled his lips away, but then his tongue was sliding between my legs. I collapsed back, resting my weight against the wall.

He wrapped his lips around my clit and sucked gently at it. Pulses of heat and pleasure emanated from my core, surging into my stomach and making my nipples tingle. I massaged my breasts and ground my crotch against his mouth. Nothing on earth mattered. Nothing was real other than the two of us and that box of glass, tile, and water.

"Oh, God," I groaned. "I want your cock, Wyatt. Give it to me."

Wyatt stood, spun me around, and bent me over. I pressed my hands on the wall to hold myself up, and with an explosion of ecstasy, the full length of his gorgeous cock filled me until his balls pressed against my clit. An inarticulate groan escaped my lips as he began to thrust into me. He reached around my body to grip my breasts, pinching the nipples as he slammed into me. I was tiptoeing on the verge of an orgasm, ready to climax at any second.

"Fuck me hard, Wyatt. Faster."

He did what I asked, our wet skin slapping together as his hips met my ass, his dick slamming into me faster and harder. His grunts of exertion and how full he made me with each thrust sent me over the edge.

"Fuck!" I screamed, and the burst of pleasure sent my legs quivering. I struggled to hold myself up, and if not for Wyatt's thick, muscled arms holding me, I would have fallen to the tile floor in a twitching mass. I hung limp in his arms as he continued to fuck me, his shaft sliding into me over and over. The world spun and shivered in my pulsing state of bliss.

Wyatt didn't slow down. A second climax built, even stronger than before as he hit that sensitive spot inside me. A mixture of fear and excitement swirled in my head. I was almost afraid of how powerful the orgasm would be.

"I'm gonna come," Wyatt gasped, breathing heavily.

"Come, baby. Come for me." I slipped a hand between my legs to rub my clit.

His motions grew erratic and spastic, and then he cried out in exultation as he came deep within me. His release sent the next wave crashing over me, making ice and fire course through my veins. This time, I did slide to the floor, though Wyatt did his best to keep me from falling. His cock slid out of me, and a moment later, I lay on my back, water raining down on me as pleasure pulsed through me. Nothing had ever felt so good.

Wyatt knelt, joining me on the tile floor, kissing my body—shoulders, chest, nipples. His lips caressed me as his hands ran the length of my body. I reached between his legs and stroked his side lovingly.

"That was amazing," he whispered, his breath hot against my ear.

"I would joke that I've had better, but that would be a lie."

We collapsed into giggles before getting our senses back. After a few minutes of cuddling under the water, we finally stood and turned off the water. I dried him with a towel, and he did the same for me. The massive walk-in closet held several robes in various sizes, and once we were both wrapped up, we stepped out into the bedroom, Wyatt's hand lingering on my back.

The TV in the room flashed with one word: **Message**. The big red letters filled me with trepidation, but I grabbed the remote and pushed play. Better to know than not know. Von's face appeared on screen, and the lovely post-coital bliss I'd been experiencing vanished in an instant.

"Good afternoon, everyone. A quick message for our hard-working contestants. The remainder of the afternoon and this evening will be yours to experience as you'd like. It was, after all, a *very* intense morning and early afternoon. We think you all could use a little rest.

"In case you were wondering, tomorrow will not be quite as dramatic. Prepare yourselves for a Q&A session with fan questions, along with a smaller challenge in the jungle later in the afternoon. Rest up and enjoy. Dinner will be served at six, but if you'd like the staff to provide room service this evening, all you need to do is call with your requests.

"Until then, we'll put on the video replay of this afternoon's festivities. I have to tell you all, that was a fantastic job. From our fans' reactions, that may have been one of the most successful challenges in our history. Even without an elimination, the fans went wild for it." Von winked. "See you all soon."

The screen shifted to a shot of Wyatt walking into the ballroom, Von at his side. My curiosity got the better of me, and part of me wanted to see what I'd missed. How close had Wyatt really come to dying?

Before the video could go much further, Wyatt yanked the remote from my hand and turned off the TV.

"I do not want to experience that again," Wyatt said, tossing the remote onto the bed.

"I kind of wanted to know how bad it was," I said. "I sort of feel bad I wasn't there."

"Don't," Wyatt said. "It was bad, but there's no need to worry about it."

I sighed and waved at the screen. "I was up here, literally napping, while you all were down there, fighting for your lives. Wouldn't you feel a little guilty if the roles were reversed?"

He took in my words, and I could see I'd hit the truth. He knew he'd be racked with guilt if I'd had to go up against that monster while he was knocked out in bed.

"Yeah, you're right," he said. "Watch it later when I'm not here or something. I can't relive that panic. Right now, I just want to be with you. I don't care if we're arguing or on that bed going for round two. As long as I get to spend some time with you, I'll feel better. No stupid *Reject Project* messing with my head."

"Round two?" I repeated, raising an eyebrow.

Wyatt grinned and opened his mouth to say something, but then a knock interrupted us. His face fell as he realized the same thing I did—the universe had a perverse sense of humor.

The knock came again, more insistent, followed by a voice calling from the other side. "Kira? Hey, are you okay? Are you in there?"

Ugh, Gavin.

"For crap's sake. I've had it with this guy," Wyatt growled. He looked mad enough to bite through steel.

"Let me go talk to him. He'll never leave otherwise," I said, cinching my robe tighter and walking toward the door.

I left the security chain on but unlocked the deadbolt. Opening the door as far as the chain would allow, I found Gavin outside, looking anxious.

He sighed in relief at the sight of me. "Oh, thank the gods. You're okay. Can I come in?"

"Uh..." I glanced over my shoulder. Wyatt sat on the far side of the room at the corner of the bed, unseen from Gavin's vantage point. "I don't know that now is the best—"

"I know Wyatt's here. Okay? I know," Gavin said. The words pained him, but he wasn't devastated or heartsick. Maybe disappointed, but otherwise, he was fine.

"Right," I said. "It's still not a great idea. Was there anything else you came to say?"

"Well, yeah, actually." He came closer, face almost in the eight-inch opening. "I don't care that Wyatt is here. I still think you and I can make this work. I get it—you've known him for a long time, emotions are running high, and things happen. I don't want you to end up with someone who isn't right for you just because of this stupid show. People do things they aren't proud of when they're stressed."

It was all I could do not to roll my eyes. "Gavin, I don't think you really get what's happening."

He closed his eyes for a second, holding up a hand. "No, you're right. I'm not in your head, so I can't say what you're thinking. After tonight, I've realized I don't know you as well as I thought I did. Down there in the ballroom, I was *positive* that it was really you. When it ended up being that... that *thing*, it got me thinking. We should really get to know each other better. I know I've said this before, but it's true—I *know* that you and I are a perfect match." He jabbed a finger into his chest over his heart. "I know it here. Deep down."

As I listened to him speak, I thought about how my life might have been different if, as he believed, our blood work had been accidentally swapped. Compared to Jayson, Gavin was an amazing guy. A little clingy, maybe, but he had an innate kindness his brother didn't have, and it appeared he really wanted what was best for me. In another world, he and I may have been happy together.

The flip side of that coin was that Wyatt wouldn't be in my life. Not the way he was now. That thought alone made my inner wolf whine and shy away in sadness. I couldn't imagine my life without Wyatt now. A few weeks ago, that thought would have been ludicrous. Gavin had to understand that there was no future for us.

"Listen, Gavin, you're a great guy. You have no idea how flattered I am. You're a really decent guy, and a much better and kinder alpha than your brother, but..." I chuckled ruefully. "I think you have this idealized vision of me in your head. If I had to guess, you've built me up into something I'm not over the years."

He shook his head vehemently. "No, that's not it at all."

"Let me finish, please."

He lowered his head, chastened. "Sorry. You're right. Go on."

"Thanks. You are desperate for a mate, and I get that. I want one, too, but the mate you're looking for isn't me."

"No, Kira. You and I are both on this show. We both came here to find our fated mate. That has to show you that this is meant to be. Maybe the goddess is trying to fix whatever mistake happened with the bloodwork. It could be that simple. She set us on this trajectory so we could come together here. Once you realize—"

"Gavin." I kept my voice gentle. "I didn't come here to find a mate."

He blinked at me, his face warped into a mask of confusion. "Wait, what?"

"I did not come here to get a fated mate. I came here to restore my pack's standing and help them survive the war that's coming."

His brow furrowed as he stared at me. I could almost hear the gears clicking in his head. When they finally snapped into place, his eyes widened. "You... you want the favor from Heline?"

I blew out a breath of relief. Maybe that would be enough for him to realize that I wasn't the person he thought I was. Knowing that I was the kind of person who could be cold-hearted enough to reject a mate in favor of a wish from the moon goddess was surely enough to end his attempted courtship.

After considering the revelation for a few seconds, he chuckled to himself. "Well, that's not something you have to worry about. If you mate with me, then my plan would go into motion. We assimilate the Ninth Pack into yours. It would make the Eleventh Pack one of the strongest packs outside First and Second. Hell, it might make us so strong that they have to rename the packs. We would be allied with the First Pack because we won. We'd be strong enough to face any war that might be coming." His smile grew wider. "See? This is all working out perfectly. You don't have to reject anyone if you pick me. Once we overthrow my pack, all the things you came here for will be realized. You won't have to take the favor."

He was like a dog with a bone. "Oh, Gavin," I said, shaking my head sadly.

Chapter 12 - Wyatt

That jackass kept going on and on. Could he not take a hint? Hell, Kira wasn't even giving him a hint; she was practically holding up a big, neon, flashing billboard.

His constant pursuit of Kira was to be expected, though. I knew why he'd come on the show, after all. The thing that really surprised me was when he outright admitted that he wanted to take his pack down and let Kira's pack absorb it. I'd honestly figured he'd be a bootlicker like his older brother, bowing down to the sanctity of the pack system. To hear him talk, he wouldn't have been upset if his whole pack disappeared. I had to admit, seeing the look on Jayson's face when his entire world was demolished would have been a nice treat.

My eyes narrowed when I heard him remind Kira that she had more options than she thought.

"We'd be strong enough to face any war that might be coming," he said, sounding like he had it all figured out. "See? This is all working out perfectly. You don't have to reject anyone if you pick me. Once we overthrow my pack, all the things you came here for will be realized."

It struck me then that I wasn't enough for Kira to succeed. She was so desperate to help her family and pack that her focus was solely on that favor from Heline. Kira would reject any man she ended up with to get that grand favor. For the first time since leaving, I mourned the Second Pack. If I had a higher standing than a lone wolf, Kira might see mating with me as a good solution. Departing and severing my ties to the pack I'd been born into had been the most freeing and happy time in my life. To this day, I considered the pack system a corrupt antique, a bygone system ripe for reform. The entire hierarchy was suffocating and stringent. Though, some things were more important. Part of me wondered if staying in my pack would have afforded me a chance with Kira.

That thought nagged at me while Kira continued to try getting rid of Gavin. I wanted her, deep in my bones and soul. It was an ache that wouldn't go away. If I did become the final guy, Kira would make sure I made it off the show safely and found my way to this Haven place that one-eyed wolf told her about. That wasn't what I wanted, though. *She* was what I wanted.

Even if we both managed to survive the show, I'd be stuck on Bloodstone Island for the foreseeable future. Alone. Hiding from anyone and everyone, dodging death every damn day. All while knowing Kira was a thousand miles away, living her life without me. The ache in my stomach became a heavy, painful knot.

"Gavin, I really need to rest," Kira said. "My brain is too fried to think about overthrowing packs right now. I'll see you later."

Gavin muttered something I couldn't hear, and a moment later, the door clicked shut.

"Sorry about that," Kira said. "He didn't want to leave."

"I heard," I said, nodding and staring at the door where Gavin had been standing a few minutes before.

Kira sat on a plush chair opposite me and shook her head in disbelief. "Can you believe what he was saying?"

Tearing my eyes from the door, I looked at her. "Is he serious about wanting to tear his pack down?

Would you help him do that? Team up with a Fell to help your pack?" The questions sounded crazy coming out of my mouth, but I couldn't stop them.

Kira rolled her eyes. "I can't even fathom the *thought* of someone wanting to turn their back on their pack, much less tear it down. And no, I wouldn't do what he's asking, even if he thinks it makes sense. The best way to save everyone is by asking Heline to help. That's the only goal here."

I gave a derisive laugh. "Well, here's my take. If I had the chance to dissolve my home pack, the Second Pack? I'd do it in a heartbeat. Those shifters in the upper packs all live a life of luxury, but they're corrupt and miserable to the core. They live in their gilded halls, sipping on champagne and nibbling on fucking caviar. They'd be better off finding new packs to see how the other side lives." I didn't want to keep going, but I was on a roll now and couldn't stop. "The lower packs all look up to the upper ones. They even make excuses for the awful shit they do. It's all because everyone in the lower packs thinks they can someday rise to the upper packs' level through hard work and loyalty, but that's bullshit. The upper packs want to keep everything the way it is. No one can rise, no one can fall. The system is rigged.

"I think that's part of why this sadistic fucking show is so popular. It gives people hope that one day, if they get really lucky, they can possibly become an honorary member of the First Pack." I took a breath, then asked the question that had been gnawing at me. "If you had to make a choice right now and pick a person for the moon goddess to tie you to, who would it be?"

With that question out in the world, I looked into Kira's eyes and waited for her answer. Since the beginning, she had been saying she wasn't in this for a mate. I was positive that was how she'd felt in the very beginning, but was it still that way? Could her mind have changed?

Kira took in my words and shot me a sarcastic grin. "Wow, that's a big question." She walked over to me, bent over, and kissed me. Her lips were warm and welcoming. After she pulled away, she said, "I guess Tate might be the frontrunner. He's been such a big fan of mine lately."

"I'm serious, Kira."

She flopped down beside me. "Well, if we're being serious, I'm more concerned with finding a way to shut down *The Reject Project* once and for all. That's what I want to do. This thing has caused enough hurt and death."

"So, is your goal to win the show or destroy it? I don't think you can do both."

Kira mulled that over, her mouth quirking to the side. "Powerful people are using this show as a glorified and legal death sentence. Look at Mika. His dad, his own fucking father, wants him out of the way. He didn't commit any real crime, but his dad forces him onto the show and then actively tries to interfere and get his child killed. And like Crew said, there's something weird going on with this island—Leif going feral so fast, this Haven place, and whoever the hell the Simon guy is that Crew mentioned. There's a ton of shit happening here that needs to be revealed to the outside world."

"You still haven't answered my question," I pointed out.

"I know." She chuckled. "I can't give you an answer yet. Both are important. If I win, then I can help my pack and maybe the whole world avoid a war.

But breaking this show might do something even bigger." She took a deep breath, letting it out slowly before changing the subject.

"I'd like to talk to Zoe again soon. Get our plan in place for the fake eliminations. I'd like to stage your exit first. Get it done ASAP and have you safe at Haven."

"Wait, what? No way. What the hell are you talking about?" Was she being serious? Send me away first? "You aren't getting rid of me that easily. You tried to send me home once, and you know how that worked out. I'm staying right here by your side until you win or until there's no other option."

Kira grimaced. "If you aren't here, then I can focus on surviving the game. You're... a distraction. Okay?"

It was my turn to laugh. "That's fine if you think that, but I've got to keep an eye on you. Make sure you don't get into worse trouble than you usually do."

Kira scowled at me for that, which I couldn't blame her for. I grinned back at her. "You know you're kind of adorable when you make that mad face, right?" Before she could respond, I kissed her again.

"That's not fair," Kira said when I pulled away. "You don't get to end an argument by trying to be all sweet and stuff."

"Sorry. I have to use secret weapons when I have to."

She rolled her eyes again, letting that part of the discussion die. "Fine. If we aren't talking about you, then who goes first?"

"I *may* have mentioned the fake elimination to Mika," I admitted. "He's desperate to get off the show. He's already tried to slip off once; in fact, that's how he almost died a few days ago in that challenge, and I had to talk him out of trying again right after that boat disaster. He might be the best choice at this point. Especially since he's already actively trying to run."

"I thought about J.D., too. He's too nice for this place. Ugh." She sighed, "I want *everyone* to get out alive, but we have to be careful. We can't tip off the viewers or showrunners."

"True. We'll have to play it by ear, at least until you can make contact with Zoe and this Crew person again. For now, we need to think big. It's the only way we'll take down this fucking show."

Von was still on my shit list for barging in on us when we were half-naked and showing the whole world what should have been a private moment. Every day, that bloodsucker seemed to do something else to piss me off. Today, it was drugging and knocking Kira out, then replacing her with that *thing*.

"We should start with Von," I said. "Find out what gets under his skin. Maybe we can figure out some of his history. If we do that, I might be able to find something that could make him unravel on air. He's a huge part of the show, and doing that might destabilize things. I've even thought about trying to stir up trouble with the staff, or sabotaging some things to cause technical difficulties. Anything to tank the ratings."

"I want to hit them hard," Kira said, clenching a fist. "But I can't figure out how. For now, I think that might work—little things here and there. It's a start. We can go with that for now."

"Cool. I'll start really antagonizing Von tomorrow. Dig at him, see if anything bothers him more than other things. For now," I added with a raised eyebrow, "I'm enjoying this time we're getting to spend together. Now that the secret is out, we don't have to be as careful."

Kira glanced down at my hand, which was sliding up her thigh. "That was pretty smooth. I never even saw you move."

"What can I say?" I said with a shrug. "You bring out the best in me."

Kira laughed. "Is that so?"

She pressed so close that her scent overpowered me, making me dizzy with desire. I wanted her again already, wanted to tear her robe off and devour her. I pushed closer to kiss her, but a knock at the door stopped me.

I growled in frustration. "The universe hates us. That's the only thing that makes any sense. It's got it in for us."

With a laugh, Kira gently moved my hand away and went to the door to see which asshole had interrupted what was about to be a really great time. I followed Kira to the foyer. If it was Gavin again, I wanted to make sure he had to look at me while he bugged Kira. But it wasn't Gavin at the door.

It was Chelsey. The woman gaped when she saw me behind Kira. Both of us were in robes and obviously naked beneath them. It didn't take a rocket scientist to figure out what we'd been doing.

"Crap," she said. "I'm sorry. I didn't mean to, uh, interrupt."

"No, no, no. You didn't," Kira said. "It's fine. What's the matter?"

"Let me grab my stuff," I said. I could tell by the way Chelsey eyeballed me that she didn't want to say whatever she'd come to say with me around. "I need to head out, anyway."

Kira escorted Chelsey into the room while I quickly put my clothes back on in the bathroom. When I came out, Kira was pouring Chelsey a glass of wine.

"See you later," I said as I walked toward the door.

"See you," Kira said. Chelsey gave me an awkward smile.

The whole walk back to the alpha den, I thought about how best to get under Von's skin. I wanted something that would make him blow up, preferably during one of the live broadcasts. Then he wouldn't have a chance to edit it out.

When I stepped into the den, I saw that several guys had turned in early and were already fast asleep. The ballroom fiasco had drained everyone. The sun wasn't even all the way down yet.

Mika was still awake. Seeing me, he stood and joined me at the door. "Can I have a word real quick?"

"Sure," I said. "What's up?"

He pointed toward the hallway. "Out here," he whispered. "Most of them are asleep, but you never know who's listening."

Mika led me into the hall and down the corridor before ducking into what looked like a small decorative office.

"Is Kira okay?" Mika asked.

"She is. I checked on her as soon as I left the ballroom."

"Good. I was worried about her as soon as I realized she'd been replaced." He chewed on the inside of his cheek for a second and glanced back out the door to see if anyone was lurking in the hall. "You said you might have a plan for getting people off the show. Is that the truth? Is it really possible?"

Time to give him the whole story. "There is a chance. Zoe, Kira's friend, didn't die out there. A guy named Crew saved her, and he has some kind of hidden enclave or camp called Haven where others are living. We're waiting to get word from Zoe to plan the fake eliminations in detail, but in short, we'll make Von and everyone else think someone has been knocked off the show, but in reality, they go into hiding at this Haven place. There's more to it, but that's basically the gist."

Mika nodded along as I spoke. When I finished, he said, "Well, if you're looking for a guinea pig to be the first to sneak off, I'm your guy. I volunteer."

I gave him an assuring nod. "I think that can be arranged."

"Seriously?" He looked as though he hadn't expected that answer.

"Someone has to be first, and you're more ready than anyone else. Why not?"

"Damn. All right, then. Do you guys have a timeline?"

I shook my head. "Not yet. Like I said, we need to get in contact with Zoe again. Once we get some info, then we'll move. We're gonna try to do it soon, though. These tasks are getting fucking ridiculous."

Mika looked more excited than I'd ever seen him, like he had a mission or a goal. Maybe it was the first time he'd had any hope since finding out his father was fucking his fated mate behind his back. Whatever it was, I liked seeing that glimmer of life in his eyes.

"Let's get back in there. We need to get some rest," I said.

"Yeah. You're right about that."

As we headed back, my mind drifted to my unofficial pack and Kolton. Other than Kira, Mika was the closest thing I had to a friend on the island. The people I'd left behind were like a dream. We were so isolated on this stupid island, it was as if nothing else existed but this place.

Kolton and his parents were probably dealing with the political fallout from the coming war, and gods only knew what kind of shit the Ninth Pack was putting them through with Jayson leading them. If I had to guess, that would be the very first skirmish that broke out in the war. Jayson and the rest of his sycophants probably couldn't wait to go after the Durst family pack lands. That thought sent a tremor of unease through me.

Kolton and I had thrown a few fists back in Fangmore City, but that was rare. Kolton had never been a fighter. If war came calling on his doorstep, I didn't have high hopes for his survival. He was the polar opposite of his sister; he did not seek out and conquer dangerous things. He sought out and conquered books.

My unofficial pack would be there, and they could handle themselves. They would align with Kira's pack since they'd given us shelter and a home, but they were nowhere big enough to be a true army. We needed to get off this stupid island and back home before war really did break out.

"Goodnight," Mika whispered as we stepped back into the alpha den.

"Night," I grunted, quietly pulling my clothes off beside my bunk.

Gavin wasn't yet asleep. He turned to see me. Our eyes locked for a second, then he grimaced and rolled over to turn his back to me. Well, at least the feeling was mutual.

I slipped under the covers and stared at the ceiling. Tomorrow, the real revolt would begin. I'd do everything I could to get under Von's skin. I wanted to see that bloodsucker squirm for once instead of making us squirm. I also resolved to find some way to break the rules about contacting people off the island. There had to be some way that these people communicated with the mainland. I was desperate to get a hold of someone back home, and by the gods, I would.

Chapter 13 - Kira

Chelsey downed the glass of wine as soon as Wyatt was out the door. "You want another?" I asked.

She put the glass down and waved a hand over it. "No, I'm good. One was enough."

I joined her on the couch. "Okay, then. What brought you over? I hadn't thought I'd see you up here this late. It's pretty close to bedtime."

Chelsey glanced into my eyes, and I could see the fear lurking inside her. "That changeling thing freaked me out. Kira, it looked *just* like you. I've never seen anything like it, and then when it changed?" She shuddered.

"I keep hearing that. Pretty bad, I guess?"

"It was awful. Honestly, the worst part was right before that thing revealed itself. Everyone thought everyone else had to be the monster. We were ready to start killing each other. Other than when they took my brother, it was possibly the scariest thing I've been through. I mean, at least out in the jungle or in the water earlier, you know what wants to kill you. This was totally different."

"You're going to think this is crazy, but I'm kinda disappointed I missed it."

Chelsey looked at me like I had three heads.

"I mean, I wish I'd been there to help fight it. It's not right that I was asleep while you guys were doing all that."

She looked relieved. "Oh. Okay, I get that." She twisted her hands together in her lap. She wanted to say something, and it was clearly something that made her feel uncomfortable. She really wasn't good at hiding her emotions.

Reaching over, I put my hand on hers to stop their fidgeting. "It's fine. Say what you need to say."

Her shoulders slumped. "I'm sorry Von burst in on you and Wyatt like that. It wasn't right. I also don't think it's right how they're targeting you two." She sighed. "I really did like Wyatt. He's great—and so are you. The two of you should get an even playing field to find a mate like the rest of us. If Wyatt is your fated mate, then that would be how this plays out."

"Thanks for that. I really appreciate it," I said.

The words *fated mate* paired with Wyatt's name made me both uncomfortable and excited. A girlish thrill went through my chest each time the subject slipped into my mind—a whole host of butterflies in my stomach and jelly in my legs. It was silly to think about such things when your life was literally on the line, but it was a thought my inner wolf liked latching onto. It was both irritating and pleasant at the same time.

Pushing away those thoughts, I tried to delve deeper into what Chelsey came here for. "I'm not sure you came all the way up here tonight to tell me that, though. Is there something else on your mind?"

She wouldn't meet my eyes. I let the silence build, giving her time to get out whatever she wanted to say.

"This is embarrassing," she said.

I laughed. "I just had about a hundred million people see me half-naked. If it had been a few minutes earlier, they would have seen *way* more. I think I know a thing or two about being embarrassed. Spit it out."

"Well, I came to see if you had any more ideas about how to bring the show down. Like, that was the *main* reason I came here." She huffed a breath. "Okay, that's a lie. That was, like, the last of the things I wanted to talk about. I miss my family. I, uh, sort of needed a friend, and I look at you as a friend. That's stupid," she added quickly. "I'm dumb for saying that, we barely know each other. I should go—"

"Hang on, chick." I smiled at her and patted her hands. "I didn't say anything. Why would you think that was dumb to say?"

That's not what I thought she would say. To tell the truth, I was happy it was something simple. I didn't make friends easily. Never had. At least not since the night of my first shift. Once that happened, I saw myself as a monster and threw all those walls up. It was a huge reason I could never see how Wyatt felt for me. Other than Zoe, I didn't really have any friends. Kolton was the person I was closest to, but a sibling relationship wasn't the same as a friendship. Not in my mind. If Zoe hadn't been so easygoing and quick to befriend me, I might not have anyone I could call a friend.

Instead of friends, I had acquaintances from work and in my pack, but those were all surface-level relationships. My mind had been so consumed with keeping people out and suppressing my wolf that I'd inadvertently isolated myself from everyone.

Noticing that I'd fallen deep into my thoughts, Chelsey leaned forward. "Sorry, did I make this weird?" She chuckled. "I can come off as intense sometimes. People say I'm intimidating. Maybe it's because I say what I think. I don't have a big filter, I guess."

I blinked, shaking away the self-analysis. "No, it's fine. Seriously. I didn't mind."

"I do think we can be friends. Do you?"

"Yes, I think so. I like you, Chelsey. Though, we may not be friends for long. Not the way this show works. We could die any day in one of these dumb challenges."

"True," Chelsey said. "Very true. Even then, we can at least have each other's backs until, um, the inevitable happens. Right?"

This woman was going through something as awful as I was. Of all the people in the world, she was the one I should be able to confide in the most. Maybe laying all the dirt out for her would help us become *real* friends and strengthen this alliance or whatever it was we were building between us.

I glanced over my shoulder at the minibar. There were some snacks left, the rest of the red wine, and an unopened bottle of white wine. I needed something with a little more kick.

Looking back at Chelsey, I raised an eyebrow. "Do you like whisky?"

"Um, I, uh... I don't know if I've ever tried it."

I stared at her in disbelief. "Well, we need to fucking fix that right now. Come on." I took her hand and tugged her to the door. I was still just wearing my robe, but I didn't give a damn.

"Where are we going?"

"You said you wanted to be friends," I said. "One of the things friends do is get drunk and tell stories. Plus, I can't call myself a true friend if I let you get off this island without drinking whisky on the rocks. Let's go."

Chelsey looked aghast and tugged on me, keeping me from dragging her out the door. "Won't Von or someone from the show be mad we're out running around this late?"

I grinned and looked her dead in the eyes. "Maybe. Fuck 'em."

She stared back at me, shocked at first, but then the worry vanished, replaced with an angry smile. "Yeah," she said with feeling. "Fuck 'em."

Laughing, I pulled her out the door and headed for the main dining area. The bar there was stocked with all the good stuff. It would be great to get hammered on *The Reject Project*'s dime.

"Where are we going?" Chelsey whispered as we hurried down the stairs.

"Hush. We're doing something bad, but who cares?"

Off to the side of the dining room area was a bar with emerald-green tile, brass fixtures, and an oiled mahogany bar top. Several shelves of bottles lined the wall behind it.

"Oh, I see," Chelsey said.

I grabbed a bottle of whisky from the top shelf and poured a glass half full, then put some ice into it from the ice maker under the counter.

"Here you go," I said, sliding the glass toward her.

She sipped at it, and her eyes bulged. She coughed and swallowed a few times. "That's... really something."

I couldn't help but laugh. "Yeah. It's a bit of an acquired taste, but so is pretty much all of this stuff." I swept a hand to the shelves.

The house was silent. All the staff members must either be in bed or editing footage. Von was probably in his room, fucking and eating someone. I shivered at the thought. Our bracelets weren't glowing green, so we weren't being filmed.

"Let's head back to the room," I said. "We can talk in peace there. What else do you wanna bring?"

Chelsey glanced at the shelves and shrugged. "Um, I've never tried gin before, either. I'm more of a wine and beer person."

"Gin it is," I said, tucking a bottle under my arm along with the whisky. "Come on."

By the time we were back in my room, Chelsey had finished her whisky and was sipping on a gin and tonic.

After pouring my own drink, I sat beside her. "Okay. Instead of worrying about all the awful ways we might die here, let's think of how to take down this stupid show. First, though, if we're going to be friends, tell me about yourself. Your background and whatnot."

"Okay. Um, my life's not very exciting, though."

"Trust me, sometimes quiet, boring lives are way better than the exciting ones. I mean, being on this island is exciting, but that's not a good thing, right?"

Chelsey chuckled. "True. Okay. I'm from the Twelfth Pack. We didn't come from a lot of power." She glanced at me and smiled awkwardly. "I guess you get that. Being from the Eleventh Pack, I mean."

"Yeah. Kinda rough at the bottom, right?"

She looked relieved that I didn't take offense at her comment. "I paired with this amazing guy. I couldn't have asked for a better fated mate. He was charming, gorgeous, smart, and kind. I *literally* fell in love with him at first sight. The problem," she said with a sigh, "was that he was in the First Pack. His parents were disgusted by the idea of him being mated to someone in such a lowly pack. They talked him into rejecting me. They did it in front of an audience. News cameras and everything."

"Oh my gosh, are you serious?" Being rejected in front of friends and family had been bad enough. I couldn't imagine how bad it would have felt if it had happened to me the way Chelsey's had.

"Yeah," Chelsey said, looking world-weary. "Ben sent me away, and I never saw him again. Not that I didn't try. Like an idiot, I went by his house twice. The first time, his mother called the cops on me for trespassing. No one was home the second time. He even changed his phone number and email address. I was fully and completely ghosted. I've been walking around with a broken heart ever since. I signed up for the show on a whim when Von made that special announcement."

"Same here," I said with a laugh. "I didn't even watch the show other than when my friend Zoe wanted to watch it."

Chelsey laughed, and this time, it was a real laugh. "Neither did I. I think I watched a few seasons when I was a kid, but for the most part, I ignored the whole thing, especially after I was rejected. It would have been too painful to watch. I wouldn't even let anyone talk about the show around me. It's pretty weird we ended up here when there are people drooling over the chance to be on this show."

"Drink up. You have to finish that before you get any more. We're supposed to be getting drunk, right? We're shifters—we have to drink fast, or we'll burn it all off before we get there."

"Oh. Right." She slammed back the last of her drink and winced. "Whew. Ready for more."

"That's my girl," I said, pouring her another.

"What about you?" Chelsey asked. "What was your rejection like? They didn't talk about it much on the show, from what I saw. Only a few hints here and there."

"A complete shitshow."

I told her about Jayson and our relationship, or lack thereof. I didn't paint the best picture of him, which was what he deserved. I told her how he and his family orchestrated my termination from the Tranquility operatives, and that my own pack was pushing my father to banish me.

"You know," I said, as a thought occurred to me, "I was *with* my fated mate for five whole years before the ceremony, but I never really felt like he was the *one*." I was starting to feel a little tipsy. "He was such a dick to me all the time. How could that douchebag be my real fated mate?"

My words startled me. I paused, thinking about what had come out of my mouth. Had I just stated what Gavin had been preaching all along? Deep down, beyond the outrageous nature of the revelation, I truly did believe it. Jayson couldn't be my fated mate. The blood test had to be wrong. That possibility, touted by

Gavin, meant that one of Heline's temple acolytes had made a mistake.

Could that have happened? Did some person, overworked and exhausted, accidentally swap my name with someone else's? Could it be that simple, or was something else going on? Regardless, it felt good to say it out loud. I decided to repeat it.

"He was not my fated mate," I said. "I don't give a damn what the test said. It took a while, but I finally realized that here on this island, I had to stop pining after what I'd lost. Especially when I knew that if I'd gotten what I wanted, I'd have spent the rest of my life miserable. And you know, people have been saying for a while that they think the fated mate connections are messing up, and I think they're right. No one wants to say it out loud, but I think everyone is beginning to notice it. I'd love to know who my true fated mate is." I sighed sadly. "I guess I'll never find out at this point."

"You're right," Chelsey said. "It seems like there are more and more fated relationships that are backward or ill-paired. And I think you hit the nail on the head. There's this weird undercurrent among the packs where everyone is starting to notice it, but no one wants to say anything. Maybe they're afraid of pissing off Heline or something. That's what made what happened to me and Ben hurt so much. We had a *real* connection. I'm angry and hurt, and all I want to do is hate him for what he did, but my wolf still wants to be with him. She refuses to let me move on. I dream about him at least once or twice a week. I want to move on, find a new mate, and leave Ben behind, but even saying that makes me ache all over. I don't know how I ever will."

Draining the last of my drink, I poured another and sipped at it. This poor woman did not deserve to be here. She was pure and unassuming. This show was a chainsaw, tearing through people like timber. Wyatt and I were highly trained and capable operatives, but the dangers and drama were almost too much for us to handle. This woman deserved to be home with the love of her life. She deserved to have someone who would never reject her because, unlike me, she was a decent shifter who wouldn't do awful things.

When I told her all that, she scoffed at me. "You act like you're some kind of monster, Kira. You aren't. You've proven over and over again that you're a wonderful person."

Maybe she had a point, maybe she didn't. I'd been struggling with what I did the night of my first shift since I was a kid, when I could barely go a month without having a nightmare of waking up, covered in blood. To this day, I wondered exactly what happened and why I did it. Whatever I did as a child didn't make the deaths on this show my fault, but part of me kept thinking I was cursed or something.

I downed the rest of my drink and poured another, gesturing for Chelsey to do the same. We were going through the drinks fast enough that even our shifter metabolism couldn't hold back the effects. My brain had gone fuzzy and a little numb. We were well and truly drunk. We spent an hour drinking more and brainstorming ways to fuck with the show. Chelsey even had the idea to purposefully cut ourselves and smear the blood on our skin to tempt Von into attacking one of us live on air. I wasn't sure that was a good idea.

"What about this?" I said, forcing myself not to slur my words. "Von's, like, really important, right? What if we, like, uh, do something to make him not be good and important no more?"

"Huh?" Chelsey squinted at me through glazed eyes.

I thought about what I'd just said and devolved into cackles of laughter. Chelsey followed suit, both of us collapsing on the bed, unable to stop laughing at my drunken, incoherent rambling. We lay there, trying to catch our breath, and within minutes, we were both asleep, the near-empty bottles sitting on the table beside the bed.

Chapter 14 - Wyatt

My dreams were chaotic and stressful. I dreamed of shifting and running through the woods back home. My paws skimmed over the leaves and moss and dirt, the scent of the outdoors filled my nostrils, the wind brushed my fur. Those images were interspersed with screaming monsters, splashes of blood, and dark figures reaching out to me. When I woke the next morning, I felt like I hadn't slept at all.

Restless, I sat up. My dreams were a symptom of being on this island. All the death and danger everywhere, coupled with the fact that I hadn't had a good run since getting here, had filled me with anxious energy. I'd run through the woods in my wolf form, but running for your life was way different from running for relaxation and enjoyment. Shifters weren't meant for this. We weren't creatures made to be caged up with no outlet for stress.

Part of me missed the grueling training of the Tranquility ops. Shifting and running through specialized courses would be better than what I was doing here. Maybe homesickness had something to do with my strange dreams? The thought struck me as strange. There'd never been a hint of that when I left my pack. Of all the things in my life to have made me wish for home, it should have been those months after I became a lone wolf. I'd been fine, though. Once my unofficial pack took me in, I felt even better. Almost like truly coming home.

Chewing on the inside of my cheek, I thought about my pack. August Evander was probably my closest friend aside from Kolton. He was one of the top lieutenants of the unofficial pack, had been since joining up with us three years ago, and I missed that son of a bitch like crazy. I'd have given my left arm to have August and Kolton here for an hour to trade some jokes, stories, maybe a few conversations about football or basketball. Anything. The longer I remained here, the more isolated and closed off I felt. I thanked the gods that I had Kira.

Before my homesickness could turn into full-fledged depression, voices from across the room pulled me out of my rapidly building despair.

"Bro, no way. Jamison would destroy that guy in man coverage. I'm not a fan of the Fangmore Beasts, but if you think the quarterback for the

Eastern Wild Manticores is good enough to throw dimes on Jamison, you're off your rocker." It was J.D.'s voice.

I glanced over and found him tying his shoes, talking football with Abel.

Abel shook his head. "Are you serious? Clinton was the freaking MVP of the league last year."

J.D. pointed at him. "MVP, but did his team win the Shifter Cup? Nope, the Flames did. That guy choked hard, threw four interceptions in the championship game. Jamison will eat him alive this year. Mark it down."

Abel snorted a laugh and waved a hand at J.D. "Whatever. I'm going for breakfast. See you down there."

"See you in a minute, dude."

As Abel walked out, I looked at J.D. and saw that he was still smiling as he finished getting his shoes on. It was nice seeing him back to himself, or at least closer than he had been for several days. J.D. was the most likable person among the alphas, and much of our group attitude played off his positivity. His renewed happiness stemmed from Kira revealing that Leif was still alive on the island. Even knowing

Leif was feral and lost in the jungle wasn't enough to dampen J.D.'s spirits. That was good.

Kira was right. After we got Mika off the show, J.D. should be next.

I dressed and headed downstairs for food. I was starving. I hadn't eaten during that damn ballroom challenge, and my stomach was about to cave in on itself.

The other guys were already munching away. At the buffet, I had the chef make me an omelet with spicy peppers, cheese, and sausage. I was craving spice this morning. While he cooked, I grabbed some buttered toast and sliced fruit, piling my plate high, then poured a massive glass of orange juice before taking my omelet and other food to sit at a table by myself.

While eating, I glanced surreptitiously at the others. Gavin looked sullen and kept casting pissed-off looks in my direction when he thought I wasn't looking. Tate also sat alone but only had eyes for his food, not bothering to look up other than to take a drink.

Mika, J.D., and Abel sat together, chatting about nothing in particular. Mika looked tense, though. He was antsy for the plan to come together soon. I couldn't blame him because I was, too. Every hour that went by was another chance for Von to screw with us and maybe get one of us killed.

I ate fast and left the dining room to poke around the mansion. If I could sneak around and be subtle about it, I might hear some of the support staff, producers, assistant directors, or tech guys drop some dirt I could use.

The main areas we typically used were pretty much always empty, only used for the cast or special things like revealing challenges or interviews. The first place I ventured to was at the back of one hallway, near the lounge Kira and I had used for a few minutes of fun and excitement a few days ago. At the end of that corridor, I found two techs and one of the fae staff members working on some of the hover cameras.

"Why does it keep wobbling?" one guy asked.

"That's what she's here to figure out," the other tech said, pointing to the fae girl.

She sighed, poking one of the cameras with a finger. "These spells don't do well after a while out in the jungle. There's a lot of magic out there, especially twisted magic. When these things get caught up in it, it screws with the spells we put on these—oh, shit! Mr. Rivers?"

She'd caught sight of me and ruined my cover. The two techs spun around, and I had to think fast.

Plastering a massive smile on my face, I shrugged. "Sorry to interrupt. I was walking down the hall and heard you guys talking."

The fae blinked rapidly at me and grinned. "This is gonna sound all kinds of corny, but can I get your autograph?"

I frowned and tilted my head. "Sorry?"

A pad of paper and a pen magically appeared in her hand and she stepped forward.

"Rhiannon, are you serious?" one of the techs said, staring at her like she'd lost her mind.

The woman looked over her shoulder and snarled. "Fuck off, Carl." She turned back to me, her smile back in place. "Sorry. Do you mind?" She held the pen and pad out to me.

"Uh. No, it's fine." I took the pen, scribbled my name on the pad, then handed it back to her.

"Wow, thanks. You and Kira are my absolute favorite. At the beginning, I thought Omar had a real shot to be the one for Kira, but after the first couple episodes, I *knew* it was all you."

Any chance I'd have to hear anything from these three was over, and if I didn't get out of here, I was afraid they'd talk my ear off and waste my time.

"Well, I'll let you get back to work." I waved and left the room. The three of them started arguing as soon as I was out of sight.

The next stop was the greenhouse-style sunroom attached to the second-floor patio. They'd outfitted the room as a staging area for witches to help with the challenges. A fallen angel was in there with the witches and techs. As soon as he saw me coming, he met me at the door, placing a hand on my chest.

"Can I help you?" He stared at me with the weird, jet-black eyes some fallen angels had. No whites, no pupils. Only solid black orbs.

With my best *let's-be-buddies* grin, I patted him on the shoulder. "Stopped by to talk."

"About?"

This was obviously not going to go how I wanted. Time to cut bait. "Maybe I should get the hell outta here."

The fallen angel nodded grimly, keeping his eyes locked on mine. "Yeah, maybe you *should* get the hell outta here."

Once he removed his hand from my chest, I managed to step away a few paces. I pointed my thumbs over my shoulder as I continued backward. "So, I guess I'm just gonna go fuck myself. Cool?"

"Cool," he grunted and shut the door with a loud click.

I'd almost given up on having any success until I found two young medical witches outside. The women looked like they were on some kind of break, both sitting with mugs of steaming liquid. There was no way I could sneak up on them from where they were sitting. That meant eavesdropping was out of the question. I'd have to rely on my charm instead.

Both women's eyes went round as they saw me step outside and walk toward them. "How are you two doing?" I asked, pulling up a chair and joining them.

The blonde looked at her friend, the brunette, and smiled in a confused manner. When she looked back at me, she was blushing.

"Sorry, Mr. Rivers, we weren't expecting you."

I shrugged nonchalantly and gave them my most charming smile. "Why would you? Anyway, how are you guys liking our season? Are we putting on a good show?"

The two shared a look, then laughed. Finally, the brunette said, "We're both team *Kwyatt*. It's the best pairing we've had in several seasons. You guys have no idea how big of a deal you are. Ratings are higher than they were for the tenth *and* twentieth anniversary seasons. Even higher than the thirtieth anniversary. Which is saying a lot."

"Interesting," I said. I couldn't care less about ratings. Though, if Kira and I were successful in sabotaging the show, the more people watching the trainwreck, the better.

"Yeah," the blonde added. "Everyone is crazy about you guys." I recognized her now. She was one of the healers who helped Chelsey after she'd been stabbed in the stomach by that monster.

The brunette put a hand on my wrist. "And Mr. Thornton is really freaking excited about the ratings. Though, he's been a little more pissy than usual. Not sure what that's about."

This was what I wanted. They were already talking about Von. If I steered the conversation further down that path, it wouldn't look like I'd brought it up.

"How is it working with Von? He's a pretty interesting guy, from what I've noticed," I said. "Like, what's his backstory? What did the guy do before the show?"

Again, that shared look between the two women. An unspoken conversation they thought was only between them, though my training saw right through it. I'd questioned enough suspects in my time, watched them try to be sneaky with their partners or lawyers or wiccan counsels. I knew what these two witches were saying. Was I trustworthy? Should they tell secrets? Sure, why not? Who's really going to know?

Anticipation and excitement coursed through me, but I managed to maintain my composure. I didn't want to seem too eager.

The brunette shrugged and her smile widened, showing off her brilliant white teeth as she leaned a bit closer to me. "We can't tell you a lot because he sort of keeps to himself when it comes to his background."

"Yeah," the blonde added. "He's more concerned with flirting and getting you up to his room for, uh, dinner, you know?"

"I can imagine," I said. Unbidden, a mental image flashed through my mind of Von, naked and surrounded by writhing bodies of men and women as he sucked the lifeblood out of a nubile young witch. I had to clamp my fist tight to prevent a shiver from running through my body.

"He tried to get me to go up a few nights ago," the brunette said.

The blonde laughed. "If you're under the age of sixty, he's probably tried to get you to come up to his room. The guy's insatiable." She pulled a face. "Not my type, though."

"Same," the brunette said. "Anyway, the only thing anyone knows is that he's several hundred years old. Some people think he was maybe born near the ocean or something. He talks about sailing a lot when the cameras are off."

"Well, the way I heard it," the blonde interjected, "was that he was a pirate. Sailing around and pillaging coastal towns until one day, he saw the daughter of a mayor of one of those towns. Saw her through a telescope and fell in love the moment he laid eyes on her. Instead of attacking the town, he decided to woo her. He became a lovesick puppy dog, trying to get her to wed him. She rejected him and broke his heart. I think maybe he went off looking for vampires to turn him. Like, purposely tried to make himself into a vampire. All to come back and turn her into one, too, forcing her to be his." She waved a hand through the air. "All gossip, though. Who knows?"

After knowing Von these last few weeks, I highly doubted he was ever *lovesick* for anyone. At best, if that story was remotely true, the mayor's daughter was probably someone Von had wanted a wild romp with—a notch on his bedpost and nothing more. Maybe she'd said no and hurt his pride. This tale was a good start, but nothing solid.

"Well, it was lovely talking to you ladies. I'll let you two get back to your break. Sorry to interrupt you." I stood and headed toward the door.

"Bye. It was nice talking to you," the blonde said.

"Yeah, good luck today," the brunette added.

I waved and ducked back into the mansion. Von's message last night had said there'd be some Q&A thing with the fans today. My free time was running out. I had no idea what time the thing was supposed to start. I might have time to talk to one more person if I hurried.

Before yesterday, I hadn't even realized there was a basement area until Von led me to the ballroom. Maybe there was more to find down there. It was worth a shot.

After finding the staircase, I hurried down and turned right instead of left toward the ballroom. There were more doors, but most were locked or just supply closets. One room looked like some sort of trophy room, with thick leather chairs, velvet wallpaper, and at least two dozen mounted heads around the wall. There were tiger, elk, and wolf heads, a massive elephant head, and also a basilisk head, a griffin, and what was either a minotaur or an actual bull. The back of the room was lined with glass cases that held multiple types of firearms and magical weapons. It was interesting, but there were no people, and that was what I needed to find.

Moving down the hall, I finally hit paydirt when I glanced into a room whose door was ajar. It looked like a monitor room, with multiple computer terminals playing video feeds. This must be where they edited the video footage.

Inside, a lone warlock sat fiddling with some dials, rewinding a video of J.D. and Abel at breakfast. If this was the editing room, it must have some form of communication with the outside world. The showrunners and staff had to be able to converse with outside people when they were cutting clips for the show.

Before I could search, I had to get that guy out of the way first. I bumped the door with my shoulder, knocking it fully open. The sound and movement caught the warlock's attention. His head snapped around, and he pinned me with his eyes. I gave him an awkward smile, unsure what else to do.

"What the hell are you doing here?" he asked.

In a split second, I formulated my plan and implemented it. "Um, yeah, Mr. Thornton was looking for you."

The warlock paled and put a hand on his chest. "Me?"

I nodded enthusiastically. "Yup. He looked kind of pissed about something. Didn't even bother asking the staff. I was the closest, so he sent me down here." I leaned farther into the room, looking into his eyes. "He is *not* happy about something. You probably want to hurry."

An anxious look passed over the guy's face. "Oh, shit. Okay."

The warlock rushed out the door, not bothering to lock the room or even glance at me as he hurried down the hall toward the stairs to search for Von. I'd have five or ten minutes, maybe longer. The mansion was huge, but the staff probably knew better where to find Von than I did.

With one last glance around the hall to make sure it was clear, I slipped inside and latched the door behind me. I hesitated for a moment, then went ahead and locked it, too.

The equipment was mostly stuff I'd never seen before. Instead of poking around with it and wasting time, I sat at a console and scanned the files on the desktop. Most of the programs weren't even password-protected, and I scrolled through at will.

It took a few minutes until I found what I'd come searching for: a voiceover internet protocol program. It turned the computer into a cell phone. All I had to do was connect it to the number I wanted. A quick scan of the history showed a ton of calls going to a number in Fangmore City. I did a reverse look-up with the computer's internet and found it was *The Reject Project* home office number. Each call was anywhere from one to twenty minutes long. That meant it worked.

I punched in Kolton's number, activated the minicam, and video-called him. When the connection was successful and Kolton's phone rang, I almost shouted for joy. A few seconds later, his face appeared. A confused scowl transformed into a shocked smile when he saw me on his screen.

"Wyatt? What the hell?"

"I know," I said. "Had to pull out all my tricks to make this happen."

"Shit," Kolton hissed. He looked to be in a store of some kind. He tucked himself between two aisles and lowered his voice. "How is this possible? You guys aren't supposed to have any contact with the outside world."

"Good to see you, too," I said sarcastically.

Kolton winced. "Fuck, sorry. Good to see you, man. Dude, are you gonna get in trouble for this? There's no way they'll let this fly." He squinted into the screen, trying to see what was behind me. "Where the hell are you, anyway?"

I snorted a laugh. "I don't know how I could get into more trouble besides being on this show. I'm in an editing room. I snuck in, and I'm using their computer to call you. If they find me..." I shrugged. "Maybe they'll try to get me killed faster."

"You're right about that. I know you can't see the feed they show us, but it's freaking obvious the showrunners have it out for you and Kira. Even the commercials for each episode talk about making sure to tune in because you guys might be eliminated at any time. It's crazy." Kolton glanced around, then looked at me again, his expression more serious. "The way they're editing the show is weird, too. They're making you and Kira look like total assholes. You can tell it's pieced together to push the narrative they want, but it doesn't add up."

"Not surprising," I said. "They want us to be the bad guys instead of the show itself. They probably want to tip fans toward hating us instead of liking us. Then there won't be as much backlash when they finally figure out how to knock us off. Don't worry about us, though. I'm still protecting Kira as best I can."

"I know. I can tell. They can't edit out everything. That changeling thing was fucking messed up. Even though they showed us which one of you was the imposter, it still freaked me out seeing my sister turn into that thing. It messed with my head."

I didn't want to think about the way Kira's face had split apart to reveal that howling mouth full of tentacles. I decided to change the subject.

"How are things back home? Any more news on whether war's gonna break out?"

"It's getting bad," Kolton admitted. "A lot has changed since you guys left. Skirmishes are breaking out daily. It's not only in the borderlands, either. There have been a few small riots in Fangmore City. Even human and wiccan cities are seeing trouble. We had a big group of teenagers from the Sixth Pack come through our lands and stir up shit. Your guys helped take care of that."

At the mention of my unofficial pack, I pressed for more information. "How are they doing?"

"Fine. Dad let them stay just for the extra manpower. A lot of the elders wanted them banished. Said it put a target on our heads, having an unofficial pack staying in our lands, but for once, Dad stood his ground. August has been my main contact since you've been gone. We've gotten to know each other pretty well the last few weeks. That guy has a *ton* of contacts. He's the one who got me the fake press pass to that 'Meet the Mega Fans' event last week."

I chuckled. "Of course he did." August had been a member of the First Pack before getting tossed out. His connections ran deep. He had amazing people skills, plus he was a hell of a computer whiz. Those two skills had helped us a lot over the years. It was good to hear that he and Kolton were getting along.

"August will help you keep things from going sideways. Keep him close, Kolton. You'll need all the help you can get if things get bad." I glanced over my shoulder at the door, then back at Kolton, my attitude more subdued. "I want you to watch out for my pack, okay? Tell August he's the main guy in charge. I'm not entirely sure I'm making it back from this place."

"Hey, none of that," Kolton said quickly. "Don't think negative stuff like that. We're working on stuff from our end to get you guys off that island. It's a massive undertaking since Bloodstone is out in the middle of nowhere. It's both the most secure and dangerous place in the world, but August and I are working on a plan."

My expression must have been hilarious because Kolton laughed outright. "All you need to worry about is staying alive. You and Kira both, okay? If we can help you, we will. Count on it."

I'd already spent too much time on the call. That warlock or someone else might be back at any moment, so I needed to get out of here before I was caught.

"Okay, I gotta go," I said. "Take care. If I get a chance, I'll contact you again, but if not..." I trailed off.

"I got you," Kolton said. "We'll see you soon. For sure. Stay strong."

"We'll try our best. See ya, bro."

I spent the next several seconds putting the computer screen and chair back exactly as I'd found them. Unlocking the door, I checked the hall, finding it deserted. My luck held until I stepped onto the first floor and ran almost directly into Von. The vampire looked surprised, then pissed.

"And where the *hell* have you been?"

"Stretching my legs. You know how it is," I said with what I hoped looked like a convincing smile.

"For your information, Wyatt, the staff started looking for you *fifteen* minutes ago. We're late for filming the Q&A segment. They looked all over the place. Where exactly were you?"

I shrugged, giving him a shit-eating grin. "Around. It's no big deal."

Von's eyes narrowed suspiciously before huffing a petulant sigh. "You know, I've told you before that I really do like you and Kira. You guys have been great for ratings. Everyone on the planet wants to know if this thing between you two will play out like a love story or a tragedy. That being said," he added, pointing a pale finger at me, "if you don't play by the rules and quit doing shit like this, I'll have no choice but to feed you to the wendigo out in that jungle with my own two hands."

"Wow," I said, heedless of my words now that Von was starting to piss me off. "Tell me how you really feel."

Von rolled his eyes in mild disgust. "I'm actually surprised you two are still here. If you ask me, one of the showrunners must have a soft spot for you." He rubbed his chin absently. "In fact, I think I know which one it is, though why she'd give a damn, I don't know. She's rarely interested in anything these days."

"Hang on," I said, my curiosity piqued. "What do you mean by that? Why is the lady on the board of directors so important?"

Von checked his watch and scowled. "Ugh, no time for that. We have to hurry. I'm flying in my personal masseuse for a massage at two, and if we don't get this filmed, I'll have to bump it. Let's go, Mr. Rivers."

Something about his comment stuck with me as we made our way down the hall. Why would that strange woman have any sway over the rest of the board? Garth Sheen was the richest and most powerful shifter on the planet. How could that weird woman in white sway anything?

"You know," Von said as we neared the room where the session would happen, "I'm pretty excited about this afternoon's challenge."

"Yeah, me too," I said dryly.

Ignoring me, Von went on. "It'll be dramatic. I don't know if it will be as entertaining as yesterday's, but it does have a shot at being fun. One can only hope, at least."

"Right." I rolled my eyes. "One can only hope."

Chapter 15 - Kira

Chelsey left early the next morning. Even with our high-shifter metabolism, we were both a little hungover. I didn't know how humans did it, and their hangovers were probably ten times worse. Ugh.

I was too queasy to eat breakfast. That would probably bite me in the ass later, but the extra few hours in bed did wonders for me. Being hungry later was a small price to pay.

We were supposed to do some kind of question-and-answer session. From the way Von made it sound in his video message, it would probably be questions from the fans sent in via email or social media. Great. An afternoon answering questions from horny housewives about which alpha I wanted to fuck, or douchebags who thought they should have been picked as cast members and were bitter. It would be just like the last time we did this. Though, I had to admit that answering dumb questions was much safer than risking my life out in the jungle or the ocean.

After finally dragging myself from bed, I took a shower and brushed my teeth. Feeling like a real person again, I dressed, letting the air dry my body.

As soon as I stepped out of the bathroom, a loud *tap-tap* at the window startled me. I wrapped my arms across my naked body, covering myself. I relaxed when I realized what it was. A magnificently colored parrot sat on the sill, another message tied to its leg. It tapped the glass again with its beak.

I rushed over to open the window, desperate to see what Zoe had sent. After opening it a crack, I checked for cameras. Once I was as sure as I could be that no one was watching, I let the parrot in. It sat on my table while I rushed back into the bathroom for my robe. When I came out, it politely held its leg out for me to untie the message. Whoever that eagle shifter was, he was a great trainer.

I unrolled the note and began reading:

Bestie, it's me, your favorite fae. Anyway, I hope things are good there. Crew said I was good to give you a little more info on Haven. We can't go into too much detail on the off-chance my little rainbow buddy there gets compromised. If stuff goes sideways, we don't want the showrunners knowing more than they already do. I'll give you all I can other than the location—that's still super-duper secret.

There are a few dozen beings living here at Haven. Most are various types of shifters, but there's a little bit of everything. We do our best to stay hidden from the producers and staff of the show. Crew says they come out every few weeks to look for us but always give up fairly soon, which means our hiding place is really good. Let's keep it that way!

He says that he's pretty sure they think our numbers are super small. Like less than a dozen beings. They'd shit themselves if they knew how many were actually here. Other than the showrunners, we also have to stay hidden from the creatures in the jungle. But the main thing that scares us is Simon Shingleman.

I stopped reading the letter for a moment. Simon Shingleman? Why did that ring a bell? Had I come across that name during work? Something tickled at the back of my mind, almost within reach, but when I focused on it, the memory slipped away again. Huffing, I sighed and went back to the note:

He's a psycho. From everything I've heard, he's some kind of magical scientist and a madman. There's a lab somewhere deep within Bloodstone Island, but Crew hasn't found it yet. One of the fae who lives here says he does some pretty shady experiments. He's a monster. He kidnaps creatures and beings to experiment on them. The word around Haven is that he uses them to create these awful weapons, potions, and other stuff. Crew and the others are certain he has outside help or funding of some sort, but they haven't found any good evidence to support that. All they know is that the few times he's managed to capture someone from Haven, they get tortured for information and then either die or turn feral. We have no clue how he does it, but he turns shifters feral. It's probably one of the weapons he's developed.

Skimming back, I read that section again. Heart hammering, I put two and two together. This Simon guy had turned Leif feral. It was the only thing that made sense. This piece of shit had drugged him or given him a potion and made him feral. If that was true, though, then maybe Simon could also reverse it.

We have a team watching the mansion from a safe distance. Crew and his second-in-command are ready to use magic to create a convincing death for the cameras. All we need from you is the name of the target and when the next challenge is. The challenge has to be outside the magic barriers, though. Mr. Feather Pants was busy, so send that info back with my newest friend, Mr. Rainbow Sprinkle Butt, and we'll be as ready as we can.

Love you! Hope to see you soon.

P.S. This one won't catch fire. Write back.

I glanced at the parrot. "Mr. Rainbow Sprinkle Butt?"

If I didn't know better, I could have sworn the bird rolled its eyes in disgust.

Suddenly, a knock sounded on my door, and I nearly jumped out of my skin. "Miss Durst? It's time for the Q&A session," a woman's voice called through the door.

"Oh, shit," I hissed, looking over my shoulder.

"Oh, shit," the bird mimicked.

"Be out in, uh, five minutes," I called back.

"Miss, we really need to go now. We'll be late."

I didn't bother responding to that. I dug around in the desk drawer for a pen, then wrote a quick reply on the back of the note.

You're taking Mika Sheen. There's a challenge this afternoon in the jungle. He'll be ready to go.

The asshole witch pounded on my door again, calling for me. My fingers shook with excitement as I rerolled the paper, tied it to the bird's leg, opened the window, and sent him off. The woman was still calling for me, but I waited until Mr. Rainbow Sprinkle Butt was out of sight before rushing back to my closet and throwing on an outfit.

By the time I finally made it to the door of my room, I looked like a hot mess—no makeup, my hair still wet. But at least I wasn't naked anymore.

"Hey, sorry," I said, pulling the door open.

The witch in the hall gave me a onceover and frowned. "Um, you're ready?"

"Yeah." I tried to make my voice sound indignant, but it came out as embarrassed.

"Well, come on then. Mr. Thornton is going to be very angry."

Biting my tongue, I stopped myself from saying something I shouldn't and followed her. Instead of worrying about Von, I enjoyed the hope that surged within me, knowing my message was on its way back to Zoe. The thought that the plan Wyatt and I were implementing might actually come to fruition filled me with an excitement I hadn't experienced in a long time.

When she led me into the room, Chelsey and the other alphas were already there. It was all I could do not to stare at Mika. I was as calm and collected as I could manage until I noticed that Wyatt wasn't in the room.

Chelsey beckoned me to sit next to her. When I did, I whispered, "Where's Wyatt?"

"Don't know. We were waiting for you both, and Von got pissed and stomped off to find him and sent the witch to get you."

"How the hell did you know what time to come?" I hissed.

"They mentioned it during breakfast, but you didn't come down, and I guess Wyatt left early." She shrugged in apology. "Sorry. I assumed they said something to you guys separately."

A few minutes later, Von and Wyatt hurried in. Wyatt immediately caught my eye and gave me a quick, almost imperceptible nod before sitting next to Mika. We didn't want to draw attention to ourselves.

Von snapped his fingers at one of his staff. "Are we ready?"

The guy tapped at a tablet and gave Von a thumbs-up. "We're good, sir."

"Penelope? Cameras?" Von barked at the witch who'd fetched me.

The witch waved her hand over two cameras sitting on a table beside her. The devices buzzed to life and rose into the air. One stayed pinned on Von, and the other floated around to get different angles.

The frazzled, frustrated look on Von's face vanished in the blink of an eye. The ivory smile, the fangs, the charm all appeared so fast, it made my head spin.

"Good afternoon, all you *Reject Project* fans. I know you've been looking forward to today. Our team has been collecting the best and brightest questions from our social media pages, our fan site, and our texting lines. Now that those questions have come in, it's time to pose them to our sexy, sizzling cast."

He waved a hand toward all of us, the cameras following his gesture. One camera buzzed by us, getting a good shot of each of our faces. I couldn't help but wonder if the lens picked up my wariness. After getting a shot of each of us, the camera returned to Von.

"I hope everyone is excited to see how fun things get over the next few days. We have some really fun challenges coming up. For now, though, questions and answers—nothing dangerous. There are simply too many questions to get through. As much as I'd love to add a little danger, that will have to wait until later this afternoon."

That was a relief. He probably wasn't joking, either. If there was a way to add danger to something, Von would do it. He could turn a baking class into a bloodbath if given enough time to prepare.

"First one," Von said, pulling a note card from a stack on the table beside him. He read from the card, "We all know the changeling disguised itself as Kira. Who did you *want* it to be?" He gave the camera a scandalized smile. "Intense. Okay, Tate, how about you answer first?"

"Uh, I didn't really have a preference," Tate said. "But I guess one of the other alphas. I don't like the idea of hurting a woman. Even if it's only a thing that *looks* like a woman."

Oh, that was a bullshit answer. The second Tate had found out Wyatt and I knew each other before the show, he'd been done with me. I had no doubt he'd have loved to jam a knife into my throat, but from what Chelsey told me during our hours-long drunken convo, he'd been backed up against a wall, scared shitless like the rest of them while Wyatt dealt with the changeling.

Von asked every contestant in turn, getting mostly canned answers. Wyatt did stir some drama when he said he wanted the changeling to be Gavin, and of course Gavin answered that he wanted it to be Wyatt. It was all quite silly, in fact.

Von snapped up another card. "Oh, this is a good one. Should get a lot of people heated up back home." He cleared his throat before asking the questions. "Which of the twelve packs is the best?"

Even as tense as things were, most of the contestants chuckled. They thought it was an easy question. One that any wolf shifter could answer from the time they were old enough to talk. Obviously, *your* pack was the best, and you'd always think so.

As Von went around the room, things went pretty much as planned. At least they did until he returned to Gavin and Wyatt.

"Wyatt? What's your answer? You originally hailed from the Second Pack, correct?" Von asked.

"I did," Wyatt answered. "But like many of the upper packs, the Second Pack is corrupt. To tell the truth, all the traditional packs are. I have to go with my unofficial pack being the best."

"Bro, that's not a real fucking pack," Tate said. "It's a bunch of mongrels who aren't fit to be in real packs."

Wyatt didn't seem fazed. "My unofficial pack is the largest in all the pack lands. We watch out for each other and are more of a family than any other pack. I stand by my answer."

Von raised his eyebrows and leaned in close to the camera. "Well, well, well, folks. A bit of intrigue, no? Do you all think any of the unofficial packs wandering around out there constitute real packs? Let us know. Our social media page is live for your comments.

"Last but not least, Gavin. What is your answer? Which pack is the best?"

Gavin glanced at me, and I knew what he'd say before he even opened his mouth. "The Eleventh Pack."

Even Abel and J.D. looked shocked at his answer. It was one thing for a shifter like Wyatt, who'd left his own pack, not to pick the one he'd been born in. As taboo as that was, it still kind of made sense. But Gavin was the brother of the Ninth Pack's alpha. He was as far up the hierarchy as anyone. For him to choose another pack was startling.

Tate snorted with disgust. "Bro, you have to get your nose out of Kira's asshole. Are you really gonna disrespect your own pack to try and get some pussy?"

"Tate!" Von barked. "Language! We're live."

I almost laughed. Bloody, violent deaths and sex were fine, but the word "pussy" wasn't? What kind of alternate reality was I living in?

Gavin looked as equally unconcerned as Wyatt. "What can I say? I've lived in the Ninth Pack. I know how crappy it is. I also know Kira and I are destined to be together. She's the best person I know. To me, that means the pack she came from has to be the best pack."

Tate only rolled his eyes. Abel looked like he wanted to say something, but kept his mouth shut. Mika had answered with his own pack as well, but when he said it, I could tell he was just parroting what the audience wanted to hear. I wished Wyatt and Gavin had done the same.

"Next question," Von said. "We'll start with J.D. Who is the one contestant you'd bring back if you could?"

"Oh, that's easy," J.D. said. "I'm sad about all the guys who got eliminated, but I really miss Leif. I'd take on anything in that jungle if it meant hanging with that dude one more time."

Even from across the room, I could see the wistfulness in J.D.'s eyes. It was sweet that he wanted

Leif back, and it made my heart hurt for him. How would I have felt if I only admitted my feelings for Wyatt to myself after he was gone, like J.D. had with Leif? The whole thing made me sad, and I promised myself I'd make sure those two were reunited.

The question went around the room, and pretty much everyone agreed on Leif. Von got to me, and all I could do was nod. "Yeah. Like J.D. said, every elimination was rough, but if I'm being selfish, I'd bring back Leif."

"My, my," Von said. "Looks like Leif had a big impact on everyone. Next question—and this is a doozy—comes from a human fan. Would any of you ever date a non-shifter?"

Oof, what a loaded question. Many shifter packs, notably wolf-shifter packs, were old-school about that. Still, I was curious about what the others would say.

Von pointed at Gavin. "You first, Mr. Fell."

He shook his head quickly. "Absolutely not. No chance."

"Same," Tate said.

"Interesting," Von said, then nodded to Abel and Chelsey.

"I don't think so, no," Abel said.

"I don't have anything against non-shifters," Chelsey said hesitantly. "I have friends who aren't shifters, but no, I don't think I could."

"Kira? What do you say?" Von asked.

For a moment, I imagined Wyatt being a human or a fae, or even something more bizarre, and I realized it didn't matter. My feelings wouldn't change. That was an interesting revelation, as I'd always considered myself traditional. A lot of my old thoughts and beliefs were changing. Lots of things had changed for me on this show.

"Um, I think I would," I said.

"Kira?" Gavin gasped.

"Why am I not surprised?" Tate muttered in disgust.

I stared back at Gavin and cocked an eyebrow at him. "What? It's a little bigoted to say you'd never date someone just because of how they were born, right? Almost as bigoted as saying you wouldn't date or mate with someone in a lower pack."

He couldn't keep eye contact with me. He knew I was right, and it shamed him that his own family had rejected me for it. The whole thing with Wyatt was nothing but pretense. Jayson had wanted out, and his father had wanted him to *get* out. They'd used that accident with the lion shifter to get rid of me, the poor little woman from a lesser pack.

Chelsey stared at the floor, absorbing my words. From the look on her face, she, too, was reconsidering her worldview. She'd had almost the same thing happen to her.

"Wyatt?" Von prompted.

He leaned back in his seat, looking as cool as I'd ever seen him look. "I've dated people who weren't shifters. Short relationships, but it happened. I don't see a problem with it. You love who you love, right?"

I'd heard a bit about Wyatt's romantic exploits over the years, so his answer came as no surprise to me. In fact, to my shame, I'd made fun of him when he'd dated a human woman a few years before. Remembering that made me feel a little dirty.

"He's right," J.D. said, leaning forward with a new fire in his eyes. "You love who you love."

"I agree with them," Mika said. "If I ever found someone I truly loved, I'd never let them go. Doesn't matter if they were a shifter, human, or even a damn mermaid. As long as she let me love her completely and we could be faithful to each other, it would be all I needed. Who gives a shit about tradition?"

Chelsey and I gaped at him. Mika wasn't one for a lot of words, so it was a bit funny, seeing him act all romantic now. I'd never have believed it from the broody, tortured alpha.

"Enough softball questions," Von added with a grin. "Let's get dirty. If you could eliminate one contestant right now, who would it be?" His eyes glimmered with malice.

The question made me uncomfortable, not only because he wanted me to answer it, but because it might stir up a lot of drama. Of course, that was exactly what Von wanted.

Abel, Chelsey, and I passed on the question. When J.D. also passed, Von rolled his eyes and groaned. "Oh, come on. We all know your lives would be a little easier if a certain person was gone. Tate, surely you have an answer?"

Tate chewed at the inside of his cheek and glared at Wyatt, then grinned. "You know, Von, now that you mention it, I wouldn't mind seeing Wyatt kick the bucket."

"Same here," Gavin chimed in, staring daggers at Wyatt.

Wyatt also passed on the question, though he gave Gavin and Tate a wink after doing so. Mika, obviously a little more confident, went last and glanced over his shoulder at Tate. "I'm tired of this guy's mouth, so I'd pick him."

Tate blinked at him in surprise. "Damn, what did I ever do to you?"

"Again," Mika said, "that mouth just won't stop, will it?"

"All right," Von said, interjecting before Tate could retort. "One more question, and I think it's a fitting one. This is *The Reject Project*, after all. As all of you here have been rejected in the past, would any of *you* reject a mate now?"

A lead ball settled into my gut while shame and remorse flooded my mind. From the very beginning, my plan was to reject whoever I ended up with if I won. My reasoning was based on the greater good of everyone, not only my pack. The favor from Heline could quite possibly prevent an entire war with hundreds of lives saved, and daily life wouldn't be turned upside down by pissed-off wolf shifters. The good should have outweighed the bad, but all I could see now was the mental devastation I would put one of these guys through. I didn't even know if I *could* reject anyone after everything I'd been through. Even if they didn't die and I somehow managed to get them to Haven, I had to consider the mental and emotional toll my rejection would exact. I'd never liked Jayson, but the rejection had still been painful. How could I possibly do that to someone else, especially if that someone was Wyatt?

Almost as though he heard me thinking about him, Wyatt caught my eye. Through his facial expression alone, I saw he understood how this question made me feel. He sat stoically, but his eyes spoke volumes.

Von went around the room, asking the others, but Wyatt and I maintained eye contact, communicating everything while saying nothing. Finally, he lifted a hand. Crossing his middle and index fingers, he slid his palm down his chest. Another TO hand signal—*everything is fine*. I nodded and tried to push my inner turmoil to the back of my mind.

"Kira?" I flinched at the sound of Von's voice. "How do you feel about that? Would you reject someone?"

For a few seconds, I thought I might come up with a diplomatic answer, but the truth came spilling out. "It's a disgusting thing to do. I'd feel like a terrible person for putting another shifter through what I've gone through. Unless there's physical or emotional abuse at play, I think you should honor the person you are fated to."

It was the truth, but it still didn't erase the reason I'd come on the show. In fact, admitting how I really felt in front of an audience made me feel like an even bigger piece of shit for what I had planned.

After Wyatt and Abel gave similar answers to mine, Von put the note card down and grinned at the camera. "There's a lot to unpack here after all these deep questions. I'm sure everyone at home will be discussing this on the message boards. Make sure you all tune in later this afternoon for our next jungle challenge. I can assure you it's going to be extra fun. You will not going to want to miss it. Be back here, and never forget, everyone loves an underdog."

The camera stopped recording, our bracelet lights flashed to yellow, and Von sighed as though he'd just finished some grueling race.

"There, now," he said to us. "That wasn't so bad was it?"

"Better than last time," Chelsey muttered. "At least I didn't almost die."

The last time we'd answered questions, she'd ended up drinking wolfsbane, so I supposed she was right on that account.

Von pointed at Chelsey and let out a belly laugh, slapping his knee as if she'd said the funniest thing he'd ever heard. "It looks like Kira's sass is rubbing off on you, Miss Rein." He made a show of wiping away tears of laughter before looking at Chelsey and me again. "I know I keep saying this, but remember, this is all a game. None of this is personal to me."

I wondered if that was true. The vampire may have been following orders, but to me, he seemed to take an unusual amount of pleasure in our discomfort.

Hopefully, we could make *him* uncomfortable soon.

Chapter 16 - Wyatt

Von's last words struck a chord with me. We were all a bit more relaxed after the Q&A, including him. Maybe now was when I could dig.

"Hey, Von?" I called.

The host turned his expectant gaze to me. "Yes, Mr. Rivers?"

"What *would* make things personal for you?"

Von made a *pfft* sound and waved my question away. "At my advanced age, not much truly bothers me. Almost all other beings have such short lifespans that it's hard to get caught up in things the way you all do. If I took everything you poor creatures did or said personally, my long life would be beyond miserable. I'd have walked into the sun without protection or fallen on a stake by now."

"Really?" J.D. asked. "It's that simple for you?"

Von shrugged. "What can I say? I love what I do and the drama I get to witness. Speaking of, I think the fans are going to love what we have coming up this afternoon."

What we needed was some way to make Von hate his job or do something to lose the fanbase. That prospect looked more difficult than ever, especially after what he'd just said. The guy acted like his entire reason for being was the show itself. Whatever we did, it needed to be aggressive.

Von clapped his hands. "I need you to go get ready for the challenge. The team has placed some outfits for you in your quarters." He glanced at his watch and huffed. "I suppose I won't get time for my massage, after all. Damn the luck. Oh, well. I'll meet all of you down at the back door in thirty minutes."

The host hopped off the stool and slinked out the door with the rest of the staff, the hovering cameras following along like dejected puppies. Two witches waited outside the door to lead the men back to the alpha den and the ladies back to their suites.

I needed a moment alone with Kira, but the pushy witch rushed her and Chelsey away before I could even try. Instead, I followed the others back to the bunk room. The whole time, I pondered all the ways I could tip Von over the edge, but none of my ideas held up under scrutiny.

The outfit laid out on my bed looked more like a uniform than the tactical outfits we'd worn in past challenges. I couldn't describe it as anything other than gaudy. I'd never seen anything like the bright golden fabric. When I picked it up, the light caught the outfit and made it shimmer like liquid gold. Weird.

The strange jumpsuit was a little tight once I had it on. Not quite as bad as a leotard or something, but still snug. I felt ridiculous, but I was sure Von would soon enlighten us as to why we were dressed like circus performers.

"What the hell is this?" Tate grumbled as he stood in front of a mirror and gawked at himself. "We look like idiots."

He was right, but I didn't want to agree with him. Instead, I headed for the door, ready to get this over with. The others followed a few moments later, their boots thumping along behind me.

At the staircase leading down to the main level, we met Chelsey and Kira coming down. I gaped at Kira. The ladies had similar suits to us, but it seemed that Von wanted to play up the sex appeal. Kira and

Chelsey's outfits were skintight, more like body paint than fabric.

Kira rolled her eyes when she saw me checking her out. "Don't say shit. I know I look ridiculous."

"You look great to me," Gavin said from behind me, and I suppressed the urge to kick him in the balls.

"There you are," Von called up the stairs. "Come on down. We'll head outside before we start."

Von strode to the door and flung it open. As soon as he stepped out, an umbrella materialized and hovered over him to keep the sunlight off his delicate face. The group trundled down the stairs to follow him. I moved to join, but Kira grabbed my hand, forcing me to stop. When I looked back to see what was wrong, she was staring at the back of Mika's head. She looked at me with wide, insistent eyes and jerked her chin toward Mika.

"Huh?"

Slowly, we descended the stairs. Kira looked at me like I was a dumbass, then jerked her head toward Mika again with more urgency. Suddenly, the pieces fell into place in my mind. I mouthed, *Zoe?*

Kira nodded and pointed at Mika once more. She'd gotten another message from Zoe. Mika would be our target for rescue during the challenge. That had to be what she wanted to tell me. Cameras and recording equipment were everywhere, and there was no way to say it out loud, but I got the gist. Through the crowd of alphas and staff, I watched Mika as we headed outside. I had to get word to him.

Doing my best not to draw attention, I quickened my stride to catch up to him. I needed to talk to him before Von launched into whatever spiel he planned to give. I touched his shoulder, and Mika turned, raising a questioning eyebrow.

"What's up?" Mika asked.

I smiled. "Hey, man. I just wanted to say good luck," I said, raising my voice to make sure everyone could hear. "You're a great guy, Mika." I leaned in and hugged him.

"Pansy assholes," Tate muttered as he walked past us.

Mika stiffened when I hugged him. He knew something was up. Before he could pull away, I put my lips to his ear. "It's happening. Heads up and be ready to be a guinea pig."

My lips were right next to his ear. Even then, my voice was so quiet, I wasn't sure if he could hear me. But when he pulled away, his eyes were blazing with excitement.

"Seriously?" he asked.

"It's time," I said with a nod.

Mika took a deep breath. "Okay. All right. I'll be ready."

I clapped a firm hand on his shoulder. "Good. Knock 'em dead out there, bro."

As we rejoined the group, I sent Kira a look. When she saw me, I gave her a hand signal as surreptitiously as I could, letting her know we were all set. She smiled back, and her face relaxed a bit. We were as prepared as we were going to be.

Cameras came swooping out of the mansion. One of them shot high into the sky, then slowly lowered. Von stood beneath it with his arms wide open, grinning up at the lens. It would probably end up being the most dramatic opening shot in history.

"Good afternoon. We come to you from Bloodstone Island for another deliciously dangerous challenge," Von said once the camera was close enough to hear him. He swept a hand toward us, showing the whole world our stupid, shimmery outfits. "Behold—our alphas and prize mates. Our numbers have dwindled, but the passion has not. Each of these lovely people is ready and willing to show you what they've got."

I flinched as someone touched my back. Whirling, I found one of the staff witches. She moved down the line, touching each cast member's zipper. A spell? Von kept yammering on while I reached over my shoulder and tried to pull the zipper down, but it was locked in place by whatever the witch had done. Panic filled my chest. Why the hell did they need to magically lock the zippers? There was nothing to do but listen and find out. I returned my attention to Von.

"Now, for today's challenge..." He pointed to the sky. "It's late afternoon. That is a very important time. Many creatures are out hunting at this time of day. Our contestants will be part of that hunt. Each member of our cast will be sent into the jungle to hunt a specific creature. Simple enough, yes?" The vampire smirked wickedly. "But there is a catch. Late afternoon is the time when the island griffins are most active in their hunts."

"Oh, fuck," I muttered, understanding dawning on me.

"Griffins," Von went on, "are typically not a danger to higher-cognition creatures. They tend to only eat fish, smaller mammals and reptiles, and the occasional deer or small river serpent. However, what they truly love is gold and treasure. For centuries, the creatures have been known to fill their nests with loot stolen from pirates, kings, and warlords. As you can see, our contestants have been dressed to be very, shall we say, conspicuous. Any griffin coming across them will take their special outfits to be a treasure and won't hesitate to rip them to shreds to get that fabric off them." Von smiled ruefully. "Our staff of witches has bewitched the suits to be unremovable, but the contestants *can* shift with them. We don't want them to be completely defenseless, now do we? Of course not. When they shift, the suit will morph around their bodies."

J.D. nudged me and whispered. "I thought you said griffins don't hurt people? When we heard one screeching the other day, you said that, didn't you?"

"I said they don't attack you *unless* you have something shiny they want. Well, now we *are* the shiny thing they want," I hissed.

"Crap." J.D. shook his head and went back to listening to Von.

"We are giving our contestants more free rein this time. They can pair up or go it alone on their hunts. They can move through the jungle as a group, like they moved through the swamps in one of the earlier challenges. To kick things up a notch, though, there is a one-hour time limit. If they have not returned from hunting their creature in one hour, the protective wards around the mansion will slam shut and lock them out."

This challenge was designed to get at least one or two eliminations. For once, that worked in our favor, as long as we didn't get killed by griffins or other monsters before getting Mika to Zoe and Crew.

"Time for our contestants to choose their prey." Von held up a hand, and two of the witches walked over, each holding a shiny brass bowl in their palm. "In one bowl, we have contestant names, and in the other, we have the creatures you will each hunt. I'll pull names and creatures at random. The slip of cotton bearing the creature's name also holds their scent. That will give you a good start on finding them." He paused for a moment to put a hand to his chest. "I do want to send my deepest condolences to the families of the staff members who retrieved these scents. A very sad day that was. Anyhow, on with the show."

Von put his free hand into the name bowl and swirled it around before pulling the first victim. He grinned. "Chelsey." He then pulled her creature. "Oh, looks like you'll be hunting a feral bear shifter."

Chelsey swallowed hard and nodded. Von went through the names and creatures. J.D. was to hunt a mad vampire. Gavin got to hunt a ghost, and a witch handed him an enchanted weapon to complete the task. Tate received a demon, and the big man did not look happy about it. Abel was given a corrupted fae, and Mika, a banshee.

It wasn't lost on me that Kira and I were the last names to be drawn. The witches had probably bewitched the bowls to ensure Von drew our names last. I wouldn't put anything past the show at this point.

Von's eyes brightened when he pulled my name. "Wyatt Rivers. Oh, let's see what you'll be going after." He dug into the other bowl and read the flapping piece of fabric. He let out a theatrical gasp, and I knew I was screwed before he even said anything. "Wendigo."

A little sigh drifted out of my chest. Of course. I'd seen one a while back during one of the challenges. It was probably the only one on the whole island since the things were incredibly rare. Of course Von would give that thing to me, but at least Kira didn't have to go after it.

The witch walked over and handed me the fabric. I sniffed it, catching the scent—rotten meat, fetid musk, and something like ammonia.

While I memorized the scent, Von pulled the final name out of the bowl. Mostly for show since everyone on earth knew Kira's name was all that remained.

"Kira Durst," Von said with a little giggle. "Who else *could* it be? Looks like you've won the prize." He pulled a final piece of cloth from the other bowl. "A surprise."

"Huh? What does that mean?" Kira asked, taking the words right out of my mouth.

Von waved the cloth toward her. "Exactly what it sounds like, silly. The creature you are to hunt is one we have no name for. It's only been glimpsed three or four times. The staff member who went in search of it managed to track it down and get the scent, but..." Von made an awkward face and shrugged. "All we found of the poor man was his severed hand holding this." Von shook the cloth again. "I think you'll be up for the task, though."

The rat bastard was screwing with her on purpose. All the rest of us knew what we were hunting. Even the ones who weren't trained could at least make some sort of game plan. Kira couldn't even use all the thousands of hours of training and research she'd done as an operative to figure out how to take down her quarry. All she would get was a few seconds before the thing tried to rip her apart.

"A little good news for everyone," Von added. "You do not have to kill the creature. Though, if you do, kudos to you. With only one hour, we understand that time will be a little tight for you to bring down most of the creatures you are going after. So, what will we require as proof? A body or head, if you are feeling very frisky, but in lieu of that, a token is all that's needed for success. A demon horn, a claw, ectoplasm, some fur—you get the idea. Any questions?"

There were none. We were all too worried about what we had to do over the next hour. Before Von could say anything else, a blood-curdling shriek came from deep in the jungle. A moment later, a responding call echoed from even deeper. Griffins.

"It sounds like our special guests are ready," Von said with a wink to the camera. He turned and pointed at an archway carved into the jungle's foliage. "That is the starting and finishing line. No paths this time. Once inside, you are free to go wherever you want on the island. On my mark, your timer will begin. Three... two... one... go!"

There was no time to think or worry, no time to formulate a plan. The others knew it, too. The mad rush of people running toward the jungle reminded me of people fleeing disaster, running from a flood or fire. The only difference was, we were running *toward* danger instead of away from it.

Tate, Chelsey, and J.D. shifted even before we entered the jungle. Von was right—the golden suits morphed to fit the wolf bodies perfectly. I decided to get my bearings first once we were in the jungle before deciding what to do next. Behind me, I could hear Von and a few of the staff members clapping as we rushed into the jungle. Kira, always a faster runner than me in human form, burst through the archway and into the shadows of the jungle. Digging my toes into the ground, I put on more speed to catch up to her. More cameras appeared and zoomed in to follow each of us.

The noise of Von and the others clapping vanished as soon as I ran through the archway and entered the jungle. Kira stood there, waiting for me. Surprised, I almost crashed into her. Her hand found mine, the warmth of her fingers a comfort to me. Around us, the others bolted in multiple directions to pursue their marks.

"I thought you were gonna leave me for a second there," I said.

Kira grinned at me. "Nah. I need you around in case I have to trip you. It's like they say—you don't have to outrun a bear; you only have to outrun the person with you."

"Very funny," I grunted. "What's the plan?"

"I think we should go for the wendigo first. We know what it looks like and have a basic idea of how to fight it. Once it's been taken down, we can go after whatever the hell I'm supposed to be hunting."

"Then Mika?" I ask.

"Yeah. We'll need to see if we can check his progress." She sighed and looked into the jungle. "I kind of wish he'd stayed with us. We could help him get—"

I pressed a finger to her lips, then looked over at the camera hovering a few feet away.

Kira's eyes popped wide. The cameras were around all the time, essentially part of the scenery. We didn't want the showrunners to know what our plan was for Mika. We had to play it off like whatever happened to Mika was what the showrunners expected.

I took my finger away, and Kira played it off well. "Getting touchy there, aren't you, big guy? We can have some fun once we're out of this death trap. Anyway, like I was saying, I want to see if we can help Mika get his banshee hunted down. But first, the wendigo. Have you caught the scent yet?"

Tilting my head back, I pulled in a deep breath, catching the creature's scent. It was at least a thousand yards away.

"That way," I said, pointing to the east.

We ran as fast as our human legs would allow, the pungent stink of the thing drawing nearer with every step. When the smell grew stronger, I put a hand on Kira's arm, signaling her to stop running.

"Are we close?" she asked.

"We are. We don't want to attack it head-on, though. They're incredibly dangerous."

"Flank it?" Kira suggested.

"Yup," I said, pointing to the northeast. "If we go that way, we'll be downwind of it. We can get close and attack before it realizes we're there."

"Are we sure that's going to work? These things aren't actually *living* creatures. It could sense us some other way."

Wendigos were one of the few magical creatures not fully understood by our world. Some legends said they were once humans who had to resort to cannibalism. Others claimed they were remnants of demigods associated with hunger and feasts from some long-forgotten religion. The one common thread between all the stories was that they had a ravenous hunger and attacked indiscriminately. In my experience, anything that hunted still used its five senses to track.

"I think it will," I said. "And if not? We improvise."

"Wow. Good plan."

"Smartass. Come on."

Kira and I moved through the jungle, angling in behind the wendigo. Even Kira could scent the thing now. I thought I could hear tearing sounds as well. I wasn't sure what that was, but it came from the same direction as the scent. In the back of my mind, the seconds ticked away on the clock. We'd already been in the jungle for more than five minutes. An hour was *not* a lot of time to accomplish everything we had to do.

After another minute or two, I finally caught sight of the beast. My hand tightened on Kira's, and I pointed through the foliage toward it. She froze and knelt, gazing out to where I pointed.

The thing shouldn't have been able to move. There were almost no muscles in its body, just skin stretched over bones. Patchy fur hung in loose clips up and down its limbs like mange. It hunched over what looked like a dead tiger—the black-and-orange stripes stood out in stark relief to the gray and brown of the wendigo. It was probably a feral tiger shifter that the monster had hunted down.

Kira and I flinched as the thing yanked its head to the side, tearing a hunk of flesh and fur from the tiger. Blood sprayed across the leaves around it.

I watched in disgust as the wendigo tilted its head back and opened its skeletal mouth. The entire mass of meat slid down its gullet. The emaciated thing swallowed, and its belly distended as the flesh settled into it. After swallowing, it went right back to the meal, burying its head and shredding more meat from the corpse.

With a few hand signals, I told Kira to wait there while I snuck up on it to take a bit of fur. If I could go silently, I might be able to get it without the creature ever knowing, but I'd have to be nearly silent. Shifting, I inched forward. My wolf paws were much quieter than my big, booted human feet.

Every inch brought me closer to a dangerous creature. If it had taken down a feral tiger shifter, there was no telling what it could do to me if I made a mistake. Keeping my eyes locked on the thing's back, I crept ever closer. I hunched directly behind it, the awful reeking stink of it making my wolf eyes water. Fuck. How would I take the fur without it noticing?

Frozen by indecision, I watched it swallow another chunk of meat. It had to be getting full. At any moment, it might turn around, satiated, and find me there. Even if it wasn't hungry, it would still try to kill me. What could I do? Reach out and yank a chunk of its fur off, bolt, and hope for the best?

Then I noticed the paw. A huge tiger paw lay beneath the undergrowth to my left. The appendage looked ragged and torn, obviously ripped off during whatever battle had taken place between the two creatures. That didn't matter. All that mattered was the hunk of ragged flesh hanging from the claw—a sliver of fur and skin from the wendigo. I glanced back and forth, making sure the color and texture matched. Relief flooded through me as I leaned forward as silently as I could and plucked the skin off the claw with my teeth.

An immediate and almost debilitating nausea filled my stomach at the taste of it, but I suppressed a shudder and slowly backed away. Inching toward Kira, I kept an eye on the monster. When I finally made it back, I felt more exhausted than I should have been. I shifted and tucked the skin into a zippered pocket on the left hip of my outfit.

Once we were away from the wendigo, I sighed with relief. "That was intense."

We stepped out into a clearing in the jungle. Kira opened her mouth to agree, but a piercing scream from above cut her off. We looked up at the massive griffin swooping out of the canopy toward us. Sunlight shimmered across our outfits, making us look like freaking gold coins. The beast's scream rattled in my brain, making my ears ring.

"Run!" I yelled, grabbing Kira's hand and ducking back into the jungle from where we'd just come.

Above us, the griffin descended like wrath itself from the sky. Its huge twenty-foot wingspan blotted out the sun as it drew near. Its front paws stretched forward, talons grazing Kira's back, but it didn't slice through her outfit. The beast pulled its wings in and tumbled on the ground before leaping up to chase us through the jungle on foot.

The thing was fast. It looked like a hawk and lion had mated and spawned some freak with the body, back legs, and tail of a lion and the head, wings, and front feet of a bird of prey. Even with its bulky wings folded at its back, it managed to duck and dodge the branches growing nearer every step.

As we ran, the panic that seized me made it hard to understand where we were going. We were running directly back toward the wendigo, but if we altered course, the griffin would be on us. It snapped at my heels with its beak, and my suit tore at my calf where it nipped me, missing the skin by a millimeter.

Ahead of me, Kira screamed and jumped to the side. For a second, my eyes widened as I came face to face with the reason she'd screamed. Drawn by the noise, the wendigo had come running toward us. The zombie-eyed creature rushed straight toward me, arms and taloned fingers extended in front of it, mouth open, tatters of flesh still hanging from its jagged teeth. I was about to be smashed between two nightmares. Copying Kira, I leaped to the side, praying to the gods I might survive.

Instead of both creatures leaping upon and devouring me, they slammed into each other. The wendigo and griffin began rolling and fighting across the ground. The griffin outweighed the other creature by at least a couple hundred pounds, but the wendigo's bizarre, mystical strength made the fight much more even than it should have been. In seconds, the wendigo had shattered the griffin's left wing. The griffin tried clawing out the wendigo's throat, but only managed to tear three deep slashes down the creature's chest.

Kira stared in wide-eyed shock as the two beasts tried to devour each other. Not giving a damn which one won, only wanting to get the hell away while they were occupied, I scrambled over and grabbed Kira's hand.

"Let's get the hell out of here. Come on." I tugged her to her feet and ran.

Behind us, the sounds of the scuffle grew even more chaotic until the griffin's triumphant screech echoed through the jungle. It had either killed the wendigo or had gotten free. Kira and I hurried on, but soon, the sounds of a thundering, hurt, and angry beast reached our ears. It was still coming for us.

The jungle had given way to a boggy swamp filled with pools of viscous mud and mangroves. Glancing behind us, I took in the silhouette of the griffin running through the forest, dragging its ruined wing behind it. How could the fucker be so fast?

Before I managed to turn back around, Kira yanked me off the side of the path and down into one of the mud pools. She dragged me under, mud coating my body and splashing around my face.

"What the fuck?" I sputtered.

"Shut up," Kira hissed. She scooped up big handfuls of mud and smeared them over every inch of my body.

Like a light switch clicking on, I understood what she was doing. I started covering her in mud, making sure to get every inch. The shimmery golden fabric vanished under the thick brown mud. The griffin came stomping through a few seconds later. It turned its baleful yellow eyes on us as it passed, but without the temptation of the gold, it continued on. Once it was well away, I lay back in the mud, sighing with relief.

"Pretty smart, huh?" Kira said.

I grinned at her. "I mean, it would have been better if we could have tried to cut the outfits off. My day would have gotten a whole lot better seeing you running around the jungle all naked and sweaty, but I guess mud-wrestling will have to suffice."

"Would you shut up? You realize we're fighting for our lives here, right?"

Wiping a glob of mud off my chin, I chuckled. "Hey, if I'm gonna die, I'll die with a smile on my face."

"Well, as romantic as your advances are, I don't think you want your dangly bits to be bitten off by some passing monster."

I winced. "Point taken. How much time do we have left?"

Kira looked at her bracelet. The bracelets all had a small display that functioned as a watch. "Shit, we only have thirty-three minutes left."

Crap. Going after the wendigo had taken far longer than I'd thought. The griffin attack had eaten away nearly ten minutes, too. We had to hurry.

"Do you have the scent of your creature?" I asked.

Kira dug her fingers through the mud to find the zippered pocket. She pulled the fabric out and took a long sniff, then scented the air and frowned. "I'm not getting anything yet. Maybe we're too far away from it?"

I sniffed the air, too. Maybe I could help. If it was unusual or strange, I might be able to pick it up. Though, it wasn't the smell of the monster I noticed. Instead, it was a couple of scents I knew very well.

Kira saw my eyes go wide. "What's wrong?"

"It's Mika and Gavin."

She smiled, but it vanished when she caught the scent. Strong and metallic. Blood. Lots of blood.

"We need to hurry," she said.

"Yeah, let's go." Hand in hand, we sprinted into the woods, following our noses in the direction of their scents. We ascended a small hill, climbing over thick, prickly bushes that choked the path. Once through, we climbed another small hill that ended on a large open plateau. What we saw stopped us in our tracks.

Blood was splattered everywhere—on the leaves and moss, the tree trunks, and the ground. Even worse, there were what looked like wolf body parts. A leg lay only a few feet from me. It had the same grayish hue as Mika's wolf.

A scream tore me from my thoughts. At the furthest end of the small plateau, Gavin lay on his back, swinging a stick at a large reptilian ghost. Gavin was not in good shape. Blood smeared his entire face, and a nasty gash ran down his left cheek all the way to his neck. Another wound must have taken him in the leg because his entire golden suit was shredded below the knee, showing nothing but red.

Gavin saw us and screamed. "Help me! Oh, gods, help me!"

The panic in his voice made me forget how much I disliked him. Kira and I rushed forward. The ghost spun when it heard us. The thing was awful to behold. Whatever it had been in life, death had twisted it into something that should have only resided in nightmares. Kira bent and scooped up the enchanted weapon—a metallic scepter that Gavin must have dropped during the fight.

The ghost drove toward me, lunging to claw out my throat with the kinetic energy ghosts drew from some unknown power source. Before he caught me, I dived to the side and rolled away. It turned, translucent eyes following me, and it left its blindside open.

Kira jammed the scepter into it. With a flash of light, the ghost rushed deep into the forest, either terrified of or injured by the magical weapon.

Unconsciously, I scooped up a jelly-like chunk of ectoplasm and shoved it into a zippered pocket on my suit, then went to Gavin. Kira was kneeling beside him, checking his injuries. It didn't look good. The ghost had almost taken his jugular.

His leg looked even worse. A deep gash in his calf exposed muscle and fascia.

"Kira?" Gavin whispered, his voice hoarse from pain and screaming. "Help me up. I'll help you hunt your creature."

"Gavin, you aren't going anywhere like that," I said as I snatched up a length of golden fabric that had been part of an outfit some time ago.

I handed it to Kira, who quickly made a tourniquet with the fabric and a stick nearby. "He's right, Gavin. We need to get you back to the mansion. The healers need to get to you before it's too late."

He struggled to his feet, wincing as he put weight on his damaged leg. To my surprise, he didn't complain or whine, just tightened the tourniquet.

What he said next surprised me even more. "You're right. I'll get in the way if I try to help you. I'll head back." It looked like it physically pained him to say those words.

"Here, man. You'll need this for them to let you back in." I dug into my pocket, pulled out the ectoplasm, and put it in his hand.

Gavin stowed it away and gave me a nod, the closest I'd ever get to a *thank you*.

"You good?" I asked, nodding to his leg.

"I'll be fine," he grunted.

"Be careful, Gavin," Kira said.

He smiled at her, but the cut on his face had him wincing. "Yeah. You too. Wyatt, you get her back in one piece or you'll answer to me. Got it?"

Now wasn't the time to argue, so I played along. "Got it, big guy."

Gavin turned to limp away, but Kira stopped him. "Gavin, wait. Was Mika here with you? It, uh, looks like he was." She glanced down at a bloody piece of fur and skin by her foot. "Did... did you see him die?"

Gavin shook his head but pointed at the flesh on the ground. "No, but you're right. I don't think he made it. I'm sorry. I know you liked him." Regardless of his words, it was obvious he didn't really give a damn that Mika might be dead.

The cameras swooped in to get a good shot of Gavin hobbling away into the forest. Kira stared at the gore surrounding the area, her face pensive and worried. Honestly, I was worried as well. The leg *really* looked like it came from Mika's wolf.

She looked ready to break down into sobs. I pulled her close, hugging her hard and pressing my lips to her ear to ensure the cameras wouldn't hear. "If Zoe took him and this is staged, she may have left a sign or something. You can send word to Zoe and find out the truth. Do not panic or freak out until we're sure. Okay?"

"What if we waited too long? What if he's actually dead? If he is, it really is my fault."

"Hush. Let's see if Zoe left any signal or clues," I said, trying to cut off Kira's negative thoughts before they destroyed any hope she had left.

We searched the area quickly. Anyone watching the video feed would have no idea what we were doing. As we looked for any sign of fae magic or some clue that Zoe and Crew had managed to get Mika out, I worried that Kira might be right. Could Mika really be dead? Torn apart by some awful creature? I'd considered him a friend. He was a guy I could have seen joining my unofficial pack.

"I don't see anything," Kira huffed.

"Neither do I," I said. "What's our time look like?"

Kira glanced at her bracelet. "Less than twenty minutes."

"We've got to go. We're running out of time to find your monster."

Kira cast a glance around again, zeroing in on the hunk of wolf leg lying at the edge of the plateau. "But what about—"

"We can't worry about that now. We have a mission to accomplish. We can think of other things when that's done."

She looked drained beyond belief, but she stepped toward me. "Okay. Yeah. Let's find it." Her voice was hollow and full of regret.

Taking her hand, I led her back into the forest, forcing myself not to look back at the remains of what might have been Mika. I could hold out hope. It was all I knew to do. There had to be a chance he'd made it.

Chapter 17 - Kira

Wyatt dragged me along, and I let him. I could barely keep my legs moving because of the dark thoughts swirling in my head. All that blood and torn body parts. Had that been Mika? If another contestant had died, I didn't know how I'd ever forgive myself.

A thousand different things rambled through my mind as we ran. Should we have tried sooner? Should we have tried to stay with him in the jungle? Had he not been focused on the dangers because he'd been too excited to get out? Dammit, I hated feeling this way.

After a few minutes of self-pity and sadness, I buckled down. We had fifteen minutes to find my creature and get back. No amount of introspection and hindsight would bring Mika back if he had died. Right now, I had to focus on what I *could* manage. Wyatt was still alive, and I needed to stay focused and do what needed to be done to keep it that way. Even though I'd been fired, I was and always would be a Tranquility operative. One thing that had been drilled into us in training was that if one member of the team went down, the rest had to go on and complete the mission. There'd be time to mourn afterward.

"This way," I said, pulling Wyatt's arm as I finally managed to catch the scent.

"You sure?"

"Yeah, I've never smelled anything like it before."

Taking the lead, I pushed my body to its limits, sprinting faster than I could ever remember running in my life. As powerful and athletic as Wyatt was, even he lagged behind me as I hurried to get to the creature.

I sensed rather than saw the vampires explode from the underbrush. The things were too emaciated and weak to have a chance at catching me. I passed them and made it twenty yards ahead before I skidded to a stop, turning to see if Wyatt was okay.

Wyatt, at a dead run, spotted the two vampires, reached out, and snapped two branches off a tree. Without breaking stride, he slammed the makeshift stakes into their chests and leaped over their tumbling bodies. He never even slowed down.

"Damn," I muttered. That had been impressive.

"Are we close?" he called as he quickly joined me.

I nodded and pointed down a small vine-choked ravine. "I think it's down there."

Wyatt glanced around and shook his head. "We're really far from the mansion. This is almost as far out as the volcano, just on the opposite side of the island. We need to hurry. It's gonna take every second to get back in time."

"Get a move on, then. Might as well see what this damn thing is."

Moving cautiously but quickly, Wyatt pushed through the vines and hanging tree branches. A cave was set back on the side of a hill. The foreboding black entrance yawned open like a gaping black maw, ready to swallow us. It gave me a moment of déjà vu. It wasn't exactly like the cave Wyatt had found me in all those years ago, but it was close enough to send a chill up my spine.

With time ticking away, we moved in less cautiously than we normally would. Typically, we'd check the perimeter, scent the area, then proceed into the cave slowly and with calculated precision. But with the time constraint hanging over us like a curse, we rushed in. Only the years of training made Wyatt and I slow to a fast walk rather than a full run.

The scent hit me first. Stronger than ever now, but it still made no sense. I smelled the mineral scent of a vampire, the muskiness of a bear shifter, and the wet-mud smell of a kappa. There were hints of other creatures as well. Had we somehow stumbled into some warren where multiple beasts nested together? That was almost too outlandish to consider.

We managed to get almost fifteen feet into the cave when the thing I'd been sent to hunt staggered out of the darkness. Wyatt and I froze. I'd assumed whatever Von sent me to hunt would be bad. Now that I witnessed what waited for us, I had a moment of worry that my brain was shattering. It shouldn't have been possible, yet here it was, walking toward us. A nightmare made real.

The cameras floated to the cave's ceiling, giving us a clear look at the monstrosity before us. It was like a bunch of beings and creatures had been thrown into a blender and made into an abomination. The back and haunches were thick and humped, covered in the brown hair of a grizzly shifter. It walked bipedally, standing upright. Further down, the fur gave way to the mottled lizard skin of a kappa, but the feet were humanoid. The toes were tipped in thick, wolfish nails.

The arms and face were the worst part. Heavily muscled, pale-skinned arms ended in paws that were some combination of bear, wolf, and human, with massive, glimmering claws hanging from each finger. The head was massive, like a bear's, but the face had a vampiric complexion and shape. Though the jaw was elongated a bit like a wolf's, when the thing opened its jaws, its vampire fangs were at least five times larger than they usually would be. The eyes were the yellowish frog-like orbs of a kappa.

I literally almost pissed myself. Nothing like this should have existed in nature. Whatever kind of magic had been at work here, I'd never seen the likes of it in any of my studies, which meant no one had ever seen anything like it before.

"What the fuck," Wyatt muttered.

At the sound of his voice, the creature swung its huge head toward us. Jaws snapped open and shut twice, the *pop-pop* sound echoing across the stone walls of the cave. But it didn't rush forward to devour us as I thought it would. Then I realized why. The yellow eyes were coated in milky cataracts. It was blind. Whether from age or from whatever horrifying spell had done this, I didn't care. It gave us a chance.

"It can't see," I said. The head swung toward me, trying to pin me down by hearing alone.

"Okay. Let's do this," Wyatt said.

As though it understood his words, the beast let out an ear-piercing shriek and lumbered forward, swinging those wickedly sharp claws at us. Tucking and rolling, I moved to the side. Wind blew past my face as it missed me by inches. When I came to a stop, I looked up at Wyatt, who lashed out with a kick, making contact with the arm and deflecting the thing's claws. Before I could stand, the other arm swung out and caught Wyatt in the shoulder. Not a damaging wound, but three long gashes appeared in his muddy outfit. Trickles of blood oozed out as he danced back out of reach.

There was no way we had time to kill it. All I had to get was a sample, and then we could run. But how? I stood, ready to attack the thing from behind, but my foot caught on something. The sound of clattering metal rang through the cave. Looking down, I saw an ancient, rusty hatchet on the ground. Some tool from the first explorers of Bloodstone? Maybe a weapon used in a past season? I didn't care—it was exactly what I needed. I scooped it up right as the creature spun on me. Its blind eyes gazed around dumbly as it tried to smell or hear me.

For its humongous size, it was fast as hell. The massive jaws snapped forward so quick that I barely had time to lean back. The teeth slammed together mere inches from my face, the stink of its breath almost making me gag. Before it could attack again, Wyatt leaped onto its back, wrapping his arms around the neck. He pulled back with all his might. The thing roared in anger and spun hard. The strength of its spin flung Wyatt off. He tumbled into a heap at the mouth of the cave.

With its back turned, I saw my chance. A strange tail hung from the thing's lower back, like a wolf's tail but hairless and almost reptilian in appearance. Before I could talk myself out of it, I rushed forward, hatchet held overhead. The tail dragged on the floor behind the creature, and when the ancient rusty tool slammed down on it, three inches of the tip sliced away. The impact snapped the hatchet to pieces.

The howl that filled the cave sent needles of pain into my ears, but I didn't bother looking at the beast. I grabbed the chunk of tail and rolled under its swinging arms. The monstrosity was still bellowing its pain and rage as I sprinted to the edge of the cave where Wyatt was struggling to his feet, a heavy gash bleeding above his eyebrow.

"I have it! Move!"

Without questioning me, Wyatt hauled ass after me. Behind us, the obscene monster screamed even louder. It was huge and strong as hell, but at least it didn't seem to want to leave its lair. It didn't even attempt to follow us.

"We have to hurry," I panted as we sprinted through the jungle. "Seven minutes left."

"Are we gonna make it?" Wyatt asked.

"Maybe, as long as nothing stops us."

Big tree leaves slapped at my face and my boots slid in the dead leaves, but I didn't slow down. Wyatt matched me step for step, and I made sure not to leave him behind. There was no reason for me to reach the mansion if he was left out here alone. At least if we were stuck out here, we could try to survive together and find Haven on our own.

"What the... fuck... could make that thing?" Wyatt said, gasping. "There's no way.... It was some... fluke of creature."

He was right. That monster *had* to have been created with some twisted magic. A warlock or fae, maybe a witch or even a human with a magically powered item. But why the fuck would anyone want to create such a thing?

"I have... no idea," I said, doing my best to save my breath. Shifters could run hard for a long time, but my strength was waning.

A faint memory of Zoe's last letter trickled into my brain. She'd mentioned some guy, Simon Shingleman. The one experimenting on the creatures on the island and the people hiding in Haven when they were caught. Could that guy have created that monster? Icy dread trickled down my spine at the thought.

"Do you think the witches on the show somehow made it?" Wyatt asked as we passed through the swamp area again.

I glanced at the ever-present camera above us. "I doubt it. Von loves to get into detail on shit like this. If he knew exactly what it was, he'd have given a ten-minute description about all the ways it would rip our guts out and feast on our corpses." I leaned close and lowered my voice so the microphone wouldn't pick it up. "I have an idea about it. I'll tell you when we get back." I finished speaking right as the hovering camera shot down to try and pick up my words. I refrained from flipping it off, but only barely.

A giant griffin fluttered overhead, looking down at us. The gigantic wings flapped as it spun in a lazy circle. Thankfully, we were still coated in dried mud, so instead of attacking, he caught an updraft and soared away.

Our luck didn't hold out for long. We were within sight of the mansion, with only two minutes left, when our path was blocked. Three snarling feral wolf shifters emerged from the jungle to stand in our way.

I felt an immediate tinge of sadness that none of them were Leif. He'd been turned feral, but maybe this time would have been different than the last. It would have been good to at least try to talk some sense into him. Instead, we faced these three things that were ready to rip our throats out.

One of the shifters leaped forward—obviously, the leader of their little pack—and the two others followed. Wyatt shifted and jumped into the fight, catching the biggest one before it could attack either of us.

The leader pounced, launching itself toward me with its mouth open, saliva-coated fangs shimmering in the late afternoon light. Without even thinking, I let my training and muscle memory take over. I jumped into a backflip, then spun, my right foot kicking out and catching the wolf in the throat. Cartilage cracked and collapsed beneath the toe of my boot, crushing the wolf's windpipe. I landed on one knee, a single hand on the ground as the lead wolf collapsed, gagging and trying to breathe through its ruined throat. Ignoring it, I stalked toward the remaining wolf.

Even feral, it must have seen something in my eyes that let it know that discretion was the better part of valor. It whined, then bolted off into the jungle.

Behind me, a loud, painful yelp cracked through my focus. Spinning on my heel, I was ready to help Wyatt, but he was already shifting back to his human form. The wolf he'd fought limped away, blood pouring from massive wounds on its chest and back leg.

Wyatt grabbed me and ran, pulling me hard enough to make my wrist pop. "Hurry!"

As we ran, I glanced down at my bracelet. We had less than fifteen seconds to get in. I could see the courtyard through the foliage. I could even see Von standing under that ridiculous umbrella of his. The fucker actually waved at us like we were friends walking up the path for a goddamned tea party.

I watched it happen. A silvery shimmer appeared near the top of the mansion's roof and spread out, lowering itself around the entire property. The standard spells kept out all the creepy nasties that would love to murder anyone in the house, but this was a spell intended for the contestants and any other sentient, sane creatures. Von was going to watch us get locked out.

Wyatt let go of my hand. "You're faster than me. Go. Leave me."

"No fucking way."

I grabbed *his* hand and poured on even more speed. It was faster than he'd ever run in his life, I knew. He might lose his footing, but either way, he'd be stuck outside. Might as well push as hard as we could.

The shimmer of the boundary spell lowered further, inching closer to the ground as the last few seconds ticked away. My mouth was stuck in a rictus grin of determination as I dragged Wyatt along behind me. Five feet from the periphery, I jumped, diving like a baseball player stealing home. Wyatt dived along with me. We slid under the lowering spell an instant before it slammed down. Rolling over, I sucked in gasping breaths as I tried to recover.

The translucent spell vanished. If I hadn't known better, I'd have never known it was there.

"My goodness!" Von shouted. "Douglas! Did you get that? Tell me you caught that shit on camera!"

"Three different cameras got it, boss," one of the techs said.

"Magnificent," Von chuckled. "Welcome back, you two. I'm being honest when I say we were all sure you two were done for. Even when I saw you coming down the path, I didn't think you had time."

I rolled over, still panting, and glared at him. "What were you doing? Waving fucking goodbye?"

Von shrugged and knelt beside us. "Well, actually, yes. Though, I am glad you made it. Things just wouldn't be the same without you."

Having caught my breath, I looked around and surveyed the damage. It seemed everyone had returned except Mika. J.D. and Gavin were being attended to by healers. Gavin still looked rough, but the wounds on his face and neck were already fading. J.D. had several bites on his neck and shoulders that had to have been from vampires. Near them, Abel paced back and forth, his golden suit torn and tattered almost to the point that it was falling off him. From the looks of it, Tate had gone through the worst. He was wrapped in a towel and appeared to be naked underneath.

Wyatt, on his hands and knees, stared at Tate. "Where the hell are your clothes?"

Tate scowled at him. "I found a sharp rock and cut them off. Did the whole thing naked."

"That poor jungle," Wyatt said with a smartass grin. "It's gonna need therapy after seeing that."

"Fuck off, Wyatt." Tate turned and stalked away to stand near Chelsey. She looked unhurt, but pretty worn out and disheveled.

Von stepped in front of a camera and clapped his hands while looking at all of us. "Bravo, everyone, bravo. I do have to let our fans know that we've had another unfortunate elimination, finally. Poor Mika Sheen is no longer an option for Kira or Chelsey. Our staff says his camera malfunctioned during the event. Thankfully, we had a backup nearby that caught the action." Von snapped his fingers, and a large flat-screen monitor floated from a tent off to the side of the courtyard. It hovered toward him like the cameras. "We don't want anyone to miss the show. So, a quick replay."

I hurried over to watch. Good or bad, I had to have some sort of closure. Part of me worried that if Zoe had taken Mika, this secondary camera might reveal them, and then the showrunners would know something was up. But even that possibility was better than the thought of Mika being dead.

On screen, Mika backed up, growling at the banshee. His wolf form had a few injuries, but he otherwise appeared healthy and mobile. He was in the clearing where we'd found Gavin, but Gavin was nowhere to be seen. His fight must have happened after this.

The banshee swept in close to Mika, opened its mouth, and let out its ear-shattering scream. As soon as it did, a flash of light obscured the camera, flickering and pulsating.

"Our team tells me," Von said, "that some types of banshees emit a flash of light when they scream. Something about the tenor and volume interacting with electrons in the air—well, far above my pay grade. Which, I have to say, is pretty high."

Von chuckled at his joke, but I kept my eyes glued to the screen. He was right—some banshees did emit a light, but it was always more of a quick flash that tended to be deep in the thing's throat. You'd only see it if you looked straight down its gullet when it screamed. It wasn't bright enough to do this. Only a TO with experience dealing with them firsthand would know that, though.

After about two seconds of the flash, the screen reappeared. The banshee was slinging chunks of wolf flesh and body parts around. Mika's *actual* death was never seen, and what was shown on screen looked exactly like Zoe's style of fae magic. That had to be what it was.

It was a hell of a convincing death. A wolf did die, but it must have been a feral. Zoe had seen enough of the season to know what Mika's wolf looked like, so she and Crew must have found one that matched Mika's. I clamped a hand over my mouth to cover my smile. Happy tears sprang to my eyes as I realized Mika had made it out. To anyone looking, I probably looked devastated.

Von gave me a simpering, paternal frown. "I know, Kira, I know. Quite tragic. Another life cut down in his prime, but..." his smile returned. "We know this is all for love, and who wouldn't risk their lives for one of these two ladies?"

Even though I was almost positive Mika was still alive, I wanted to kick Von in his shriveled-up vampire balls. *He* thought Mika had died, yet he still used him as something to get ratings. I called on all of my training and acting skills to keep the angry scowl off my face. Instead, I buried my face in my hands and pretended to sob. Wyatt grabbed me and wrapped me in a hug, acting along with me.

"It's okay," he murmured to me. "He's in a better place now."

All around me, the others looked stricken and upset to varying degrees. J.D.'s face was the one that sent the worst shame through me. He looked ready to cry himself. He kept staring at the screen in shocked horror as Mika's fake death replayed over and over again. I wanted to tell him the truth without the others knowing, but J.D. had a hard time lying and keeping secrets, so it would have to wait. Maybe until right before we tried to get him off the show, too.

"Very tragic indeed," Von said. "Mika will be missed." Von left us and moved back to address one of the cameras. "Now that we are down to only five alphas, we are getting to a more intense portion of the season. Many times, this is when the alphas begin to grow more desperate and pull out all the stops to impress the prize mate. I, and of course our fans out there, are excited to see how these remaining studs try to win over Chelsey and Kira.

"To that point, we want to dial up the drama a bit. Tonight, the entire cast will be participating in a group date. As always, there'll be a twist. Make sure you tune in to find out the surprise."

A twist? I did not like the sound of that. At this point, though, I would have been surprised if Von *didn't* throw in a twist to make things more dangerous, dramatic, or terrifying.

"Tune in tonight, and remember, everyone loves an underdog," Von signed off from the broadcast.

The camera floated away, and he slipped his sunglasses back on. "Whew, it's bright out here, isn't it?" He pulled out a tube of sunscreen and began to slather it on his skin. "You know, that was a decent challenge, but not quite as fun as it could have been."

Abel sneered. "I'm sorry we weren't more entertaining."

Von, either ignoring or not noticing the sarcasm, waved Abel away jovially. "Oh, it's not your fault, Abel. Tomorrow is a new day. Now, go rest up. I've been in contact with the showrunners and producers. We've worked with the writers and techs to make something really special happen tomorrow. Something totally new and exciting to test the remaining contestants. I think it'll really spice things up."

How much spice did this fucker want? But I could read between the lines. He was basically saying they'd found a new way to try to eliminate me and

Wyatt. They were probably starting to get worried we'd survive the whole show. The last few challenges had been set up for us to fail.

Wyatt let me go when Von strolled back to the mansion, his head down as he tapped away at his phone. The first thing I did was console J.D. He looked devastated and heartsick. It hurt my own heart to see him like that. Sitting down next to him, I wrapped an arm around his shoulders.

"I can't believe he's dead," J.D. muttered. He didn't look as upset as when he thought Leif had died, but he was obviously hurting.

"I know." I felt like shit for lying. "But like Wyatt said, he's in a better place now. Up with the gods. He's probably drinking some beers with the whole pantheon right now, laughing about how scared we all are."

J.D.'s chuckle held no humor; it was hollow and sad. "Yeah. Maybe."

"Come on. Let's head up," I said.

"Okay."

J.D. went inside, leaving the rest of us behind. Wyatt came up in the rear of the group, and I fell in with Chelsey. The two of us made eye contact and smiled but didn't talk. Even though I was sure Mika had made it out, the sadness and tension was palpable among the others.

As we stepped through the mansion doors, Tate hurried to slide between us. He didn't push me, just nudged me aside with his shoulder. It was enough to piss me off, but I concealed my irritation.

"Hey, can you give me and Chelsey a minute to talk?" Tate asked, though it sounded more like a demand.

"Is that okay?" I asked Chelsey.

"Yeah, it's fine," she said with a nod.

It seemed odd, but I left the two of them alone and headed up to my room. I was coated in mud. It was caked in my hair, and if I didn't take a shower soon, I would scream. I didn't even want to know what I looked like. If Wyatt's appearance was any clue, it was bad. Gray mud smeared his face, and flakes of dirt fell off him as we walked. When I glanced down, I noticed the same thing. Every step taken left behind dirty footprints.

Wyatt gave me a nod of assurance, then veered off to the alpha den. I went straight up the stairs to my room. The spell on the zipper must have broken when the challenge was over because I easily peeled myself out of my outfit. I tossed the filthy thing into the trashcan and jumped in the shower.

As I soaped, scrubbed, and shampooed myself multiple times, I let my mind drift. It was lonely in my room without Zoe here. I missed her more than I could say. It would have been nice to sit and gossip about everything going on. To talk, blow off steam, and try to work through what I should do next. Over the years, I'd grown accustomed to bouncing ideas off her. What I wanted most was to talk to her about the revelation I'd had.

I was in love with Wyatt.

That realization alone was one of the biggest things I'd ever discovered in my life. Maybe *the* biggest, yet I couldn't talk to my best friend about it. I also couldn't do anything about it. We were stuck on this stupid island, fighting tooth and claw to stay alive, with no chance to explore our feelings. I wanted to explode with frustration.

Turning off the water, I stepped out of the shower and dried off. My mind turned to darker matters. The showrunners were using me as a toy, and that infuriated the fuck out of me. All I was to them was some pretty little thing to be dangled in front of the fans and pushed into deadly situations for nothing more than ratings. Yes, we'd managed to save Mika without them knowing, but I needed more. I wanted to lash out and hit *The Reject Project* right where it hurt, and soon.

Wyatt was dead-set on targeting Von and the rest of the staff in some way. It might work, but as much sway as the staff held, the fans had the true power. They determined whether this show succeeded or failed. In the big scheme of things, everything revolved around eyes on screens. Could I use that in some way? Maybe. The votes on certain challenges and tasks could be swayed if I did it right, as long as the people running the show didn't decide to intercede like they had in the past. Of course, there was no guarantee that the audience would even want to be generous or benevolent with their votes. Many of the fans enjoyed the brutal, tragic traditions of the show.

I paused while brushing my hair, staring into my eyes in the mirror. Maybe we could appeal to the softer, romantic side of the fans. Could one of us get through to them and make them see how fucked up the show truly was? If that was possible, I didn't know if I was the one to do that. Hell, I'd been on board with rejecting someone just to benefit myself and my pack. Others would benefit, too, but deep down, I had to admit it was mostly for my own people. Did that make me any better than the sadistic fans drooling over us as we got ripped to shreds by monsters? In hindsight, this entire thing had been a terrible decision on my part. Now, I was stuck here.

"Well, well, well," I muttered to my reflection. "If it isn't the consequences of my own actions. Shit."

I finished getting ready, and a deep restlessness made me pace my room. Every few minutes, I checked my window, hoping for one of those parrots with ridiculous names to come flying back with a message from Zoe. I had a soul-deep need to know whether or not Mika was in Haven. I was ninety-nine percent sure of what I'd seen on the replay, but until I had confirmation from Zoe, the nagging worry would eat away at me.

After an hour cooped up in my room, I finally decided I needed to get my mind off things. Wyatt would most likely be in the alpha den, so I wouldn't be able to talk to him in private. Chelsey, however, was probably alone in her room. I wasn't as close to her as I was to Zoe, so baring my soul to her was more than likely out of the question. But I could at least check in with her, see how she was doing, and maybe talk about something—anything—to keep my mind occupied.

Before I could talk myself out of it, I left my room and made my way to her suite. After I knocked, Chelsey answered by peering out, eyes suspicious until she saw who was there.

"Oh, Kira. Come on in."

She stepped out of the way, and I stepped inside. She closed and locked the door quickly behind her. She looked stressed and haggard.

"Is something wrong?" I asked.

She ran a hand through her hair and glanced at the door again. "Stay away from Tate."

"I wasn't planning on asking him out on a date. No worries there."

"Ugh, no, I mean *really* stay away from him. He left a few minutes ago. He spent, like, an hour trying to convince me that he and I should team up to knock you off the show. He said it was a great idea because of the extra bonus Von gave me. He could be my mate, and we could claim the favor from Heline."

Wow. Tate had gone that far? He'd thought he could talk Chelsey into helping him either murder me directly or put me in a position where some other creature took me out. The guy really hadn't gotten to know Chelsey well.

"That's not good," I said.

"Right? He said that since you've been lying for the duration of the show, it was obvious the showrunners were targeting you and you'd be dead soon, anyway. His theory was that we should take you out first to get the biggest prize possible. That I might as well benefit if you were going to end up dead regardless." She shook her head and shivered. "It was creepy. He was almost too convincing with how romantic he was being, acting all concerned for me."

Tate had flown under the radar until the alphas had been whittled down. He'd since shown that he was more calculated and conniving than the others. He'd been able to hide it when other assholes like Omar and Nathaniel had been around, but now that most of the remaining guys were all decent—I still wasn't sure if Gavin fell under that umbrella—his true colors were showing. It also sounded like he was getting desperate to win. Didn't surprise me.

"Thanks for the heads-up," I said.

"I thought you should know to watch your back."

"Well, don't worry about me. Better men than Tate have tried to take me down, and they've all failed."

Chelsey grinned. "I wish I was a badass like you sometimes."

"You've survived the show this long," I said. "That makes you stronger than almost the entire population. Now, let's talk about stuff that doesn't have to do with this stupid show."

Chapter 18 - Wyatt

There had been an obvious change with the other alphas. The tension in the alpha den was thick as oil, almost suffocating. Abel sat on his bunk, fingers interlocked, staring at the ground, not at all like his usual self. J.D. lay on his bed, staring morosely at the ceiling. The only bonus was that Tate and Gavin were nowhere to be seen, so I didn't have to suffer their snide comments.

With only five of us left, things were looking grim. Every day might bring a challenge that would leave us dead. Of the five of us, only two were getting off the island alive—one, if the show killed me and Kira off—and that knowledge was starting to weigh on the others.

The stress of everything was having an effect on them, and part of me wondered if it would be better if I went ahead and told them the truth. If they knew Kira and I were faking eliminations to safely get them off the show, it might bring us all together as one team. If there was more hope that they could survive, it would be better for everyone's mental health and give them something to strive for other than the show. They could help us bring down the entire show.

As nice as that thought was, I had to brush it away as soon as it crossed my mind. Telling all of them at once would be too dangerous. While I was almost positive J.D. would be down for it, and possibly Abel, I had no such illusions with Gavin and Tate. Those two would be the most difficult to persuade. In fact, I had a suspicion that if they knew our plans, they'd go tattle to Von. The promise of getting a mate, prize money, and membership in the First Pack was too much for them to turn their backs on. Tate would throw Kira and me under the bus, and Gavin would try to find some way to make it all my fault to keep Kira for himself.

No. I had to stick to the original plan.

I headed straight to the bathroom to rinse the mud off myself. I stayed in the shower, letting the water soothe my aches away until the hot water ran out. By the time I came back out freshly washed, everyone but J.D. had left. He looked less devastated than when he'd thought Leif was dead, but he was still mourning for Mika.

"How's it going?" I asked as I sank down beside him on his bed.

J.D. sat up, a tired sigh leaving him as he did. "Fine, I guess. I'm sitting here thinking how stupid it was to come on this show. How stupid it was for *all* of us."

I patted his shoulder. "It's all gonna work out."

"I'd love to believe that, but at this point, I don't know."

I glanced around the room. It was clear. My bracelet showed no cameras were nearby. Even so, I kept my next words low and quiet. "There's more going on here than you understand, man. Things aren't as bad as they seem."

"I don't know what you're talking about, Wyatt. All I know is that I'm sick of seeing good people—my friends—get killed. I've never been an angry person. My inner wolf has always been mellow and laid back, but I'll tell you what—it's ready to jump out and tear Von's throat out. I've never been so fed up in my life."

"Stay calm," I said. "Things are probably gonna get worse before they get better, but there is a light at the end of the tunnel."

J.D. turned and fixed me with a glare. "Are you serious? Do you really believe that?"

"I do. I can't tell you why yet, but I believe we're gonna get out of this."

J.D. laughed humorlessly, but the expression on his face told me he took some solace in my words. "Okay, bro. Whatever you say. I hope you're right, though. I'm gonna take a nap. That shit in the jungle wore me out."

"Sounds good," I said as I stood.

The other man rolled over and tucked his pillow under his head. With nothing more to say, I left the bunk room to give him some peace and quiet. What I really wanted to do was check on Kira. She'd probably be back in her room by now.

Mind made up, I headed toward her suite. I made it less than twenty feet before I ran into Gavin. He looked like he'd come fresh from the healers, his cuts and wounds all gone now. When he saw me, a wicked little grin spread across his face and he blocked my way.

"Look, Gavin," I said. "I don't have the energy for this shit right now."

"Well, you better find the energy, okay? We need to have a discussion. Man to man."

"About Kira?"

He nodded. "Exactly. I'll be honest with you. Over the last few challenges, you've earned my respect. That's more than I anticipated."

"Thanks, I guess."

Ignoring me, he went on. "That being said, you and I both know you aren't a good match for Kira. You never will be."

I narrowed my eyes. "Let me guess. I'm not, but you are?"

"That's exactly what I'm saying. You must see it. If you're honest with yourself, you'll know it's true. Her best bet, and the thing that will give her the best chance at a happy and safe life, is if she chooses me as a mate."

Laughter bubbled up out of me. This guy really had a high opinion of himself. Gavin's face darkened, but he stayed silent.

"Can you tell me exactly why that is? During this whole thing, I think Kira has saved your ass more than you've saved hers."

His face flamed and he chopped his hand through the air as if cutting my words in half. "Stop. That's not true, and you know it. You know what I'm talking about. I've got a plan to use my pack to strengthen hers. That's all she really wants. And once her pack is safe in whatever war might or might not be happening, she'll have everything—a strong pack, a mate who loves and cares for her, and a life. What kind of life will she have with a lone wolf? Seriously? All you're doing is getting in the way and putting her in more danger."

I kept my cool. Nothing would come of me kicking his ass. Why let myself get drawn into that here in this stupid hallway? But that didn't mean I couldn't try to set his ass straight.

"Here's the deal, Gavin. I've known Kira *much* longer than you or even your douchebag brother, okay? I think I know her better than you do. You *think* you know Kira, but that's nothing but infatuation. A fucking crush, man. Kira knows me almost better than I know myself, and that goes both ways. Please stop acting like you two are star-crossed lovers separated by fate. It's silly and ridiculous." I should have stopped, but once I started, I couldn't hold myself back. It was cathartic to let him know exactly how I felt. The rage written on his face only spurred me on.

"If you haven't noticed by now, Kira doesn't want the same things she did when she first came on the show. You'd see that if you *actually* knew her as well as you think you do. Yes, she wants her pack safe. Yes, she wants to avoid war. That's about all you really know about her. She's not the same person she was when this all began. She deserves to choose her own mate. She doesn't need you pressuring her to choose you because you think it's the *logical* choice, for fuck's sake."

Gavin smiled, but it looked more like a grimace. "You think you know so much. I know you two have..." He trailed off, looking like he didn't want to say what was next. "You guys have been *intimate*, but that's none of my concern—"

"You're damn right it's not your business."

"But I can look past that," he continued, unperturbed by my outburst. "People have needs and bodily desires. I wasn't there for her, but you were. She's confused, and having you around makes it worse for her. That's why I'm saying this. She needs to be practical and follow her heart, not her, uh, hormones or whatever."

"God, you're dense," I said. "If you truly understood Kira, you'd know she has a hell of a temper. She'll almost always give up the practical to protect the people she cares about, especially when she's mad. Right now, she's pissed at this show and trying to keep all the contestants alive."

Gavin rolled his eyes and barked a laugh. "Well, that isn't working too well, is it? Not with Mika torn to shreds and the jungle painted with his blood. If she—"

"I think you should stop talking now," Kira said from behind Gavin.

The look on Gavin's face was priceless. I'd have given my left nut for a camera to catch it. Even before he turned, his face went pale and slack. It was all I could do to keep a straight face as he turned to find her glaring at him. "Kira? I didn't—"

"I *know* you didn't. That's the fucking point," she said. "I appreciate your vote of confidence, Gavin." Her voice was thick with sarcasm and condescension.

Gavin held his hands out in a pleading gesture. "Wait, no, that wasn't what I meant. Can we talk?"

Completely ignoring him, Kira walked up to me and took my hand. "I need to talk to you." She glanced at Gavin. "Alone."

Kira tugged at my hand and pulled me down the hall, but we didn't make it far before Gavin tried one more time.

"Wait," he said, looking desperate and frustrated. "Kira, I know you're mad, but you have to play the game the right way. Playing is the only way to win. Can't you see that?"

Kira released my hand and whirled on Gavin. The other man jerked back, and I again had to bite my lip to stop myself from laughing.

She jabbed a finger into Gavin's chest. "I'd rather break the entire game than play the stupid thing. I don't enjoy sadistic games. Let me make this crystal clear once and for all: I have no intention of being at your side, Gavin. I know you have these feelings inside that you think are for me, and I'm sorry, but they aren't in me. You need to get over it." Before he could respond, she turned back and grabbed me again, hurtling down the hall, leaving Gavin to stand and stare at us as we left.

"That was impressive," I whispered.

"Fucking Fell boys. If they aren't aloof and soulless assholes, they're clingy, lovesick assholes," she muttered.

We'd left him far behind when Kira finally looked up at me and saw the smile on my face.

"What exactly is funny about all this?" she demanded.

The grin vanished and I apologized. "Sorry, sir. No smiling, sir. I've been a very bad boy, sir."

She swatted at my chest. "There's nothing funny about this, Wyatt."

"I know," I admitted. "I just like seeing that temper come out, especially when it's not aimed at me. It's kinda hot, actually. Your passion has always turned me on. I've always tried to ignore it or act like it annoyed me, but..." I slid a hand up her back. "No need anymore."

She blinked, caught off-guard by my statement. "I don't, uh, I don't—"

"Yeah, I know," I said, rolling my eyes. "Kira Durst doesn't do well talking about feelings."

"Can we not do this right now? Sexy talk later. I have *other* things to say."

She glanced around before dragging me into the nearest room. It was small for the mansion and appeared to be some sort of wine cellar. Three walls held wine bottles encased behind glass doors. In the middle of the room, a huge sofa sat in front of a wooden table, probably for wine tastings or something.

"What's up?"

"I heard from Zoe," she hissed.

"What? When?"

"I went to see Chelsey after the challenge. When I went back to my room, Mr. Rainbow Sprinkle Butt was waiting for me on my desk—"

"Hang on," I said, holding up a hand. "*Who* was waiting in your room?"

"Rainbow Sprinkle Butt. He's a bird, follow along. Anyway, he had a message on his leg. A letter from Zoe."

I knew this was what we'd been waiting for—confirmation that Mika had indeed been swept away by the fae and her new allies, or that he'd been murdered by a monster in the jungle.

I swallowed hard, terrified to hear the answer. "And?"

Kira smiled, hints of tears glistening in her eyes. "He made it. He's there. Mika's alive in Haven."

A shuddering sigh left my chest at the news. "Can I see the note?"

Kira shook her head and showed me the black smudges on her fingers. "It burst into flames as I read the last word. It's Zoe's way of keeping everything a secret. Nothing but ashes now."

"Okay, that's fine. What did she say? Is he all right?"

"She said he's still his same old self. I think the exact terminology she used was 'His Broodiness.' It seems like he's safe and sound otherwise."

It had been a long time since I'd experienced such relief. Mika had been through more shit than pretty much anyone else on the show. Hell, he'd been through more shit than me. My fated mate had been a controlling monster, but at least my father hadn't been fucking her behind my back. My father had loved me in his own way. It wasn't a tender or close love, but he'd never have done what Mika's father did. When I rejected Serenity and left the pack, I knew it had hurt him. His position in the pack had made it impossible for him to do more than give me a hug and a pat on the back as I departed.

If anyone here deserved a happy ending, it was Mika. Whether he would be happy remained to be seen, but at least he was safe and far away from this sadistic shitshow.

"Thank fuck," I said. "Do you have any idea how decent of a place this Haven is? Like, are they pooping in the woods? Hunting their own food? What?"

"I don't know. Zoe isn't complaining about stuff like that in her letters, but it could be she's got more to worry about than creature comforts. It has to be better than here, though."

"True," I agreed. "I'm sure it's not a five-star accommodation. They are living and surviving on Bloodstone Island, after all. Speaking of..."

"What are you doing?" Kira asked as I ran my hands up her arms.

"I'm checking to see if all your wounds are healing okay. Anything still hurt?"

"Wyatt, you fuss over me too much. I'm fine. Really."

I lifted her shirt to check her stomach. A fading bruise sat below her ribs. "What about this?" I drew a finger across it, barely gliding over the skin.

"Now you're being silly. You know what kind of injuries I've had during missions. This is nothing compared to some of those. This will heal in no time, even without the witches."

"Don't remind me. Do you have any idea how hard it was to control myself when I saw you get hurt at work? God, Kira. It always bothered me. Like that time we hunted that bear shifter, the serial killer who went after humans? That guy tried to drown you in a pond. I thought you were dead until you coughed up all that water. Every time I see you get hurt or injured, another sliver of my heart breaks off."

Kira looked away, almost like she couldn't bring herself to look me in the eyes. "Really? Every time?"

"Every time. And don't even ask how it affected my wolf. He *freaked* when it happened. It's part of why I was always trying to jump in and save you, even if you might not have needed it. I knew it pissed you off, but he wouldn't let me sit back. He was always desperate to swoop in and rescue you. And it's getting worse. I can't help but get a little testy when I see you hurt. Even if it's nothing more than a bruise."

Kira finally looked at me, her face thoughtful rather than angry. "You know, after all those years of suppressing her, my wolf finally has some emotional freedom. I never noticed it before, but I think she feels the same way about you that your wolf feels about me. Weird."

A tremor ran through my chest. The thought that Kira might have the same feelings I'd nurtured all these years had my wolf doing a joyful Cirque de Soleil routine.

"Uh, why do you think that is?" I asked lamely.

"I don't know. Maybe it's the familiarity? Probably because she views you as a safe place? Almost like you're part of my pack? Just a guess." She trailed off and seemed to drift back into deep thought.

"Well, since we're on the same page, let me alleviate my worries." I tugged her shirt up again to check her lower back.

"Jeez. Fine," she said, but if my ears hadn't deceived me, she didn't sound irritated. More like she was happy for me to run my hands across her body.

An excited fire filled my belly at that. After a few moments of checking her back, I moved up to her shoulders, gently kneading the muscles around her neck. "How's that feel?" I whispered into her ear.

"Uh, good. Really good," she said with a sigh.

I leaned down and kissed the back of her neck. "What about that?"

"Mmm. Good."

My cock was getting hard in my pants, pressing painfully against my underwear. I pushed my hips against her, letting her feel it.

Kira chuckled. "Is that a flashlight in your pocket, or are you happy to see me?"

Releasing her shoulders, I trailed my fingers down her back, around her midsection, then up to her chest, finally cupping her breasts through her shirt.

"How about this?"

Kira groaned and pressed her ass back into me, grinding on my throbbing dick. "Lock the damn door."

"Yes, ma'am."

I turned, locked the door, and turned back. Kira was now naked to the waist. Her breasts drew my eyes like water to a man in a desert. She was the most beautiful thing in the world. Nothing on earth was as amazing as she was. I could barely contain myself.

I shoved the table out of the way, not even registering the screeching of its legs on the floor. I nearly tore my shirt as I ripped it over my head. When my shirt cleared my eyes, Kira was completely naked, her skin flushed with the same excitement I felt.

She locked her eyes on me and sat back on the sprawling leather couch. Biting her lip, she let her legs fall open. A jackhammer rumbled in my rib cage, thudding and slamming away, ready to burst from my chest. The rest of my clothes and shoes went flying across the room. Naked, I joined her. The fiery heat of her skin slipped across my chest and stomach as I slid on top of her. Her nipples were hard and dragged across my flesh, sending my brain into a frenzy. Before anything, I *needed* to kiss her.

When our lips met, Kira ran her fingers through my hair, slipping her tongue into mine. The slippery wetness of her mouth somehow made me even harder. My cock pressed against her pussy, urgent and demanding, but not yet.

I pulled away, lowering myself down her body, trailing kisses across her chest, flicking a nipple with my tongue to make her giggle, then going lower. I slid my tongue across her until I slipped deep into the cleft between her legs—warm, wet, and soft. Kira arched her back, sucking in a breath. The movement had her crotch pressing into my face.

My tongue slid and probed and circled deeper and deeper. She tasted like honey and sex. I stroked myself as I feasted on her. Looking up from my task, I met her eyes as she stared down at me, her fingers tugging at her nipples, pinching, stroking, pinching, then stroking again. It was the most erotic thing I'd ever seen, and I moved my hand faster, stroking my shaft at an almost frenzied speed.

Pulling my tongue free, I wrapped my lips around her engorged clit and sucked at her. Her gasp was a heavenly melody. I finally released myself and grabbed her ass with both hands, pulling her as close as I could, devouring her with an abandon I'd never felt before.

"Come here," Kira said. "I want you inside me. Now, please, Wyatt."

I did as she asked, but not quickly. I inched my way up her body, kissing every ounce of flesh I could reach. When I reached her breasts, I took her left nipple into my mouth, sliding my tongue across it before sucking and gently nibbling.

"Wyatt. Fuck. Please. I need you."

My wolf growled in delight, and with a single thrust of my hips, I entered her, slipping home all the way to my balls. The exquisite warmth and heat of her on my shaft made me groan in pleasure.

"Gods, Wyatt." Kira wrapped her arms around me, moving her hips against me as I slowly thrust into her.

Again, we kissed. This time, almost breathlessly. My tongue slid in and out of her mouth in time with my cock sliding in and out of her pussy. Kira trailed her finger down my back until she cupped my ass, urging me deeper with every movement.

Pulling away to catch my breath, I slammed into her with everything I had. Kira pressed her forehead to mine, making eye contact.

"Look into my eyes," she gasped. "I want to see your eyes when you come."

I did as she asked, my balls tightening as my climax built.

Kira slipped a hand between us, rubbing at her clit as I fucked her. Knowing she was touching herself made it all even hotter.

"Are you gonna come for me?"

Mouth slightly agape, she nodded. Sensing she was close, I moved even faster, pulling my full length almost all the way out before entering her again fully. Each time, it was like coming home, going back to the place I'd always belonged.

Kira's face flushed, the pulse in her neck visibly pounding as she came. She clenched beneath me, pulsing around my cock and sending me over the edge. Our eyes remained locked, and a moan tore from me as I came. The connection was like nothing I'd ever experienced. Waves of pleasure crashed over us, but we never lost eye contact. It was a moment I would never forget. Possibly the most amazing moment of my life.

Spent, we collapsed together. We lay like that for several minutes, and once the initial bliss wore away, I could tell Kira's mind was still whirring.

Putting my weight on my elbow, I looked at her. "What's wrong? You're thinking about something."

"Nothing." She pursed her lips, then said, "Okay, actually, I am." She turned to look at me. "I think Gavin is on to something."

"Ugh. I really don't want to hear his name while we're naked."

"I know, but it's not about his usual bullshit. It's his theory about fated mates. He thinks something is wrong with the system. I think he's right."

"What do you mean? What part?" Where was she going with this?

"Well, some of the matches work like they're supposed to, but for the most part, things aren't right. Rejections used to be fairly rare, but now there are huge numbers of failed fated mate connections. People who are miserable together, bad matches, or simply don't like each other. Look at me and Jayson. I don't really believe I was ever supposed to be with that idiot. We had no spark between us, no desire, no nothing. Always so blah, you know?"

Hearing her talk that way about Jayson made me unreasonably happy. The guy *had* been a total dick. I'd spent years biting my tongue about their lackadaisical relationship. I'd always kept my mouth shut because, for one, it had been Kira's life and her decision, and second, the moon goddess had chosen Jayson to be her mate. Who the hell was I to say that a god could be wrong or inaccurate? Though, I should have been more suspicious. My own fated connection had been so poor, I should have come to the same conclusion years ago about Kira's.

"I have to agree," I said. "You were never meant to be with that asshole. No way. For the record, I don't think I was ever meant to be with Serenity, either. From the moment I met her, I despised her. That's definitely not the way it's supposed to be, right? We're not crazy or something, are we?"

"No, we're not. I think we're figuring something out."

Her words sat heavy in my mind. The fated mate crap was what drove me out of my pack in the first place. It had basically ruined my life for a while.

I looked into her eyes again, this time with trepidation and worry instead of carnal desire. "Something is really wrong. Like, world-changing wrong if this is accurate."

"There's no *if* to it," Kira said firmly. "We *are* right."

Chapter 19 - Kira

My initial feeling about the fated-mate pairings somehow getting messed up was dread. Existential, foreboding dread. After all, one of the main underpinnings of wolf-shifter society was the pairings. Fated mates were what formalized the pack system. If everyone was meant to be together, that made the packs more stable. If it was found that hundreds, maybe thousands of pairings were the products of mistakes or purposeful alterations by one of Heline's acolytes, chaos would ensue.

"What do you think will happen when everyone knows?" I asked Wyatt. "I mean, if we can get proof and then tell everyone?"

A line formed between Wyatt's eyebrows. "I have no idea. Anger, panic, maybe some relief?"

"Relief?" I sat up on my elbow to get a better look at him. "Why would people be relieved?"

"Well, think about it. You were allegedly paired with Jayson. How fucking miserable would your life have been if he hadn't rejected you? Awful, right? Well, what if you'd turned on the TV one day and someone said, 'Hey, to make everyone aware, your fated mate may not *actually* be your fated mate.' Wouldn't you be relieved? Happy that you weren't stuck with someone you weren't supposed to be with?"

He had a point. This revelation might not be as devastating as I'd first anticipated. This could be good news. Excitement flared in my chest.

"If we brought attention to this on the show, maybe we could affect the audience back home," I said.

"What? How?"

"It's like we said—I think everyone subconsciously knows something is wrong. I think people are either too blinded by loyalty to the system or unable to think outside the box to say it out loud. If we bring it up and push that narrative, it could get people on the mainland talking and thinking. If they realize it, they might revolt against the show. If nothing else, they might stop tuning in while they have a life crisis or something."

Realization dawned in Wyatt's eyes. "You're right. This whole stupid show is literally *built* on the fated-mate paradigm. If we showed that it was all bullshit or a mistake and that a lot of the rejects weren't true rejects, then the show has no leg to stand on. Why sign up to be on a show when all you need to do is go out and find your *actual* fated mate? Don't risk your life on this godsforsaken island when you can go out on your own and look for them."

My excitement gave way to nerves. "We need to find the right time to bring it up. It must be at a point when it can stir up the most trouble."

Before Wyatt could answer, one of the glass doors of the wine room flashed opaque then black, before revealing Von Thornton's grinning face.

"Fucking hell," Wyatt yelped, covering his crotch with a throw pillow from the couch.

"It's a TV. Wow," I said calmly despite the shock of it. They really had spared no expense on this place.

"Good afternoon, my lovely cast. I hope this message finds you well wherever you are."

I lowered my hands from my naked breasts now that I knew the vampire wasn't actually looking at us. Nonetheless, being interrupted during post-coital pillow talk and snuggling by that damn bloodsucker's leering face was a shock.

"A quick update. Make sure you all dress in your finest outfits. Tonight, we'll be having a rooftop dining experience on the terrace. It's always good to look your best and sexiest.

"I am so excited for what we'll be revealing tonight. It's a never-before-seen experience. We've been leaving little hints that something big is coming on our social media accounts and website. The fans are absolutely foaming at the mouth and waiting with bated breath to hear what it is. I think all of you will be pretty excited.

"One last thing. Try to contain your excitement, but I think we are rapidly coming to the end of this season. Everyone loves an underdog, and I think all these underdogs are going to get picked off soon. The finale may be just around the corner. Maybe even only in a couple of days." Von rolled his eyes to the back of his head in mock pleasure. "Ooh, I can't wait. Very exciting. Until tonight."

The screen went black, then opaque, and eventually returned to the fully translucent glass. Wyatt and I stared at nothing but wine bottles, taking in Von's words. They were a terrible reminder that danger lurked right around the corner.

"As soon as I hear from Zoe again, we need to work on getting someone else off the show," I said.

"Yeah. I'm thinking J.D."

"That's my thought, too. Who knows, maybe when he gets to Haven, Zoe and Crew can catch Leif and figure out how to help him." I chewed my lip and ran a hand down Wyatt's arm. "I'm nervous."

"Me too, but it'll all be okay. I know it."

He pulled me close and kissed me again. For a few seconds, it was just me and him again. The awful world we found ourselves in vanished while we were together. I was desperate to get off this island with him and see where our relationship could go. First, we had to get off the island alive. Then we could see.

With a collective sigh, we stood and gathered up our clothes. Wyatt dressed first and gave me one last kiss goodbye before slipping out the door. Once he was gone, I locked the door and took my time getting dressed.

A strange, deep loneliness settled over me. It wasn't only Wyatt I missed, but Zoe as well. Her sporadic letters were better than nothing, but I missed having her around. So much had happened since she'd been gone, and I would have loved nothing more than to bounce ideas off her, unload my emotional baggage, and chat about stupid stuff. Plus, I had to go to my room and try to get ready for a fancy dinner, and she was way better at hair and makeup than I was. The only bright side was that she couldn't dress me in some ridiculous getup. Her idea of a "nice" dress was one that had my tits hanging out and my ass showing. I loved her, and she had an amazing eye for fashion, but her tastes ran more scandalous than mine.

One bonus was that with Von's announcement, all the other contestants were in their rooms, getting ready. The halls were deserted while I made my way back to my suite. Even though I'd just received a message from Zoe, I was still a little disappointed that one of the messenger parrots wasn't sitting in my window when I got back.

I found a slinky red dress in my wardrobe that might be sexy enough to make Zoe proud, but was still modest enough for me to feel comfortable in. After getting dressed, I did my best with my hair and makeup. I'd put in some pretty decent practice since she'd been gone, and I had to admit, I looked pretty good by the time I finished.

I slipped on a pair of heels and headed out to go up to the rooftop terrace. Halfway there, I crossed paths with Chelsey. Abel was with her, escorting her with his arm interlocked with hers. Abel gave me a nervous nod, but Chelsey smiled as we approached each other.

"Hey. You look fantastic," she said.

"So do you. Are you guys ready for this?"

"I guess," Abel said, but worry laced his tone.

"I'm nervous," Chelsey admitted. "I don't like the way Von was talking earlier. Sounds like something bad's coming."

"I don't think he says anything that doesn't allude to us getting screwed over in some way," I said, failing to keep the bitterness out of my tone.

Chelsey patted Abel on the arm. "Can you give us a few minutes? You head on up."

He blinked in surprise but obliged by removing his arm from hers. "Yeah, sure. No problem. See you up there."

Chelsey smiled, and as soon as Abel was out of earshot, she grabbed me and pulled me into a small alcove in the hallway. "I want to do something tonight or tomorrow to throw the show off-course."

The vehemence and venom in her voice caught me off-guard.

"Um, okay, what do you have planned? Why now?"

"After you left, I thought about it, and Mika didn't deserve to die like that," she hissed. "It's bullshit. Von more or less said they're going to try and kill everyone else soon. We talked about this, but the more I think about it, the angrier I get."

"Hang on," I said, leaning out to check the hallway and then my bracelet. Once I was sure we weren't being overheard, I pulled her close, pressing my lips to her ear. "Mika is alive."

She jerked back like I'd slapped her. "What?"

"I can't get into it right now, but if we get time alone later, I can fill you in. As for your other idea, I think Wyatt and I know how to make trouble for the show. Watch for me to say some stuff at dinner. It'll sound crazy at first, but follow my lead."

The vicious smile that spread across Chelsey's face warmed my heart. "I can't wait."

"Shall we?" I asked, putting my arm out.

"It would be my pleasure," she said, interlocking her arm with mine.

We strolled up the last steps that led to the rooftop terrace. The last time I'd been up here, the showrunners and owners had been present to decide my fate. Now, I was going to find out whatever awful thing Von had planned for us.

Hopefully, the food would be good.

The terrace had been transformed. Fae lights floated around, illuminating everything. Tropical flowers had been woven into garlands and hung from almost every wall and rail. Faint music played from somewhere, and the staff had set up multiple high-top tables with platters of hors d'oeuvres. A few staff members moved around, filling wine glasses and smiling. Chelsey separated herself from me and went to speak to J.D. and Abel.

My eyes locked on Wyatt. He was leaning on a railing, a half-full glass of red wine in his hand. He looked good enough to eat in his tuxedo. He made his look better than any of the others, and that was saying a lot. All the alphas were handsome and attractive in their own way, but they couldn't compare to Wyatt.

Despite how good he looked, I could tell he felt uncomfortable in the attire. Having been born and raised in the Second Pack, he must have had to wear dressy clothes all the time. Knowing Wyatt the way I did, he'd probably always felt out of place in that world. Fancy dinner parties, orchestral concerts, caviar, and champagne? They weren't his style. He was more at home watching football in pajamas or hanging out with friends in a bar. This wasn't who he was.

Von appeared behind me in a solid white tuxedo. Had the sun not almost set, the color would have blinded me. It was accented with a blood-red pocket square and bow tie.

"Good evening," he said. The cameras whirred to life, sweeping through the crowd and zeroing in on Von. "We are coming to you live from Bloodstone Island. As you can see by the setting, things are getting quite romantic here. Love is in the air in this tropical paradise. Danger around every corner, but also desire. Our remaining contestants are doing everything they can to ensure they step onto that helicopter with their fated mate on their arm. We are nearing the end, but for some of these folks, it will only be the beginning."

I did my best not to gag as he winked at the camera. He was so full of bullshit.

"And why wouldn't these hunks want to be with these lovely ladies." Von stepped over and put his arm around my shoulders. "The fiery and feisty Kira Durst."

His hand sat unnaturally cold on my shoulder, but I was a professional. I didn't shudder or pull away. Instead, I smiled at the camera. "It's a gorgeous night, Von. Absolutely amazing."

The host chuckled. "Indeed it is. Something else that is gorgeous is our other prize mate." He stepped away to accost Chelsey. "The delightfully demure Chelsey Rein." Chelsey wasn't as good an actor as me and had to mask the look of disquiet that naturally accompanied a vampire touching you like you were long-lost lovers.

"Uh, hi, Von. It's very nice. Thank you," Chelsey said.

"Have you got your eye on any of these remaining alphas, Miss Rein?" Von asked.

Chelsey flushed but stayed composed. "Still biding my time. You, um, can't let them know what you're thinking, can you?"

Von pinched her cheek and swept away from her. "That is correct. Always keep them guessing. That could almost be the tagline for this show.

"We are giving all these folks a chance they might never have had on the mainland: the opportunity to find their perfect match. It's a good thing we here at *The Reject Project* are completely invested in love. Beyond all other things, that is what this show is about."

"What a load of crap," J.D. muttered.

I turned to see him shaking his head with a disgusted look. Of all the people to speak up, I hadn't anticipated it being him. His words were also loud enough for the cameras to pick up.

Von's perfect façade slipped a fraction, but he recovered quickly, though the smile looked much more forced than it had a few seconds before. He gestured toward a round table on the opposite side of the terrace—the same table the showrunners had sat at.

"Please, have a seat. I'm sure you enjoyed the canapes, but a fantastic four-course dinner awaits you."

We all took our seats at the table. As silly as I thought all this was, ravenous hunger clawed at my insides. I couldn't remember the last thing I ate. My mind braced itself for whatever curveball Von was about to throw, but when the wait staff brought out salads for the first course, I stuffed my face.

Von stood to the side of the table as wine was poured into our glasses. "Go on, chat. Don't mind us. Enjoy dinner."

Enjoying dinner was difficult with all the cameras flitting about, but we did our best. Abel sat to my left. I decided to see how he was doing while the others chatted among themselves.

"How's your day?"

Abel glanced up and smiled. "Fine."

"I'm glad things worked out today. With you making it back to the mansion okay, I mean."

"Uh, yeah. Same to you," he muttered and went back to his salad.

He was not acting like his usual pleasant self. Across from me, J.D. also looked upset and tense. In fact, the strange tension was palpable all around the table. From the corner of my eye, I saw Gavin trying to catch my attention. He was obviously upset that I'd called him out on his bullshit and that I continued to ignore him.

At the other end of the table, Tate acted as though nothing at all was wrong. He even asked me to pass him a roll and was genuinely polite about it. That alone made me more suspicious.

"Here you go," I said, passing the bread platter to him.

"Thanks," he said with a wink. "You're a doll."

I saw straight through his act. He wanted to get my guard down. I had no doubt that he was still plotting to convince Chelsey to knock me off so he could get both prizes.

Wyatt noticed the interaction and gave me a knowing look. He was almost as good as I was at staying in character. He and I had been trained for situations like this. Well, maybe not *exactly* like this, but similar. By the time the third course came out—a filet with creamed potatoes and roasted mushrooms—I could almost convince myself that I was at a run-of-the-mill dinner party.

After the entrees had been cleared, the staff set out dessert silverware and champagne flutes. Another staff member followed behind, pouring the bubbling liquid into the glasses. They'd already given us a few glasses of white and one of red that were delicious. Might as well enjoy myself while I had the chance. I picked up the new glass to see how the champagne stacked up.

The drink slid down the glass, pale yellow, and an instant before it touched my lips, I smelled something that sent a shockwave of memory through me—a lion shifter glaring at me in shocked and angry surprise. "*Lying cunt,*" he'd spat at me before flipping the table over.

The champagne touched my tongue, the barest sip coating the tip of it before I tossed the glass aside. The others flinched at the sound of shattered glass. Leaping up from my chair, I reached across the table to slap the glass from Chelsey's hand before it touched her lips.

"What the fuck, Kira?" Tate barked, wiping splattered champagne from his tux.

"Don't drink that. No one fucking drink a drop of that shit."

I couldn't believe the anger surging inside me. The absolute rage. It was the exact same drug the lion shifter had given me in the restaurant. It felt like a lifetime ago, but that moment had caused my life to go off the rails. Already, I could feel the barest effects of the chemical. I'd had less than a sip, but the strange heat was already building inside me.

Wyatt stared at me, and I could see the gears turning in his head. He glanced at the shattered glass on the ground, then back at me, and his jaw dropped. He'd put it together. Then, the others began to notice.

Abel sniffed the air and frowned. "What the hell?"

My scent had changed. I smelled like I was going into heat. And alpha male shifters surrounded me. Fuck. They would be drawn to me.

Abel touched my thigh. "Are you okay?"

I swatted his hand aside. Tate rose from his chair, sniffing the air as well. "Yeah, are you good? Come here, let me check you out."

Wyatt exploded from his chair and shoved Tate in the chest, sending the alpha tumbling backward to the ground. "Get away from her, asshole!"

"What is going on?" Chelsey asked in a panic as she glanced around at everyone.

Gavin gazed at me with a renewed longing and desire. He stood, and I could already see the erection pressing through his pants. Gross.

Gritting my teeth, I did my best to ignore the effects of the drug. It wasn't nearly as bad as that first time. I'd had a much smaller dose, but I still felt it. Thoughts and fantasies I'd never imagine if I wasn't drugged flashed across my mind.

Wyatt thrusting into me with vicious force, sucking at my nipple, me screaming out in pleasure.

Wyatt bending me over, taking me from behind.

Wyatt's cock buried in my throat, gagging me.

I clamped my eyes shut and tried to focus. When I opened them, the anger in Wyatt's eyes had faded, and now he was looking at me with deep need and desire. It was an even stronger reaction than the others were having.

"Kira?" He stepped toward me.

Just looking into his eyes was enough to make me almost lose myself. Wet heat pulsed between my legs. If he came over here, I'd be fucking him in seconds. I didn't give a damn that we were surrounded by people and cameras. The moment he touched me, it would be over. I had zero control. Not with that shit working its way through my system.

"Oh, it appears things have gotten a bit out of control," Von said, hurrying to the table. "Wyatt, let's get you back to your seat."

Von put a hand on Wyatt's chest. The rest was surreal and happened fast, like a sped-up dream. Wyatt, seeing the vampire's hand on his chest, snarled, his eyes filling with indignant rage. He shifted faster than I'd ever seen, his wolf appearing in the blink of an eye. Von yelped in surprise, and Wyatt lunged forward, his teeth clamping on Von's throat. With a savage twist of the head, Wyatt tore Von's throat out. A spray of blood arced through the air, landing on the white tablecloth as a fan of red droplets.

Von clutched at his neck, coughing and choking before tipping over and slamming to the ground. His white tuxedo was a mess of red gore. He stared up at me sightlessly as his body went still.

All around us, attendants and servers screamed and backed away, pressing themselves against the walls and handrails that ringed the terrace.

"What the fuck?" Abel shouted, backing away from Von, lying in a spreading pool of blood.

Von would be fine. He was already dead before Wyatt had torn his throat out. Unless Wyatt slammed a stake into his heart or ripped his head clear off his body, Von would be up again in moments. That didn't make the sight any less shocking.

Wyatt gnashed his teeth, chewing on the vampire flesh before flicking his head and tossing the hunk of throat aside. He then paced and whined, alternating between growling and whimpering. Every few seconds, he'd look at me and start all over again. He wasn't fully in control of his wolf, which was strange. He'd always been so focused and in sync with his inner wolf.

Chelsey rushed around the table and pulled me away, dragging me to the far corner of the terrace. The other alphas were still looking at me with hungry and confused expressions. Even J.D. was giving me a strange look. Whatever this drug was, it was beyond powerful.

"Are you okay?" Chelsey asked.

"Umm, I think so."

I squeezed my legs together, and a shiver of pleasure went up my spine. It was all I could do to stay in my right mind and focus. Memories of my first time with the drug came flooding back. The sexual need wasn't as painfully brutal, but I was still in bad shape. If even another drop had passed my lips, I'd have been out of my mind like the last time. All that was keeping me focused was my anger.

A few of the braver staff members were with Von, patting his cheek, trying to wake him up. From where I was, I could already see his wound healing. He would be up anytime now. The cameras were still flying around, taking in the carnage and chaos.

Through it all, I realized now was my chance. This was when I could shine a light on the dark, dirt secrets of the show. Von was still out; most of the staff had run off. There was no one to stop me.

Taking a breath and focusing my mind, I pushed through the drug's chemical effects and moved toward the nearest camera. Chelsey tried to stop me, but I gently pried her hand off me.

"It's okay," I said. "I know what I'm doing."

As I approached the camera, whatever spell was propelling it must have sensed that something big was coming. It spun from watching Wyatt pace to lock its lens on me.

"*The Reject Project* just tried to use a highly illegal substance on me and Chelsey," I began. "A drug that forces a female shifter into heat. I know this for a *fact* because I've seen this chemical before in my work as a licensed and trained Tranquility operative."

The other alphas, still fighting off the effect I was having on them, turned to listen. I needed to throw the whole show under the bus.

"The show has lost all credibility by doing something so underhanded, disgusting, and vile. They wanted to drug Chelsey and me to force some kind of orgy or something. This drug has an unknown origin and is being investigated at the highest levels by the Tranquility Council. This act of deception and pure abuse of power comes straight from the showrunners and the owners of the company behind *The Reject Project*. Anyone watching needs to know that this show is not out to showcase love. This is the most-viewed program in the world, and all the producers want is drama and blood, sex and torture, pain and deception. They operate without any fear of being held accountable, and I call for someone—*anyone*—to form an inquest into their actions."

I glanced over to see that Von was still not awake. I could go in for the kill. It was now or never.

"Every year, this show kills rejected wolves, all in the name of finding love. Each season, there are almost a dozen rejects here. On top of that, *thousands* of others are not chosen for the show. How is that possible? How can there be so many rejects every single year? If Heline's acolytes *truly* paired them with their fated mates, how can there be this many rejections? Think about it. We all know something is wrong. If you look deep down, you'll know it, too. There is something terribly wrong here, and I think it's like a cancer, causing issues throughout all the packs. It's possibly the reason for the tension that's leading us all to war. The First Pack's alpha had his own son sent here. Mika took a chance *here* on Bloodstone Island—the most dangerous place on the planet—rather than stay in his pack after his own father had an affair with Mika's fated mate. That's right, Garth Sheen himself, the most powerful alpha in the world and one of the highest-ranking members of *The Reject Project* board of directors, engaged in behavior that undermines the entire fated mate tradition."

The few staff members still on the terrace were staring at me in open-mouthed horror, but they didn't move. If their expressions were any indication, I was making my point. If even five percent of the people watching believed what I was saying, this was all worth it. Damn the consequences. Sometimes, speaking the truth meant more than worrying about what might happen to you.

"Since coming on this show, my eyes have opened," I continued. "I see how problematic the entire pack mentality has become. Any romantic illusions I had about fated mates have been shattered. Why the hell shouldn't you be able to love whoever you want? Why should someone from the Tenth Pack be rejected simply because their fated mate is from Fourth? Why did Chelsey get rejected because she was in the Twelfth Pack? Can anyone give a coherent answer as to why we continually do this to each other? I've seen from my own experiences that the blood tests the moon goddess's acolytes perform mean nothing. They are bullshit.

"*The Reject Project* isn't about finding a mate. It's not about finding your true love. How do I know? Because I love Wyatt Rivers, and all the show is trying to do is tear us apart by killing one or both of us for ratings. If the show is not about finding love, then what is it about? From what I can see, it's nothing more than a glorified death sentence. A way for powerful pack leaders and elders to get rid of people they don't want around anymore. A way for them to sweep problems under the rug. This... this *abomination* of a show is a mockery of real fated mate connections. I do believe they are real and that everyone deserves that kind of love. We aren't getting that right now, and we need to tell the people in charge that we are sick and tired of it. Whether it be the rich and powerful, the acolytes, or Heline her-fucking-self."

My breath came in heavy gasps, panic setting in when I realized what I'd done, the huge step I'd taken. Not only had I basically declared war on everything about *The Reject Project,* but I'd admitted on live TV that I was in love with Wyatt.

The other alphas were looking at me with strange expressions on their faces. Gone were the looks of suspicion and confusion at my drug-fueled scent of heat. Now, they were caught in shocked introspection. Even the staff on the terrace looked like they were considering how much sense I made. They were frontline workers; most were only doing what they were told. They hadn't thought about what was happening any more than the average fan did. My words had startled them into introspection. Maybe it was doing the same around the world.

A sudden sense of profound power gripped me. Staring into an inky-black camera lens was one thing, but knowing hundreds of millions of people were watching me was like staring into the void.

"She's right!" J.D. shouted, taking a hesitant step toward me. "None of it is right. The fated mate connections haven't been working for a long time."

A grin formed on my lips when Chelsey spoke up, too.

"I believe Kira," she said. "If this show has shown me anything, it's that it has nothing to do with love and mates. It's a bloodbath. All of it is a lie, orchestrated for ratings. It's bullshit."

Wyatt, finally coming down from whatever reaction his wolf had to the drug in my system, shifted back to his human form and stared at me. The intensity wasn't sexual, not at the moment. It was more than that. He'd heard me confess my love for him.

"Cut!" Von's rough voice screamed from the ground. "Cut now."

The cameras almost immediately bobbed away, their lights flashing off. My chance to say more was gone, but was there really any more to say? I'd gotten it all out, and more than one contestant had agreed with me. What might be happening on the mainland now that I'd put this worm in everyone's ear?

Von had rolled to his stomach and was pushing himself onto his feet. I'd *never* seen him look so furious. His usual cool façade had given way to rage and vulgarity.

"Stupid motherfucker." He staggered as he retook his feet.

He glanced around and saw that something was wrong. The staff beside him looked shell-shocked. The other cast members were all either glaring at him or staring off into space.

"What happened here? What the hell did you say while I was out?" Von demanded. "What the absolute *fuck* did you say?"

I opened my mouth to answer. I was going to be honest with him, but his attention span must have been on the fritz from having his throat torn out. He spun away from me before the first word could come out of my mouth and leveled a finger at Wyatt.

"And you!" Von howled, his voice cracking. "This tuxedo cost ten thousand fucking dollars. What in the blue hell is wrong with you?" He gestured down at the suit that was now sprayed with blood. Von slapped his hands to his face and groaned. "I am never going to hear the end of this."

The vampire visibly restrained himself, pulling back from his rage. The game show host returned. "Well, it's out of my hands now. Whatever you all did while I was out can't be taken back. Hopefully, it was for ratings. You realize I haven't been killed on this show since season two?" He held up two shaking fingers. "Almost thirty years. It's the reason I don't go out in the jungle anymore. My gods. I'm going to go watch the replay." He eyed me suspiciously. "I hope you didn't do anything too foolish, Miss Durst." He chuckled to himself and shook his head. "Though if you did, I'm sure she'll find this evening even more entertaining than she'd hoped. She's like me in that way. She loves seeing new things."

"She who?" I asked.

Von didn't answer, just snapped his fingers. "Security?" He looked around, baffled. "Where the hell is security?"

"You, uh, sent them away," one of the serving staff said. "You didn't want them on camera. Said it didn't set the right mood."

"Ugh, yes, that's right. Thank you, Pamela."

He pulled his phone from a pocket in his ruined jacket and hit a button. Ten seconds later, six burly security guards burst through the terrace door—two fallen angels, a demon, a half-demon, and two humans who looked like they'd been surviving on a diet of steroids and muscle-enhancing potions for the last two decades.

"Take them to their rooms."

The guards separated us and ushered us away from the terrace patio.

"Who the hell were you talking about, Von?" I asked before I was pushed through the door.

He ignored me and put his phone to his ear. The security guys kept each of us far enough apart that we couldn't talk. When J.D. tried to speak, the half-demon shouted him down.

The two fallen angels separated Chelsey and me and escorted us to our rooms. Once I was in, I pressed my ear to the door and could hear the gigantic guard breathing. He was obviously standing guard. Stomping away from the door, I hurried to the window, hopeful. The absence of a messenger bird only enraged me further. What the hell had Von been trying to do? If Chelsey and I'd taken a full swig of that drink, it would have been a disaster. I could still recall the painfully carnal way the drug had worked on me all those weeks ago, causing uncontrollable, agonized desire. Just looking at Wyatt on the roof had sent my mind into a frenzy.

My cheeks burned with embarrassment. A hundred million people would have seen me jump Wyatt. Gods, my own parents might have had to watch me try to devour him on live TV. I almost gagged at the thought. I lashed out, slamming my fist into the wall. The drywall gave way beneath my fist. It felt cathartic, but did nothing to alleviate my anger.

All I could do was hope that my words had gotten through. That people back home were, at this very moment, questioning everything they knew. If one good thing could come out of this awful day, I hoped that was it.

I stared out my window, looking into the jungle and praying to all the gods I knew that I'd done all I could.

Chapter 20 - Wyatt

The guards shoved us into the alpha den and slammed the door shut behind us. The other alphas all drifted off toward their bunks. Tate looked more disturbed than I thought he would. Either Kira's words had really gotten to him, or he was pissed he hadn't gotten more time with Chelsey during dinner.

Abel was staring contemplatively at his feet. Gavin had a distinct look of sadness and depression on his face, almost like he'd lost something important. J.D., on the other hand, was pale with shock, either from what had happened with Kira or from his brazenness in vocally agreeing with her tirade.

As for myself, I was experiencing a schoolboy elation. It was childish and silly, but I couldn't help it. Kira had said that she loved me. Maybe that was what had Gavin looking like he'd sucked on a lemon. For the first time ever, she admitted her true feelings for me. Not only that, but she'd done it in front of the whole world. There was no taking it back.

The door of the den loomed large. I stared at it for several seconds, my inner wolf urging me to try it.

I stood and hurried to the door, grabbing the knob and opening it. It swung out three inches before it stopped dead. The dark face of the demon bodyguard peered in with one dark eye.

"You need something?" he asked.

"Uh, I was going to walk around. Blow off some steam, you know." I tried to smile.

"Sit your ass down, lover boy. No one leaves right now. Boss ordered it." He pulled his suit jacket aside to show the pistol in his shoulder holster. Even from where I was, I could smell the acrid stench of silver. "You want to push it, I can push back. Wanna try?"

Silver bullet? They were serious. "I guess not," I mumbled.

Before I could say anything more, he pulled the door shut. Dejected, I stalked back to my bunk and flopped down. It was ridiculous. All these years, all the waiting and hoping, and now that Kira had finally said the one thing I'd been waiting for, I couldn't be with her. All I wanted was to be with her, maybe even teasing her about it a bit. A few good-natured laughs about this thing we'd finally figured out. She'd get annoyed and needle me back. Then I could take her in my arms and show her exactly how much I loved her. How much I *wanted* her.

One bit of solace I could take was thinking of Von. He'd been half dead, healing from the wound I'd inflicted, but even then, the scene had been obvious. The looks on our faces, the way Kira was standing in front of the camera, the way his own staff had looked gobsmacked. He'd known then that we'd thrown a car-sized wrench into the program. By now, he'd have made contact with the showrunners and seen the replay of Kira's speech.

Plus, the armed guard at the door had told me all I needed to know. We'd fucked with them. *The Reject Project* had big problems. If only I could get out of here and see it with my own eyes. I craved to see Von look like a struggling worm on a hook. Hell, he was the face of the show, the main authority on the island. If anyone was going to be a fall guy, it would probably end up being him.

"Was it true?"

I spun, finding Abel looking up at me from where he sat on his bed.

"What Kira said. Was all that true? The fated mate connections aren't accurate anymore? Is it really all a big lie?" The sorrow in his eyes almost broke my heart. He looked miserable.

All I could do was nod. "We think so. It's the only thing that makes any sense."

He broke eye contact with me, staring off into space. "So... the girl who rejected me? That means she wasn't actually supposed to be with me. I took that shit hard, Wyatt." He looked at me again. Horror and anger had replaced his sorrow. "That's the whole reason I came on this stupid show. Risked my fucking life."

"Hang on, man," Tate said, interjecting himself into our conversation. "There's no way things have gotten that screwed up."

"Really? How else do you explain this? Do you know how many rejected mates there have been in the last few decades? Tons of them," Abel said.

Tate winced in irritation. "Just because a bunch of people have been rejected doesn't mean the entire system is fucked up. There's not a problem with the connections. I mean, the moon goddess herself is in charge of that."

But Tate's voice didn't sound as cocksure as usual. It sounded like he was trying to convince himself rather than Abel. It made sense. If you heard something as earth-shattering and world-altering as what we'd just heard, there would be pushback. You'd go through shock, fear, anger, disbelief, and a dozen other feelings.

"Abel's right." This time, it was Gavin adding his two cents. "I've thought something like this has been going on for a while. It's how I knew Kira and I were supposed to have been matched up all along."

I let that idiocy slide. We had bigger things to deal with than Gavin's crush on Kira.

"Look," I said, "there's something big happening. Bigger than this show, or us and our rejections. The only way we can truly know who we're *actually* supposed to be paired with is to ask Heline herself."

Of all of us, only J.D. looked relieved. He smiled up at me. "I know you guys are upset, but I'm actually happy."

"The hell is there to be happy about?" Tate barked.

J.D. shook his head sadly. "When my blood test came back, it said that I was fated to a woman I'd never met. I went to find her, but it turned out she had already met and mated with the love of her life. Everyone said I needed to tear them apart, to assert myself and take her as my mate. The blood test said she was mine fair and square, so they said that meant I should have her. They all said she was with someone she wasn't supposed to be with.

"When I finally saw her, I could see how happy she was, even from a distance. How in love they were with each other. I couldn't break them apart, so I rejected her and pissed my pack off in the process. This means I did the right thing. You have no idea how guilty I've felt about this. It's like a weight has been lifted off me."

"If it's true," Tate said, heavy skepticism coloring his tone.

"Right," J.D. said. "But if it is, that means our real fated mates are still out there somewhere. Waiting for us to find them."

Those words pierced my mind like an arrow. Waiting for us to find them? What if mine was still waiting for me to find her? Or, what if she'd been right in front of me the whole time?

Could Kira be my fated mate? The thought alone filled me with wonder and hope.

I tamped it down immediately. That was wishful thinking. I was drawn to her because of my feelings. That didn't necessarily mean we were fated. I had to keep a level head. Once she and I made it off this island alive, we could figure out what it all meant.

"Any of you wonder what's going on back home?" J.D. asked. He smiled in wonder. "She said all that stuff on live television. Can you imagine the reaction?"

He was right. Kira had tossed a stick of dynamite into an already volatile situation. It had to be done, but there would be chaos.

"I think it's bad," I said. "The fact that they have us locked up in here tells us everything. Bad shit. Panic."

Abel gave me a worried look. "So, uh, is that bad for us?"

"We'll have to wait and see," I answered. "Though, I doubt it'll be good. I think Kira's speech is going to have a bigger impact than even she thinks."

"Speaking of Kira," Tate said, "what the fuck was up with you, Wyatt? Why'd you flip out because she started giving off the barest hint of heat scent? A little heat wave shouldn't have done that. I thought you were going to rip all our throats out like you did with Von. Kinda scary."

Tate was spoiling for a fight, but I didn't rise to the bait. "You guys all reacted, too. Don't forget."

"Well, yeah," Tate said, rolling his eyes. "She was going into heat. Of course we'd *react*, but we weren't ripping fucking throats out."

There was no point answering him, because I didn't know why I'd reacted so violently. It reminded me of the day Kira was drugged by the lion shifter. I remembered how painfully I'd wanted her in that parking lot, though this time had been even stronger. Maybe because now I knew what it was like to be with her.

When I'd caught her scent on the roof and realized she was going into heat, my wolf had lost it. It had taken total control of me, something I'd never experienced before. I'd had one single goal—keep the other men away from her. That had included Von. When he'd touched me and stood between Kira and me, my mind had snapped. Was that what being feral was like?

It made me uncomfortable. When I probed my mind to get answers from my wolf, all he gave me was sullen silence. Why the hell had I become so enraged and possessive? The other alphas had reacted less than half as strongly as I had.

When Tate realized I wasn't going to answer him, he snorted a laugh and lay down on his bed. I did the same. Might as well try to rest. Who knew how long we'd be in here?

The minutes turned into hours. Around the time I was starting to wonder how long they'd keep us locked in here, there was a knock at the door. It opened, and the security guys led in a few staff witches and fae, carrying trays of food.

"I know your dinner was interrupted. Sorry about that. We brought a few things for you to munch on," one of the witches said.

"How long are we going to be kept here?" Abel asked. "Are we prisoners or something?"

"Right," Gavin added. "Do they think we're a threat to Von, or that we're going to burn the palace down?"

The witch gasped, looking scandalized. "Oh, absolutely not. We're simply sorting some things out." She swallowed and bit her lip. "Um, but they have shut the show down temporarily."

I sat up quickly, surprised by the news. "Seriously?"

The witch looked worried that she'd said anything, but continued. "Yes. A couple of the showrunners have come to the island via magic teleportation. They and Mr. Thornton will be sorting things out fairly quickly. Until then, the leading ladies and all of you will be contained."

"Contained? I don't like the sound of that," I said.

"Yeah," Gavin echoed. "Isn't it going a little overboard to shut the show down and lock us in here?" He pointed at me. "He's the one who attacked Von. Kick him off so we can get back to it. You can't keep us here against our will."

Tate chimed in. "Right, like how *contained* are we, anyway? We could shift and take on almost the whole staff if we really wanted to."

The staff members glanced at each other nervously, and the security guys became more rigid. One of them inched his hand closer to the concealed holster under his arm. This would go bad fast if I didn't calm everyone down.

"Hey," I said to them with a smile. "Don't mind those guys. It's in their nature to be pricks. No one is going to attack anyone."

My words calmed them a bit, though they still looked tense. They finished setting the trays of food on a table near the door. When the staff turned to go, I realized I had one chance to get a message to Kira.

"Excuse me, miss?" I called to a young fae.

"Yes?" she asked.

I hurried over to her. "Can you get a quick message to Kira for me?"

She looked uncomfortable and glanced behind her. The other staff members had gone, though a security guard glared at me for interfering.

"Mr. Thornton doesn't want any contestants talking right now," she replied. "Not until things get figured out."

"I get that, I really do, but this won't be any kind of message that will get you in trouble. I promise."

For a moment, I thought she would decline, but then she said, "Okay, what is it?"

I grinned at her. "Thanks. Tell Kira that she's an annoying little brat, okay?"

The fae's brow furrowed in confusion. "That's your message?"

"Yeah."

"I guess I can do that."

She hurried out the door, and I turned around to find J.D. gaping at me.

"A brat? Bro, you are the harshest person I've ever met. Didn't you just hear her confess her freaking undying love for you?"

"Oh, I heard her," I said with a grin. In fact, it was all I could think about.

For once, Gavin wasn't reacting to my words about Kira. Instead, he said something that chilled my blood. "I think I know why the show's been shut down."

"What's that?" Abel asked.

"To get them to freeze production on this show, especially when we're so far along, something bad has to have happened. Something momentous." He glanced around the room at all of us, meeting each of our eyes as he went. "War. I think it may have finally happened."

Gooseflesh rose on my arms and neck. He might be right. Probably was right. This show was the biggest thing on the planet. To shut it down meant something had to have gone to hell. Immediately, worry welled up in my chest for my unofficial pack and Kolton. If war had finally broken out among the packs, what was happening in the Eleventh Pack's lands?

The last time we'd spoken, Kolton had mentioned that he had some sort of plan to get Kira and me off the island. That was all well and good, but we had our own plan to stay alive here for the time being.

Kolton needed to focus on his own family and pack. Protecting them should be his main objective, and he shouldn't be worrying about his sister. I was determined to keep her safe no matter what happened next.

Chapter 21 - Kira

After some time staring out the window, I decided to do what I could to take my mind off everything. I took a shower, brushed my teeth, and put on more comfortable clothes. But doing all the little mundane things to prepare for bed didn't help me feel better. Instead, it made the whole situation even more surreal, almost like I was in a dream within a dream.

I paced my room, replaying my speech in my mind over and over again. I didn't see how I could have added more to it. I didn't regret doing it. Spur-of-the-moment decisions didn't usually turn out well for me, but I thought I did good. Someone needed to point out how messed up shifter society had become, how cruel and pointless *The Reject Project* was.

After being stuck in my room for an hour, though, I was starting to worry. I'd assumed Von would come speak to me after seeing the video replay. He'd chide me, perhaps give me a warning. If I was really lucky, he might look scared or worried. Hell, at this point, I would have been happy to have him in my room, raging at me and calling me an ungrateful bitch. Anything was better than this silence.

Von loved to hear himself talk. He also liked to throw his weight around. Something about the continued silent confinement made me uneasy.

The minutes ticked by, and eventually, I got tired of pacing. I sat on my bed, then grew restless and moved to the couch, then the chair by the door, then the windowsill before returning to the bed. I was antsy and twitchy, and my wolf was uneasy. It had been two hours since they'd locked me in here.

Needing fresh air, I opened my window, letting the tropical breeze flutter in. The air was humid, but it was better than the staleness of the room. Again, I wished I could get a message to or from Zoe. I pleaded with the gods to see those red, blue, and green flapping wings heading my way. But all I saw was the rapidly darkening jungle. Night had fallen, and with it, some of my hope.

In the distance, something else caused my mood to lower even more. Massive dark thunderheads appeared to be sliding across the sea, headed straight toward Bloodstone Island. If that was coming to dump a tropical storm on us, there was even less chance that

Zoe would be able to send her messenger birds anytime soon. And unless they had some sort of way to view the show in Haven, Zoe had no way of knowing what had happened. All of it made me feel more isolated.

When the knock came at the door, I flinched. I'd been so sure no one was coming that I was trying to talk myself into going to bed. I nearly tripped over myself as I rushed to the door. It opened a moment before I stepped into the foyer. Instead of Von, a young fae and witch stepped in, followed by a guard.

"Good evening, Miss Durst," the fae said. "We brought you a late dinner since your meal was... er, well, since you didn't get to finish."

On the tray was a grilled panini, potato chips, and the biggest chocolate cupcake I'd ever seen in my life. I was hungry, but I wasn't worried about food at the moment.

"Where's Von? What's going on?"

The fae shook her head and shrugged helplessly. "I'm sorry, I can't tell you any of that. Mr. Thornton will need to update you. All I know is that a few of the showrunners have arrived on the island to...

well, they said they needed to sort some things out. Not sure what that means."

I groaned. "Can you tell me *anything*?"

The fae glanced hesitantly at the witch. The older woman lifted an eyebrow. "Tell her. I don't think you'll get in trouble for it."

Hope surged in my chest. She had news. Some bit of information, maybe?

"I did speak with Mr. Rivers earlier," she said haltingly.

An even warmer ball of longing filled my chest. "Wyatt? What did he say?"

"Well, he asked me to pass on a message."

"And? Spit it out."

She looked embarrassed before finally speaking. "He said to tell you that, uh, that you're an annoying little brat."

I frowned at her, then I remembered the code words we'd set up. When it clicked, I laughed in delight, eliciting a confused scowl from the witch. I smiled at her, blinking away tears of happiness.

I cleared my throat. "Thanks. Um, if you see him again, tell him that he's really pissing me off." My code for *thank you*.

The fae and witch shared a confused look. Finally, the witch turned to leave. "You shifters are weird."

The fae nodded, though she looked bewildered. "If I see him, I'll tell him."

When they left, I carried my tray to the table in front of the window. I took a bottle of sparkling water from my minibar and sat down to eat. It wasn't world-class cuisine, but I barely tasted anything as I ate. Boiled cardboard would have tasted the same. The meal was nothing but calories, fuel for whatever might be coming next.

What were the others going through? Was an example being made of me? I couldn't rule out that Chelsey and the alphas were also locked in their rooms, but it was equally likely that the showrunners had sequestered me here as a punishment for speaking out. I could almost see them huddled with Von, thinking of the most entertaining way to kill me off. They'd want my death to be as big and bombastic as my speech.

But that seemed petty, even by the show's standards. Was something else happening? Could my words have had an even bigger impact than I thought?

I tossed the cupcake wrapper into the trash and slumped back in my chair. I wanted Wyatt. I would have given anything for him to be here with me. I longed to have him next to me, to be curled in his arms in bed and just forget the outside world. Being with him sounded like the most amazing thing in the world. I was beginning to realize I wanted more and more of that every day.

I'd come up with this plan to protect my family, to keep them and my pack safe. I would still do anything to make sure that happened, but now I'd also do anything to keep Wyatt safe. In my heart, he *was* my family, too.

Eventually, I was too tired to think. I closed the window to block out the strange sounds of the creatures that lived in the jungle, turned off the lights, and fell into a fitful sleep. My dreams were chaotic things that made no sense, morphing shapes and twisting colors with no coherent narrative. So when the screaming began, I thought it was part of my dreams.

When the screams finally roused me, I finally realized they weren't products of my own mind. The room was still inky black, but wind and rain lashed at my window, the only light from bursts and flashes of lightning outside. Groggy, I sat up, trying to figure out whether the screams were real or just the roar of the storm outside.

Shouts in the hallway shattered the night. The screams were right down the hall, and they were loud. Adrenaline shot through me. Those were not normal screams, and they weren't coming from an argument or fight. These were screams of terror and horror, and they were growing louder.

Years of ingrained training kicked in. I was out of my bed and dressed in tactical gear in minutes. I was lacing up my boots when the door burst in.

Yelping, I stood, ready to fight, but instead of an enemy, the guards rushed in. Heedless of me, the two massive fallen angels nearly fell over each other as they pushed through the door. The biggest one slammed the door shut behind him while the other grabbed a decorative cabinet and shoved it against the door. Then, the two shoved every piece of movable furniture into a barricade against the doorway.

"What the fuck is going on?" I demanded.

The two men looked absolutely terrified. Sweat sheened their faces.

"Are you gonna answer me?" I walked over to them. One was on his ass, pressed against the barricade. The other was bent over, hands on his knees and panting.

I glanced at the door and heard the screams outside. Uneasy fear filled me. What were they trying to keep out?

They still hadn't answered me. I grabbed the one who was bent over and slapped him. "Tell me what the fuck is going on. Now!"

My slap sobered him a bit. He blinked at me. "It's not good. The show was shut down, but when the showrunners arrived..." he trailed off, shaking his head in disbelief. "They had some kind of argument. That was when news came that war had broken out on the mainland. First reports are that the Eighth Pack invaded the lands of Seventh, trying to get a jump on them before they were attacked. It's gone to chaos back home—riots, fighting in the streets. Even the human city of Black Rock has been overrun with fighting wolf shifters.

"Anyway, a bunch of the magic staff heard their families back home weren't safe. Von and the others tried to calm them down." He took a few deep breaths and looked into my eyes. The fear I saw there made my knees weak. "But they left."

"Wait. What do you mean they left?"

"Gone. Not all of them, but most." He grabbed my shoulders, almost as if he was trying to hold himself up. "When they left, the wards around the mansion were weakened. It takes a full staff of witches and fae to keep the barriers up."

"What are you saying?" My voice trembled.

"Reject Mansion is no longer safe. The creatures and beasts of the island are infiltrating the grounds. They're inside the fucking house."

The news sent me reeling. War back home? I was too late. If the fighting had already started, my pack was in grave danger. Any of the more powerful packs could descend on our pack lands and try to lay waste to them. But right now, everyone inside the mansion was in even worse peril. The monsters were loose inside the walls.

"Where the fuck is Von? The other show—"

A wolf's howl cut me off. It was full of rage—the battle cry of a shifter. I recognized it immediately. Wyatt.

Leaving the guard, I ran to the window. The howl had come from outside. I peered through the glass, but the rain made it impossible to see anything. If Wyatt was out there, it meant he was fighting.

A few minutes later, his howl came again, but this time, it was from downstairs. He was inside now. He was trying to get to me.

"Get out of the way!" I shouted, rushing toward the door.

I pulled a chair away from the door, slinging it aside. When I heard the *snap-snap* of a bullet being chambered, I froze, turning to find both guards leveling their weapons at me. I sniffed the air, catching the metallic and bitter stench of silver. Both men looked terrified. *The Reject Project* had probably hired the biggest, baddest-looking motherfuckers they could, but being big and able to bench press four-hundred pounds didn't mean you were battle-tested.

"You freeze right fucking there," the smaller one said.

"I need to go help my friends," I said, the seconds ticking away like bomb blasts in my head.

"Nope. Not today, bitch. Show's shut down. We don't have to protect you anymore. Now, it's every man for himself. If you move that barricade, I will fill you with so much silver, they'll make fucking jewelry out of your guts. Back up and get away from the door."

"Yeah," the other one said. "Von's already gone, left on the only fucking helicopter with the other showrunners. They all left us here high and dry. If you put us in danger, we will blow your pretty little head off. Got it?"

My mind was still having trouble wrapping itself around all this. What could have caused this much chaos this fast? Von was gone? Had he really just cut and run?

These two assholes weren't going to stop me. I'd dealt with worse in the TO. Dammit, I'd dealt with worse on this stupid island. Panic and fear did weird things to people. They became irrational and dangerous. These two guys were massive, and yes, they had silver bullets aimed at my head, but Wyatt was out there. Wyatt needed my help, and I would be damned if these two fuckers stopped me.

Holding up my hands in surrender, I said, "It's okay. I get it. We're safe here. Sorry. I lost my head."

The two didn't lower their guns, but relief crossed over their faces. The one on the right raised his pistol, pointing the barrel at the ceiling. The other moved his finger off the trigger guard. Both were mistakes. Mistakes they would pay for.

With one swift movement, I kicked at the chair I'd pulled off the barricade, catching it with my toe and flinging it toward them. Even as the chair flew, I was moving. When the chair hit the guy on the left, it struck his hand, knocking his gun away. I slid, kicking out at his leg, knocking him off-balance. He fell forward. As he did, I grabbed his outstretched hand, pulled it away, and pressed on the back of his head, forcing him to the ground even faster. His face smashed into the hardwood with a sickening crack, blood spurting from his broken nose. He was snoring before I leaped to my feet.

The other guard, dazed by the rapid escalation of events, barely had time to turn his gun toward me. My left foot lashed out at him, breaking his wrist, and sent the pistol tumbling. I slammed my elbow into his chin, knocking a tooth loose. My fist crashed into his sternum, sending an explosion of breath out of his lungs. Before he could gasp for air, I kicked, my foot connecting with his stomach. He flew backward, his head slamming into the wall. He slid to the floor, vomiting on himself.

I glared at him as he gagged and desperately tried to suck in a few breaths with his broken jaw. "What did you learn?"

"Ugh... ugh..."

"That's what I thought. Be glad you're still alive." I went back to pulling the barricade apart.

Once the door was free, I tore through it. The hallway was in chaos. An assistant director I'd met once or twice was lying in a pool of blood down the corridor, a maddened vampire drinking greedily from his throat.

"Shit," I muttered.

From elsewhere, more screams, growls, and snarls of beasts echoed through the mansion. Hell had descended on Reject Manor. I ran down the hall and grabbed the vampire by its neck, twisting my hips and slamming it to the ground. Dazed, it blinked up at me with its mad eyes. That gave me the chance to break off one of the heavy oak spindles on the handrail. I rammed it into its chest right as it was sitting up.

It twitched and died, and from the next level down, a voice called out in fear, feminine and familiar.

Chelsey. Yanking my makeshift weapon from the dead vampire, I rushed downstairs. Chelsey was struggling with another bloodsucker. She had her hands around its neck, pushing it away. The creature was snapping at her with razor-sharp canines.

Taking the final seven steps in one massive leap, I slammed my shoulder into the vampire. When we both crashed to the ground, I dealt the killing blow as I stabbed the stake into its heart.

"Kira? Oh, gods, I thought I was dead." Chelsey looked terrified.

Standing, I took her by the shoulder. "Stay with me. Wyatt's nearby—we need to meet up with him. Come on."

The two of us hurried down the next set of steps, coming to the landing on the second floor. A banshee at the far end of the corridor screamed in rage and burst through a door. From the room, screams of panic escalated as the monster rushed in, followed by the bloody sounds of torn flesh and the eardrum-bursting shrieks of the banshee. Whoever had been hiding there was gone. There was nothing we could do. I tugged Chelsey in the opposite direction.

It seemed that once the wards around the mansion had dropped, every terrifying thing on the island had converged here, drawn like moths to a flame.

As though it heard my thoughts, a ragged feral bear shifter came barreling down the hallway, bellowing in rage, eyes mad, with foam frothing at its massive teeth.

"Watch out!" I shoved Chelsey aside to take on the bear.

Waiting until it was almost right upon me, I jumped and spun in the air. As I landed on my back, I slid right beneath its gigantic head. The giant ran straight over me, my movement too fast for it to alter course. One huge paw came down on my shoulder, sending lancing pain down my arm, but with my free hand, I shoved the wooden spindle into its chest. It continued on for several feet, not realizing it was dying. Splatters of blood trailed after it as its life pumped out of its chest. It turned and glared at me, but then it fell over, finally dead.

"Wow," Chelsey muttered. "That was... crazy."

I stood, wincing as I moved the arm it had stepped on. It wasn't broken, but I'd have a hell of a bruise to heal from, but even that would be gone in no time. All in all, I came out pretty good, especially compared to the bear.

This place was open territory, and nearly every creature on the island was territorial in some way. It was probably why they were converging on it. Each of them was ready to claim this area as their own.

We had to get out of here. This house had been a beacon of safety, but now it was the most dangerous place on the island. We had to find the others and head into the jungle. For once, the safest place would be out in the wilderness. Our only hope of survival was to find Haven.

I dragged Chelsey along behind me, trying to stay out of sight of monstrous, feral creatures. We saw a basilisk slithering up the stairs toward the top floor, a manticore devouring some poor woman, and a shadowy something that smelled like rotten meat and ammonia slipping into a room.

The second floor was devoid of any life that wasn't intent on killing us. Chelsey and I went for the stairs to head for the ground floor when I heard Wyatt's howl again. This time, it was accompanied by two more howls. Hope surged inside me when I realized how close he was.

"Move!" I shouted, hauling poor Chelsey's arm.

She almost stumbled but regained her footing, following me to the rear stairwell. Behind us, an explosion of movement and noise drew our attention. Two feral tiger shifters came crashing through a door where we'd just been. They were too busy clawing and biting each other to bother with us. Chelsey and I hurried down the stairs toward the sound of another battle.

Coming to the ground floor, I almost sobbed with relief. Wyatt was there. In his wolf form, he and two other wolves that looked like J.D. and Gavin were fighting off a hulking minotaur. The monster swung its head side to side, trying to gore them with the huge sharp horns on its head. Gavin had his jaws clamped on the thing's throat, the minotaur swinging him around like a rag doll.

As we watched, J.D. and Wyatt caught the beast by its hands and pulled it onto its back. The floor shuddered beneath me as it came crashing down. Wyatt rushed over and locked his teeth on a horn, pulling the head back to give Gavin more room to work. A moment later, the creature gurgled as Gavin's teeth crushed its windpipe. For a moment, it flailed, and then it went still.

"Wyatt!" I called.

His wolf head snapped around. When our eyes met, I felt safe for the first time since waking up to chaos. The three men shifted back, and Wyatt ran to me, pulling me into his arms. J.D. limped toward us. His back leg was severely injured. It looked like the minotaur had managed to stab him. Gavin put his arm around his shoulders, helping him walk.

"Are you guys okay?" I asked.

Wyatt nodded, eyes darting around warily. "We have to get out of here."

"We need to get to the jungle. Maybe we can find Haven."

"What the hell is Haven?" Gavin asked.

"No time," Wyatt said, taking my hand. "Let's move."

Wyatt led us down the hall. We stumbled upon two guards. They'd been torn apart by something. It must have been fast because they never had time to pull their guns.

"Grab their weapons," Wyatt commanded.

Chelsey and I grabbed the pistols. I checked them both—fully loaded with silver rounds. I nudged Wyatt, and we moved on. We didn't move as fast as we could have. J.D. was hurt, and until he healed, it would be slow-going. The screams on the upper floors had started to die down. Dread hung over me. Fewer screams meant fewer people. The monsters were wiping out the entire crew. Anyone and everyone was fair game.

I felt sick to my stomach. As much as I hated this show, most of these people had just been doing their jobs, following orders given by upper management. Now they'd been killed in numerous horrifying ways.

I flinched and gasped as three quick gunshots sounded behind me. Turning, I found Chelsey panting heavily, the gun in her hand smoking. At our rear, a feral panther shifter writhed in pain as the silver bullets sent it into the agonizing throes of death.

"Good job," I said.

There was terror in her eyes when she looked at me. "Yeah." She lowered the gun and followed.

The massive foyer had turned into an abattoir. The white marble floors were smeared with blood.

Bodies lay strewn about, and red paw and footprints were everywhere. The doors had been torn off the hinges and lay shattered on either side of the entrance.

"Hurry," Wyatt said.

He took the lead, followed by Gavin and J.D. Chelsey and I stayed at the rear with the guns. We were almost to the door when movement to my right caught my eye. A blood-coated hand was waving feebly at us.

I skidded to a stop, slipping in blood and almost falling over. Once I focused on the figure and made out his features through the blood on his face, I realized who it was.

"Abel?"

"Help!" he shouted hoarsely.

"Holy hell," Gavin muttered.

Chelsey and I ran over to help him. His body was covered in bites and gashes. It looked like a lot of the blood was his, but some must have come from elsewhere. If it was all his, he'd have been dead already.

"What happened?" I asked as we dragged him toward the front door.

"I got, ugh..." He moaned in pain. "Got caught between a couple of ghosts and ferals." He coughed and hacked out a wad of bloody spit. "It was like being inside a buzzsaw."

"Can you stand?"

"I can limp. My right foot is broken."

"That will have to do," I said.

Chelsey and I groaned in unison as we hauled him up, supporting him between us.

"Let me carry him," Wyatt said, stepping forward.

I shook him off. "No. We need you to lead. You're the strongest fighter. Here." I shoved my gun into his hand. "We've got him. Let's move."

Wyatt looked like he wanted to argue, but he took the gun with a grunt and we started moving again. Outside, the howling wind and rain drowned out the cacophony in the mansion. The storm lashed at us, washing the blood from Abel and J.D. as we went. Descending the front steps with two injured men was slow-going, but we made it to the front courtyard. Knowing it was hopeless, I still glanced toward the helipad. Sure enough, no aircraft was visible. I gritted my teeth and swore to every god in the heavens that I wouldn't be happy until I drove a stake through Von Thornton's fucking chest.

"Help! Hey, help me!" The scream was barely audible above the storm.

"It's Tate!" J.D. shouted.

Sure enough, the rapid-fire lighting in the sky illuminated the other alpha. He was leaning against a tree, looking harried. His face was smeared with blood, and his hair was matted and sweaty.

Wyatt waved to him. "Hurry! Come on!"

Tate burst from the cover and came running. I frowned. Something was wrong. The shadows behind him were moving, and there was a flash of silver. Was it my imagination? Maybe the storm was playing tricks on my vision. I wiped the rain from my face and peered harder into the distance.

Wyatt gasped. "Tate!" he shrieked. "Run! Run, dammit!" I couldn't remember the last time he'd sounded so scared.

Something out of a nightmare emerged from the forest. The hood of its filthy black cloak hid its head, but even through the storm, I could see the malevolent red eyes. A revenant. My heart stuttered. I never thought I'd see one in real life.

All of us shouted for him to run. Tate looked confused as he jogged toward us. Could he not hear us? Fear ate at my guts. The thing in the forest swept forward, almost floating above the ground. Even as I watched, it hefted a massive silver scythe, the blade at least three feet long.

"Tate!" His name exploded from my throat.

The revenant swung down hard. The silver blade caught Tate between the neck and shoulder, cleaving him in half diagonally. The shock on Tate's face faded to the blank stare of death as his top half tumbled forward and smashed into the sodden ground. His lower half stayed upright for a moment, spewing blood and gore, then slumped on top of the rest of his body.

Chelsey screamed, covering her eyes with her free hand.

The revenant looked down at Tate's corpse. Behind it, an animalistic scream erupted, and the creature swept back into the jungle to hunt whatever had caused it. I stared at the pile of limbs and blood. Tate had wanted me dead, had been plotting to get rid of me. His death should have filled me with cathartic happiness, but all I felt was bone-chilling horror.

Of all the deaths on the island, this was the first I'd seen with my own eyes. I'd promised myself I would get everyone out alive, and I'd failed. Tate's desire to do me in had been fueled by this stupid fucking show. Who was to say if our roles had been reversed, I wouldn't have done the same thing? He was a victim of circumstance, one more mark on the tally. Another coin added to the debt the showrunners owed us. And by gods, I would make them pay that debt in blood if I could.

"Come on," Wyatt said. "There's nothing we can do. If that thing is trying to stake its claim on the mansion, it won't stop until all living creatures are dead, including us. We're lucky something distracted it. We need to hurry."

Without another word, we moved toward the tree line opposite where the revenant had gone. Wyatt stayed close to us. Chelsey held her gun out, ready for anything to attack us. A vicious, victorious roar came from the mansion. Something had won a fight. More strange noises erupted from the jungle as we entered.

A new fear gripped me. We were in the wilderness, in the dark, during a storm, and with no idea where to go. I couldn't shake the thought that we'd traded one danger for a worse one. At any moment, something could come rushing at us from the darkness. With two of our party injured, we would not fare well. The only good thing was that the dense jungle dampened the cacophony of the storm and provided meager shelter from most of the rain and wind.

"Man," J.D. groaned. "This is so not cool. I just learned I may have a real fated mate out there, but I'm about to get eaten by the gods only know what. That, or get blown out to sea by this stupid storm."

That low mood spread to the others. Abel looked miserable, and it wasn't from his pain; there was a hopelessness to his face that I didn't like. Chelsey was biting her lower lip hard enough to draw blood, fighting back tears of despair. I wanted to tell her and the others to keep their heads up and stay focused on surviving, but I kept my mouth shut. They didn't have the training Wyatt and I had. These were normal people who'd never dealt with ferals or mad vampires until coming here. Wyatt and I were battle-hardened Tranquility operatives. How could I possibly ask them to stay strong?

"Abel, can you walk? Are you healing?" I asked.

He put pressure on his foot, then winced but nodded. "Yeah. I think so. It wasn't a bad break, and it's already getting better."

"Okay, Chelsey, you keep helping him walk. I'm going to take point with Wyatt."

"What's the play?" Wyatt asked when I joined him.

I looked up, the sheets of rain pouring through the canopy into my face, then turned to him. "Shelter until this storm passes. Until this is over, we'll end up walking in circles. Once it's clear, we can search for Haven."

"Sounds good to me," Wyatt said. "Let's go, everyone."

"We are so dead, aren't we?" J.D. asked.

I put a hand on his shoulder. "There's one good thing about this. With the mansion overrun and the storm, most creatures will either be ransacking the house or hiding for shelter. They won't be out looking for food."

Hope glimmered faintly in J.D.'s eyes. "Seriously?"

"Yeah. We're lucky. Well, as lucky as we can be right now," I added. "Let's go."

What I'd said was probably a lie. There was every possibility that awful things were still on the prowl out here. But hope was a powerful motivator, and I'd be damned if I would take that away from them.

Chapter 22 - Wyatt

The storm raged around us, picking up strength as we trudged through the jungle. Even the canopy overhead wasn't doing much to keep the rain off us anymore. Between the wind, the trees, and the water slamming into us, I could barely see more than ten feet in front of me. None of my other enhanced senses were any good, either. We were walking blind.

I grabbed Kira, putting my face close to her ear. "We need to find cover soon! Have you seen anything? A cave or something?"

She shook her head, rivulets of rain streaming down her cheeks and chin. "Not yet, but you're right—we have to find a spot to hole up. J.D. and Abel need time to heal. They aren't in a good way."

Glancing over my shoulder to look at them, I saw she was right. Both men were putting up a good fight, but neither looked great. For shifter healing to work, you needed to rest and let your body work at getting itself mended.

"We stay the course," Kira said. "Stay on this path and try to find something. As long as we don't get turned around and walk in circles, we'll find something eventually."

As terrifying as the situation was, I loved having Kira by my side. Her clipped, no-nonsense, and professional demeanor was exactly what we needed right now. We were in a survival situation, and having a trained partner gave me hope that we might have a chance at getting out alive.

It was all the better that my partner was the woman I was in love with. I'd do whatever I could to keep her safe, and she'd have my back as well.

We managed to get another hundred yards before we were accosted. A gnarled, decrepit vampire came stumbling out of the jungle. It held a squirrel creature to its mouth, sucking the blood from it. Kira grabbed the others, stopping them before the creature saw us. Two more bloodsuckers appeared behind the first one. It was a full coven.

The things fought over the squirrel's body, hissing and snapping at each other. They could survive on the blood of animals, but they preferred the lifeblood of sentient creatures. They'd be on us in a moment once they noticed us. With a few hand signals, I told Kira to get the two injured men and Chelsey behind a tree.

I leaned toward Gavin. "Can you fight?" I whispered.

He nodded as Kira returned. "I'm good."

"Okay. You take the one on the right. I'll go for the biggest one on the left. Kira, you take the middle. Do it fast before—"

A shriek pierced through the roar of the storm. I'd been about to say "before they see us," but it was too late. The middle vampire leveled a finger in our direction and screeched again.

We rushed forward. I kicked out, my foot catching the vampire in the shoulder. The blow made it spin and fall, bashing its face against the ground. I jumped on its back, grabbed it under the chin, and snapped the neck. It popped like a dry twig under my hands. That would keep it down for at least ten minutes. Maybe longer, given its weak and emaciated state.

Done with mine, I turned to find Kira shoving her target face-first into a tree. A branch took the monster in the chest. Beside her, Gavin was plunging a stick into the monster he fought. I breathed a sigh of relief. We'd done it.

Gavin looked over at me and gave a thumbs-up. I saw it before he did. A fourth vampire ran at a dead sprint.

"Gavin, behind you!"

Before he had time to look, the monster leaped onto his back, shoving him directly onto the same stick he'd killed the other one with. It slammed into Gavin's body.

Kira dashed forward. The last vampire reared its head back, fangs exposed, and drove its mouth toward Gavin's exposed neck. Instead of making contact with flesh and blood, it met Kira's boot. Blood and sharp fangs flew into the air, and the creature tumbled aside. I rammed a branch into its ribcage, ending the fucker there and then.

"Oh, gods. Oh no," Kira muttered as I joined her.

She was above Gavin, staring at his back where he lay like a lover on the rapidly decomposing body of the vampire he'd killed a few seconds earlier. There was only one way to know how bad it was. I grabbed his shoulder and rolled him over. The stick slid out of his body. He'd been stabbed high in the chest, right below the collarbone. It was a nasty wound, but it didn't look fatal. Blood still oozed from the injury, but it didn't pulse out like an artery had been struck.

He blinked at us through the rain and coughed before wincing in pain. "What the fuck was that?"

"Can you stand?" I asked.

He nodded, blood oozing from his puncture. "I can make it, yeah."

I reached out and took his hand, helping him to his feet.

He grunted and put a hand to his wound. "That fucking hurt."

Watching him try to hide his pain as we went to get the others, I had to admit to myself that this Fell brother was different from Jayson. Gavin was able to keep his head and shrug off the pain. Jayson would have screamed about how unfair all of this was, how he was a special boy and deserved better. The injury alone would have sent him into screaming hysterics like a toddler. I still held no love for Gavin, but after everything he'd done tonight, I had to give him my grudging respect.

Once our group was together again, we moved on. The next twenty minutes were hell on earth. We stayed on the path Kira had pointed out, but it led up a steep incline. With three injured people in tow, it was awful. The rain had turned the ground into mud that was inches deep. We trudged up, sludge trying to suck up our shoes with every step. I was soaked through to the bone, and even in the tropical location and warmth, the blasting wind of the storm made me shiver from the cold.

As we neared the hill's apex, Kira fired two quick shots into the darkness. I staggered back, then saw the feral bear shifter stumble and fall dead at her feet. The thing had come out of nowhere.

"Good shot," I said.

Kira was still looking into the darkness. She turned and locked eyes with me, nodding in the direction the bear had just come.

I furrowed my brow in confusion but followed, keeping my gun up. I looked at the others as we went. "Stay with us, but keep back until we find out what she's looking for."

Chelsey and the others quickly agreed. All of them looked too tired and drained to argue. Creeping along behind Kira, I saw why she'd led us here. A gaping black hole yawned open, almost hidden by the branches and palm fronds. How Kira had noticed it, I had no clue.

As we drew nearer, she pointed at the ground. I saw bear tracks, already being washed away by the rain but still visible. They led from the opening of the cave.

"Stay here," I told the others. "We'll be right back."

When I stepped in, the immediate relief of not having rain pound on my head almost made me groan with delight.

Kira came close, pressing her lips to my ear. "If we see anything, unload on it."

"You don't have to tell me twice."

The cave went back almost fifteen feet before turning at a near-ninety-degree angle. There, we found the end, along with two more feral bear shifters. Whether they'd smelled us or heard our footsteps, they were rousing themselves from sleep before we'd fully realized what we found.

Kira and I backed away, turning the corner and retreating to the cave entrance. Both bears roared at our unwelcome visit and broke into a run. Kira and I leveled our pistols and unleashed fiery death on both of them. The one I aimed at was a grizzly larger than any I'd ever seen before, and it took the entire clip to put him down. Thankfully, he collapsed at my feet, unmoving, as the slide on the gun locked back.

Kira had killed the other bear. She gave me a look and nodded, her mind still locked in operative mode. It was amazing to see how she could compartmentalize everything and stay on track. I didn't have that same killer instinct she had. I was good at what I did, but Kira was better.

We dragged both bears out of the cave and left them with the other one she'd killed a few minutes before. The things weighed a ton. By the time we were done, the four others had made their way into the cave and had settled at the back, huddling together for warmth.

Kira and I joined them, and instead of settling down to rest, Kira checked on the wounded. I watched her as she checked Abel's broken foot and many gashes and wounds, moved to examine Gavin and his injury, and then made sure J.D. was comfortable. Finally, once everyone was settled and as safe as she could make them, the mask dropped, and I could see how wiped out Kira was. It wasn't only the exhaustion that had her looking tense, though. I knew it also came from our location. We were in a cave, similar to the one I'd found her in all those years ago.

"I'm going to sit at the front," Kira said. "Keep watch right by the opening. I still have three bullets left in this pistol."

"No," Chelsey said, pushing herself to her feet. "You've done enough. I'm not hurt. I'll be the lookout. You and Wyatt need to rest."

Kira was shaking her head to disagree, but before she could voice her dissent, Gavin rose as well.

He gestured toward Chelsey. "I'll sit with her. I'm not that injured. We can keep each other awake. And you two really need to rest."

I knew Kira well enough to know she wanted to fight, but her shoulders sagged in defeat. She handed the pistol to Chelsey. "Don't rely on your eyes alone," Kira warned. "Use your ears and nose. I know the storm makes it hard, but you might catch a whiff of something before it's right on you."

Chelsey took the gun and grinned at Kira. "Got it, boss."

They left to man the mouth of the cave. Kira sat against the far wall, pulling her knees to her chest and hugging them close to her body. Abel and J.D. were still huddled together for warmth. I sat next to her, letting her be silent for several minutes before speaking.

"How are you doing?"

She looked at me blankly before shrugging. "As good as I can be, I guess. This is all kind of surreal, isn't it?"

I thought about it for a moment, then nodded. "It does sort of feel like I'm still asleep."

Kira snorted a laugh. "I mean, what, two hours ago, I was asleep in bed in a mansion. A prize mate on a TV show, planning how to get everyone out alive. Now? Here we are. Huddled up in a cave with dozens and dozens of monsters hunting us across the island."

"You know, those bunks we had in the alpha den weren't super comfortable, but they sure beat the hell out of this." I knocked on the stony ground.

"I'm serious, Wyatt. I'm not talking about missing the nice sheets and food. I mean that we were trying to bring the damn show down. At this point, who knows if we'll get a chance? Von's gone, the show's over. There's no way to get word to the outside world, and there's a war going on."

"I know," I said. "But maybe that's what all this is about. The war, the mansion, Von running? It all went down after your little speech. Maybe you did do what you planned to do."

The expression on her face told me she wasn't buying it. She didn't have as much faith in herself as I did.

She changed the subject. "We can't get ahold of Zoe, but our only chance to survive is getting to Haven. As soon as the storm lets up, we need to head out to look."

"What's Haven? Abel asked. J.D. stirred beside him.

Kira sighed deeply, then proceeded to tell them everything. Zoe being alive, the one-eyed wolf, Haven, taking the show down—all of it. While she laid out everything, I tried to take stock of where we were and what needed to be done. We needed to get everyone to Haven, but Kira was my main objective. Her survival was my priority. I also worried about my unofficial pack and Kolton and his parents, wondering how they were dealing with everything going on. Everyone Kira and I cared for was in danger, and we were helpless to do anything.

After a while, Kira stood and brushed her pants off. "It's been a long day, and none of you had a good night's sleep. Get some rest. I'll take watch." She glanced around at the stone walls with trepidation. "I can't sleep in caves, anyway."

"I'll go with you," I said.

Kira didn't argue, and once we'd sent Chelsey and Gavin to sleep, she took a seat only a few inches from where the rain was pouring down at the entrance. I took a seat beside her and set the pistol on my lap.

We watched the storm for a little while. The wind might have been dying down a bit, but even if it was, it was still the strongest thunderstorm I'd lived through. If this wasn't a hurricane, I hoped never to see one.

Eventually, I broke the silence. "So, uh, your family—"

"I know. Trying not to think about it."

I put my arm around her and pulled her closer. For a moment, I was sure she'd pull away, say she was fine, tell me to stay focused. But she warmed my heart by leaning into me. She rested her head on my shoulder and let me hold her.

"Not that it means much, given our current situation," I said. "But I promise to do anything I can to make things okay again."

"Would you do it again?"

"Huh?" I looked down at her, but she was still staring into the storm. "What do you mean?"

"This. Would you do it again? If you knew what you know now, would you come on the show? Knowing that you'd end up right here hiding in a cave, our chances of survival dwindling by the second, no way to get back home, going through everything we've been through so far... would you do it again?"

"Of course." I didn't hesitate. "Even if I'd died in one of the past challenges, I'd still do it again. As long as it meant you were safe, I'd do it all again in a heartbeat."

She finally pulled her eyes from the storm to look at me, a faint smile on her lips. "You really would, wouldn't you?"

"I'm a man of my word," I said with a grin.

Her eyes went soft and introspective. "You know I meant it, right?" she whispered. "I do love you." She blinked and huffed, almost like she'd come back to herself. "I can't believe I fell for the bossiest, nosiest, and most overprotective wolf in the world—and a lone wolf, no less." A playful spark twinkled in her eyes. "But I can't deny how strongly I feel for you, Wyatt. You're also pretty hot. That helps."

I laughed and leaned forward, kissing her hard and fast. Our lips merged for what might have been a few hours or a few seconds—time seemed to stand still. When I pulled back, I gazed deep into her eyes. In my heart, I had to admit the odds of all of us making it to Haven in one piece were low. Kira knew it, too, and there was no reason to dredge it up. She'd been through too much already. All I could do was vow to myself that I'd get her to safety. No matter what.

The storm continued to rage on and on. Finally, an hour before dawn, the trees stopped swaying as hard and the torrential downpour transitioned to a steady drizzle. Lighting still flashed every few seconds, but the thunder was fainter.

"Do you think we should give it a try?" I asked.

Kira stood and dusted her butt off. "Probably now or never. The storm could be passing, or maybe we're in the eye. Either way, we need to move. Once things look less terrifying, the creatures will be stirring again."

"Let's scout a bit before we get the others out in this. At least find a direction that looks the least strenuous."

Kira agreed, and we let the others know what was going on. Chelsey looked nervous for us to go, but I assured her we'd be back soon.

"Okay. Be careful, guys," she said.

I left the gun with her and headed out with Kira. I'd completely dried off in the cave, so stepping back out into the rain—even though it was only drizzling now—was a psychological gut punch. Being wet and miserable was way worse than being dry and miserable.

Kira and I continued up the hill. We found the carcasses of the bear shifters, and they'd definitely been fed on. I was grateful that we'd hauled them this far from the cave entrance.

"What do you think was here?" Kira asked, poking one of the bodies with the toe of her boot.

I looked down at the creature. All that was left of one was a bloody skeleton. "No idea, but better it happened to this guy than us. Come on."

The hill grew ever steeper. It was more of a small mountain than a hill. At the top, we had a good vantage point to see a large swath of the island. In the distance, the dormant volcano stood sentinel over the jungle.

I pointed to it. "Whichever way we go, let's steer clear of that thing."

"The volcano?"

"Yeah. It's got some cave or cavern where Leif was trying to drag me into. I can't imagine it's a place we want to be."

Kira pointed north. "Someplace near the mountains would be the best place for an encampment like Haven. Mountains to your back give you less area to watch. It looks like a river flows right beside that stretch, which would give them fresh water. We can try that way. It'll take us past the volcano, but we should be able to swing wide and keep a safe distance."

"Okay. I can't think of anything better," I said, but my mind replayed that strange whirring sound I'd heard coming from the cave in the volcano. I shivered, and it wasn't from being wet.

We plotted a route down the hill toward the river beside the mountain. The rain slacked off even more, and we decided to head back and check on the others. On the way down, I stopped dead in my tracks and looked back over my shoulder. The hair on the back of my neck stood on end.

"Do you feel it, too?" Kira asked.

I gazed into the jungle, trying to see what had caught my attention. I had the strongest feeling that something was watching us.

"Like we're being stalked?" I asked.

"Yeah. I wasn't sure if it was all in my head or not. All that time with cameras everywhere, I'd sort of gotten used to it."

"This is different."

Kira took my hand and pulled me along. "I know. It's weird, whatever it is, but we need to get back to the others."

She was right, but I kept my senses sharp as we returned to the cave. I never heard or scented anything more, but that weird sense of being watched never ceased.

We'd almost made it back to the cave when a lizard-like creature came slithering out of the jungle toward us. The thing was covered in mud and soaking wet. It was a cockatrice, a smaller creature that resembled a dragon but with a head that looked like a rooster's. It rushed us, screeching a battle cry. It only came to hip height, though from the aggression it showed, you'd think it was ten feet tall.

A group of them would have been dangerous, but one was easy to deal with. Kira kicked it in the face right before it could attack us. The thing flipped over, either knocked out or dead. We didn't stick around to find out.

Back at the cave, the others still looked exhausted despite their naps. Thankfully, J.D. and Abel had managed to heal up a bit more. They could walk unassisted, though both were limping.

"Everyone stay alert," I said as we exited the cave. "If you see something, say something, and say it fast. Understood?"

They all agreed, and we headed out, again ascending the hill. The storm had almost completely passed. Any monsters who had taken shelter would be out and about, looking for a meal. As silently as we could, we moved up the hill and down the path Kira and I had chosen.

"Does anyone else feel like a rabbit instead of a wolf?" J.D. hissed. "I feel like we're being hunted."

So Kira and I weren't the only ones who felt it. I glanced over my shoulder to see that our entire group was feeling it. Whatever or whoever was watching us was still there.

"We feel it, too," I said. "Kira and I noticed it earlier. Just stay the course and keep a lookout."

After descending the hill, we found ourselves in an area of the island I'd never been to before. The jungle wasn't as thick with trees, but heavy vines stretched between every trunk, creating a sort of spiderweb.

Gavin grabbed one of the vines and tugged at it. "These things are tough. We'll need to either go around or find some way to cut through—fuck!"

A roar exploded from beyond the heavy wall of vines, and a massive head ripped through the plants, sending shreds of leaves flying. Gavin stumbled backward, backpedaling with his feet and his good arm. Beyond the torn vines, nightmares emerged, the mutations Kira and I had encountered on the last challenge. Multiple beasts had been melded into a single creature by some strange combination of science and magic.

An explosion went off next to my ear, and I jumped. Kira stood, gun forward, barrel smoking. The bullet tore through the skull of the first monster, a thing with the head of an alligator, the body of a lion, and the arms of a human but with thick talons for nails. I gaped at the body as it fell forward, blocking the way for the two other monsters behind it. One had strangely stunted and twisted wings on the back of a body made up of equal parts tiger and human. The other had the head of a massive snake atop a body with the mottled gray-green flesh of a kappa and the legs and arms of a bear.

"What the fuck is that?" Gavin shouted.

Before I could answer, the creatures burst through the barrier and were on us. Kira fired the last two rounds of the gun, but the snake-headed beast struck her, making her shots go wild.

Chaos erupted. Gavin grabbed Chelsey and pulled her aside as the winged tiger monster tried to bite her face, its teeth missing her by inches. I shifted and leaped onto its back, biting and tearing at a stunted wing. The scream that came from the maw of the thing made my guts go cold. It sounded almost human. Hearing that noise come from that thing was like a nightmare come to life. Once again, I was hit with a strange sense of surrealness.

J.D. was trying to help Kira fight off the snake-headed creature. It swung an arm out and caught him in the chest, cutting four shallow wounds below his collar bone. He fell backward, but Kira managed to keep him from hitting the ground.

"Run! That way." She pointed through the hole in the vegetation the creatures had created.

These things were too strong to take on without either weapons or fighting-fit people. As it was, almost our entire party was wounded in some way. Kira took J.D.'s hand and ran for it. My teeth were still locked on the wing of my quarry, but as the others rushed through the opening, it roared its strange alien cry again and threw me off. Tumbling through the air, I looked down. The huge tiger mouth opened. A combination of human incisors, tiger canines, and jagged, serrated teeth snapped at me. I hit the ground in a roll and ran after the others.

Dirt flew up as my paws slammed into the ground. I caught up to the others fifty yards on, but something was wrong. Kira was screaming, and Gavin and J.D. were holding her back.

"We have to go back for him!" Kira shrieked.

I shifted back to my human form and grabbed her shoulders, looking into her eyes. "What's wrong? Who are you talking about?"

The guilt, horror, and devastation in her eyes tore at my heart. There was guilt, horror, and devastation. "Abel. He's not here. We left him."

My stomach sank, and I whipped my head around. Abel wasn't there. Had he been left with the monsters? I didn't remember seeing him in my rush to escape. As though they sensed me thinking about them, the sound of stampeding feet raced towards us. I turned in time to see both monstrosities rushing us. Wild and hungry eyes locked on us all.

I shoved Kira behind me and stepped forward, screaming at them to come on. If I was going to die, then by the gods, I would do it fighting.

When they were only twenty feet away, the sky erupted in the fluttering and flapping of wings. Despite what was coming, I looked up. Hundreds of bats swooped from overhead, coalescing before me in the naked form of a woman.

The Shadowkeeper.

The small shadows of the forest surged forward to cloak her and cover her body in a robe of darkness. The beasts, seeing new prey appear from seemingly out of nowhere, altered their course and rushed her.

The Shadowkeeper looked at the two monsters with unfiltered disgust. She clapped her hands, and more shadows emerged from the jungle, forming two heavy blocks of darkness. They slammed into the creatures, one on either side, crushing the beasts in a spray of blood, bone, and gore.

The remains of the beasts splattered to the ground, and I gaped as the Shadowkeeper brushed her hands together, sending the huge blocks of shadow melting back into the jungle.

"Hello again, Wyatt," she said, raising an eyebrow at me.

I swallowed hard. "Uh... hey. Good to see you again."

Chapter 23 - Kira

The woman before us had a strange and powerful presence, almost like gravity pulling at us. There was also a faint and somehow familiar scent in the air. It tickled at the back of my memory. She smelled like... something I'd scented before. Not exactly the same, but similar, though I couldn't place it.

The Shadowkeeper. Everyone had heard legends about her. She had a cult following even outside the show. I didn't know what I'd expected her to look like, but it wasn't this. She strolled forward, confident as the shadows rippled around her body like a living dress. As she looked at us each in turn, I couldn't help but feel like she was weighing and measuring each member of our party.

"Thank you," Chelsey blurted. "For saving us, I mean."

The Shadowkeeper smiled at Chelsey, though it looked more like she was smiling to herself. She glanced over her shoulder at the bloody remains of the twisted creatures. "Perhaps it is time I get involved in my sister's spectacle, after all," she said, though she sounded like she was only talking to herself. "Meddling may indeed be necessary."

"What does that mean?" Wyatt asked.

She raised her arms and the shadows vanished from her body. She was perfect, like a form carved from pale marble. An instant later, she exploded into a cloud of bats that surged straight toward us. Was she about to kill us? My heart hammered in my chest, fear overtaking all other thoughts. The tiny creatures swarmed us, surrounded us. A flash of light blinded me, and I knew I was dead.

Then, I opened my eyes to find we were nowhere near where we'd been. The jungle was gone, and we stood in an area nestled right against the mountains. A heavy wall of trees ran around the perimeter of a small clearing. This had to be close to Haven. Why else would the Shadowkeeper teleport us here?

"Ugh." J.D. was wiping at his arms and shivering in disgust. "Man, I freaking *hate* bats." He actually gagged, then wrapped himself in a hug. "Gross. Yuck. Blech. I have a thing about bats," he added when he saw our expressions.

"I thought we were dead," Gavin said.

"Same," J.D. said. "I just *knew* that was it. All done. Now I still have a chance to look for Leif."

"Leif?" Chelsey turned to look at him, forehead creased with lines. "What are you talking about? Leif's dead."

Gavin turned to look at me. "Looks like there's a lot we aren't aware of. Kira? Want to fill us in on what exactly the fuck is going on?"

I couldn't answer him. Now that we were momentarily safe, I couldn't stop thinking about Abel. He was back in the forest. At best, he was on his own and injured. At worst, he was already dead. The weight of that thought almost brought me to my knees. After watching Tate die, I didn't think I could handle losing Abel, too. Unlike Tate, Abel had been kind and good. His death would hurt even worse.

Wyatt pulled me close. I sagged into his embrace.

"This is not your fault," he whispered.

"Well, it kind of is," Gavin muttered. "Both of yours. If you'd told us what was going on sooner, we might have been better prepared."

"Gods, Gavin, shut up," Chelsey snapped.

There was no reason to let Gavin's words get to me. They weren't a dig at me or Wyatt, but the truth. But there was no way we could have told them sooner. If I'd revealed my plan to fake the eliminations too early to too many people, it never would have worked. Someone would have let something slip. So, yes, it was partially my fault, but that didn't change the fact that we'd made the right decision.

"Come on," I said, glancing around. "We need to find Zoe if she's here."

A flash of light lit up the early morning, and a second later, I was being tackled in a bear hug. When the arms wrapped around me, I struggled against it, terrified that some other horror had me in its grip. Then, the familiar scent hit my nose, and I relaxed, gratefully allowing the arms to embrace me.

"Kira! You made it!" Zoe screamed as she tried to pop my head off with her hug.

I wrapped my arms around Zoe and held back my tears. My best friend, alive and well. If nothing else had gone right today, at least I'd found her. That meant we were in Haven. There was no other explanation.

I noticed the person who'd appeared along with Zoe—a beautiful fallen angel in military garb. "Who's your friend, Zoe?"

She released me and turned, giggling. "Oh, sorry. This is Eliana, Eli for short. She's Crew's second-in-command. I told you about her."

If this was Crew's right hand, she wasn't what I'd expected. I'd assumed that person would be some grizzled, battle-worn shifter, not the stunning fallen angel who stood before us. Eli nodded to us in greeting but remained silent.

"We don't have any time to lose," Zoe said. "We only found out a little while ago about the mansion being overrun. I need all the details on how that happened, but first we need to get to Haven. Simon is probably out hunting for anyone who escaped the mansion. He'll want anyone he can find to use in his experiments."

"Kira, you're sure we can trust these people?" Gavin asked, eyeing Eli warily.

"I'd trust Zoe with my life," I said. "Come on."

"Follow me," Eli said.

Zoe hurried to join Eli in leading us out of the clearing into another line of trees before coming to a steep rock face of the mountain. Eli walked straight into the stone and vanished.

"What the..." J.D. sputtered.

"It's a concealment barrier spell," Zoe explained. "Pretty simple and keeps us hidden. Come on."

Zoe took my hand and led me through the faux rock. The world blurred for a split second, and then I was in a tunnel. This wasn't quite a cave; more like a mine shaft, dug out by hands and magic rather than by millions of years of erosion.

"Stay close," Zoe said, this time addressing all of us instead of just me. "There's a ton of tunnels down here and loads of booby traps. If you don't want to end up in a bloody spot on the floor, stay nose to ass, people."

"Nose to ass?" I asked.

Zoe grinned and tilted her head toward the fallen angel. "That's one of Eli's favorite sayings. Let's hurry."

We watched Eli and Zoe disarm three different traps as we made our way deeper into the honeycomb of passages.

J.D. looked around like a kid who'd fallen into his favorite movie. "This is so dope! A legit guerilla warfare underground base. Nobody's gonna believe this when I get back home." He called up to Eli. "Do you guys actually live *in* the mountains?"

She didn't look back. "We live in a system of caves beneath the mountain, yes." She finally stopped and turned to address us. "Our leader escaped the mansion and the show attached to it two years ago. He created the tunnels you're in now, and the ones lower. He used an elemental fae weapon to create the caves. When he was a contestant on the show, they gave him the weapon for one of the challenges. It lets him manipulate stone and earth."

J.D. pumped his fist and laughed. "Yes! A secret shadowy leader with a freaking magic wand? I think I played a video game like this once."

While J.D. geeked out, Eli went on. "He created this place to be exactly what it's called—a haven. It's open to anyone who has been sent to Bloodstone Island to die. We used the fae weapon to hollow out the mountain, and have expanded it and fortified it as well. We've worked hard to make this place as self-sustaining as possible. We rarely need to venture out into the island itself. The only time we leave is for emergencies or to help any poor unfortunate souls who get sent here."

The story was amazing, and from the look on everyone's faces, I wasn't the only one who was impressed. The fact that all this was going on without *anyone* on the show knowing was the most impressive part.

"This leader of yours sounds like a really amazing person," Chelsey said.

"Yes, miss, he's really something. Come. Let's go meet him."

We continued following Eli and Zoe through the many corridors. The place wasn't massive by any means, but it was expansive. I figured two or three dozen people probably lived here. Not a huge number of people, but enough that the logistics could get difficult. This Crew guy was one hell of a leader to keep this running. Not only that, but he'd made this place as damn near impregnable as he could. The sheer number of traps they'd set in the entry tunnels boggled my mind.

The farther we went into the tunnels, the more became visible to us. We passed one room that was made into an entire underground garden. Two shifters and a fae woman walked around, plucking tomatoes and squash from plants. Above them, a fae light shone what must have been UV rays on the plants. Another chamber revealed what looked like bunk rooms. A man sat on one of the beds, his head down as he stared at the floor. As we passed him, he looked up and I slid to a stop.

"Mika!" I smiled at the sight of him.

His broody frown slowly gave way to surprise, followed by a smile as he stood and walked to meet us. "How the hell did all of you get here?"

"Long story," Wyatt said as he shook Mika's hand.

The others seemed equally happy to see the other alpha alive again. While the reunion was quick, I noticed something strange. Rather than keeping eye contact with any of us, his eyes continued to slide away. To Zoe.

I looked at my friend and raised an eyebrow. What the hell?

Zoe saw my face and rolled her eyes. "Mister Broody? His Broodiness? Broodypants McSadface? I think he's finally starting to get into the swing of things here," she whispered.

Was Zoe really that blind to the way Mika was checking her out? Mika could be difficult, but I wondered what he'd been like before his father and mate ripped his life apart. If he could get out of his head, he could still try to have a happy life.

"I can't wait to hear about what happened at the mansion," Zoe said.

"Yeah," Eli said. "But let's wait until we're all together. We need to make sure Crew hears this, too."

Chelsey's face went deathly white and she stumbled backward. J.D. had to catch her to keep her from falling.

"Whoa, what's wrong?" I asked her.

Once she'd steadied herself, Chelsey leaned toward Eli. "Wha... what did you say? Repeat that name, please."

Eli looked confused. "Um, you mean Crew?"

Chelsey nodded quickly. "Is that a first name or a last name?"

Eli glanced behind us and smiled. "You can ask him yourself. He's right there."

Chelsey spun around, her eyes wild. There came a sharp intake of breath behind me. Once I turned around, I found Crew staring at Chelsey like she was the first light he'd seen in years. Like she was a river, and he was a man dying of thirst. His jaw moved, but no words came out, like he couldn't find the words to speak.

Chelsey had a similar look on her face. "Ben?"

My eyes widened. Ben? Her fated mate who'd rejected her two years ago? My head snapped back and forth between her and Crew. This was the same guy who'd broken her heart to pieces?

I should have hated the asshole for what he'd done to Chelsey, but when I looked into Crew's face, one thing was certain: he was still in love with her. There was no hiding that look. It was how Wyatt looked at me, and probably how I looked at him, too.

Chapter 24 - Wyatt

Crew stared at Chelsey, Chelsey stared at Crew, and I stood there like a dumbass, looking back and forth at them like I was watching a tennis match. Was this really happening?

"Hang on," J.D. said. "You two know each other?"

Whatever spell Chelsey had been under shattered. She blinked and sputtered. "Uh, I think... well... I don't know him anymore. Maybe once—"

"Yes, we know each other," Crew said, his voice more assured than Chelsey's.

Things grew ever more awkward as they continued to gaze into the other's eyes. If everyone else felt like me right now, then we all felt like intruders in something that should have been happening in private. Chelsey's face grew more anguished while Crew kept staring at her in stunned silence. He looked like the happier of the two for some reason, yet from what I remembered of Chelsey's story, *he'd* rejected *her*. Why the hell he'd be happy to see her was beyond me.

Zoe stepped forward, giving Crew and Chelsey a weird look before speaking. "Okay, this has been fun, but can we maybe go to the meeting hall? Once we're there, you two can keep staring holes through each other while we figure out what happened at the mansion."

Crew, still unable to take his eyes off Chelsey, nodded. "Yeah. Okay." Finally, he shook his head, trying to clear his thoughts. He grabbed a passing person. "Can you take these two to our healer?" He gestured at J.D. and Gavin.

The man glanced at the two alphas and stepped forward. "Sure thing, boss."

"Don't call me boss, Daven. You know I hate that," Crew said with a smile. He was calm and assured with the people here, and I was already starting to warm up to him.

"Oh, shit. Sorry, I forgot. My fault, boss."

Crew rolled his eyes. "Anyway, make sure they're taken care of once they're with the healer. Get them water, food, whatever they need."

"I'm on it," Daven said. He turned to J.D. and Gavin. "If you two want to follow me?"

Gavin glanced at Kira, and I was sure he was going to protest about being taken from her. But surprising me yet again, he lowered his gaze and followed the man helping J.D. limp down the corridor.

Crew, still casting desperately confused glances at Chelsey, led the way along with Eli and Zoe. Taking in more of the compound, I grew more impressed with what I was seeing. If Crew had really done all this, even with the help of a fae weapon, then he was very focused and able to command the respect of everyone here. It wasn't just that Haven was well-thought-out and organized, it was that it felt *safe*. My wolf relaxed as it became more and more clear that we—and most importantly, Kira—would be safe here.

The meeting hall Zoe had mentioned was a natural cave with multiple corridors leading off it. We approached a table with mismatched chairs around it. Crew and his people were scavengers, by the looks of it. Rather than a general's ready room, it looked more like a humble dining room than anything else.

Chelsey was no longer looking at Crew the way she had before. In fact, she kept her head down, trying not to look at him.

Thankfully, Crew managed to pull his attention from Chelsey long enough to address the rest of us. "Can anyone tell us what exactly went down at the mansion? All we know is that some of our scouts saw a chopper take off like a bat out of hell, and then the wards went down a few minutes later. The place is infested now. Dead bodies everywhere."

Kira cleared her throat and gave Crew a quick run-down. Mika had apparently told them what he knew, but he hadn't known everything. Crew and Eli listened intently as Kira recounted the meeting with the showrunners, her suspicion that the fated-mate pairings weren't working, our plan to take down the show, and everything that happened the evening before.

"Von drugged me," Kira went on. "I came across the substance in my time as TO. It forces you into a heat. Not any regular heat, either. Imagine the most painful and indescribably powerful desire you've ever felt. The alphas all reacted to it, Wyatt worst of all. He ripped Von's throat out when he got between us."

"No shit?" Zoe said with a gasp, turning to look at me with what I thought was admiration. All I could do was shrug.

"That gave me an opening," Kira said. "All the staff members were too scared to interfere, so I made an appeal on camera. We were live, which means I basically told the whole world the show was corrupt, the fated-mate pairings weren't accurate, the whole nine yards. It was dumb; I wish I'd had more time to plan what I was going to say. It was probably pointless and ended up getting us all in trouble." She looked more tired than I'd ever seen her.

"That's not entirely accurate," I said. "Your speech was amazing. You're underselling yourself, Kira."

"It really wasn't anything special. Just the facts."

"You also helped get most of us out of the mansion alive, you stood up for us when no one else would, you led us through the jungle to get here. I could go on," I said.

Kira grinned and shoved me. "Okay, enough."

I grabbed her hand and held it. Kira's face went red and she tried to pull away. The public display of affection obviously made her uncomfortable, but Zoe had already noticed it.

"Aww, you guys," Zoe said, putting her hands to her face. "Did you both finally pull your heads out of your asses? I've thought for years that you two would make the *cutest* couple."

"Zoe, shut up," Kira growled, looking around at all the others watching us. "We have more important things to talk about."

She smacked my hand away playfully, but I still felt smug. I agreed with Zoe, and the way Kira blushed only made me feel better about the whole situation. We might have been stuck on a dangerous island, but I'd finally gotten the girl. Now, we just had to stay alive long enough to enjoy it.

"*Anyway,*" Kira said, trying to get the conversation back on track. "It looks like the reason the show shut down is because war broke out back on the mainland."

"Really?" Mika asked. "War?"

Kira nodded. "That's what one of the security guys told me—full-scale war. Apparently, it's really bad."

Crew and Eli shared a worried look, while Zoe and Mika looked solemn.

"We've done okay here, but still don't have much true technology," Crew said. "All we have are some magic users. We can't make contact with the outside world, so this is all news to us. All very bad news."

"Without *The Reject Project*'s presence on the island," Eli said, "Simon will have free rein to hunt for his experiments. He has no reason to hide now. He can send his abominations out day or night to look for us and drag us back to his laboratory. He has to suspect we're somewhere on the island. The only thing that ever hindered him was the worry that the show's team would sniff him out."

There was that name again: Simon. Kira had mentioned him before. It was odd to me that this guy could be living here without anyone knowing. Bloodstone Island held many more secrets and horrors than I'd ever thought possible. It filled me with a sense of foreboding that our seemingly safe place could already be in danger. Having Kira be in perpetual danger all the time had grown old.

"Who is this Simon guy?" I asked. "I keep hearing this name in passing. Is there really some mad scientist living on this island? What's the plan to deal with him?"

Crew shared another look with Eli, then sighed. "We don't know a lot about him. All we know is that he's been on the island for several years. With you mentioning war, it makes me think things with him will start to escalate."

Kira frowned, showing the same confusion I felt. I held up a hand for Crew to stop. "Wait, why would war on the mainland have anything to do with him?"

"You want to say it?" Crew asked Eli.

The fallen angel shook her head. "You go ahead."

"Fine," Crew said. He cleared his throat and took a second to think before answering. "I'm positive the war will impact him because I have a theory that Simon was sent here on purpose. He's doing horrifying experiments, warping science and magic together to create biological weapons. Drugs, monsters, anything and everything that you can think of. My theory is that someone is funding his work.

There's no other way to explain the level of equipment he has. He's also never been seen searching for food or anything else. To get all of that onto this island without being noticed takes someone powerful. I think Simon is in that person's pocket."

Kira leaned forward on the table and gazed down at the floor. Even though she didn't say anything, I knew she was thinking about her family back home—Kolton, her parents, the rest of her pack. We needed rest.

"Are we done here?" I asked. "It's been a *really* long twelve hours. I'd like to get Kira somewhere to get taken care of."

"Oh, I *bet* you want to *take care of her*," Zoe said with a wicked grin.

Kira's face flamed and she shot a glare at her friend. "Please shut up, Zoe. Unless you want to see a pissed-off female alpha wolf in here."

Zoe giggled and waved off Kira's comment. "Ugh, you people. So serious." She turned to Crew. "I'll show the newbies around and get them settled somewhere to rest."

"That's fine." Crew looked over at Chelsey. "Can we talk for a second?"

Chelsey, ignoring him, addressed Eli. "Is there a bathroom or something around here?"

Eli glanced between Crew and Chelsey, then nodded. "Yes, miss. I can show you."

Crew's face fell as she departed with the fallen angel. The rest of us followed Zoe down an opposite corridor.

"We don't have many nice private areas down here," Zoe explained. "There was only so much Crew could do with that fae weapon before it ran out of juice. I have no idea how to make something like it. I was never big on earth magic, anyway." She led us to a small cave room. "This can be your spot. It doesn't echo too much. Hopefully, people won't hear you moaning—uh, sorry, I mean *snoring*."

Kira gave Zoe a sidelong glance. "You are on thin ice right now. Enough sex jokes."

Zoe's smile faded a bit, but I didn't think it was from Kira's comment. Instead, I thought it probably had to do with the fact that the two friends were finally reunited. Zoe always exuded a flippant and silly demeanor, but deep down, she truly cared for Kira.

The fae woman lunged toward Kira and wrapped her in another hug. "I missed you so much."

Kira grinned and hugged Zoe back, rubbing her back. "I missed you, too. I was worried sick about you all the time."

Zoe laughed. "Me? I was safe here. You were the one in that toilet bowl of danger."

"I guess that's true. This place does seem safer than the mansion. Even if it has dirt floors instead of mahogany."

When she pulled away from the hug, Zoe wiped tears from her eyes and cheeks. "If you guys want, there are some storage areas in some of the bigger caverns we've carved. Lots of supplies there. Crew and Eli have managed to raid some of the supply drops for the mansion. They've stolen a lot of stuff, plus there are some things we've managed to make with magic. It's not a department store or anything, but there's plenty of what anyone would need. If you need anything, please ask any of us. Everyone here in Haven is really nice."

"Speaking of that," I said. "Where the hell did all these people come from? I was thinking there'd be like five or six of you here, but I've already seen over a dozen people."

"Some were escaped contestants from *The Reject Project*, like Mika and Crew. Others are former staff of the show who were totally and completely screwed over." She put a hand on her chest. "Like yours truly here. There are a couple of people who worked for the show, but got lost and left for dead in the jungle. Most are folks who were sent to Bloodstone as a death sentence, though."

"That happens?" Kira asked.

"More often than you'd think," Zoe said. "What better place to get rid of someone without a trace? Plus, you can justify it to yourself by saying *you* didn't kill them; you just left them on an island. Like there's any difference between shooting someone in the head and leaving them defenseless on an island to get eaten by a feral shifter." Zoe rolled her eyes. "Crew found all of us and saved us. We owe him our lives. In return, we try our best to take care of this place."

"This place is amazing," Kira remarked.

"It's not bad. You two rest up. I think someone will bring you something to eat in a second. I'll find you later after you've had time to get settled."

"Thank you, Zoe," I said. "You have no idea how much this means to us. Without you, we'd probably be dead."

"Thank Crew. Without him, I'd be dead. See you later."

The room was not luxurious, but it was warm, dry, and safe. I couldn't ask for more. A stone plinth had been carved as a makeshift bed. Palm frond matting had been piled on it to make a sort of mattress. On any other day, I'd say it didn't look comfortable, but I was so tired, I could have slept on broken glass. Though, I did want something more than leaves to sleep on.

Zoe's promise of food was fulfilled a few minutes later when another resident brought us bowls of vegetable soup and some kind of cornbread. It was simple fare, but we devoured it.

"I'm going to go find some supplies. You wait here," I said.

"No arguments from me," Kira said, leaning back against the bed.

The passageways weren't too serpentine, and after a few minutes, I found one of the supply caches Zoe had described. I dug out two sleeping bags and some basic toiletries. Still hungry, I grabbed a few granola bars from a shelf. When I got back, Kira was lying on the palm fronds, nearly asleep.

"Hang on," I said, holding up the sleeping bags. "I found something to make things more comfortable."

"Oh, thank you," Kira said, sitting up. "This is better than the ground, but not by much."

I laid out the sleeping bags, then joined Kira on the bed. The rooms were all lit with fae lights, but the shadows were dark enough that I could feel myself slipping under as soon as Kira nestled against me. The warmth of her body pressed to mine sent a wave of desire through me. I wanted her badly, but I was more concerned with her comfort and safety right now.

Kira snuggled her back into my chest. "I needed this," she murmured.

I smiled to myself and wrapped an arm around her. "I think I did, too. I could get used to falling asleep with you in my arms for the rest of my life."

My smile grew wider as Kira spluttered a response. "The rest of... uh, I meant, well, what I meant was that I needed to relax. Sleep, you know."

"I know *exactly* what you meant."

She sighed and her body softened, sinking further into me. "Though, I have to admit, this would be nice to have every night. I wouldn't mind it in the least."

Rolling her onto her back, I leaned in and kissed her lips. She kissed me back, running a hand along my jaw.

When we pulled away, she looked into my eyes. "There's something I need to tell you."

"Uh oh. Sounds serious."

She rolled her eyes. "I *am* serious. Now that the show is over, and my whole reason for coming here is gone, I can be honest."

"About?"

She chewed her lower lip. The silence dragged on for several seconds before she finally answered. "Originally, I came here to reject whoever I ended up with at the end of the show and get Heline's favor. The problem is, I've pretty much talked myself out of that." Her voice dropped to a whisper. "If things had continued, and you and I were left alive at the end, I wasn't going to take her gift. I was going to choose you as my mate."

Her revelation stunned me. I'd hoped to hear something like that, but her words still floored me, knowing how fiercely loyal she was to her pack and family. She'd been so emotionally and mentally driven to stop this war before it even began. I knew she'd always choose the greater good over what her heart truly desired. Now she was saying she'd been planning to forgo all that for me.

"I couldn't stand the idea of leaving you here to die," she said. "Never seeing you again? Never hearing your voice, feeling your hands on me, your arms around me? I would have never been able to live with myself."

Words wouldn't come, and I was utterly giddy. I'd fantasized about her picking me and hearing her say she chose me. Now she was, and I had a hard time figuring out how to respond. Knowing she cared for me as deeply as I did for her was almost more than I could imagine.

My face must have said it all. Kira smiled, ran a finger across my lips, and snuggled against me. "I thought you should know."

She was asleep in seconds, her breathing steady and deep. While she slept, my brain went into overdrive. What happened next? Despite what Kolton said during our last conversation, I didn't think it was possible for him to get us off the island. Our loved ones and friends would have to deal with the fallout of the war on their own. We would be stuck here, dealing with Simon and whoever pulled his strings.

It was like everything we'd worked so hard for had slipped away. All the agony and terror of *The Reject Project* had been for nothing. Well, maybe not for nothing. I pulled Kira even closer. I'd meant what I'd said to her back in the cave. I wouldn't do anything different because now I had her. And she had me.

Chapter 25 - Kira

When my eyes snapped open hours later, I had a moment of terror. Where was I? Was I safe? Then Wyatt's strong arm circled my waist, and I breathed a sigh of relief. We were in Haven. Safe.

With the fear gone, I realized I was better rested than I'd been in a long time. Sleeping on a thick, soft mattress with cool, smooth sheets and heavy, luxurious blankets in the mansion was nothing compared to sleeping in the arms of the man I loved. Even here, on a bed made of rock, leaves, and sleeping bags, I couldn't remember ever feeling so rejuvenated and relaxed.

Rolling over, I pressed myself against him, breathing in his scent and letting the warm surge of contentment that followed wash over me. My movement stirred him. His eyes blinked open, squinting at the fae lights in the corners of the room.

"Are you okay? Nightmare?" Wyatt asked groggily. "Do you need something?"

He looked cute with his eyes swollen from sleep and his hair all mussed. I slithered my hand between us and caressed his cock through his pants.

"Since you're offering," I whispered.

His eyes snapped open, wide awake and already hardening beneath my fingers. He glanced around furtively at the door. "I swear, if someone tries to walk in here and interrupt us, I'm gonna lose it and let my wolf have full control."

I leaned forward and gently bit his lower lip. "Is that a promise? Are you going to turn your wolf loose on me?"

A hungry, desperate growl erupted from his throat, and a moment later, he was on me. Kissing me hard, he cupped my ass. We'd survived a night of horrors and death. I needed a release, and I was certain he did, too. We needed to feel each other, to remember why we'd fought this hard to escape. I rolled him onto his back, pulled my lips from his, and grinned at him.

"What are you doing?" he asked as I slid down his body.

As an answer, I yanked his waistband down, freeing his thick, throbbing cock. I caught it deftly in my mouth, sliding my lips to the base. Wyatt clasped a hand to his mouth to stifle his moan of delight as I worked on him, caressing his shaft with my tongue and sucking at the head with each stroke.

As I brought him close to orgasm, he writhed and groaned beneath me. When he was right on the edge, I pulled away, leaving his dick rigid and glistening. I made quick work of disrobing and nestled myself above him.

"I want you, Kira," Wyatt whispered, his cock barely brushing my pussy.

Waves of heat cascaded through me, surging from between my legs. When I lowered my hips and impaled myself on him, I sighed in ecstasy. The pleasure of being stretched tight, filled with him, made me dizzy with delight.

I kissed him again, though neither of us moved. Our passion made everything else disappear. For the moment, nothing mattered but the two of us. Wyatt's hands roved up my back and around my chest until he cupped my breasts. He flicked my nipples with his thumbs, making me groan into his mouth. That groan must have unleashed something in him because he began thrusting his hips, sliding the full length of his shaft in and out of me.

"Oh." I collapsed against his chest, wrapping my arms around his neck and pressing my lips to his ears. "Take me, Wyatt. I want it."

"Fuck," he rasped, moving his hips faster.

With each thrust, he filled me to the brim. I let him take me, let contentment and happiness wash over me. We were free of the house, free of the show. We could be open with our love. I loved him. Just saying the words in my head gave me indescribable joy I never knew I could have.

Moving my hips to meet his, we slammed together. I sucked and kissed his neck and ear as he clutched my ass, pulling me down onto him as he rose to meet me. For a moment, I had the almost insatiable urge to bite him, to claim him as mine. My mouth opened, ready to bite down, but I cast that thought aside. Claiming wasn't something you did in the heat of the moment.

I focused again on our pleasure, pushing away those deeper ideas. I sat up, resting my weight with my hands on his chest, and ground my hips against him. Wyatt, breathing hard, reached up and took my breasts in his hands again, caressing and massaging while I rode him. I was getting close. It was like a grenade was inside me and the pin had been pulled, ready to explode.

Wyatt's right hand slid away from my breast, drifting across my stomach until it found my clit. His thumb pressed against it, circled it. An earth-shattering orgasm began to erupt from deep within me.

"I'm coming, Wyatt," I groaned. "Oh, fuck, I'm coming."

Wyatt slammed his cock into me even faster. His body tensed, and the full length of him spasmed and clenched inside me.

My own climax didn't seem to want to end. My mouth hung open in abject ecstasy as I was lifted to a precipice, then plunged again and again.

Finally, when I was totally spent, I collapsed against his chest, gasping for breath. We were both sweaty and tired, but I'd never felt anything so amazing in my life. For the first time, in Wyatt's arms, I was home.

Unlike every other tryst we'd had, we had all the time in the world this time. We basked in the afterglow, hands caressing and exploring, kissing and snuggling together. Now that the haze of passion was fading, I wondered about my inexplicable desire to bite him. That was only something officially mated wolves ever did.

"Okay, I'm gonna call this half-time," Wyatt said. "I'm going to find us some more food. We need energy to continue this lovely morning."

I laughed. "We can't just eat and screw all day."

Wyatt sat up and gaped at me. "And who the hell said we couldn't? That sounds like a great way to spend the day in an underground bunker on a dangerous island in the middle of nowhere. In fact, I think I watched a dirty movie like that once. It worked well for those people."

I sat up beside him. "I'm sure they had a great time, but we have more things to deal with. We need to get acquainted with Haven. Learn the caves and passages, meet the people, all that."

"We can do that later. There's not a lot to do other than hide from Simon. Besides..." he slid a hand along my ribs and cupped the side of my breast. "I think you could really use some more rest and relaxation."

"Oh, is that what we're calling it now?" I asked with a grin.

"It's what I call it."

I took his hand and plucked it off my chest. "You're a very horny boy, yes, I know. There will be plenty of time for that later. Right now? I want to explore." I swung my legs off the bed and grabbed my clothes.

Wyatt gave me an overly dramatic sigh. "Fine. Have it your way. I'm just telling you, walking around dirt hallways is nowhere near as fun as sitting on my face, but who asked me?"

Wyatt put his shoes on and left to find food. I chose a corridor and walked down it, deciding to wander around to see what I could find. In the first big room I came across, I found Zoe in deep conversation with a few other residents of Haven. She didn't notice me in the doorway. Neither did Mika, who sat at the back of the room, holding a mug of steaming liquid. His eyes were locked on Zoe. Earlier, I hadn't been entirely sure what I'd seen in his furtive glances at her. Now? There was no denying it. Mika had it bad for my friend.

Zoe seemed completely oblivious to the alpha's attention. If she didn't notice it soon, I'd have to point it out to her. The more I thought about it, the more I thought they might make a nice couple. Mike had been through a lot in his life, and having a bright ray of sunshine like Zoe around might pull him out of the depressed, insular façade he'd cloaked himself in.

I moved on, not wanting to interrupt. Whatever Zoe was discussing with the others sounded important. Maybe I could see how the other alphas and Chelsey were settling in.

Gavin was passed out when I found him in a bunk room. I let him sleep, glad to see that his injuries had been dealt with. Down the hall, echoes of laughter rang out along with J.D.'s voice. I hurried down to what looked like a makeshift cafeteria. J.D. sat at a table surrounded by others, all of them laughing along with him.

"So then, Wyatt goes full werewolf horror movie and rips Von's throat out," J.D. said gleefully.

The others around the table gaped at him. A woman reached forward and swatted J.D.'s arm. "No freaking way."

"Yes freaking way. I saw it. Swear on my life, I saw the whole thing." He paused, his eyes brightening as he spotted me hovering at the edge of the doorway. "Kira, come on in. Meet my new friends."

Feeling out of place, I did as he asked, waving awkwardly at the others. "Hey. I'm Kira."

J.D. pointed around the table at the others. "Doug, tiger shifter. Michelle, fae. Salvador, fallen angel. That big sack of muscle is Valurion, a demon, but he's actually a good demon."

"Have you met everyone in Haven already?" I asked, amused.

J.D. chuckled. "I got bored, so I walked around."

The people at the table seemed to enjoy his presence. Not surprising—I couldn't see how anyone wouldn't like J.D. Hating him was like hating a puppy or kitten; it felt wrong. Being safe and sound with people to talk to had obviously lifted J.D.'s mood as well.

He stood and put a hand on my arm. "Can we talk for a second?"

"Sure. What's up?"

J.D. looked at the others. "Excuse me, guys. I'll be back in a minute."

We moved back to the corridor out of earshot. He was still grinning, which meant he wasn't planning to say anything really bad.

"Man, I'm glad we found this place," he said. "It's super cool."

His happiness was rubbing off on me. "I'm glad you approve."

He glanced around, making sure no one was around to hear. "They do have, like, *really* strict rules about going outside, though. Have you seen any way to sneak out without causing trouble?"

I furrowed my brow in confusion. J.D. wasn't the type to buck the rules or be a troublemaker. "Why would you want to do that?" I asked, but even as the words slipped from my lips, I figured it out.

"Well, I want to see if Leif is out there. I mean, even if he's feral, I want to know that he's all right. And we could go look for Abel. We can't be sure that he... well, you know. There's no telling what actually happened to him."

Once shifters went feral, there wasn't much you could do. Those few who came back from it only did so before they fully changed. The only thing to do once they fully turned was to either kill them or heavily sedate them to be sent to this island. It should have meant there was no hope for Leif, but the fact that he'd turned feral so quickly, so violently... there had to be something unnatural causing it. Simon and his weird experiments came to mind first. If he'd been altered with some strange drug or potion, there might very well be a way to reverse it. Even Wyatt had said Leif seemed to be struggling with something internally, almost like he didn't *want* to be feral and still tried to fight it. That was something I'd never heard of before. If we had even the slightest chance of saving him, he deserved our help.

"I'll see what I can do. Okay?"

J.D.'s smile returned, lighting his face up like fireworks. "Really? You will?"

"Yeah. The next time I see Crew, I'll tell him what's going on. Maybe he'll let us venture out to search or something."

Before I knew what was happening, J.D. crushed me in a hug. "Thank you, thank you, thank you. Oh, man, that means more than you know. Kira, you're the best."

"Easy," I said, prying his arms off me but unable to keep the grin off my face. "Get back to your new friends. I'm going to explore the place some more."

"All right. See you later." He headed back into the cafeteria.

As I wandered through the compound, I met a few more people, some working to build furniture with wood from the jungle, others using magic to purify water, and more repairing clothes and tending the underground farms. It really was like a tiny town tucked under the mountains.

Eventually, I made my way back to the original meeting room where we'd first met Crew. He was discussing some kind of plan with Eli and a few other fae residents.

"With the help of some fae magic, I think we can harvest it," he said. "Yes, it's a little dangerous since we'll need to go above ground, but I think it's worth it."

"Are you guys planning a mission to go outside?" I asked, stepping into the room.

The fae flinched in surprise, but Crew and Eli glanced up at me lazily, obviously having sensed my approach. Crew eyed me warily. "Possibly. Are you looking to volunteer?"

I shrugged, not wanting to show my cards, but J.D.'s words echoed in my head. If there was a way to get out of Haven to search for Leif or Abel, I wasn't going to pass it up. "If you need help."

Crew's eyes narrowed. "You just got here. From what I hear, you barely made it here alive. Why would you want to go back out so soon?"

From what I'd learned from Zoe's letters and Chelsey's description, Crew came from a privileged background, similar to Wyatt and Mika. Being stuck on this island had obviously hardened him, turned him into some sort of survivalist warrior. I wasn't scared of him, though. Everyone who lived here revered him as a savior. Anyone who could garner that type of devotion had to be an honorable person. Maybe he'd understand what I wanted to do.

"Question," I said, ignoring his own for the moment. "Is there a way to find a specific feral on the island?"

He straightened up. "Not likely. There are dozens of ferals. Actually, more like hundreds. Tell me why you want a feral." His voice was still cordial, but there was a hard edge when he added, "Don't lie."

"One of our friends, an alpha from the show, is out there. He vanished during a challenge, then showed up again less than two days later, completely feral. He had no symptoms before leaving. It doesn't make sense. We think if we find him, there might be a way to save him."

Instead of scoffing at the idea, Crew locked eyes with Eli. The two shared a look, and I could see an unspoken conversation was taking place.

"We have a theory about that," Crew said.

"Wait, really?"

He gestured toward the fae sitting at the table. "We've noticed a lot of newly turned ferals, more than would happen naturally. Many of the magic users here in Haven think there could be a way to help them change back and regain their sanity, so to speak. At least for the recently turned, that is. Like your friend."

"Hang on," I said. "So this is a thing? Can ferals be brought back? I've never heard of this before." I paused. "Sorry, I don't want you to get the wrong idea. I *want* to help Leif, but I thought it was a long shot. Nearly impossible."

Crew tilted his head and grinned sadly. "Typically, it is, but we've been here long enough to see what Simon is doing on this island. Most of the time, only Eli or myself go out, but every now and then, others go foraging, too. We've had a few folks escape while he or one of his experiments tries to drag them back to the lab he has near the volcano. Those few times, our people saw enough to know this guy is really fucked up. We think he's causing these rapid transitions to madness with one of his experiments. Once we had our suspicions, we tried to keep tabs on him when possible. Again, we think we can help them, but once they're driven to become feral, it takes me weeks or months to find them. At that point, it's been too long. Nothing can be done if we don't get to them in the first week or so."

Hope soared within my chest. "Well, Leif only changed a few days ago. There could still be time."

Crew nodded slowly. "Possibly. If he is that recent of a case, we may very well be able to help him. I have to admit, it would be huge for morale in Haven if we actually succeed." He eyed me closely with his one piercing blue eye. "Are you saying you want to go? If we agree to this?"

"I do," I blurted.

"All right. If you're really sure about it, you can leave Haven with me. It'll be a short excursion. I need to harvest some things for us here, but while we're out, we can check for your friend."

"The hell you will!"

I closed my eyes. Wyatt came stomping out of the hall behind me. He'd heard everything. I didn't even need to see his face to know how pissed he was.

"Kira isn't going anywhere. There's no way she's leaving to go back out in that hell hole," Wyatt said.

"Wyatt, this is to help Leif," I said. "Don't you want that?"

"What I want," he said, glaring at me, "is for you to stop putting yourself in danger. I have to be here to keep you from doing something stupid like this."

My own anger surged now. Did he not see what we had at stake? The life of our friend?

"Can you really say that Leif doesn't deserve our help?" I asked, then waved to Crew and the others. "Especially if these people say they can help him?"

Wyatt held his hands up almost in surrender. "I feel bad for Leif, I really do, but he is not your responsibility."

"Oh, well, then whose responsibility is he?'

Wyatt sputtered. "Well, I don't know. I guess all I know is that he's not *yours*. That's all that matters."

I jammed my fists into my sides and pressed my face close to his. "And if it was me out there? Feral and running around like a lunatic? Who would be the one to go and save *me*?"

"I would," Wyatt bellowed, jabbing himself in the chest with a thumb.

"Fine. Now you see how I feel. It's final, I'm going. You can get on board, or you can go pout about it. Up to you, big guy."

Wyatt gritted his teeth and ran his hands through his hair. "You drive me crazy. If that's the way you feel, then do what you want, but I'm going, too." He turned and glared at Crew. "I'm not happy with you, either," he said, leveling a finger at the leader of Haven. "Why did you give her permission to do this, anyway?"

Crew and Eli looked at us like we were crazy, and I didn't blame them. Our fighting was not a great way to start our residence here in Haven.

"I'm not a pack alpha," Crew said. "I'm not a monarch or anything like that. I do what I can to keep this place safe and save anyone who needs saving. I won't tell anyone what they can or can't do unless it puts the rest of these people at risk. Kira is free to make any decision she feels is best. I'm pretty sure she wouldn't have made it this far on *The Reject Project* if she was an idiot or couldn't handle herself. From what Zoe says, she was a decorated Tranquility operative. I'm sure she can do what needs to be done."

I had to bite my lip to prevent myself from grinning at Crew's vote of confidence. Wyatt looked ready to explode, but he couldn't argue with straight facts. Crew had stayed calm even under the withering glare of Wyatt Rivers. He'd gained even more of my respect in a few short seconds.

"Dammit," Wyatt muttered. "Fine. If we're doing this craziness, I'm going to get ready."

He stomped away, and I let him go. He'd need some time to blow off steam. Once we headed out, he'd be locked in and focused.

As he departed, Chelsey appeared around the corner, walking down the hall toward the dining area J.D. had been in earlier. I noticed the way Crew watched her. The sad longing in his eye made my heart hurt, but I still wondered exactly what was going on there. Why reject her if he truly had feelings for her? Or maybe he only realized he had those feelings when it was too late?

Chelsey clearly still wanted nothing to do with him. She glanced at us as she passed, but looked away from Crew, walking faster until she was out of sight.

Something about this relationship didn't make sense. I was starting to think some awful, heartbreaking mix-up may have occurred between them. Maybe once we found and saved Leif, I could dig a little more. Who knew, I might end up playing matchmaker for more than one couple in this underground compound.

"Meet us at the cave entrance in ten minutes," Eli said. "We'll have a fae or witch there to disable the traps for you. I'll send a runner to tell Wyatt."

I didn't bother waiting and headed straight there. When Crew and Eli arrived a few minutes after me, they seemed surprised to find me ready to go.

"You're punctual. I'll give you that," Crew said.

Wyatt came down the corridor a few moments later, looking dour but ready. He looked at me and shrugged apologetically. "Sorry I blew up at you."

"Apology accepted."

"But remember, we will look for Leif out there, though it has to be quick," Wyatt warned. "Not a long, drawn-out thing. I hope we find him, but it's no good if one or more of us are killed trying to save him. We aren't even completely sure we *can* help him. Don't endanger yourself for what might not be a sure thing."

"We're on the same page," I said. "I promise. I'll play it safe."

He smiled and sealed my promise with a kiss. It still felt weird to be open about our relationship after hiding everything for so long around the cameras and staff of the show.

Crew raised an eyebrow. "Are we good? Or..."

"We're good, yeah," I said. My cheeks went a little red at how ridiculous Wyatt and I had been acting in front of our new host.

Crew glanced at Eli. "Do you have what we need?"

Eli handed him a pair of gloves and a small pouch. "Fae finished these up a few minutes ago. It'll keep the plants from burning us."

Crew took them and stuffed the items in his back pocket before looking at me. "Let's go."

A witch walked with us, disarming and rearming the traps as we went until we were at the hidden mouth of the entrance cave.

Crew turned to the witch. "We'll be back in a little while. Wait for my howl."

"Be careful." The woman looked at Crew with what could only be called reverence.

In the jungle, the sun was high in the sky, which made no sense. "How long were we asleep?" I asked.

Eli smirked. "Over fourteen hours. You guys were wiped out."

Fourteen hours? Jeez, we really must have been tired. I pushed that information away and followed Crew and Eli deeper into the jungle. The two crept along carefully and quietly. I couldn't even hear their footsteps. I thought Wyatt and I were good at stalking, but compared to them, we sounded like lumbering elephants.

"What are we looking for, exactly?" I hissed.

Crew knelt, inspecting the ground. "There are certain plants we need to run Haven. We use them for potions, medicines, and to help things run smoothly. Today, we're looking for sunburst vines. If the fae have enough of those, they can mix it in the soil with some spells, and our fruit and vegetable plants can produce more fruit even though they don't get full sunlight." He plucked a leaf from a nearby plant and rubbed it between his fingers. "All we have is a huge fae light in the farm chambers, but that isn't quite enough. It doesn't produce as much light as the sun, obviously."

"Is that what the gloves are for?" Wyatt asked.

Eli nodded and patted her pocket. "Sunburst is highly caustic until it's been refined with magic. The sap will burn right through most things. Fabric, leather, even metal. We need these to harvest it safely."

"Can we help with anything?" I asked.

Crew gestured toward the jungle around us. "Eli and I know what we're looking for. You two keep an eye out for danger, and for your friend."

We proceed along. I swiveled my head around constantly, peering into the trees and trying to catch Leif's scent in the air. Behind me, Wyatt did the same. No dangerous creatures found us, but we also found no sign of Leif.

Under a thickly canopied knoll, Eli and Crew found what they were looking for. The sunburst vines weren't what I'd expected. I'd thought they'd be thick ropes ascending a massive tree. Instead, they were thin web-like vines stretched between two saplings, with huge bright yellow flowers hanging from them. Eli and Crew worked efficiently but carefully to harvest as much as they could fit into the special pouches before cinching them tight and putting them away.

Looking relieved to be done with that task, Crew turned to us, still keeping his voice low. "Done. We've still got some time. If you want to find a feral wolf, there's an area near here that's popular with wolves. They spend a lot of time there. If you want to try there, I know a path that will bypass most danger. What do you say?"

Wyatt tensed beside me. He probably wanted to speak up and say we'd already been out too long, that it was too dangerous.

I beat him to the punch. "Let's do it."

Wyatt growled but kept his mouth shut. He didn't want to argue in front of Crew again, especially not out here where noise could bring out hordes of things to kill us.

Crew looked at Eli and pointed to the back of our group. "You take the rear. You know where we're going, right?"

She nodded and stepped aside so Wyatt and I could pass. Crew led us on a circuitous route to the destination. At one point, we skirted the very edges of the swamp, getting close enough that I could hear the ghosts inside screeching and moaning. It sent shivers up my spine.

The path he led us on took us up a jagged trail to a precipice that overlooked a clearing fifty yards below. Even before I came to the edge to look down, I could hear the snarls, barks, and growls of at least a dozen wolves.

Wyatt and I lay on our stomachs and inched toward the sharp edge of the outcropping to join Crew. My jaw dropped at what lay before me.

At least twenty feral wolves stalked the clearing. The area looked to have been struck by a storm a long time ago. Lots of trees were down and partially or totally rotten. Saplings and shrubs had sprouted up to compete for the newly revealed sunlight, but wolf feet had trodden most of them down, creating an oval-shaped opening for them to congregate.

The wolves were in various states of filth. Most had matted or mangy fur. One barely looked like a wolf at all. Its fur was deeply tangled and covered in mud, and it almost appeared to have armor hanging from its body. The beasts rolled their heads, snapped at nothing, and dug at the ground in pointless bursts of activity. As I watched, two of the creatures snapped at one another until they exploded into a fight, with gnashing teeth, open jaws, and clawing feet. The fight didn't end until one of the wolves lay dead, its throat torn out, the victor howling at the sky.

It broke my heart. They'd all been people once. At one point, they'd been shifters like me or Wyatt, men and women with packs and families, but they were now stark-raving mad and stuck here forever.

My heartache vanished when I saw Leif's familiar wolf form lope into the clearing. Excitement and hope filled me at the sight of him, even if he was obviously out of his mind. He stopped mid-stride, shook his head, batted at his face with his paw, then growled savagely at a sapling. He even stalked toward the plant like it was an enemy before biting and clawing at it until he either grew bored or decided it wasn't worth it. Tears filled my eyes.

"That's him," Wyatt whispered, pointing to Leif. "We've found him. What the hell do we do now?"

"Is there a way to get him back to Haven safely?" I asked.

Crew nodded, keeping his eye locked on the wolves below. "We have a holding area at Haven. It's never been used, though. Originally, it was made in case we had to restrain an angry shifter or people I rescued who might be a little out of it at first. It should hold a feral shifter." He glanced back at Eli, who sat hunched behind us. "Do you think you can help?"

Eli nodded. "I can calm his mind and induce sleep if I get close enough. My powers should be able to put him under deep enough that he won't wake during the return trip." She raised an eyebrow. "We have to get him alone first. I'm not strong enough to do it to more than one creature at once."

"We wait, then," Crew said. "Watch and see if he separates himself from the rest. I'll give it an hour. Then we call it."

"Okay," I said, though it was a grudging agreement. I didn't want to leave Leif here. We'd just found him, and there was no guarantee we'd find him again. But I was a guest here, and I had to follow Crew and his rules.

The minutes ticked by in silence. All we could do was watch the shifters below us wallow in their misery and madness, waiting and hoping Leif would venture off alone.

"What are you going to do about Chelsey?" Wyatt asked, and I jerked my head around.

"It's easy to see you're still into her, but she's acting like she wishes you didn't exist," Wyatt went on.

Emotional agony darkened Crew's face. Eli was looking at him with interest. Surely the residents of Haven were curious about their leader's past, and his past relationship with Chelsey looked like a doorway right into it.

"That's a long story," Crew said. "I can't say I'm surprised she doesn't want to talk to me, though."

"Maybe I could talk to her," I offered. "I can at least ask if she'd discuss things with you. Get her feelings off her chest, if nothing else."

His face betrayed the hope he must have felt. But Crew disagreed. "Nope. I don't want to bother her. She's been through too much already. She hates me, and I deserve it."

"He's breaking off," Eli hissed, jabbing a finger to point at Leif.

We turned to look. Leif was walking away from the others, trying to get away from a fight that had broken out among three other wolves.

"This is good," Crew said. "He's going north, downwind of the others. Come on."

We scrambled after Crew, who was navigating the rocky outcropping like he'd been born on them. The guy would have made an amazing Tranquility operative. I watched as he eyed Leif through the trees. Crew kept us far enough away that Leif wouldn't hear or scent us, but close enough to continue tracking him. I had no idea where he was heading, but Wyatt was getting more tense by the moment.

Finally, Wyatt touched Crew's shoulder. "We need to turn back. We're getting too close to the volcano."

I looked up and saw the volcano was indeed looming over us ahead. Leif was heading straight toward it. That's why Wyatt was so nervous. It was where he'd been taken and almost dragged to some unknown doom.

Before Crew could answer, an undead shriek of rage shattered the silence of the jungle around us. A cold wind blew, and a moment later, a monstrous ghost shimmered into view, rushing straight toward us.

My heart thundered. We had no enchanted weapons, no way of fighting the thing. We had to run. It was the only way.

My mind was already set to grab Wyatt's hand and drag him to safety when Eli stepped toward the specter, almost as though she were wholly unconcerned. She slipped her fist directly into the thing's chest.

"Be at rest, brother," she muttered.

At her words, the ghost burst apart in a haze of mist. A glob of ectoplasm splattered to the forest floor at her feet.

"Holy shit," Wyatt muttered.

Eli wiped the ectoplasm on her hand against her fatigues. "It should have known better than to approach an angel, fallen or not."

"We've got bigger problems," Crew hissed, sniffing the air. "Wendigo. Hide. Now."

I caught the scent as well, and my fear grew. It looked like our quiet walk in the woods had gone to shit.

"Run!" Crew screamed.

Ahead of us, I saw the creature. It had already spotted us, so there was no time to hide. It burst forward with inhuman speed, snarling as it went.

Our group scattered, rushing in all directions. I wanted to stay with Wyatt, but it was better to split up. With more targets to hunt, it might grow confused and give up. I didn't look behind, didn't think, just ran as fast and hard as I could. Eventually, I dived behind an outcropping of rocks in a thickly wooded area. I rolled over, hugged my knees to my chest, and waited, listening intently.

Distant screams echoed toward me, all of them from the wendigo or other creatures that had been stirred by its hunt. I tried to calm myself with the fact that I didn't hear any shouts or screams from my friends. I forced myself to wait.

There was no way of knowing how long I sat there, but I eventually stood and scented the air, trying to catch Wyatt or the others. The scent I found was not the one I'd been looking for, but it was familiar. Leif.

Maybe this operation hadn't been a complete disaster. If I could find his trail again, we could salvage the rescue mission. Kneeling low, I followed the scent and looked for signs of his passing. Above me, the volcano loomed larger. In my haste to escape the wendigo, I'd rushed right toward it. The mountain cast a shadow over the jungle here. Had it not been so dark, I might have seen what awaited me.

From under a thick tangle of branches, vines, and fronds, a deep, angry growl rattled to life. Freezing where I was, I glanced over and saw the shimmering golden eyes of a wolf emerge from the shadows. Leif.

"Shit!" I whispered.

His growl grew deeper for an instant before he snarled and lunged toward me. He slammed into me, knocking me down. His jaws clamped on my foot and he began to drag me toward the volcano. I thrashed against his grip, but he was too strong, and his teeth were cutting into my skin.

Panic surged, and my inner wolf leaped forward, taking control, again throwing off the years of suppression to save my life. I shifted, and even in my terror, the feeling was pleasant. Like coming home.

Leif released my leg and backed away, hackles raised, mad eyes glaring at me. I stalked toward him, growling and ready to fight. I readied myself to leap upon him, to fight him to the ground, when a sharp, stabbing pain shot through my hindquarters. Snarling in surprise, I turned to see some sort of dart protruding from my flesh. Nausea swept over me, and the world began to spin. I tumbled to my side, already shifting back to my human form.

Whatever drug the dart had contained was now flooding my body. I couldn't lift my arms or stand. It slowly paralyzed me, taking all movement but my lungs and eyes. First, I feared Leif would shred my body in my weakened state, but he stood twenty paces from me, sitting on his haunches, staring behind me. Only then did I notice the footsteps, crinkling through the leaves and growing ever nearer.

Gods, I'd never been so scared. If I hadn't been immobile, I'd have been shivering in terror. I lay there motionless as fear tried to take over every other emotion.

A foot stepped over my body, then a fae man stood above me, wearing a dirty lab coat. This had to be Simon, and... I recognized him. His features were familiar, but I couldn't place from where. He knelt and looked into my face. His eyes were curious at first, then they went bright with recognition. When he spoke, all the memories came crashing down.

"My, my, my. How you have grown. I never thought I'd see you here, my little friend. It seems the fates and gods do have a sense of irony."

The only part of my body that could move was my eyes, and they widened in shocked horror. That voice. It came from the depths of my memory, from that awful night of my first shift when I was at the fae party. It was the last thing I remembered before finding myself covered in blood and running—a voice calling to me from the darkness.

Those few words echoed like nightmarish bells in my head. *"Young one? Come. I want to show you something."*

Simon crossed his arms over his knees and gazed at me. "I want to thank you for helping me fake my death all those years ago. None of this would have been possible without you, dear girl." He reached down and caressed my cheek, then stood and looked at Leif. "Bring her."

He strolled away from me. My vision went gray, blackness covering the periphery. The last thing I saw before going under was Leif grabbing my foot and dragging me across the jungle floor, following Simon toward the volcano.

All I wanted was to call out to Wyatt, to scream for help. Instead, my eyes slipped closed. Just before I fell into the endless black depths, I heard Simon speaking to me again.

"My first truly successful experiment. You were the beginning. Perhaps now, you'll be the end as well."

Printed in Great Britain
by Amazon